Bra

BRIDES

———❖———

Brandywine BRIDES

AMBER STOCKTON

BARBOUR BOOKS
An Imprint of Barbour Publishing, Inc.

Bound by Grace © 2011 by Amber Stockton
Stealing Hearts © 2012 by Amber Stockton
Antique Dreams © 2012 by Amber Stockton

Print ISBN 978-1-63058-454-2

eBook Editions:
Adobe Digital Edition (.epub) 978-1-63409-184-8
Kindle and MobiPocket Edition (.prc) 978-1-63409-185-5

All scripture quotations are taken from the King James Version of the Bible.

This book is a work of fiction. Names, characters, places, and incidents are either products of the author's imagination or used fictitiously. Any similarity to actual people, organizations, and/or events is purely coincidental.

Published by Barbour Books, an imprint of Barbour Publishing, Inc., P.O. Box 719, Uhrichsville, Ohio 44683, www.barbourbooks.com

Our mission is to publish and distribute inspirational products offering exceptional value and biblical encouragement to the masses.

Member of the
Evangelical Christian
Publishers Association

Printed in the United States of America.

Dear Readers,

I'd like to give you a warm and personal welcome to the fascinating and often overlooked significance of the tiny state of Delaware, the setting for this series of three historical novels. Though I now live in the mountainous state of Colorado, thirty years of my life were spent in Delaware, and I spent a lot of that time exploring its rich history and unique contributions to what made America what it is today. For those who have read my books before, you might be familiar with Liberty's Promise, my previous historical collection set in Colonial Delaware. This series continues that family's story and highlights a family heirloom book featured in my very first novel.

Through each of these novels, you'll also venture into the world of shipyard business industries and the rediscovery of a lost dream in the reopening of a family-owned bookstore. Through the challenges they face in life and with each other, they each learn to let go and trust God, allowing their faith to guide them down the river toward a more rewarding life, and discovering abiding love along the way.

I hope you enjoy visiting historical Delaware and the Brandywine River Valley within the pages of this book as much as I enjoyed journeying with the characters along their journeys. I look forward to hearing from you.

Wishing you God's blessings along *your* life's journey,
Amber Stockton
www.amberstockton.com

BOUND BY GRACE

Dedication

I want to thank JoAnne Simmons for the golden opportunity to write for this club and for helping me get my foot in the door. I also want to thank my copyeditors, Rachel Overton and Becky Fish. My writing has only improved because of you. Finally, this book is dedicated to my readers, who have faithfully continued to purchase and read my books. I wouldn't be an author without you!

Chapter 1

Brandywine, Delaware, 1881

So, was your venture successful? Did the gentleman have what he promised? Were you able to locate it?"

Charlotte Pringle's youngest sister barely allowed her to step through the door to the bookshop before the verbal interrogation began. Her assistant, Laura, looked up from behind the front counter, the same place Charlotte had left her nearly two hours ago.

Charlotte pushed back and untied the hood on her cape. After inhaling the familiar smells of leather, wood, and vanilla incense, she gave Anastasia a teasing grin. "Might I have a moment to relax from my journey before you plague me with questions? I might need to burn some lavender incense if you continue in this fashion."

Anastasia looked as if she might bust a seam in her daffodil walking dress, but she could wait a few more moments.

"Laura." Charlotte addressed her assistant. "Thank you for tending the store in my absence."

"It was my pleasure, Miss Charlotte." Laura averted her gaze and wrung her hands on the apron she wore. "If you have no other need for me at the front, I'll return to reconciling our inventory."

"That will be fine, Laura. Thank you again."

Just one year younger than Charlotte's own age of twenty, Laura wasn't much for conversation. But she worked hard and was quite thorough. Given Anastasia's fanciful notions, Charlotte appreciated having someone dependable to help her.

"So–o. . ." Anastasia splayed her hands on the edge of one of the front tables, barely acknowledging Laura's departure. "What was the result?"

With a calm that contradicted the butterflies fluttering in her stomach, Charlotte reached into her satchel and withdrew a worn but well-kept volume of *Robinson Crusoe*. She closed her eyes and ran her fingers across the smooth surface of the binding, her mind replaying the name written just inside the front cover. A first edition. Once owned by her great-grandmother's great-grandmother, Raelene Strattford. Charlotte's mother loved telling the story of how the book played into the courting of Gustaf and Raelene. But somewhere along the line, the book had been lost. A chance meeting with a bookstore

9

owner in Philadelphia alerted Charlotte to the book's location. After six generations of history, she had finally brought it back into the family once more.

"You did find it!" Anastasia clasped her hands together just beneath her chin, her bright eyes resembling those of a child who'd just stepped into an ice-cream shop. Leave it to her sister to be overly dramatic.

Charlotte shook her head. "Yes, although judging by your reaction, one might think *you* were the one who had been searching for three years to find this treasure."

"Can a girl not be truly happy for her sister?" The gleam in Anastasia's eyes matched Charlotte's excitement. "I love books as much as you do." An impish grin overtook her lips as she turned away and moved from behind the counter, assuming an air of nonchalance. "Besides, one day some of these cherished tomes may very well become mine. And I have already been making a list."

Charlotte raised one eyebrow. "Oh, you have, have you?" She crossed her arms. "Suppose I decide to live far longer than you. What will you do then?"

"Borrow them when you are not looking," her sister said with a shrug.

Anastasia winked and pranced away toward the four long aisles of books, but not before Charlotte reached out and tugged one of the bouncing locks hanging down her back. How nice it must be. So carefree and young. Of course, Anastasia was almost fourteen. And she'd already had at least two young men express interest in pursuing a courtship with her. Not so young, after all.

If only those young men had older brothers or knew of some men who weren't already engaged or married. The selection seemed to grow thinner with each passing day. Charlotte sometimes wondered if she'd ever meet a man who understood her passion. Her friends told her she needed to give up the bookshop if she hoped to find a suitable match, but that was out of the question. She loved her books too much. And if a man couldn't love her along with everything she brought to the relationship, she'd rather remain alone.

As the eldest daughter, however, she owed it to her parents to make a suitable match. With her older brother married and poised to follow in their father's footsteps in gunpowder manufacturing, working closely with the du Pont family, the mantle now rested on her shoulders. If another season passed without any prospects, her parents might be forced to choose someone for her. She prayed that wouldn't be the case, but she'd honor them if it happened.

"Charlotte?" Anastasia called from the back of the shop. "Where did you shelve that copy of *Emma* you had last week? I can't seem to find it. Someone didn't borrow it, did they?" She gasped. "Or purchase it? I have wanted to read it for several days, but I had to finish *Pride and Prejudice* first. I shall simply swoon if it's gone."

Charlotte erupted into laughter. "It's the next aisle over, you silly goose, with the rest of the books by Jane Austen." She peeked down the aisle and caught her sister's eye. "As much time as you spend here, you would think you'd know the location of every book by heart."

"No, that honor belongs only to you, dear sister." Anastasia grinned as she flounced around the corner to the appropriate shelf.

Charlotte smiled. Yes, she did know each and every precious volume and the treasured locations where they rested. She reached out and caressed the spine of the nearest title. Some days, the books served as better companions than her friends or the latest unsuitable suitor her parents attempted to send her way.

"Found it!" Her sister's voice floated to the front of the shop, preceding Anastasia's appearance by mere seconds. She clutched the book to her chest. "I'll have it back to you in less than a week. No one will know it's gone." She pursed her lips. "Except you, of course."

Charlotte reached out and tipped her sister's chin with her finger. "Just be certain you don't allow any more matchmaking ideas to enter that pretty little head of yours. Remember what happened the last time you attempted to orchestrate a rendezvous between Jeremiah Graham and Amanda Stewart?"

"Oh, must you remind me of that again?" Anastasia held up the book to hide her face. "You have to admit they did appear rather fond of each other." She peered over the top of the book. "How was I to know their grandmothers were sisters?"

"You would have had you been paying more attention to the conversations around you and less to your latest matchmaking schemes." Charlotte rolled her eyes. "Honestly, I can't fathom why you continue to interfere in other people's lives in such a manner. Why not allow young ladies and gentlemen to choose for themselves who they shall marry? The results are so much better that way."

"Not always." Anastasia wagged one finger. "Do you recall how I arranged for shy and unassuming Paulina Whetstone to accidentally bump into the much-sought-after Matthew Adams? Those two likely would never have given each other a moment's notice had I not moved things along a bit." She took on an air of smug triumph. "Even you cannot deny how perfectly suited they are for each other."

"It is true." Charlotte pressed a finger to her lips. "I have never seen either one of them so happy, nor more suitably matched." She shook a warning finger in her sister's direction. "But that is not the case with most of your attempts. And I fear reading that book"—she gestured toward the volume her sister held—"will only make matters worse."

"Or it might improve my skills," Anastasia countered. "Perhaps I only need a lesson or two in observation skills. If I paid closer attention, I might become far more successful than I have been."

"And if you do not, I shall be forced to go behind you to clean up the pieces of your failed attempts." Charlotte covered her sister's hands with her own, imploring her with her eyes. "Just promise to be more careful next time. Please?"

Anastasia tilted her head, peering up at Charlotte. "Very well," she sighed. "But I suppose I should tell you I have already selected the fortunate young lady who will become the next focus of my attentions."

Charlotte raised both eyebrows. "Oh? And who might that be?"

Her sister stepped out of reach and fairly skipped the few steps toward the back door of the shop. She placed one hand on the doorknob and pulled open the door leading to the common courtyard area behind the buildings. Peering over her shoulder, she tossed her sister an impish grin. "You." With that, she was gone.

The final word hung in the air like an ominous storm cloud about to release everything it held. Charlotte turned her face heavenward and sent up a silent prayer asking when the cloud finally did burst, she wouldn't get too wet.

*

More than a week later, Charlotte marveled over how many new customers had visited her shop. It seemed as if someone had posted banners around the area, announcing the shop's location. But she wasn't about to complain. She *did* own the only shop that both sold and loaned books between here and Philadelphia. The increased patronage helped both her sales and the shop's reputation. If each one of those who visited her shop told one or two other people, she might have to consider taking on another assistant and extending the hours she was open to the public.

Even the courier had been making more frequent visits. He seemed to deliver a letter every other day from someone inquiring about this title or that, asking if she had it in stock and if she might set it aside for them until they had the opportunity to come in person. One such letter had just been delivered yesterday, but Charlotte had read it at least a dozen times since. She kept it folded and tucked in her pocket. During a brief lull, she withdrew the now-worn paper again and read:

To the Owner of Cobblestone Books:

I have recently learned of the existence of your shop from various acquaintances. It appears I might need to pay a visit, but I wanted to write and notify you of my possible arrival beforehand, for I did not wish to appear unannounced. Since the purpose of my visit is to locate a handful of specific titles, I would like to make you aware of those titles in the hopes you might secure them beforehand and have them ready. My niece is rather fond of reading, and she has read everything I've given her at least twice over. Enclosed is a complete list of titles I would like to locate. Any of them will suffice, as I do not expect you to have them all available. I shall be happy to compensate you for your time and assistance. Please use the address accompanying this letter for any reply. Thank you for your time. I look forward to visiting as soon as time permits.

With regards,
Richard Baxton

Charlotte couldn't place her finger on exactly what drew her to the letter, but something about the words the gentleman chose and the manner in which he framed them spoke to her. His obvious love for his niece might be part of the attraction, as well. After all, how could she turn away a doting uncle who wanted to appease his niece's insatiable appetite for reading? She felt a kinship with the girl already.

Not wanting to allow any more time to pass, Charlotte opened a drawer of her desk behind the counter and withdrew a sheet of paper. She reached for the pen and dipped it in ink, preparing to compose a reply.

Dear Mr. Baxton:
I have received your note and would be honored to welcome you to my shop. The books you listed are ones I already have among my inventory. So you need not allow any more time to pass before making arrangements to visit. I have set the titles aside as you requested. Please come at your earliest convenience. I look forward to meeting you.

Sincerely,
Miss Charlotte Pringle
Owner

That should do it. Charlotte read over her response three times, making certain it didn't sound too forward but wanting it to be both sincere and professional. With a nod of satisfaction, she folded the page and tucked it inside an envelope, sealing it with wax and addressing the outside as Mr. Baxton had instructed. The next time the courier arrived, she would give him the letter to post. After that, she had only to wait for Mr. Baxton's arrival.

Oh, how she prayed it wouldn't be long.

❧

Richard Baxton stepped into the dark study, illuminated by the lone gas lamp on the desk. He'd been procrastinating for several weeks, but this task needed attention. Everything about the room seemed to bear a direct connection to his older brother. From the rich Aubusson rug covering most of the floor and the heavy velvet drapes at the windows to the custom-built, floor-to-ceiling shelves holding a wide selection of books, references, and ledgers, every nook and cranny said Elliott Baxton had once spent most of his time here.

Even the leather chair bore evidence of Elliott's presence. Richard pulled the chair away from the desk and sat down. He felt like a traitor, sitting there. This seat didn't belong to him. It belonged to his brother. What right did he have to sit in it now? Maybe he should take the work needing to be done and return to his own place. But that would mean taking his niece away from the only home she'd ever known. It had been only two months since the accident, and barely four weeks since she'd come home from the hospital. Richard didn't have the heart to pull her away.

He raised his head and gazed at the wall. Portraits of his family's patriarchs going back a half dozen generations lined the wall. They seemed to stare at him in condescension, their expectations high that he not be the one to see the family business fall to ruin. And he'd do everything in his power to see that it didn't. Even if working with his hands and managing the building of the ships suited him better than overseeing business affairs, he wouldn't disappoint his family.

With a sigh, Richard shifted his attention to the ledger on the desk in front of him. He'd happily pass on this task to someone else—anyone else—but at the moment, no one available possessed the necessary skills. Truth be told, he didn't either. But their accountant had left just before the accident, and Richard hadn't hired anyone else yet. As the new owner, he had to get it done.

Numbers had never been his strength. He'd left that to his more studious older brother. Now, with Elliott gone, the task fell to him. How he wished he'd paid more attention during his schooling. But if Richard allowed his thoughts to drift anymore, another week would pass and the ledgers still wouldn't be settled. The release of the funds associated with his brother's estate depended on the accounts being balanced. Like it or not, he had to get to work.

Three hours later, Richard drummed his fingers on top of the ledger, tempted to let his head fall to the desktop. He'd been over the numbers in every column at least a dozen times, and they simply refused to cooperate. How had the accounting gotten so out of hand in such a short time? Or was it him? Could his figuring be that rusty?

His brother had repeatedly told him how organized the financial side of the business was. Their former accountant possessed a degree from one of the finest schools in Philadelphia. So why could Richard not balance the spreadsheet? What was he doing wrong?

Steady footfalls sounded in the hallway outside the study. Eager for the interruption, Richard looked up as the butler appeared in the doorway. The man cleared his throat.

"Pardon the interruption, sir, but a missive has just arrived for you."

"Harrison, please tell me it isn't another note from our lawyer." Richard stood and rubbed his temples with his fingers. "I might be tempted to ask you to return it without my reading it."

"No, sir. This is not from the lawyer." The butler glanced down at the envelope. "It is from a Miss Charlotte Pringle, sir. Of Cobblestone Books." He started to turn away. "Shall I leave it on the tray in the front hall?"

Charlotte Pringle? From the bookstore Richard had contacted? He'd expected the owner to be a gentleman.

"No!" Richard stood and nearly toppled his leather chair. He spoke more calmly. "I will take it." He held out his hand.

Harrison stepped to the dark cherry desk and handed the letter to Richard. "Will that be all, sir?"

"Thank you, Harrison. Yes, that will be all. I will call upon you if a reply is necessary."

"Very good, sir."

Richard lowered himself into the well-worn chair once more and stared at the envelope. If this response was as he hoped, one of his less pressing dilemmas would be solved. He slit the seal and removed the single sheet of paper.

So, the owner was a lady. Or perhaps a matron. She might even be an old spinster with poor matrimonial prospects who had chosen to run an old bookshop instead. Glancing at the distinctive feminine script, Richard made up his mind. Definitely a lady. And judging by the feel of the paper as well as the words chosen, a lady of class. The carefully centered seal in the wax should have told him that from the start.

Richard read the letter three times, a pleased smile forming on his lips. The owner had signed the letter with a *Miss* preceding her name. That usually indicated a young lady, although it didn't rule out the spinster possibility. Nevertheless, he had a mission in mind, and Miss Pringle had not only obliged him with a response, but she had also set aside every title he'd requested. His niece would be thrilled.

"Are you busy?"

Richard started at the young voice. "Grace, what did I tell you about sneaking up on me like that?" It had been almost a month, yet sharing a home with a child still felt foreign.

Grace gave him an apologetic look mixed with a hint of indignation. "I didn't sneak up on you, Uncle Richard. I came down the hall as I normally do." She placed her hands on the large wheels to each side of her chair and moved them forward, bringing her into the study. Her expression reflected both sorrow and melancholy. "Besides, one cannot exactly be silent in a contraption like this."

"You have a point." Richard nodded, his heart going out to his niece, confined to a chair after the carriage accident that took her parents. "I suppose I was lost in thought. Do forgive me for snapping."

"Oh, I could never be cross with you, Uncle." Her eyes reflected sadness, yet a pixie-like smile graced her face. "Who else is going to get me every book I could ever want? As well as all the sugar sticks I can eat?"

An answering grin parted his lips. "Now who said anything about sugar sticks?"

She pressed her hands against the wheels and raised herself up. "You mean I truly can have any book I want?" Grace wheeled closer. "Does that mean you heard back from one of the shops?"

"As a matter of fact..." Richard stood and moved around the desk to stand in front of his niece. He kneeled to be at eye level with her, placing his hands over hers. "Yes, I did."

Eagerness filled her expression. "What did they say?"

Richard glanced back toward the desk then again at Grace. "The owner has each and every title on your list, and she has set them aside for us to come see."

Grace's eyes widened. "She?" A wrinkle formed in the middle of her brow, and she pressed her lips into a thin line. "That doesn't mean the owner is a dour old spinster, does it?"

"That will be enough of that, young lady," Richard reprimanded. "We have yet to meet Miss Pringle. I'll not have you forming assumptions and passing judgment before we meet her." Of course he had done that very thing moments before. He'd do well to heed his own instructions.

Appearing immediately contrite, Grace lowered her gaze. "Yes, sir. I'm sorry."

Richard tipped up her chin with the crook of his finger. "Very well. Shall we begin making plans for our journey?"

"Do you mean I can join you?" The shift from contrition to joy nearly caused Richard to fall back. Ah, the exuberance of youth.

"I would not have it any other way, my dear." He tapped Grace's nose and smiled, silently praying Cobblestone Books had street-level access.

Chapter 2

W hat do you think he looks like?" Anastasia held the feather duster in one hand, swiping at every visible surface in the bookshop. Charlotte's parents didn't force her to work, but Anastasia said she enjoyed helping. "Do you think he's an older, portly sort of gentleman? Or perhaps one of those men who do nothing but read books, wear spectacles, and hide away in their houses?" She paused and held the duster across her chest, a dreamy-eyed look entering her eyes. "Oh! Perhaps he's dashing and young and charming, and he'll come to sweep you off your feet!" Anastasia punctuated her remark by sweeping the duster across the floor.

Charlotte continued straightening the front counter and sighed. She needed to limit the number of romance stories her sister read. Having dreams was one thing, but Anastasia almost always went overboard with her fanciful imagination. Men like the ones in her stories simply didn't exist.

The bell above the front door jingled, and Charlotte looked up with a start, her breath catching in her throat. Anastasia even had *her* anticipating Mr. Baxton's arrival. A moment later, she exhaled. "Good morning, Mr. Read," she said, greeting one of her regular customers. "Have you finished the *Canterbury Tales* already?"

The diminutive, slender man doffed his top hat and tucked it under one arm, revealing his customary center-parted hairstyle, the honey-gold strands pressed close to his head. "Good afternoon, Miss Pringle." He offered a congenial smile. "As a matter of fact, I have. I must confess, I found the Miller's Tale to be the most enjoyable. *And* I've come seeking another treasure, hoping you might point me in the right direction. Your recommendation was spot on, and I have no doubt you'll do the same again." He winked.

Charlotte smiled in return. What Mr. Read lacked in stature, he made up for in social graces and personality. And his two sons, not long in their britches, were already showing signs of growing up to be just like their father.

"If you found Mr. Chaucer's storytelling to your liking, you should next read the stories of Grendel and Beowulf." She led Mr. Read down the first aisle, running her fingers across the titles and moving just a little beyond another copy of Chaucer's tales to retrieve a book. "Beowulf is a hero of the Geats and battles against Grendel, Grendel's mother, and a dragon, then becomes king of the Geats. It's an epic poem I am certain you will find engaging."

Mr. Read held the book in his hands and glanced at the cover. He ran his fingers over the title, and then he opened the book to the first few pages. Moments later, he closed the cover and looked up at Charlotte. "I shall take it." He gestured for her to precede him back up the aisle toward the front, continuing as he followed. "Under normal circumstances, I would preview an unfamiliar text before purchasing, but I know you would not steer me wrong." He reached for his billfold then paused. "Oh, and while I am here, might you also have something I could read to my sons? The tales penned by Chaucer fair well enough, but I fear Beowulf's story might be a bit beyond them."

"Of course." Charlotte nodded and looked toward her sister. "Anastasia, would you mind pulling two or three of Hans Christian Andersen's fairy tales for Mr. Read, please?"

"Right away." Her sister disappeared down the far aisle and returned moments later. Having someone else who knew the bookshop well was a definite asset. "Here you are." Anastasia set the three books on the counter with the other.

Mr. Read bestowed a pleased grin on Anastasia. "Thank you, my dear." He glanced at the titles and read them aloud. "*The Steadfast Tin Soldier*, *The Ugly Duckling*, and *The Emperor's New Clothes*." With a nod, he pushed the stack toward Charlotte. "These shall do nicely." After laying his hat on the counter, he retrieved his billfold, withdrew a few bills and some change, and paid for his purchases.

"Thank you again, Mr. Read." Charlotte noted the titles on her inventory ledger and slid the stack back toward him.

"No, thank *you*, Miss Pringle." He nodded toward Anastasia. "And to the younger Miss Pringle, as well." Taking the books and setting his hat atop his head, he bowed toward them both. "It is the endless hours of enjoyment you provide with your bookshop that is the greater gift. My dear wife, sons, and I all appreciate your service." With a tip of his hat, he left the shop, the door jingling the bell with his departure.

"I'm glad I was here to see Mr. Read," Anastasia remarked as soon as the door closed. The two sisters watched the street outside as their recent customer crossed to the park on the other side and disappeared from view. "He is one of your nicest customers."

"I cannot disagree with you, although Mrs. Merriweather and Miss Constance are among my most loyal."

Anastasia giggled. "And most talkative."

"This is true." Charlotte smiled. "Let's not forget the brooding Mr.

Cramer, with his dark eyes and pinched lips."

Warming to the little game, her sister brightened. "Or the pensive and serious Mrs. Standish. Every time I see her, I wonder if she knows what a smile is." A twinkle lit Anastasia's eyes as a teasing grin formed on her lips. "And what about Mr. Charles du Pont II? He seems to enjoy frequenting this bookshop, although it's curious how often he leaves without making a purchase." She tapped her index finger to her pursed lips. "I wonder what it is that appeals to him so much about this little shop."

"Mr. Charles du Pont is charming, I agree." Charlotte raised one eyebrow. "But have you not also noticed how often he walks in the park across the street with Miss Amelia on his arm? Besides"—Charlotte returned her sister's teasing grin—"I happen to believe Thomas and Alfred du Pont present a much better diversion and are far better topics of conversation."

A telltale blush stole into Anastasia's cheeks as the young girl dipped her head. She clasped her hands in front of her, her gaze fastened to the floor. Just as Charlotte expected. Her sister couldn't deny the way those two young lads doted on her every word or how often they went out of their way to catch a glimpse of her in the shop. Charlotte had lost count of how many times they walked by the windows, pretending not to look inside. At least they came from good families. Father couldn't fault their lineage, nor the powder mills their family operated along the banks of the Brandywine. It was the only reason Charlotte encouraged the antics. She had to look out for her sister's interests, after all.

Further banter was interrupted by the jingle of the bell. Anastasia retrieved the duster and returned to her work, leaving Charlotte to greet their new customer. Her sister could be quite adept at disappearing. With a glance at the front door, Charlotte was surprised to see a dark-haired gentleman backing into the shop, his shoulders slightly hunched and his hip pushing against the door as if he was pulling something heavy.

She immediately rushed from behind the counter to lend her assistance but froze when the man maneuvered his way beyond the door and pivoted to face her. His long fingers wrapped around the handles of a wheeled chair carrying a young girl who looked to be about ten or eleven years old. A top hat sat on top of a blanket that rested across her legs and covered most of her simple yet stylish black frock. Charlotte didn't often see an apparatus such as this, and her imagination immediately began to form several stories to explain the background she envisioned for her two visitors.

Charlotte shook her head and remembered her manners. She stepped forward as the gentleman's smooth cocoa gaze met hers. His breath came in labored yet measured spurts, but his expression held no sign of weariness or strain.

"Welcome to Cobblestone Books, sir. I am Miss Pringle, the owner. How may we be of service this morning?"

Surprise flickered in the gentleman's eyes as he tilted his head a fraction of an inch. He glanced around the shop then turned his attention to Charlotte. Stepping around the wheeled chair, whose occupant observed Charlotte with pensive curiosity, the gentleman placed one hand on the lapels of his overcoat. "Miss Pringle, I am Mr. Baxton. We have exchanged correspondence regarding my visit." Extending a hand toward her, he waited for her to return the gesture before continuing. "It is a pleasure to make your acquaintance," he said as he bowed over her hand, his mouth hovering just a hair's breadth above her knuckles.

With her hand tucked back against the folds of her skirts, Charlotte forced herself to reconcile the image she'd had of Mr. Baxton with the reality standing before her. Snippets of her sister's earlier repartee came to mind, but she brushed them aside.

Business. The single word served to set her thoughts straight again. A customer needed her help. She must remain focused. Never mind if the man's angled jaw line and high cheekbones gave him an air of distinction.

"Yes, yes, of course, Mr. Baxton. It is a pleasure to meet you as well."

He placed a hand on the young girl's shoulder and smiled. "Allow me to introduce my charming yet precocious niece, Grace Baxton." With a glance down at the blue-eyed girl, he winked and looked up again at Charlotte. "It is for her that we have journeyed to your shop. She has read every book in my possession, and we are in dire need of additional stories to keep her occupied."

Grace swatted at her uncle and gave him a stern yet amused stare. "That is not true, Uncle Richard. There are lots more books on the shelves in your library. But those are boring. You can have those."

Charlotte held back a grin at the girl's forthrightness then stepped forward and extended her right hand. "Grace, I am honored to meet you. And I'm very happy you have chosen my bookshop to satisfy your insatiable love of reading."

Grace shook Charlotte's hand and dipped slightly forward, as close to a curtsey as she could no doubt perform. "It's a pleasure, Miss Pringle." She tilted her tawny-haired head and scrunched her eyebrows together, two lines forming at the center. "What's *insatiable*?" she asked, sounding out each syllable.

"It means you have a love of reading that knows no end."

"Oh." The girl nodded. "Yes. That's true. I just love books. So many stories.

So much adventure." A dreamy expression crossed her face. "I could get lost for hours."

Charlotte winked. "I know exactly what you mean."

Grace beamed at the shared understanding. Then her attention shifted to somewhere over Charlotte's shoulder. "Who's that?"

Charlotte glanced behind her. So much for remembering her manners. "Oh, that is my sister." She beckoned Anastasia with a wave of her hand. "Anastasia, I'd like you to meet Mr. Baxton and his niece, Grace." Once her sister was at her side, Charlotte shifted her focus to the other pair. "Mr. Baxton, Grace, this is Anastasia Pringle."

Anastasia dipped into a quick curtsey. "Pleased to meet you both."

"My sister often spends her spare time with me, keeping the shop clean and shelving new books I've acquired. She also helps with customer purchases and is a tremendous assistant. I don't know what I would do without her."

Her sister bent low and leaned toward Grace, answering in a loud whisper. "Don't let my sister fool you. Charlotte and I have a lot of fun."

Grace giggled, and Anastasia straightened. "Would you like to come with me and take a tour of the shop?" She looked to Mr. Baxton and gestured toward the handles of the wheeled chair. "May I?"

Mr. Baxton hesitated, but at Grace's eager nod, he relinquished control and stepped back. "Grace can maneuver quite well on her own, too. Don't allow her to get lazy."

Anastasia led Grace away, chattering with the younger girl as they began their tour. Charlotte addressed Mr. Baxton. "The books you requested are here. I believe I found each and every one." She retrieved the small stack from behind the counter and placed it on top. Mr. Baxton closed the distance in three long steps. "Of course, you are under no obligation to purchase them all. I merely wanted to have them on hand for your perusal."

Mr. Baxton reached out and picked up each book in turn, holding them in his hands, turning them over, and flipping through the first few pages. He recognized the value of books. Charlotte could see that in the way he handled them. As he set the last book on top of the stack, he nodded. His expression reflected satisfaction. "They're in excellent condition."

Pride brought a smile to Charlotte's lips. "I insist that my books remain in the best form possible. Books available for purchase are guaranteed brand-new, and those available for borrowing are of the highest quality. If a book becomes tattered or torn, I do what I can to restore it, but if it is beyond repair, I offer it for sale at a lower price to anyone who wishes to purchase it. I also sell a few antique titles."

"Sounds perfectly reasonable. It's no wonder you have established a reputation that has spread as far as Ashbourne Hills, although I have a feeling knowledge of your shop extends further than that." Mr. Baxton glanced over his shoulder toward the doors. "And you couldn't have found a more perfect location. Customers can come here to acquire a book then venture to the park where they can relax and read." He turned back to face her with a twinkle in his eyes. "A winning combination."

Charlotte couldn't help responding to his congenial manner. A pleasant feeling sent warmth flowing through her veins. "It *has* proven to be good for business."

Mr. Baxton placed one well-manicured hand on top of the stack of books. These were not the hands of a common laborer, though the small scars and scrapes bore evidence of some form of work. "I'm pleased to hear that. Too many bookshops are forced to close their doors because of lack of business." He sighed. "Often, it's due to location. Other times, it's because the proprietor"—he gave her an acknowledging nod—"or proprietress doesn't truly love what he or she does. That's why my niece and I traveled here from Ashbourne Hills." He wrapped both hands around the books. "Well, I don't want to keep you any longer than necessary. How much do I owe you?"

Charlotte stated the total amount, and Mr. Baxton paid without hesitation. She procured a burlap sack and slid his books inside.

"I suppose it's time for us to depart. That is, if my niece will be willing to leave," he said with a wink. "Grace?"

"Yes, Uncle Richard?" The voice came from the back corner of the store, opposite where they stood.

"I have your books, and it is time to take our leave."

"Aw, Uncle Richard. Do we have to go so soon?"

Charlotte could almost picture the pouty lips and the woeful expression on the girl's face.

"I promise we shall return soon. Besides, you have a great deal of reading to do. We need to go home so you can get started."

Anastasia poked her head around a corner of one of the shelves. Grace appeared a moment later. Wheeling herself to the front of the store, Grace joined her uncle at the counter.

"All right. I'm ready to go." She crossed her arms. "But you must know how much I protest this departure."

Mr. Baxton turned to Charlotte, his mouth pressed into a thin line as he held back his laughter. With the sack held securely in his left hand, he extended his right. The warmth in his long fingers as they enveloped her own threatened to send a shiver up her back. But she resisted. Instead, she took a deep breath as he bowed slightly and raised her hand toward his lips.

"We shall return. You have my word on that." Mr. Baxton released her hand and stepped behind Grace. He placed the sack of books in her lap then positioned his hands on the wheeled chair. "Thank you again for your time, Miss Pringle. It has been a distinct pleasure."

As they reached the entrance, Mr. Baxton grabbed the door, but Anastasia beat him to it. She held it open, and Mr. Baxton backed Grace out to the sidewalk. He replaced his hat then touched two fingers to the brim in farewell, and before Charlotte knew it, the pair disappeared from view.

Charlotte stared out the bowed-front window, not seeing anything. It took several moments to realize her sister was speaking to her. She turned with a start.

"I'm sorry, Anastasia, what did you say?"

Her sister narrowed her eyes in silent assessment. "I said Grace is an amazing girl. I don't know if I could be as good-natured as she is if I were the one confined to a chair all day. But I like her." She raised one brow. "And her uncle seemed rather taken with you, as well."

Uh-oh. Charlotte recognized that look in her sister's eyes. It meant only one thing. Trouble. She'd better put a stop to things before any more ideas started stirring in that fanciful mind Anastasia possessed.

"Mr. Baxton was very cordial."

"Cordial?" Both eyebrows raised. "That's all you're willing to admit?"

Charlotte shrugged. "He was here only for a brief visit. What more could I possibly say about him? We didn't exactly have long to converse."

"Grace and I had the same amount of time, and I learned all about the accident that led to her being in the wheeled chair, how she came to live with her uncle, and the hope she has to one day walk again." She crossed her arms and glowered. "If she and I can talk about all of that, you and her uncle should have been able to discuss at least that much."

"Well, we primarily spoke of the bookshop and of Grace's love of reading. There truly wasn't time for much else."

"But he did promise to return. So maybe you can do better next time."

"Better?" Charlotte gave her sister a wry grin. "Are you insinuating I did a poor job with this conversation?"

Anastasia took a step back and held up her hands. "No, not at all. You were likely your usual self, keeping all talk to the bookshop, books, and reading."

"And what else is there to discuss when a customer comes in to shop?"

"Well, you could share a little about yourself."

"With someone I've just met? I wouldn't be so presumptuous."

Her sister sighed and rolled her eyes. "You're hopeless."

"No," Charlotte countered. "Merely practical." She had such fun baiting her sister and playing to her conniving, matchmaking schemes. But the last thing she needed was a young girl interfering with her customers.

"And that will never secure you a man," her sister said under her breath.

"What was that?"

Anastasia jerked up her head. "I said, uh, as the owner, I can understand."

Charlotte closed her eyes and shook her head. Some days, her sister could try her nerves. But most of the time having Anastasia at the shop brightened Charlotte's day.

"All right." Charlotte clapped her hands together. "What do you say we close up for lunch and a walk in the park?"

"I would love it!"

"You retrieve our lunches, and let Laura know it's time for a break."

Once on the cobblestone sidewalk, Charlotte turned the key in the lock and pivoted to stand beside her sister. She glanced up and down the busy street. Although she'd deny it, her thoughts dwelled on Mr. Baxton and his niece. A slow grin formed. She looked over her shoulder at the front of her shop, wondering when she would see them again.

❧

"How did your day go, Charlotte?" Her mother took the seat Father held out for her in their formal dining room. "Did you have many customers?"

Charlotte took her seat across from her mother. She had arrived home with barely enough time to dress for dinner. The rich aromas of braised beef and au gratin potatoes teased her nose. "It seemed to be a typical day by all accounts. I had a handful of my customers who frequent the shop on a regular basis." Her stomach rumbled, and she swallowed, anticipating the delicious meal about to be served.

"And one new one," Anastasia added. "Or two, if you count his niece. I am certain they will become regular customers before long."

The older of her two younger sisters stared at Charlotte in surprise. "You never told me about this." Bethany leaned in close and lowered her voice. "I shall expect a full report once dinner is completed."

"New customers are always good," Father said, leaning to allow the staff ample room to serve the meal.

Charlotte smiled and spoke a low "thank you" to Fiona as the girl served her. The young girl bobbed a curtsey and continued in silence. "Yes," Charlotte replied. "A great number of new patrons have visited my shop in the past few weeks. If this continues, I might have to consider hiring an additional assistant. Laura is quite adept, but I am not certain she is free to work to that capacity."

Father extended his hands toward his wife and Charlotte. "Shall we bless the meal?"

Charlotte joined hands with Bethany, and Anastasia took their mother's hand as Father said grace. The table was far too wide to complete the circle. Not like when Devon still lived with them. Some days it felt like mere days instead of four months since he'd married and moved out. Charlotte missed his teasing, jovial presence but missed her big brother's counsel and protectiveness more. So much now fell on her shoulders. She didn't know if she could handle it. Bethany filled part of the void with her level-headed advice. It wasn't the same, though.

Once grace had been said, Mother took a sip of water and dabbed her lips. "Perhaps you could allow that assistant to assume more of your responsibilities," she said, continuing the earlier conversation. "It would free you to pursue other interests rather than spend all your time in that dusty shop."

"Or take walks in the park should a certain gentleman ask." Anastasia patted her stylish blond curls and batted her eyelashes.

"Shush," Charlotte reprimanded her sister, narrowing her eyes and leveling a glare her way. The girl could be absolutely incorrigible.

"So Anastasia has met this gentleman, yet you neglect to share such important information with me?" Bethany gave a dramatic sigh. "I see where I rank in matters of importance."

"Bethany, it isn't like that at all," Charlotte protested. "Anastasia simply happened to be present when he arrived this afternoon. Had she not, it is likely neither one of you would be aware of him."

Father raised one eyebrow and regarded his three daughters. "It seems this gentleman has made quite an impact on all three of you." He cut a sliver of beef then stabbed it with his fork and paused before raising it to his mouth. "But you need to mind your manners and save your squabbles for the drawing room or your private chambers."

"Yes, Father."

"I'm sorry, Father."

The girls all nodded their dutiful obedience. Bethany nudged Charlotte, and they both shared a private grin with Anastasia across the table. This conversation would definitely continue later.

A few moments of silence ensued before Mother cleared her throat. "Does this gentleman have a name?"

Charlotte patted her mouth and returned her napkin to her lap. "Mr. Richard Baxton."

Mother's eyes widened. "Of the Ashbourne Hills Baxtons?"

"And Baxton Shipping?" Father added.

"I'm not certain." Charlotte furrowed her brow and tilted her head. "We did not speak much about personal matters during his brief visit." She recalled the return address on his letter. "Oh, but I do believe he *does* live in Ashbourne Hills."

Mother looked at Father. "Is that not the family who has recently suffered the loss of one of its sons?"

Father stroked his slightly graying moustache and beard. "If this gentleman is indeed from the family who owns Baxton Shipping, then yes." He looked again at Charlotte. "Did he not mention anything today that might confirm this?"

"Oh, it must be!" Anastasia jumped in. "I spoke with his niece this afternoon, and she told me about her recent accident. She was in a wheeled chair, too!"

"Anastasia." Father's low warning served its purpose.

"I'm sorry, Father." Anastasia lapsed into instant silence.

"Anastasia is correct," Charlotte continued. "Mr. Baxton's niece Grace was with him today. And she was in a rather ornate wheeled chair." She sipped her water. "It would seem this is the same Baxton family of which you and Mother have heard."

"Not only heard, Charlotte," Father countered. "We have engaged in business dealings with Baxton Shipping on more than one occasion, supplying gunpowder barrels for some of their ships over the years. Your Mother and I have also attended one or two social events at one of their homes."

What a small world. Charlotte could hardly believe a man who this afternoon seemed to be completely disconnected from her life had turned out to be entwined with her family's business.

Mother glanced across the table and caught Charlotte's eye. "If this Mr. Baxton becomes a regular customer, we shall have to invite him to join us one evening for dinner."

"Yes," Father agreed. "I would like to discuss a few business matters with him, and we will be sure to have Devon and his wife join us, too."

Charlotte's excitement over this potential friendship dimmed a little at the prospect of Mr. Baxton spending time in their home. That was the way things were done, but she had secretly hoped to have him to herself to some extent. . .at least at the bookshop. Then again, having him involved with her family could prove advantageous. She would have to wait and see.

Chapter 3

The bell above the shop door jingled, and Charlotte looked up, her breath catching in her throat. A second later, her shoulders slumped. Foolishness. Utter foolishness.

It had been nearly two weeks since Mr. Baxton and his niece had left her shop, promising to return. Her head told her it was too soon. Despite Grace's obvious love of reading, her uncle had purchased four books. It took time to read that many books. And the girl most likely had daily studies, as well. Charlotte felt guilty for expecting to see them so soon, but she couldn't persuade her mind and heart to react otherwise.

"Good afternoon, Mr. Couper." He might not be the man she hoped to see, but at least she could enjoy visiting with one of her regular patrons.

"Ah, good afternoon, Miss Pringle." The elderly gentleman removed his top hat, his ornate walking cane preceding him by one step. "And how are you on this grand and fortuitous day?"

He certainly seemed in a much brighter mood than normal. Charlotte could use an infusion of cheer to offset her disappointment.

"I am quite well, thank you. Have you received good news recently?"

A gleam in his eyes accompanied a teasing grin on his lips. "Why do you ask?" He was baiting her. She knew it.

"As much as I would like to believe otherwise, I can hardly imagine your enthusiasm is reserved solely for the joy of coming to this shop and finding another book to read."

"Touché," he countered. "Although I must correct you on one point. I do enjoy discovering new books. So my delight is partially reserved for my visits here every other week." Pressing his index finger to the counter in front of her, he fixed his reprimanding glance on her. "Do have more confidence in the appeal of this quaint shop. You have no idea how many lives you are impacting, nor how many pleased customers you are serving."

Chagrin filled her. "You are right, Mr. Couper. I shall endeavor to remember that in the future." She lightly grasped the edge of the counter with her fingers. "Now, do tell me about this good news. Then we can see about finding a new book for you."

"If you insist," he said with a mock sigh. Tucking his hat under his arm, he assumed a stance similar to one about to give a great speech. "You are familiar with the gardens adjoining my home on the Strand."

"Oh yes. I don't venture south to New Castle often, but when I am there, I always stroll along the cobblestone streets and marvel at the unique architecture of the homes. Yours stands sentinel over the Delaware River in a magnificent manner."

"Thank you. I quite agree, although I certainly can't presume to take credit for the beauty of its architecture. That honor distinctly belongs to Mr. George Read II. After his son passed away and the fire in town damaged so many homes, my brother was fortunate to acquire the land at public auction. Together, we repaired the damaged areas and created the formal gardens adjacent to the house."

"So those weren't always a part of the property?"

"No. From what I gather, when it was built, the focus was only on the stately and rather expansive home. Mr. Read spared no expense, right down to the silver-plated doorknobs."

Charlotte covered her mouth and giggled. Such extravagance. Then again, from what she'd heard and read about Mr. Read, profligacy and excessive behavior were apt descriptions.

"I recently hired a gardener to bring a fresh, new look to the various trees and flower beds," Mr. Couper continued. "He suggested adding one or two fountains and perhaps a few benches along a brick walking path. I hear tell he even spent time working for Joshua and Samuel Peirce on Peirce's Park."

"Oh! I adore that park. The gardens and fountains are beautiful." Charlotte nodded toward the park across the street. "As much as I enjoy time spent right here, there is something special about those gardens. They are no doubt the most beautiful in all of the Brandywine Valley. The Peirce brothers obviously had a deep love for the arboretum they planted."

"Yes, and it being open to public viewing enhances its beauty and appeal."

"So when is this renovation set to commence?"

"I am not certain, but I believe within the month."

"The next time I am in New Castle, I shall be certain to pay a visit and see the results of this gardener's handiwork."

Mr. Couper rapped his cane on the floor, the impact making a muffled thump against the woven carpet on which he stood. "Yes, you must. And tell me," he directed, glancing about to the left and right, "where is that charming little sister of yours? I don't believe I've seen her walking about the shop today."

"No, she isn't here this afternoon. She's working on a special project with two other students from her school. This is her last year, and she wants to finish with top honors."

"If she is anything like her older sister, I am certain she will," Mr. Couper said. "Now, let us talk about the real reason for my visit today."

Charlotte smiled. Mr. Couper always had some story to tell or news to report whenever he paid a visit. Some might find his eccentric ways a bother, but she enjoyed his company. He always returned the books he borrowed in excellent condition and had been a loyal customer almost since the day she opened her doors.

"So," Charlotte began, "what type of literature would you like to explore this time?"

"Actually"—he hooked his cane over his arm and turned toward the shelves behind him—"I'm here for my two grandsons. They have been creating their own adventures for some time now, and I'd like them to take a few adventures through books. What do you have that might appeal to them?"

"I know just where to direct you." Charlotte led Mr. Couper toward the shelves marked for younger readers. Locating the section she was seeking, she explained, "Just about anything written by Mark Twain, Jules Verne, or Lewis Carroll will be perfect for them."

Mr. Couper stepped closer to the shelves, and Charlotte moved to give him more room.

"I'll leave you to peruse these titles. If you have any questions, don't hesitate to ask."

"Thank you," he said without looking up, his eagerness keeping his attention locked on the books.

Charlotte continued the rest of the way up the aisle and heard the bell above the front door jingle just as she stepped into the open section of her shop. Stopping to straighten a few books on one of her feature displays, she didn't see her latest customer until he spoke.

"Good afternoon, Miss Pringle."

Mr. Baxton's voice was like warm, velvety chocolate being poured over vanilla ice cream. Charlotte tried to remain calm and professional, but she knew a silly grin had formed on her lips, and she couldn't will it away.

"Good afternoon, Mr. Baxton. I'm happy to see you have returned." Excited, eager, and relieved might be more accurate. At least now she could stop watching the door every minute. "But aren't you missing someone?" Charlotte looked behind him as if Grace might be waiting outside.

Mr. Baxton moved the scarf that hung around his neck to the side and unbuttoned the top two buttons of his overcoat. "Yes, I wasn't able to bring my niece with me today. She had an appointment with a specialist in Philadelphia that will last for most of the day. My mother, her grandmother, is with her, overseeing the appointment, so I decided now would be an excellent time to return. That way, I can have a surprise for her when I meet her after she's done."

The obvious affection he held for his niece touched a special place in Charlotte's heart.

"I'm certain she will be overcome with joy when she sees what you've brought. Now if you don't mind my asking, how did you come to be Grace's caretaker and guardian? And please don't hesitate to tell me if I'm being presumptuous. My curious nature often goes several steps ahead of my better judgment."

Mr. Baxton chuckled, alleviating Charlotte's concerns. "I don't mind talking about it. . .at least not now. Two months ago, my reaction would have been quite different. But time does allow the pain to heal." He moved toward one of the front tables and perched on the edge. His eyes took on a faraway look. With a deep breath, he began. "Grace was in a carriage with my brother and his wife. The carriage hit a deep rut in the road, causing one of the axles to break. It spooked the horses, and they bolted, broken axle and all."

A soft gasp escaped Charlotte's lips, but Mr. Baxton didn't seem to notice. He barely broke his stride in the retelling, seemingly lost in the memories.

"Elliott tried to persuade his wife and daughter to jump to safety ahead of him, but just as he managed to get the door open, the carriage careened over the edge of a fairly steep drop-off. Grace was thrown clear, but Elliott and Constance were trapped inside."

Charlotte closed her eyes against the horrific images his words created. How completely awful for Grace to have to endure something like that. And for Mr. Baxton, too.

"My brother and his wife didn't survive the crash, and as you have seen, Grace suffers from paralysis of the legs."

To lose a brother and a sister-in-law and then to become the sole caretaker of an injured niece—Charlotte could barely fathom the shock. Yet Mr. Baxton appeared to have adjusted rather well. And Grace obviously adored him. Respect for the man increased tenfold.

"You mentioned an appointment with a specialist today. So I assume the doctors haven't determined if Grace's injury is permanent?"

Mr. Baxton ran a hand through his hair, making a few stubborn locks stick out and one curl fall below his well-styled hairline. "No." He sighed. "And we have seen far too many, if you ask me. I have a hard time being patient when doctors who are supposed to have answers don't have any to offer me." A growl escaped his lips. "And Grace. It's not easy seeing the hope spark in her eyes with each new specialist we see, only to witness it being snuffed out like the gas streetlamps every morning at dawn. I don't know how much more of this I can take."

Charlotte tried to put herself in his shoes, tried to imagine what it might be like if she were the sole caretaker of a child such as Grace. Would she be able to handle it as well as Mr. Baxton apparently did? He still struggled. Anyone would. But the fact that he accepted the responsibility thrust at him spoke volumes. A lesser man would have walked away.

"And. . ." Charlotte began, uncertain if she should proceed.

"Yes?" Mr. Baxton replied, his tone and expression encouraging her to continue.

"And other children? Did Grace have any brothers or sisters?"

"No." He sighed. His eyes held such sadness. "Elliott and Constance. . ." He stopped, appearing to rethink what he was about to say. "No, there weren't," he finally said.

Charlotte wanted to reach out and cover his hands with her own, but she didn't want to overstep the bounds of propriety. Instead, she put all her sympathy into her voice, hoping her eyes conveyed what physical touch couldn't. "I truly am sorry for your loss. You and Grace both." She placed her hands on the countertop and leaned forward. "I have a feeling God has something very special planned for that little girl."

"Yes," he said, regarding her with a curious expression. He tugged on the two ends of his scarf. "I admit it's difficult trying to figure out why God would allow something so tragic to happen to such an innocent little girl. And there have been times I haven't been the best role model for Grace," he added with a rueful grin.

"Anyone in your circumstances would react the same way. And given the situation, I would say you are entitled to a few weak moments." If it had been her, Charlotte would have had more than her fair share of weak moments.

One side of Mr. Baxton's mouth turned up. The first sign their conversation was taking a lighter turn. "Why, thank you, Miss Pringle. It is a comfort to know you understand."

Charlotte held up one hand. "I am not certain I understand, as much as I can sympathize with what you're facing." She clasped her hands tightly, offered what she hoped was an air of lightheartedness, and prayed he wouldn't consider it inappropriate. "It seems all those books I've read haven't been for naught."

The genuine smile he'd worn when he first entered her shop returned.

"You are correct. And whether it's empathy or sympathy"—he stood and bestowed upon her a formal bow, his eyes twinkling as his gaze met hers—"I shall take either one. I make no qualms about particulars."

Relaxing her grip, Charlotte exhaled slowly and quietly. She often couldn't determine when the right moment came to interject a little humor, especially when the conversation leading up to that point had been melancholy. But Mr. Baxton didn't seem to mind, and now they could move beyond the unpleasant memories of his recent loss.

"So." Mr. Baxton's voice interrupted her musings. "Now that you know all about my recent state of affairs, what do you say we discuss the object of those affairs and locate a few more books to help Grace pass the time?"

Charlotte shifted her focus and became a bookshop owner once more. It wouldn't be easy treating Mr. Baxton as just another customer, but she'd see to his needs and allow him to take the lead.

"Yes, of course." She joined him in front of the counter as they faced the aisles and shelves of books. "I recall the books you purchased on your last visit. But they contained a wide variety of stories and writing styles. Why don't you tell me the types of things Grace likes? Then we shall see which of the many books will suit her interests best."

He nodded. "Sounds logical." Mr. Baxton cocked his head. "Let me see. I know she loved this book about island adventures, but I don't recall the title or the author."

Charlotte mentally scanned the list of titles she could bring to mind. "Could it be *The Swiss Family Robinson* by Johann David Wyss?"

Mr. Baxton snapped his fingers. "Yes! That's the one. She spoke endlessly of it for days. I almost felt I was right there with the family by the time Grace found another book to capture her attention."

Charlotte jotted down the title on a piece of paper. "Books do have a way of doing that to a person." She spoke from experience. She couldn't recall the number of times her parents had had to reprimand her and tell her to focus on her studies more than her pleasure reading. They of course had been right, and now that her school days were behind her, Charlotte could read to her heart's content.

"All right," Mr. Baxton continued, "we have that one book as an example. But Grace also loves reading about faraway places and adores the stories where the princess must be rescued by the handsome prince."

"What girl doesn't? You never outgrow that tale," Charlotte said without thinking, as she wrote down a few more notes.

"It doesn't always have to be a fairy tale," he said softly.

Charlotte glanced up to see a wry grin on Mr. Baxton's lips and a teasing twinkle in his eyes. She was tempted to allow a glimpse of her own dreams and desires but instead chose the safe and impersonal route. "You are correct. It is a timeless story that manifests itself in a variety of ways through many different lives. Just when you start to believe the happily-ever-after is out of reach, the prince makes an appearance and a satisfying conclusion is reached."

"Which brings me to another favorite of Grace's. She cannot seem to get enough of the stories about fighting against seemingly impossible odds and winning. It's what gives me hope that her paralysis won't become a permanent part of her life."

Charlotte touched the unsharpened end of the pencil to her chin. "I have only spoken to Grace the one time, and I certainly don't know her as well as you, but she doesn't appear to be a girl who gives up easily." She pointed the pencil in Mr. Baxton's direction. "I can imagine how exhausting the visits to the specialists can become. And if she loves those stories about impossible odds, she will find a way to win over her circumstances."

He nodded. "You are correct. Despite the repetitive cycle of disappointing news or no answers at all, Grace's determination is what keeps me fighting for her."

Once again, she pointed the pencil toward Mr. Baxton. "You are a constant source of strength for your niece. Do not forget that a champion for the handsome prince is just as important in the battle as the actual fight the prince must endure."

"True."

Charlotte straightened and picked up the pad of paper. "I think I have enough information to make some recommendations."

A few minutes later, Mr. Baxton followed Charlotte to the front, his arms laden with copies of *Ivanhoe*, *Oliver Twist*, *Nicholas Nickleby*, *The Three Musketeers*, and *Alice's Adventures in Wonderland*. He quickly paid for his purchases and waited while Charlotte placed them in a sack.

"Once again," he said as he tipped his imaginary hat, "I am in your debt. Grace will be beside herself when I collect her from the specialist's office and present her with these surprises."

"And once again, it is my pleasure. I look forward to hearing how she liked these and which one was her favorite." Perhaps Mr. Baxton would bring Grace again so the little girl could answer for herself. Charlotte wouldn't mind seeing either one of them again.

After buttoning the top buttons of his overcoat, Mr. Baxton tucked the sack against him with his left arm and bowed over her hand. "Miss Pringle, I bid you good day and offer my deepest appreciation for your time."

"You are most welcome, Mr. Baxton." He held her gaze a moment longer, and Charlotte swallowed in an attempt to calm her erratic heartbeat. "Good day," she managed, although her voice sounded forced to her own ears.

He turned and headed for the door, casting one final look over his shoulder and waving as he left the shop.

"Now, that man fancies you. There's no doubt about it."

Startled by Mr. Couper's voice, Charlotte turned with a jolt to face him. He wore a wide grin as he stood supported by his walking cane.

"And judging from the bits of conversation I heard, I believe the attraction is reciprocated."

Warmth crept up Charlotte's neck, and she took a deep breath in an attempt to prevent it from reaching her face. "Shame on you, Mr. Couper, for eavesdropping," she said without irritation. "You were supposed to be looking for books for your grandsons."

"But I was," he countered, holding up three titles. "And I have found them." He walked to the counter, his expression one of pure mischief. "Can you truly fault a man who merely wishes happiness for his favorite bookshop owner?"

Charlotte pursed her lips and regarded the gentleman. How could she possibly be cross with him? In many ways, he reminded her of her father. He'd even told her on more than one occasion that he'd never had a daughter. She certainly couldn't begrudge him some harmless banter.

"All right, Mr. Couper, I shall forgive you...this time," she said with a grin.

"Ah," he sighed as he ran his fingers over his well-groomed mustache, "if only I could be here when that young gentleman returns." He winked. "I should like to hear the reason he gives for prolonging his stay."

"You, Mr. Couper, are up to no good."

"I wouldn't have it any other way, Miss Pringle."

She obviously wasn't going to win this argument, so she should probably redirect their conversation. "Shall I total your purchases for you?"

He placed the three books on the counter and nodded. "If you must."

She gave him the amount, and he counted out the coins.

With the three books in one hand and his cane in the other, he sauntered to the door. "I expect to hear about Mr. Baxton's return and perhaps even his niece when I next visit your shop."

"I will do my best to oblige."

Mr. Couper pointed his cane at her. "See that you do, young lady." Tipping his hat, he took his leave.

Charlotte leaned back against the shelf behind her and smiled. Days like this one made being a bookshop owner a true delight.

Chapter 4

"Mr. Baxton, might I have a word with you?"

The doctor summoned Richard from the waiting room, where he and Mother sat, as a dark-haired nurse escorted Grace out from an examining room. The woman's stark white uniform blended almost too well with the white-painted walls and immaculate marble floors.

"Grace, I will only keep your uncle for a moment. I am sure your grandmother will be more than happy to continue keeping you company." The doctor gave Grace and Mother a kind smile, compassion reflecting in his eyes. He turned to Richard and gestured toward the room Grace just left. "If you please, Mr. Baxton?"

Richard preceded the doctor into the room and waited while the man closed the door. He'd been in a number of similar rooms, but this one possessed a warmth he'd not felt in any of the others. The color of the walls, the furniture, and the various items on the table welcomed anyone entering.

"Will you have a seat?"

Richard took one of the two cushioned chairs opposite the doctor's desk and was surprised when the doctor took the other. The man reached for a folder on the edge of his desk and flipped it open.

"I promised your niece I would only keep you for a moment, Mr. Baxton, and I intend to keep my word."

"So what is the prognosis?" Richard wasn't in the mood to waste any time. "Grace and I have been through this several times. If what you have to say isn't encouraging, we might as well get right to it."

The specialist sighed. "I know how tiring this must be for you both. But I am glad you came to see me. As you are aware, I have done extensive research and study on the subject of paralysis. Your niece's case is not unique."

Richard moved to the edge of the seat. "Do you mean you have seen this before?"

"Yes, and I have seen it cured, as well."

Finally! Richard's heart beat faster. At long last, they might have some good news. Of course the doctor hadn't exactly said anything one way or another.

The doctor held up a hand of caution. "I do not want what I am about to say to be construed in the wrong manner. But based upon my examination of your niece and her response to some of the more detailed tests, she has a chance at walking again."

"A chance? Does that mean there is also a chance she might not walk again?"

"Correct. The odds are as much in Grace's favor as they are against her. But it's going to take a lot of hard work on Grace's part, as well as yours."

"We are no strangers to hard work, Doctor. I can assure you of that." Richard pressed his palms to his knees. "Ever since the accident, we have worked daily on exercises, both of us hoping it would do some good and that one day we'd start to see results. When I am unavailable to assist, her grandmother helps in my place." Those exercises hadn't been easy. It nearly broke his heart to see his niece struggle so often. Not to mention how hard she tried with seemingly no improvement.

"You and your mother are to be commended, Mr. Baxton. Those very exercises can be credited with putting your niece in such a favorable position. Unfortunately, the dedication of many of the patients I see isn't nearly as serious, nor are they as determined as the three of you obviously have been." The doctor consulted his notes, flipping through several pages. "Because you have remained faithful in exercising even when you haven't seen evidence of it making any difference, Grace's muscle tone and reflexes have remained strong. Far too often, I witness atrophy of the muscles and no sign whatsoever of any reflexive response. For those patients, my prognosis isn't as encouraging. Now, Grace does have a measure of atrophy, but that is to be expected."

"So what happens next?" Richard didn't want to press the doctor, but he wanted to rejoin Grace. His mother would need relief from her long day as well.

"Next, we schedule another appointment." He closed the folder and regarded Richard with a serious look. "I will perform a handful of more extensive tests, and if those produce the results I expect, we will discuss the details of an operation."

Richard was about to jump up from the chair. He froze at that last word. "Operation?" Just repeating it produced a sinking feeling in his gut. "What kind of operation?"

"There is no need to be concerned. Not at this stage." The doctor's voice held a practiced calm. "We'll know more after Grace's next appointment. And at that time, we will discuss the matter further." He rose, and Richard did the same. "I have a great deal of hope for your niece, Mr. Baxton. You have done an admirable job keeping her limber and making her an excellent candidate to proceed further."

"Doctor, that is music to my ears." Richard glanced over his shoulder toward the door. "Does Grace know? Have you said anything to her?"

The doctor smiled. "Not yet. I wanted to leave the honor to you." He gestured toward the door, silently inviting Richard to precede him.

Richard pushed the door open, revealing an anxious Grace, who sat with her arms braced against the arms of the wheeled chair, almost lifting herself out of it in anticipation.

"Doctor, thank you again." Richard held out his hand, and the doctor gave him a firm handshake. Richard always appreciated such handshakes as well as direct eye contact in all of his business dealings. The doctor didn't disappoint.

The doctor gestured toward the front desk. "If you speak with my assistant, she will see that your next appointment is scheduled, and we can proceed from there."

Richard made quick work of the appointment then joined Grace and his mother.

"What did you find out?" His niece's anxiety was obvious in her voice and facial expression, while Mother looked bemused.

Richard stepped behind Grace's chair and took hold of the handles, silently propelling her toward the main doors.

"You're not going to tell me yet, are you Uncle Richard?"

He smiled as she looked up at him. "Not right now, no. We will have plenty of time to talk in the carriage on the way home." Two attendants held open the double doors for them, and Richard nodded his thanks. "I'm afraid you will simply have to be patient for a bit longer."

She sighed and turned around. "Very well. If you insist."

Richard almost laughed at how stoically Grace sat in her chair. She stared straight ahead and didn't utter a single word until they reached their carriage. The footman greeted them and assisted Mother first before helping Richard get Grace safely tucked inside. Once again, Richard was grateful for the use of his brother's carriages and staff. The affairs of the family business might not be settled, but at least he could continue to make use of his brother's employees and belongings in the interim.

"Are we headed home, sir?" the driver called down from his perch.

"Yes, Jacob, we are."

"Very good, sir."

Richard climbed inside, and the footman closed the door. As soon as the carriage started moving, Grace commenced with the interrogation. She pulled the blanket over her legs up to her waist and twisted her upper torso as best she could to face him.

"So, what did the doctor say? Did he tell you anything different? Why did you smile and seem so pleased when you came out of his office? Why did we have to make another appointment? And is anything in that sack for me?"

Mother sighed and leaned back against the cushioned interior. "I'm certainly happy to know you shall handle this barrage of questions. I believe I'll take advantage of our long ride and rest a spell."

Richard patted his mother's hand. "It's been a long day, and I appreciate your being available to stay with Grace. Now close your eyes and don't give us another thought."

His mother did just that, and Richard focused his attention on his niece. Her last question stuck out. He glanced at the sack from Cobblestone Books, lying on the bench. He should have known she'd see that right away. He couldn't hide it anywhere other than with the driver, but he'd wanted the books with them inside the carriage so he could present them to Grace.

"All right. One question at a time. First, the doctor complimented us on continuing with the exercises every day, and he said it has helped you stay strong despite your paralysis. He was quite impressed with how you responded to the tests he performed, and he wants to see you again so he can conduct a few more tests before deciding if you're able to have surgery."

"Surgery?" Her eyes brightened. "You mean he thinks something can be done to help me? He actually said he can do it?"

"He didn't say he could guarantee anything, but he did say he had a good feeling about it all. He'll know more after your next appointment. We can talk more about it then."

"All right." She placed her hands primly in her lap and smiled. "Now, what is in the sack? Is it for me?"

"As a matter of fact"—he moved the sack to his lap—"there is something in here for you." He peeked inside then gave Grace a teasing grin. "But I am not certain I should show you everything at once. Perhaps just one at a time."

"One at a time is fine with me!" Grace clapped in rapid succession. "I can make the fun last longer that way."

"Very well." Richard reached inside the sack, intentionally making a grand show of retrieving the first book. He nearly laughed at the anxious expression on Grace's face and the way her fingers wiggled, as if they itched to hold the treasure he would soon produce. "This is your first surprise."

"Oh! A new book!" Grace reached across the space between the two seats to take possession of the copy of *Ivanhoe* Richard handed to her. "Sir Walter Scott," she read then looked at her uncle. "So what is this one about?"

Richard breathed a silent prayer of thanks that Miss Pringle had given him a brief summary of each book as she pulled it from the shelves. "That one is about a man named Ivanhoe who comes home from the Crusades and gets caught in the middle of a battle between King Richard, the Lionheart, and his brother, John. But all he really wants to do is claim his inheritance and the woman he loves, Rowena."

"King Richard? That's your name."

He chuckled again. "Well, yes, only I am not a king."

"I bet you could be one if you had to be."

Ah, the unfailing trust of a child. It warmed his heart to see how much his niece loved him. "Thank you for that, Grace. But I think I'll leave the kingdom ruling to those in royalty. I have enough to worry about here without having to think about making decisions for an entire country."

Grace tilted her head and stared at the cover of the book. "I think I agree. I would much rather read about them than live like them." She set the book down and held out a hand for the next. "Can I see the next surprise?"

"Please?"

"Please," she added dutifully.

He reached in and pulled out *Oliver Twist,* hesitating a moment before handing it to her. "Now, this one I only want you reading during the day, and I would like you to read it when I am nearby."

She took the book and looked at the title. "Why? Is it scary?"

"Not so much scary as it contains some parts that could make you very sad, and some people in the story are very cruel. I want you nearby so you can ask questions or talk about the book when you want."

"All right." She shrugged.

Richard hadn't been too sure about that book when Miss Pringle had suggested it. He'd read it himself as a boy, but that was just it. He was a boy. And he didn't mind the fights or the orphanage or the street scenes. Some might say it wasn't proper reading for a young girl, but that had never stopped him before. Besides, his brother and sister-in-law had told him many times about the kinds of books Grace read. She was wise beyond her years, and he was confident she could handle the story.

"I'm going to give you the rest of the books all at once. No sense prolonging the surprise since you already have two of them."

Her eyes widened, and excitement lit up her face. "How many more are there?"

"Three," he replied, "for a total of five." He handed *Nicholas Nickleby, The Three Musketeers,* and *Alice's Adventures in Wonderland* to her and waited for her to read the titles.

"I haven't heard of this Nicholas one, but I know the other two. Mother loved to read—" She fell silent.

Richard leaned forward and touched her hand. "It's all right, Grace. It's only been a few months. Memories of your mother and father and all the good times you shared are sure to make you sad. You miss them a lot. So do I."

She looked up with unshed tears gathering in her eyes. He wanted nothing more than to pull her onto his lap and comfort her. So he moved from his seat and squeezed in between her and the side of the carriage then lifted her into his lap. Several tears fell and moistened his coat, leaving a damp spot where they soaked into the material.

He brushed back her hair from her face and kissed the top of her head. "And now we have another reason for you to have these new books. Every one you read will help you remember your mother and father that much more, and we can discuss those memories together. Miss Pringle assured me you would love all five books, and I have no doubt about that."

"Miss Pringle?" Grace leaned back and looked at him. She wiped at her eyes and sniffled. "You saw Miss Pringle today? So you went to Cobblestone Books for these."

The abrupt change in her demeanor made him press back against the cushion. One minute, she was mourning the loss of her beloved parents, and the next, her eyes were bright with inquisitiveness and a spark of mischief. It felt like night and day.

"Yes. Yes, I did." Richard wiped the tear track on one of her cheeks and smiled. "Your appointment with the specialist was going to take a while, so I decided to make the journey and get you something special after having to endure all that testing."

"What did you say to her? How long were you at the shop? Did she ask about me? About why I wasn't there? Was her sister Anastasia there? When will you be seeing her again?"

He held up his hands. "Whoa! Again the barrage of questions. I can only answer so many." Carefully shifting his position, Richard placed Grace back on the seat and arranged the blanket across her legs. Then he returned to his seat next to his dozing mother so he could see his niece better. She obviously didn't need comforting anymore, so there was no reason for either one of them to be uncomfortable.

A sheepish grin appeared on her lips, and she ducked her head. "I'm sorry, Uncle Richard. But I wish I could have been there. I wish I could have seen you talking to her."

"We'll have to make sure you go next time." Then his mind focused on the last part of her statement. "Wait a moment. Why do you wish you could have seen me talking to her?"

The excitement returned. "When will we be going back?" she asked, ignoring his question.

Richard laughed. "I don't know. I suppose it all depends on how long it takes you to read those books I just purchased for you and when you will need more material to read."

Grace looked down at the books in her lap. "Oh, right. I will get started on them right away." She placed both hands on top of the stack then fixed him with a probing gaze. "So what did the two of you talk about, and how long did you stay?"

If he hadn't known any better, Richard might have thought his niece had turned into a detective or newspaper reporter.

"You answer my question, and I will answer yours. Fair is fair. Why do you wish you could have seen me talking to Miss Pringle?"

"No reason." She looked away. "She seemed so nice, and you were in a better than good mood after meeting her. I spent most of the time with her sister, and I want to know more about Miss Pringle. That's all."

Richard wasn't sure he believed that to be the only reason. Grace didn't generally keep secrets from him. At least not that he noticed. But this time, she seemed to be acting more evasive than normal. Perhaps more would come out if he kept her talking.

"We talked about you, mostly," he said, returning to her list of questions. "When I entered the shop, she looked around and remarked that I appeared to be missing someone."

Grace smiled. "She remembered me."

"Of course she did, you silly goose. You aren't exactly easy to forget."

A self-satisfied smile formed on her lips. "I know."

Richard shook his head. Leave it to an eleven-year-old to be blunt and precocious. But at least he always knew how she felt and usually knew what she was thinking.

"What did you tell her about me?"

"Let's see." He placed his thumb and index finger on either side of his clean-shaven chin. "I told her about your appointment today and the other specialists we've seen. I told her about the accident, everything you told me about it."

"Was she sad, too?"

"Yes. She was sad to hear you had to go through all of that. And sad you lost your parents." He forced a brighter tone to his voice. "But she believes as I do that God has something very special planned for you. We just have to wait and see what He has up His sleeve."

Grace giggled. "God doesn't have sleeves."

"And how do you know? Have you seen Him?"

"Nobody can see Him. He's invisible and everywhere at once. But I know He doesn't have sleeves."

"And you are absolutely certain about that?"

She gave a succinct and determined nod of her head. "Absolutely."

"Well, I'll take your word for it. But I think I'm going to save my opinion until I can see for myself."

"Then I will, too." She again placed her hands in her lap. "Now, what else did you say to Miss Pringle about me?"

"Oh, we are back to that again, are we?" He grinned. "I thought we were done."

"But you didn't get to the best part."

"What best part?"

She crossed her arms. "The part where you talked about the books I like."

"And how do you know we talked about that?"

"Because she picked out these five books"—Grace touched the stack on her lap—"just for me. She wouldn't have known which books to pick if you hadn't told her what I liked."

"How very astute of you."

"I'm smart just like you, Uncle Richard."

"Actually, I think your intelligence comes from your parents." Best to keep his brother's memory alive, along with Grace's mother. He wanted her to be proud of them and of being their daughter.

"But you are my father's brother," she countered with stubborn certainty. "So you could have it, too."

How could he argue with that logic? If she was this smart now, there was no telling what she'd be like as she got older. He might be in for quite the adventure. He only prayed he could keep up with her and give her everything she needed. If it weren't for his mother's assistance, he didn't know how he'd manage. His life and their livelihood remained up in the air until the family business affairs were settled. But he didn't want to think about that now.

"All right. You win." He relaxed against the back of the seat cushion. "Intelligence runs in our family, and we all have it." Richard glanced out the window and took note of their surroundings. "Why don't you start reading one of your books? I'm going to close my eyes for a little rest until we reach home."

"Very well."

If only all instructions and decisions were received and made so easily.

Chapter 5

Charlotte pulled the needle through the cotton shift she was mending. Good thing the task didn't require much of her attention. She doubted she could muster up much more concentration.

"Ouch!"

"Be careful, Charlotte," Anastasia warned. "That's the third time in the last ten minutes you've stuck yourself with the needle. You're usually more attentive than that."

She was. But lately she had trouble keeping her mind on anything other than her bookshop, Mr. Baxton, and his darling niece. After hearing the story of Grace's accident, Charlotte felt her heart going out to the girl even more.

Three weeks. It had been three weeks since Charlotte had last seen Mr. Baxton. Despite it being foolish, she had begun watching for him after only one week. Common sense told her it had been a little over two weeks between his first and second visits, and this time, she had sent him home with one more book. But try telling that to her heart and the hope it held of seeing him again.

At least Anastasia had been occupied with her special school project. She'd only been at the bookshop one day a week, so Charlotte hadn't had to endure too much teasing when she watched the door for Mr. Baxton's appearance. At home, though, her sister was ruthless. She'd even managed to get their more peaceful sister, Bethany, involved.

"Charlotte? Are you all right?"

A hand on her arm made her stop midstitch. "What?" She turned to see Anastasia looking at her with concern.

"I asked if you were all right. Bethany and I have been telling you about the cotillion you missed last weekend. But you were miles away, lost in thought."

Look at what daydreaming of Mr. Baxton did. She had to stop this.

"I'm sorry." She dropped her shoulders and sighed, letting her hands and the shift fall to her lap. "I'm afraid my thoughts have been centered on the bookshop of late."

Bethany glanced up. "Your shop—or on a certain gentleman customer?"

Anastasia giggled. "And his resilient niece." The two younger sisters shared a private look. "Is it any wonder she's managed to put the needle into her thumb more times than through the shift she's mending?"

"This gentleman has our sister rather besotted."

Charlotte sighed. She truly needed this. Straightforward, no-nonsense talk to help her clear her head...even if it was delivered courtesy of her scheming younger sisters.

Bethany leveled a suspicious look in her direction. "So is what Anastasia tells me true? You hear the bell above your shop door chime and every time hope it's this Mr. Baxton returning to see you?"

"Yes," she admitted in a whisper.

"I told you so." Anastasia clapped her hands and bounced up and down as much as the wingback chair would allow. "Our dear Charlotte has finally met a man who has captured her attention. And now she wishes to make him her beau."

"I never said I wanted him for a beau," Charlotte protested.

Then again, perhaps her sister was right. She might not know much about Mr. Baxton, but she knew what was important. That he trusted God, cared deeply for his niece, accepted responsibility when it was given to him, and was a man of his word. She could certainly do far worse. But as of right now, their relationship was nothing more than friendship. If she could even call it that.

"You didn't." Anastasia nodded. "But you didn't say you *didn't* want him for a beau either," she added with a smirk. "And with Mother called away to tend to dinner preparations, we have the freedom to pursue this line of questioning."

Charlotte leveled a glare at her younger sister, but the girl wouldn't be dissuaded.

"Come now, Anastasia." Bethany maintained a level tone to her voice. "Let's not take things too far."

Ah good. A voice of reason. At least she had Bethany on her side.

"After all," Bethany continued, turning back toward Charlotte with a gleam in her eyes. "If we're not careful, we might cause our dear Charlotte to become exasperated and despondent. Then we'd never find out the secrets this gentleman possesses that have so enraptured our dear sister as to make her lose her concentration while performing the simple task of sewing."

Charlotte slapped her hands on the arms of her chair. "That is not the way it is, at all, you two. You're turning two minor little exchanges into something of extraordinary proportions."

"But of course!" Anastasia spread her arms wide. "It's what we do best! How else would we manage to extract the necessary information from you if not by extreme measures?"

Charlotte looked at her two sisters. Their faces indicated genuine earnestness. Then the corner of Anastasia's mouth twitched.

"Ah-ha!" Charlotte pointed a finger at each one in turn, mirth bubbling up from inside. "I knew it. You two couldn't fool anyone with that ruse."

Bethany placed one hand on her chest and faked an innocent expression. "Why, whatever do you mean?" The batting of her eyelashes only made it worse.

Charlotte pressed her lips tight to hold back the laughter, and it came out more like a loud snort. That was all it took. The three sisters leaned toward one another as giggles and merriment overtook them.

Bethany recovered first, straightening and taking several deep breaths to regain her composure. Anastasia sat up as well, her arms holding her middle as she gasped for air. Charlotte struggled to catch her own breath. Her sides hadn't hurt that much in months.

"All right. All right." Bethany splayed her hands, palms down, as if attempting to quiet a rowdy group of children. "Let's make an attempt at being civil, shall we?"

Leave it to Bethany to get everything back under control. Always the voice of reason. She led by example as she picked up the pieces of fabric she was stitching to make a skirt. When they all settled back to their respective tasks, Bethany inhaled then released a single breath.

"Now, Charlotte, *dear*. Why don't you finish telling us about this gentleman before our efforts to find out more are waylaid yet again?"

Charlotte could not escape. She crossed her ankles and adjusted her skirts. Looking straight ahead, she delivered the answer she hoped they wanted to hear.

"It's really not as significant as the two of you make it sound." Charlotte rushed to continue. "Yes, I will admit Mr. Baxton and his niece have touched a chord in my heart with little Grace's plight. But I do not wish to make Mr. Baxton my beau," she said with a brief pointed look at Anastasia, who ducked her head. "Right now, considering him a friend might be presumptuous of me. So let's call him a potential faithful customer, all right?"

"And has he asked you to call him by his first name yet?" Bethany asked. "Or are you still using formal address when you greet one another?"

"I only know him as Mr. Baxton." Charlotte placed her palms on her skirt and slid them toward her knees. "As I said, I am not certain he wishes to be a friend, but even if he had made that request of me, I likely would not tell you, lest it provide you with more ammunition for your cross-examination."

Bethany gasped. "We would never take advantage of something such as that!"

"Oh, I would!" Anastasia piped up. "Anything to begin arranging a potential suit between them."

Charlotte shrugged. "I do so hate to disappoint you both, but there truly isn't much more to say." Actually, there was, but disclosing the unspoken mannerisms she'd observed might not be the best thing to do right now.

"When are you going to see him again?" Bethany asked.

"I am not sure. It has been three weeks since he was last in my shop, and he promised he would return." She knew him to be a man of his word, but she wished he had given a more specific time frame.

"Very well." Bethany assumed a nonchalant air. "Since it appears there isn't anything further to extract from you, I suppose we have no choice but to return to our sewing."

Anastasia narrowed her eyes. "Yes." She jutted her chin into the air. "But I'm certain there will be more. We'll discover it all eventually. And when we do. . ." A teasing gleam entered her eyes, and she rubbed her hands together.

"Discover what?" Mother asked as she entered the room to join them in their sewing. "Thank goodness the matter of dinner has been settled," she said as she settled into the chair she'd recently vacated. "Now what have you three girls been discussing in my absence?"

"Oh, just the repeat visit of a certain Mr. Baxton to Charlotte's bookshop," Anastasia replied with a coy smile.

Mother's face showed interest. "So he returned?" She directed her question at Charlotte.

"Yes, but his niece was not with him."

"Did you extend the invitation your father and I discussed?"

Charlotte relayed what she hoped was an apologetic expression to her mother. "No, ma'am. I am sorry. It completely slipped my mind."

"No doubt because something else occupied it," Bethany said under her breath.

Charlotte gave her sister a swift kick, but Bethany anticipated the action and moved her legs out of reach. "I promise, Mother, the next time I see him, I will extend your invitation." That conversation would likely be awkward, so another thought came to mind. "Perhaps to aid my memory, I can give him a letter stating your wishes."

"Yes, that would be most appropriate." Mother nodded. "I shall compose it later this evening and leave it for you to take with you to the shop tomorrow." She began the methodical motion of needlepoint as an amused smile formed on her lips. "I gather from the end of the conversation I interrupted that there is some uncertainty regarding this Mr. Baxton?"

Bethany waved a hand in the air. "Oh, it is merely Charlotte being overly cautious and not willing to admit the possibilities."

Mother gave Charlotte an approving glance before shifting her focus to her middle daughter. "Being cautious is not a negative trait. I applaud it."

"Bethany and Anastasia are merely reading more into the situation than presently exists. As I told them, I am not certain anything further will develop."

"Something will happen," Anastasia stated. "I am sure of it."

"Be that as it may," Mother replied, "it hasn't happened yet. And I believe we owe it to Charlotte to respect her privacy and not meddle any further on the subject."

Charlotte picked up her shift to resume making repairs. Her sisters didn't seem hurt or offended, and for that she was grateful. Still, it wouldn't hurt to reassure them, just in case.

"If that time comes, I promise you'll be the first to know."

"We'd better be!" Anastasia threatened in a nonaggressive manner.

In the meantime, Charlotte prayed she could maintain her focus as well as her professionalism when it came to seeing Mr. Baxton again.

❧

"Mother, you cannot expect me to be in attendance at every one of these social functions." Charlotte looked over the list again. She saw enough events to keep three young women busy, let alone one.

Her mother glanced up from where she stood repositioning flowers in the vase on the table in the front hall. "I expect you to do as you're told, the same as all the other times the cotillion season has come to a close."

"But I'm at the bookshop all day. I have work to do."

"And I don't?" Her mother gestured loosely about the expanse of the manor. "It isn't easy managing a home of this size, along with the household staff we employ."

"I didn't mean that, Mother." Charlotte held up the list. "I meant there simply won't be time for me to come home, dress, and be ready for each of these events. You are already here and can make time in your day to dress."

"Then you will simply have to leave your shop early enough to allow adequate time to prepare." Her mother sighed. "I am not the one who decided to begin a profession when you had a more than ample livelihood provided for you right here at home."

Charlotte had lost count of how many times she'd had this conversation with her mother over the past year and a half. Her father had been the one to provide the funds for her to purchase the shop. He had arranged for his colleagues to donate books so she wouldn't have to buy everything. He had even called in a favor with one of his friends to craft the artistic wooden shingle that hung over the entrance. And all of this he'd done in spite of her mother's censure.

It just wasn't worth it to go down that path again. There was no changing her mother's mind, although just the other day, Mother had seemed to be congenial about the bookshop. Or perhaps she'd been expressing support of the potential Mr. Baxton brought. That would be more in line with Mother's view of things.

"And before you say anything further"—her mother broke into her thoughts—"allow me to remind you that our family has a reputation among our friends and business associates." The matriarch of the Pringle family smoothed her hands down the front of her tailored day dress. "We are expected to make our appearance at these functions."

Charlotte could almost mouth the words verbatim, as often as she'd heard the speech. *Expected to perform.* Just like puppets on a string controlled by a marionette.

With a look that brooked no argument, her mother continued. "Your sisters will also be there, so perhaps with them by your side, the events will be more bearable."

Charlotte could see beyond her mother's facade of being in control and unaffected. The pinched expression, the look of betrayal, and the hint of disappointment that touched her mother's face revealed she likely feared the worst—her eldest daughter becoming a spinster and a blight on the family name. Mother only wanted Charlotte to blend with the other young ladies of her station, but she'd done that for years. Her compliance had been fruitless. Either the young men only saw her for her dowry and impressive inheritance, or they were so boorish she couldn't bear to spend more than five minutes in their presence. Still, she loved her mother and didn't wish to intentionally bring her pain of any kind.

"Very well, Mother." Charlotte made a mental note to plan for the dizzying merry-go-round of social events soon to be upon them. "I shall post modified hours at the bookshop and make certain I leave with enough time to prepare for any evening engagement."

Her mother brightened and closed the distance between them. Taking Charlotte's hands, she smiled. "I do appreciate your concession, dear. Please know I don't ask this of you as punishment but as opportunity. You simply never know whom you might meet."

Charlotte didn't want to contradict her mother. But if the gentlemen this season were anything like those of the past six, there would be no surprises.

"I know, Mother. And I promise to do my part. I will also try to enjoy myself." She paused for effect. "No matter how dull the evening might be."

Her mother gave a sardonic grin. "I suppose that is all I can ask." She squeezed Charlotte's hands and released them then turned in the direction of the kitchen. "Now if you'll excuse me, I have to discuss this week's meals with the cook."

As her mother walked away, Charlotte watched her, shoulders erect, head held high, and a certainty of who she was and of her purpose. Although Charlotte possessed some of that same confidence in regard to her bookshop, her purpose within the home had yet to be developed. Charlotte had believed by now she'd be married and starting a family. But that obviously wasn't in God's plan. And until He showed her what His plan was, she'd continue with what she was doing.

She only prayed He wouldn't wait too long.

&

"I cannot believe you would rather be in your dusty old bookshop than here among these fine ladies and gentlemen, dancing, sharing in the merriment, and wearing your finest gown."

Bethany stood in one of the entryways to the grand room where the dancing had already commenced. Her face was flushed from her recent turn about the floor with the latest gentleman on her dance card. Anastasia had been escorted onto the floor almost as many times as Bethany, each of them leaving Charlotte to wait because her dance-card slot had been empty. Why had she bothered selecting the right gown or fashioning her hair in the latest style? It wasn't as if anyone noticed. Even the men she usually went out of her way to avoid seemed otherwise engaged.

"It is not the dancing and the actual event I detest," Charlotte countered. "It's the boorish gentlemen bent on showcasing every reason they might be considered eligible and the money mongers only interested in my dowry and inheritance."

She glanced around, taking in the crowded yet resplendent ballroom, with a gilded, floor-to-ceiling mirror taking up almost all of one long wall. Two crystal chandeliers hung suspended from the ceiling, ablaze with light.

"I can understand that," Bethany said. "After all, it isn't pleasant to be in the company of a gentleman who speaks highly only of himself."

Charlotte nodded and glanced at her sister. "That is exactly how I feel. It's good to know someone shares my feelings." She turned her focus to the room.

The far wall featured two paned windows, just one section shy of reaching the ceiling, and french doors leading out to the marble terrace. Rich burgundy draperies hung at the windows, but they'd been tied back to allow a view of the gardens. Charlotte had been in her fair share of ballrooms, but the Stuyvesants had done a beautiful job with the overall design and craftsmanship of their home. Even the polished hardwood floors gleamed, despite the overabundance of people treading on the surface.

"But if you don't give them a chance," her sister continued, "how will you know if they become more suitable?" Bethany always tried to present the logical side of the situation. She smoothed her right hand down the front of her pale yellow silk and satin gown, her fingers running across the gathered seams at the empire waistline. The color set off her milk chocolate tresses and warm skin tones to perfection. "After all," she continued, fluffing out her skirts, "some men simply aren't adept at conversation upon the initial introduction. Perhaps they need a little time to grow accustomed to you before their true intentions or personalities can be appreciated."

Charlotte had considered that possibility, but she'd also observed many of these men in other situations. From what she could tell, there hadn't been much difference in their behavior.

"I have given a number of them a chance, and they have yet to prove me wrong. It makes it very difficult to believe any differently."

"And an attitude like that might very well keep you unattached and on your way to spinsterhood."

"Bethany! You shouldn't be so merciless." Anastasia curtsied to the young man who had escorted her from the dance floor and turned to face her sisters only once her dance partner was safely out of hearing. "Now what is this about being a spinster?" She tucked her hand into the crook of Charlotte's arm. "Surely you aren't referring to our dear sister, here."

"Yes." Bethany turned to face Charlotte with an apologetic expression. "I am sorry if I sounded callous. That wasn't my intention." She reached out and took Charlotte's free hand. "But you and I both must face the reality that we are not getting any younger. The number of suitable partners is dwindling every day."

Charlotte nodded. "Yes, Mother reminds me of that quite often. How could I possibly forget?"

"Well, you are the eldest daughter." Anastasia squeezed her arm. "It's up to you to set an example for Bethany and me."

Charlotte looked down into the amused face of her youngest sister. "I've attempted to set an example for you both in many other ways, all of which you have disregarded. Why should my engagement, or lack thereof, be any different?"

Anastasia shrugged. "We need to have at least *one* aspect of your life upon which to pattern our own." She cracked an impish grin.

"Thank you very much." Charlotte pressed her lips into a thin line. "I am pleased to hear at least something in my life and character has the possibility of containing a morsel of interest."

Her two sisters immediately leaned close and embraced her from each side.

"Oh Charlotte," Anastasia said. "You know we are only teasing you."

"Yes," Bethany added. "I am certain you have at least two traits to which we aspire." She winked.

"You two are incorrigible!"

Anastasia smiled. "And you wouldn't have it any other way."

Charlotte returned their hugs, placing her arms around each of their waists. "On that point, you are correct. As to the rest, we will have to wait and see." She glanced toward the dance floor where some gentlemen were leading ladies away from the center and others were seeking their next partners. "Now if I'm not mistaken, you both have the next dance claimed on your dance cards."

"And for the one after that, you have the privilege of dancing with Beauregard Parrish." Anastasia covered her mouth with her hand and muted her giggle.

"Now, now. He isn't that bad," Bethany added, fighting hard to maintain her composure. "If you can get past his clumsy feet and sweaty palms."

Two gentlemen approached at that moment, seeking to claim Anastasia and Bethany for the next dance and saving Charlotte from having to respond. She shook her head. She might not have a full dance card, but her sisters' merriment—and especially Anastasia's escapades—more than made up for it. She could simply live vicariously through them.

If only the gentlemen she encountered could be half as good at conversation as Mr. Baxton, she might actually enjoy the time she spent with them. But for now, she had no choice but to be polite and represent her family well. In the back of her mind, though, she'd count the days until Mr. Baxton's return.

Chapter 6

Now, make these windows sparkle and shine, Zachariah, and I might be able to find another nickel or two for you." Charlotte tousled the boy's hair and winked.

"Yes, ma'am, Miss Charlotte!" The lad gave her a quick salute, his uncombed, light brown hair falling across his forehead and nearly covering his eyes. He grabbed his bucket of sudsy water and went straight to work.

Charlotte reached for the handle on the door just as another hand grasped it. "Allow me," the now familiar, velvety timbred voice offered.

Her cheeks warmed, and Charlotte nodded to Mr. Baxton as he held the door for her. "Thank you," she said, preceding him into the bookshop and silently chastising herself for her telltale reaction to seeing him again.

Mr. Baxton didn't seem to notice. Instead, he removed his hat and held it loosely at his side; then he turned back toward the front of the shop. As he glanced out the windows, she took note of his beaver hat with the fine fabric lining and leather hatband. It sported a bound edge sewn on the brim. From his clothing and mannerisms, she already suspected he didn't come from the working class and could well be a member of the family her parents knew. The high quality of his hat served to confirm her assessment.

"Does that young lad work for you often?" Mr. Baxton turned and gestured with his head toward Zachariah meticulously scrubbing at the front windows.

Charlotte tapped a finger to her lips. "It's been several months, now. Of course he doesn't come around much during the winter."

"He appears to be quite thorough."

"Yes, he does excellent work." Charlotte took two steps closer to Mr. Baxton and peered out the window. She didn't want Zachariah to see her watching him, so she straightened an already tidy display. "He first approached me last summer, offering to wash my windows and complete any other tasks I might have."

"Does he live nearby?"

Charlotte couldn't determine why Mr. Baxton showed such interest in the lad. "Actually, he lives down by Brandywine Creek, but he spends a great deal of time in and around the park." She picked up two books and held them against her chest. "From what he has told me, he comes here to look for work because there isn't much opportunity where he lives."

Mr. Baxton turned to face her, compassion in his eyes. "It appears you hired well. I am certain some of my household staff would love to have a lad like him around to help with odd jobs." A quick glance over his shoulder preceded a brief sigh. "Pity he doesn't live closer to Ashbourne Hills."

Charlotte chuckled. "You might tell him that before he leaves. It's sure to give him a great deal of pleasure coming from a gentleman such as yourself."

Mr. Baxton gave a succinct nod. "I believe I shall." He turned to fully face her, merriment dancing in eyes the color of caramel. "Now, before we proceed any further with our conversation, Miss Pringle, allow me to apologize for not bestowing a greeting upon my arrival. I must confess I overheard your instructions to the lad and saw how he set right to work, and it distracted me."

"That is quite all right, Mr. Baxton. But to reassure you, your apology is accepted."

He gave a slight bow. "Thank you very much."

Instead of stepping behind the counter, Charlotte remained at the end of it. Far too often, she felt the counter placed a barrier between her and her customers. Sometimes she needed that distance. But at times like this one, the obstruction hindered the conversation.

"Has Grace finished the books I sent home with you last, and might you be here for more?"

"Yes." He followed her to the counter. "And once again, I must praise you for your excellent selections. I had a great deal of difficulty pulling Grace away from those books to see to her studies."

She placed one hand over her chest. "Oh, I am truly sorry."

He brushed off her apology with a wave of his hand, his gaze direct. "I didn't say that to cause contrition on your part; rather, I meant to demonstrate how much she enjoyed reading those stories." He snapped his fingers. "Ah yes, and *Oliver Twist*. She had the most questions about that one, but I did as you suggested and only allowed her to read it when she was in my presence. It worked out rather well. She read parts of it aloud." A smile formed on his lips. "Brought back memories of when I read it as a boy."

"I am pleased to hear she handled it well. Some younger readers become quite affected when they read it. Either they are frightened by the characters of Fagin and Bill Sykes, or they are overcome with remorse about the situations. Mr. Dickens went into great detail in that dark tale."

As if life for some children didn't already come with its fair share of challenges. To read such a grim story and to see the corrupt institutions in England depicted in such a vile manner would make even the most stalwart reader experience a strong pang of conscience.

Mr. Baxton allowed a half grin and placed his free hand in his pocket. "Well, perhaps the next collection of books I bring her will not contain any brooding stories."

"I shall endeavor to make certain of that."

The bell above the door jingled, and Charlotte looked up to see an acquaintance of hers enter. Amelia Devonshire had been a self-named friend for many years, but she also spent most of her time seeking out gossip-worthy details to share with everyone she knew. Most of the time, she did so without malicious intent. A few times, however, the gossip had turned sour, and the object of Amelia's tales had suffered greatly.

"Good afternoon, my dear Charlotte." Amelia swept into the shop like a feather on a cloud, full of grace and effortless elegance.

"Good afternoon, Amelia. How nice of you to come for a visit."

Charlotte cast a quick glance at Mr. Baxton, grateful his back was to Amelia. He narrowed his eyes slightly and seemed to pick up on something she conveyed. Had she visibly reacted to Amelia's appearance? If so, she hoped Amelia hadn't seen it, too. Regardless, Mr. Baxton stepped away from the counter, allowing Amelia the chance to approach.

"Miss Pringle, thank you again for your suggestion," he said. "I believe I shall spend a little time browsing before making my final decision." With a nod, he disappeared down the aisle that housed books similar to the ones he'd purchased earlier.

"Should you have any questions, please do not hesitate to ask," she called to his retreating back.

"Well, it isn't often I have the opportunity to visit while you actually have a customer." Amelia stepped closer. Taking Charlotte's hands in hers, she gave them a light squeeze and smiled. "It appears most of what I have been hearing about your increased patronage of late is true. How have you been, dear?"

❧

Richard stayed close to the front, peeking around the books in order to observe Miss Pringle interacting with the other young woman. They kept their voices low, but he could read Miss Pringle's facial expressions. The conversation made her both wary and uncomfortable. He didn't dare move closer and risk revealing his attempt at eavesdropping. He shouldn't be doing it anyway. But something about Miss Pringle's mannerisms compelled him to keep watch. The other young lady likely didn't intend any harm, but Richard still felt protective.

"Is the gentleman in question present in your shop this very moment?"

Uh-oh! Richard hadn't heard Miss Pringle's response or even the comment that led to the woman's question. But since he was the object of their conversation, he should appear preoccupied. Unfortunately, Richard couldn't determine what these books in front of him had in common. Since he *should* be browsing through the books suitable for Grace, he would have no choice but to confess his guilt were someone to ask.

Richard developed an odd sense that someone watched him as he stood in the aisle, staring at the shelves. From the corner of his eye, he cast a look to his left and caught sight of the young woman Miss Pringle addressed as Amelia. The lady—if one could call her that—unabashedly stared at him and made no attempt to hide her lack of discretion. He did his best to remain still, appearing as unaffected as he could manage, until she disappeared from view.

A few moments later, Charlotte's visitor turned toward the door, but not before casting a final glance in his direction. The young woman departed, leaving him alone again with Miss Pringle. A moment or two later, another customer entered, but he went straight to a specific section of books without a word to anyone.

Richard waited several more minutes before locating the section where he'd find books for Grace. After pulling two from the shelf, he made his way to the front of the shop. Miss Pringle looked up when he approached then quickly averted her gaze, busying herself with straightening an already immaculate area around the cash register. He had seen only one other such register during his time spent along the Ohio River. It had been invented in Dayton, and he had spoken to James Ritty in Cincinnati about the inspiration behind the creation. He'd have to ask Miss Pringle how she came to acquire one, but not now. She glanced over his shoulder toward the back of the shop, no doubt looking after her most recent customer.

"I believe I've found two more books Grace will enjoy," he said without preamble.

Miss Pringle turned to face him, fully composed. "Wonderful." Her smile seemed genuine, but a hint of wariness lay just behind it. She took the books from him and looked at the titles. "Ah yes. *Little Women* and *The Adventures of Tom Sawyer*." She totaled them on the register, and he handed her the cash. "Both excellent choices," she said as the drawer popped open with a loud bell. She placed his money inside then handed him his change. "They will give her several hours of entertainment."

"Yes. I wanted to give her a little easy reading after the last set." He narrowed his eyes slightly and studied her face. "Forgive me for being presumptuous, Miss Pringle, but is everything all right? You do not seem quite yourself today." Richard jerked a thumb toward the door. "I hope your last visitor didn't upset you."

"No, no. Amelia can be rather trying, but speaking with her didn't affect me adversely." She glanced down at her hands, as if trying to decide whether to share anything with him.

Richard held up a hand. "If you do not wish to speak of it, I understand. As I said, I don't wish to pry."

A soft smile formed on her lips. "Thank you. I appreciate your concern. Since you did ask, however. . ." She paused then sighed. "I am rather troubled over my mother and the many social engagements she has arranged for me to attend this season. She seems to have no interest in my responsibilities here at the shop. Instead, she tells me repeatedly that I must see to my duty as the eldest daughter and attend because it's expected of me."

"And I am certain you have spoken with her about this." He might not know Miss Pringle well, but certain aspects of her character shone clear and bright. She didn't strike him as a young woman who would avoid speaking her mind when the situation called for it.

Sadness overtook her features. "Yes, but every time we speak of it, the result is the same."

"Let me guess. She would prefer you remain home and attend these social affairs rather than be involved with this bookshop at all."

"Yes, that is it exactly." She brightened somewhat. "My father is responsible for securing this location and assisting me with the loan, as well as collecting books initially so I could open with inventory. My mother didn't want any part of it."

Richard nodded. "And now she feels the bookshop is interfering with you being present as her oldest daughter at these events."

"I'm afraid that is true."

He placed a hand lightly over her fingers, and she startled but didn't pull away. It was a bold move, but he felt the situation warranted it. After waiting for her to make eye contact, Richard softened his expression and allowed the corners of his mouth to turn upward.

"This might not be much consolation, but my older sister endured a similar situation with our mother. Laura didn't care much for the social affairs. She preferred to spend her time reading and studying mathematics. But after much coaxing, she heeded our mother's wishes and met the man she eventually married. Now she lives with him in Ohio, where together, they own a general store." He chuckled. "And she manages their accounting books."

"If only it were that simple. The only thing my mother wants is to see me suitably matched. My happiness doesn't seem to be of any concern to her."

Richard gave her hand a slight squeeze. "Don't give up, Miss Pringle.

It might not seem possible right now, but circumstances can change rather quickly. Before you know it, you, too, could find happiness *and* a match that pleases your mother."

"I truly hope it happens that way."

If only he were in a position to be more than a friend. But not yet. He had a few business matters to settle first. An idea struck him. He removed his hand and snapped his fingers then pointed in her direction.

"I know exactly what you need. And it would be perfect for Grace as well."

Her brow knitted in confusion, and for the briefest of seconds, she glanced down at her hand, as if missing the physical contact. He thought he imagined it, but when she looked at him again, he saw a spark in her eyes.

"And what is that, Mr. Baxton?"

"First, I would like to invite you to join Grace and me on a picnic in the park the next time we visit. My cook will provide all the food." He gave her what he hoped was an inviting look paired with a hint of playfulness. "You only need to bring yourself and your smile."

It worked.

The smile absent from her face since Miss Amelia first came through the door returned. "I should like that very much. Thank you." A twinkle entered her eyes. "And second?"

Second? He blinked a few times to clear his head. Why had he allowed himself to be distracted by her smile and the softness in her features?

"Second. Yes. I would like you to call me Richard." He held up a hand and stayed her potential protest. "You have become an important part of Grace's life. . .and mine. And I feel situations like ours allow for less formality."

She nodded. "Very well. But only if you will also call me Charlotte."

Richard almost took a step back at her easy agreement. He thought for sure he'd have to persuade with more than that one argument. Perhaps she had been thinking along the same lines, but propriety prevented her from saying anything.

"Consider it done." He reached out and raised her fingers to his lips. "Until next time, Miss Charlotte Pringle," he said with a wink. "I shall return in two weeks' time."

"I look forward to it and to seeing Grace, as well."

He released her hand, took his two books, replaced his hat, and turned to leave. At the front door, he tipped the edge of his hat in her direction, maintaining eye contact until the door closed between them. With her blush-tinged face indelibly printed on his mind, he knew the next two weeks would be the longest yet.

Chapter 7

"Are we almost there, Uncle Richard?" Grace's pleading made Richard smile. "How much longer?"

Richard looked out the carriage window and saw one of the mills along the Brandywine. "I would estimate about five more minutes." He raised one eyebrow. "Are you certain you can manage patience for that long?"

"I cannot guarantee it, but I shall try."

Honest to a fault. He always knew where he stood with her or what she was feeling. Some might consider that to be brazen in a young girl of her age, but Richard found it refreshing and endearing. It only made him love her that much more. Oh, what his brother was missing. Why had God chosen to take those two lives now? Just when Grace needed them most.

"I can see the river. We're almost there!" Grace clapped in rapid succession, her eyes fixed on the window opposite her.

Good. He could let Grace watch for the bookshop. He needed to plan a little on what he would say to Miss Pringle—that is, Charlotte—once they arrived. Her given name didn't yet come easily to his mind or his lips. He'd been working on it every day since their last meeting. It had nothing to do with the familiarity he'd requested. That he wanted more than anything. But he still battled with whether he overstepped the bounds of propriety in making the request. And he left so soon after. Was Charlotte regretting her agreement? Did she think him ill-mannered or disrespectful? He certainly hoped not.

"Uncle Richard! We're here!"

Grace didn't exactly have to announce their arrival. Richard heard the *clip-clop* of the horse's hooves on the cobblestone street, the noise of the barking dogs in the park, and the echo of voices carried on the wind. Their carriage stopped, and a moment later, the footman opened the door to help them out. Richard lifted Grace against his chest, and she draped her arms around his neck. As he bent through the opening, the footman reached up to take Grace from him. Once she was situated in her chair, Richard turned to retrieve the picnic basket from the boot of the carriage.

"Feel free to move the carriage to a quieter spot along the park," he told the footman. "We will be there for at least an hour, perhaps a little more."

"Very good, sir." The man tipped his hat, and the driver did the same. A moment later, they headed up the street then turned the corner and pulled the carriage to a stop under the shade of a few maple trees.

The setting was so picturesque. He could hardly wait to walk with Charlotte along the path and sit with her as they shared lunch. They wouldn't be alone, but it was close enough for now.

"Can we go to the bookshop?"

Richard glanced down to see Grace looking up at him. No, he and Charlotte wouldn't be alone. Perhaps that was a good thing. With Grace present, there'd be no chance for any other possible proprieties to be trampled.

"Yes Grace. We're going."

After looking up and down the street, Richard hooked the basket on one handle and maneuvered Grace off the sidewalk and across the bumpy cobblestones. Once they made it to the sidewalk on the other side, Richard immediately looked in the direction of the bookshop.

There she was.

Charlotte stood outside, leaning against one of the windows to her shop, her eyes closed and her face upturned. She looked so peaceful. He hadn't expected to find her here, and all the words he'd rehearsed vanished, leaving him unprepared to greet her. But he had to say something, especially before she opened her eyes and saw them.

"Good morning, Miss Pringle." Grace took care of the introduction for him.

"Oh!" Charlotte straightened and pushed off the wall. Her hand went to her chest. "Grace. You startled me."

"I'm sorry, Miss Pringle. I didn't mean to scare you."

She chuckled. "No, no, dear. It's quite all right." Charlotte stepped forward and bent to brush a hand across Grace's cheek. "You didn't frighten me. Startled means surprised more than scared. . .at least in this instance."

"I'm glad to hear that."

Richard smiled. Charlotte appeared more relaxed today. It showed in the smooth lines of her cheeks, the absence of strain in her eyes, and the soft way her mouth curved up when she spoke to Grace.

"You are earlier than I expected." She directed this statement more at him than Grace. "I thought you wouldn't be here until Thursday."

Richard felt the odd urge to stub his toe against the ground and duck his head. Just like when he'd been caught stuffing firecrackers in the stove at school as a young boy. Instead, he met her questioning gaze and offered an apologetic smile.

"Yes. But Grace was so excited to come see you again, and we had today free, so we decided to come."

"That's not true, Uncle Richard," Grace said. "You asked if I wanted to come today because you couldn't focus on your work."

Amusement danced across Charlotte's face. Richard shrugged and held out his hands in a hopeless gesture. What else could he do?

"I suppose it's a good thing I decided not to bring my lunch with me today." Charlotte glanced at the picnic basket hanging from Grace's chair. "I see you came prepared despite the change of days. So now that you are both here, shall we proceed as originally planned?"

"Do you not have to close your shop?"

"No. I haven't had a customer in the past thirty minutes, and this is usually when I take time to have lunch, so there shouldn't be anyone coming until later this afternoon."

Richard nodded. "Very well, then. I believe we'll allow Grace to lead the way."

The three of them crossed the street and headed straight for the park. Grace chattered away as Richard pushed her chair, but her voice and words became nothing but noise with each step they took. His attention remained on Charlotte.

The way she'd swept up her hair gave her a more feminine appearance overall. Not that she lacked femininity in any way. Her gown hugged her trim form nicely, and the rosy shade complemented her complexion. Richard mentally compared her to some of the women he encountered at social engagements back home and in Philadelphia. He sometimes spent more time there than at the shipyards in Wilmington. But those women were besotted with their appearance, and he was grateful Charlotte didn't seem obsessed with having the tiniest waist or the gown with the most frills. No, she had substance to her yet remained trim and healthy.

A second later, Charlotte turned and caught him staring. He quickly averted his gaze and looked straight ahead. From the corner of his eye, he caught her slow grin, but he held the answering one back from his own lips.

"I like this spot. Right here," Grace announced. "Let's set up our picnic on the grass under the tall oak."

Richard glanced at Charlotte. "Will that meet with your approval?"

"Of course," she replied, not really looking at him. She stepped in front of Grace so that the girl could see her. "Grace, you picked a beautiful location."

His niece beamed at the praise. Charlotte was right. The place was perfect. Just enough shade, not a lot of passersby on this particular path, and near enough to the creek to hear the water rushing over the rocks.

In no time, they had the checkered blanket spread on the ground and the food set out for lunch.

"What an amazing meal your cook has prepared!"

"Yes," Richard replied, "she does tend to overdo it, or outdo herself, whichever the case may be."

"I smelled that fried chicken the entire carriage ride and all the while the basket hung on the back of my chair." Grace pouted, looking much younger than her eleven years. "Can we please eat now?"

"Of course." Richard gestured for Charlotte to take a seat, and he lowered himself on the other side of his niece. "Would you like to bless the food, Grace?"

"Yes." The girl bowed her head and closed her eyes, folding her hands in her lap. "Dear Jesus, thank You for the beautiful day You gave us and for the delicious food our cook has made for us to enjoy. I'm especially grateful for Miss Pringle joining us for lunch and a walk in the park. Please help us to have fun and for Uncle Richard to behave himself. Amen."

Charlotte giggled and remained with her head bowed.

"Just what was that all about, young lady?" Richard tried to sound firm, but the innocent expression on his niece's face made it impossible.

"Sometimes you make jokes, and other people don't understand them. Or you try too hard to get people to like you. Miss Pringle already does, or she wouldn't be here with us today. And you know I love you." She shrugged. "So I prayed for Jesus to help you be yourself."

Spoken from the mouth of a babe, just as scripture stated in the book of Matthew. He should listen more to his niece. It might help him avoid embarrassment. Of course in this case, it only made the embarrassment worse.

"So shall we eat?" he asked, holding up the plate of fried chicken to Charlotte. It was easier to move things along than dig himself a deeper hole.

Charlotte had her lips pressed in a thin line, no doubt attempting to hold back the mirth caused by Grace's prayer. It didn't bother Richard. His niece meant no harm, and he'd rather let Charlotte see the real him than some fake version with the real self buried several layers deep. She seemed to appreciate it and find enjoyment in it as well. And that set the tone for their meal rather nicely.

"Tell me, Grace," Charlotte said once they had served themselves food. "You have read ten or eleven books from my shop. Which one was your favorite, and why?"

Richard had discussed this topic with Grace many times, so he mentally removed himself from the conversation and once again observed Charlotte. She seemed so at ease with Grace. Their interaction was effortless and natural.

He was pleased to see his niece warm up to Charlotte so easily. Then again, Grace warmed easily to folks, and almost everyone had trouble resisting her infectious personality.

Propping himself on his left side, Richard enjoyed watching the two interact as he ate his lunch. Every once in a while, Charlotte stole a glance in his direction, and he smiled in return. But for the most part, she remained focused on Grace, giving the girl her undivided attention. And Grace relished it. She needed a younger female influence in her life again. Richard wouldn't mind at all if that person was Charlotte. He had to get these two together more often.

❧

Charlotte kept her legs tucked beneath her and relaxed her pose as she looked up at Grace. The way the tall oak formed a canopy above them lent a sense of privacy to their little lunch. She wished she owned one of those cameras she'd seen a few times. It could capture this moment and preserve it forever as a photograph. But all those chemicals, and the fragile glass plates. Not to mention lugging the various parts of the contraption around. It was likely more trouble than it was worth. She'd just have to stick with preserving the memory in her mind.

She smiled at Grace. "So *Little Women* is your favorite?"

"I just finished that one on the way to and from my last visit to the doctor." Grace ate her last bite of lemon meringue pie, wiped her mouth, and folded her napkin in her lap, placing her hands on top.

"Was that appointment any better than the others?" Charlotte loved discussing books with Grace, but she also wanted to hear about the chances of the young girl walking again.

Grace looked at her uncle, who nodded. Some unspoken communication took place between them, an understanding to which Charlotte wasn't privy. Again, she marveled at the closeness the two obviously shared. Their relationship prior to the accident must have been special for that bond to have solidified so quickly. She'd met others in similar circumstances, and sometimes the ones thrown together never fully developed an intimate relationship.

"Well, the one before this one was. We heard something new that time," Grace began with hesitation.

"And what was that?" Charlotte asked. "Good news, I hope."

"We aren't sure," the girl said with a tinge of dejection. "The doctor said he thinks there is a chance for me to walk again. And he repeated that at this appointment, too."

Praise God!

"That is wonderful!" she said aloud. But Grace didn't appear to share her enthusiasm. "Why do you not seem to be happy about hearing this?"

Again Grace looked to her uncle before answering. "Because I have to have an operation, and it's very expensive."

That shouldn't be a problem. From his tailored clothing, to his personal carriage complete with a driver and footman, down to his mannerisms and speech, Richard had demonstrated signs that money was not an issue. And he had to have substantial funds to be able to keep taking Grace to these special doctors so often. Unless of course, the money came from a trust fund for Grace, dispensed following the death of her parents. Still, if she had that, surely they could use those resources to cover the operation. From the looks on both their faces, though, that didn't seem to be an option. Charlotte wanted to learn more, but she wouldn't be discourteous by asking.

"Yes, from what I have heard, operations do cost a great deal of money."

Richard leaned forward to lend his input to the conversation. "The profits from our family's shipping business have been tied up in the transfer of ownership. I have been working on the details every day amidst overseeing the day-to-day running of the business. But some legal issues and personal concerns are causing several problems." He ran his hand across his face. "I am trying to solve them, but each day that passes is one more day from the accident."

He didn't have to say more. With each passing day, the chances grew slimmer for a successful operation. Something like that shouldn't be stated in front of Grace, but the girl had likely figured it out on her own. The hope in her eyes had dimmed almost immediately after mentioning the operation. And the anguish on Richard's face only made the situation more hopeless. Compassion filled Charlotte.

She wished she could do something. But what? Any extra money she had went right back into the bookshop, paying the rent or restocking books. She didn't have much left over, let alone enough to help with an expensive operation. And she certainly couldn't ask her father for help. He'd already established a dowry along with her inheritance, but both of those were off limits until she married.

"Isn't there a way for you to pay for the operation in smaller amounts over time?" Charlotte ran through possible scenarios in her mind. "I would think it prudent for the hospital and doctor to work with you. At least that way, they would know the money is coming."

Richard nodded. "We did discuss that with the doctor, but their policy is payment in full at the time of services rendered." He massaged an area just above his eyes. "So we departed with the promise we would look into the matter and get back to him as soon as possible."

"And this doctor is your only option? No other doctors perform this operation who might have a different payment policy?" They no doubt had gone through all the options, but Charlotte refused to believe the situation was this hopeless.

"The only other doctors who have ever had success with this procedure live in Chicago, New York, and St. Louis." Richard's mouth drooped into a frown. "At this critical juncture with the family business, we simply cannot afford to make a journey of that distance. And even if we did, we have no guarantee their policy would be any different."

"That's why we have to wait," Grace said.

Her quiet yet despondent tone sounded like all her hope had shattered. Charlotte longed to put a smile back on the girl's face, but how? It was her fault she'd led them down this path in their conversation. The picnic had been going so well up to that point. They'd laughed, talked about books, shared a delicious meal, and enjoyed each other's company. She had to make things right.

"Look on the bright side," Charlotte began. "At least while you wait, you can enjoy the fun of a wheeled chair to help you get around. I must confess, many days I wish *I* could ride in one. . .especially down a hill. It would be almost like sledding, only not as cold."

A little squeak of a giggle escaped Grace's lips, and her eyes showed a faint glimmer of brightness. Charlotte smiled, hoping they were on their way toward more lighthearted topics. She wouldn't forget about their need for funds, but right now, she wanted to enjoy the time they shared.

"Actually, Grace has already experienced the fun of a hill not too far from where we live." A sheepish grin showed on Richard's face. "Of course, that little ride wasn't intentional."

Grace covered her mouth with one hand and laughed. "No, but it was fun." She cast a loving and forgiving glance at her uncle. "And it wasn't your fault you forgot to stop the wheels."

"You're right." Richard offered a crooked grin. "I was still getting used to helping you get around. Everything was all so new to us both."

Good. She'd managed to help them get back to more pleasant memories and conversation. "I gather this experience was both memorable and beneficial to future travels."

"Yes, I have been overly careful ever since."

"Even when I *wanted* to go for a ride," Grace added.

Richard reached for their plates and started to pack them away in the basket.

"Here," Charlotte offered, "let me see to that."

She reached for a plate at the same time, and their hands touched, two of his fingers covering hers. Charlotte froze and stared at the plate. Richard froze, too, but when she looked up, his gaze was fastened on her, not the plate. She tried to break the hypnotic effect of his warm brown eyes, but it was no use.

"If you two don't move faster, we might have to eat what's left for dinner."

Grace's voice broke the spell, and Richard released the plate. A roguish grin formed on his lips as he handed Charlotte the other plates. He helped her gather the remaining food, and in just a few minutes, they had the meal put away. Once Richard hooked the basket on the back of Grace's chair, it made the reality of the end of their time together come crashing in like a wave on the sand. Now would be a good time to extend her thanks.

Charlotte stood and brushed off the loose grass blades from her skirts, sending the dirt to the ground as well. She bent to retrieve her straw hat, set it on her head, and tied the wide ribbon beneath her chin.

"As much as I have enjoyed our time together, I do have to return to the bookshop." Charlotte looked at Grace and Richard. "But I hope to see you both again very soon."

"Oh!" Grace sat up in her chair. "I almost forgot." She withdrew an envelope from a little pocket sewn into her dress. After handing it to Charlotte, she continued. "I would like you to come to my birthday party next month. That invitation"—she nodded at the envelope Charlotte now held—"has all the details. Please say you'll come. And Anastasia is welcome, too."

Charlotte turned the envelope over in her hand. She hadn't expected this. Grace must consider her someone special to invite her to such a personal event. She looked first at Grace then to Richard. His eyes showed his desire for her to join them. How could she turn either one of them down?

"I would be both pleased and honored to accept. Thank you, Grace."

The girl clapped and grinned like the Cheshire Cat in that book by Lewis Carroll.

"It appears to be settled." Richard placed both hands on the handles of Grace's chair. "I'll be sure to send a carriage for you on the day of the party. I'm not certain we'll be seeing you again before then, as Grace has a substantial amount of work to complete to wrap up her studies for this year." He looked down at her just as Grace tipped her head to look up at him.

"He made me promise to finish it all before the party, or he'd tell everyone the party was canceled." Her adorable pout gave her a pixie-like appearance.

Charlotte pressed her mouth into a thin line to avoid laughing. Grace looked so serious.

"Well, I suppose you'd better head straight home so you can get started. We certainly don't want a party to be canceled. They are far too much fun." Charlotte stepped forward until she was nearly toe to toe with Grace. She tipped up the girl's chin with her forefinger and smiled. "And if I know you, you'll have everything completed long beforehand. You'll probably have time left over where you will be twiddling your thumbs, looking for something else to do as you wait."

The pout transformed into a smile, and Grace's entire demeanor changed.

She tapped the arms of her chair. "Let's go, Uncle Richard. I want to get started on my studies."

Richard mouthed a thank-you to Charlotte over Grace's head. Charlotte nodded. Anything she could do to help.

"Shall we make our way back to the shop?" Richard invited.

Charlotte nodded. "I believe we shall."

The trio walked along in silence. Only the thumping of the wheels on Grace's chair against the cobblestone interrupted the stillness. When they reached the front of her shop, Charlotte turned to thank Richard, but the words died in her throat. He looked like he was about to say something. Instead, he stood and shifted from one foot to the other, alternating between licking his lips and looking down at Grace then back up at Charlotte.

Was he going to say anything or not? She didn't know. The awkward silence seemed to stretch for several minutes, when in reality it was only a few moments. This was ridiculous. She had to say something.

"Thank you again for a truly delightful picnic. I very much enjoyed our afternoon together and look forward to coming to your birthday party, Grace." Charlotte winked. "And I am certain Anastasia will be excited to come, as well." She turned partway toward her shop then included both Richard and Grace in her parting words. "As much as I wish I didn't have to leave such charming company, work inside needs my immediate attention. So, I must say good-bye."

Whatever Richard might have eventually said never happened. He did sigh though. Perhaps in frustration at being unable to vocalize his thoughts. Charlotte would likely never know.

"Good-bye, Miss Pringle," Grace called as Richard steered them toward the path.

"Good-bye, Grace. Good-bye, Mr. Ba—I mean Richard."

He grinned and dipped his head. "Have a nice afternoon, Charlotte. Thank you again for joining us."

Charlotte opened the door and headed into her shop. As she shut the door, she looked out the window. After spotting Richard and Grace across the street, she started to turn away but caught Richard pivoting Grace's chair toward the shop. An enthusiastic wave from the young girl accompanied a reserved but meaningful wave from Richard. She returned the wave and finally began her work.

The next month couldn't pass by fast enough.

Chapter 8

The entire experience felt like an exercise in futility. Charlotte didn't know why she bothered attending so many of these events, other than obedience to her mother's wishes. At twenty, she should be able to make her own decisions. Yet here she stood, feeling more like wall decor than an invited attendee at the soiree. This made the fifth event this month, and while it helped time pass more quickly, it didn't make her evenings any more enjoyable.

At least the orchestra was playing some of her favorite pieces. Between turns about the floor with her scarce dance-card signers, she could listen to the soothing strains of the music.

"So is it just me, or do these events become more intolerable each passing year?"

Charlotte startled at the familiar voice of Margaret Howard, an old schoolmate who'd also suffered through six seasons of social affairs with no success.

"It isn't just you," Charlotte replied. "But I must say it's nice to see someone else who abhors the repetitive carousel of introductions and attempted pairings that accompany these events."

"Oh, I more than abhor them. I no longer attend them for those reasons." Margaret waved her left hand in the air like royalty waving to her subjects. "Now it's become a social expectation."

Charlotte gasped. "Is that what I think it is? Are you wearing an engagement ring and a wedding band?" She took hold of Margaret's hand and inspected the rings. *Stunning.* It was the only word that came to mind, but it fit. She looked up at the twinkling eyes of her friend. "When did this all occur, and how did I miss it? And your last name obviously isn't Howard anymore. So how do I address you?"

Margaret placed her hand in the crook of Charlotte's elbow and leaned in close. "Come with me, and I shall share the entire story."

Her friend led her toward the double doors opposite them, and the two young women stepped out onto the veranda. Charlotte could hardly wait to hear what had happened.

"Are you going to share your fascinating story now?"

Margaret narrowed her gaze and crossed her arms. "Who told you it was fascinating?"

"Any story where you conclude one season without any offers and appear at the next with a ring on your hand must be fascinating." Charlotte raised one eyebrow and grinned. "Do you deny it?"

The young woman laughed. "No. How could I?" She gestured toward the waist-high wall at the edge of the veranda. "Come, let's stand over there. It affords a much better view."

Charlotte regarded her friend carefully. First, she didn't want to talk inside. Now she wanted to share her story but in a specific place on the veranda. Just what was Margaret going to tell her? And why all the secrecy? Not that Charlotte minded, of course. This was the first thing to pique her interest at one of these events all season.

"All right." Charlotte rested her left forearm on the cool stone wall and draped her right hand over her wrist. "We are here. Now tell me before I perish from anticipation." A bit dramatic, yes, but she felt like having a little fun.

"Well. . ." Margaret drew out the word with a grin. "I suppose I should start by saying it all happened unexpectedly. It isn't merely the occurrence of the engagement as much as who made the offer for my hand."

"You already have me intrigued. I should like to learn the identity of this mysterious gentleman before the evening comes to a close and the clock chimes twelve times."

Her friend cast her a glance, one corner of her mouth turning upward in an impish grin. "You always were rather theatrical. Perhaps I should lengthen the anticipation by starting at the beginning and withhold his identity a while longer."

Charlotte faced the gardens below them. White lights illuminated the flower beds and finely trimmed hedges. Even the fountains had been illuminated. It would be the perfect setting to walk with a suitor or potential intended. But since Charlotte didn't have such a man, she could enjoy her friend's story and pretend it was hers.

She shrugged, acting as if it didn't matter either way. She wanted to tease Margaret as much as her friend taunted her. "If you do that, I shall simply walk away and learn the tale from someone else."

Margaret folded her arms. "And just who would you find to divulge every detail to you?"

"I am certain I could find someone."

"Yes, but would they be able to point out the gentleman in question as easily as I?" She extended one long, graceful arm out over the wall toward the gardens.

Charlotte's gaze followed her friend's movement. She peered into the evening twilight. How did Margaret expect her to locate the man among the myriad of people out there? It wasn't as if he wore a shingle advertising his identity. And he likely wouldn't be dressed any differently—

Charlotte blinked several times as her gaze landed on a certain gentleman surrounded by a handful of others as if he were holding court. She recalled the way Margaret had waved her hand to show off her rings. No. That couldn't be the man she meant. Charlotte never had the privilege or the pleasure of a formal introduction, but she just couldn't believe he would be the one Margaret married.

A quick glance back at Margaret and Charlotte had her answer. The gleam in her friend's eyes and the broad smile on her face confirmed it.

"How did you ever manage that?" Charlotte stood in amazement. To think while she was occupied with running a bookstore, her friend had married into royalty. Well, almost. "You, of all people. Married to a baron from England." She shook her head. "This has to be the finest unveiling of the entire season."

"I am pleased to see you approve."

"How could I not?" As if she would ever begrudge anyone happiness, especially the kind that guaranteed her friend's future.

A momentary pang of melancholy crossed Margaret's face. "I have been the recipient of some rather malicious and vindictive remarks from a select few. But overall, the response and welcoming of my husband has been quite pleasant."

"As well it should be. Don't pay any attention to those who speak ill of you. They are merely jealous they weren't the ones to attract the attention of a baron." She reached out and clasped Margaret's hands. "You, my dear, are now a baroness, and you have earned every bit of the honor and grace the title bestows."

A shimmer of tears glistened in her friend's eyes. "Thank you. That truly means a lot to me," she said.

"You are quite welcome." Charlotte released Margaret's hands and turned back toward the double doors leading inside. She listened to the music floating on the air and tried to recall the order of the dances. "Now I believe I should make my way back to the ballroom so my next dance partner will be able to locate me."

"Very well." Margaret stepped forward and embraced Charlotte. "I do thank you for being supportive."

Charlotte returned the hug then stepped back. "My pleasure. Be sure and come find me before you depart so I might have a proper introduction to the baron." She winked. "And enjoy yourself this evening, Baroness," she added, stressing the final word.

"I shall."

How much fun it was to even say that word, let alone put it together with a young woman she'd known since the two of them were in pinafores and braids. She still couldn't believe it. A glance over her shoulder as she reached the double doors confirmed it wasn't a dream. As Charlotte watched, the baron joined Margaret on the terrace. If only she could be so fortunate.

Charlotte stepped into the ballroom and made her way around the perimeter. If she walked slowly, her next dance partner might have a better chance of locating her. She sidestepped one rather vigorous couple who danced in a wide arc from the rest; then she paused near one of the hallways leading into the rest of the manor. As she peered across the room, a low voice just beyond her right shoulder caught her ear.

"I cannot understand why Charlotte spends so much time attending these events and dressing in her finest." She'd recognize that voice anywhere. Amelia Devonshire. The mention of her name and the biting tone set Charlotte's senses on high alert. "It hasn't resulted in any success in previous seasons. Why would this year be any different?"

"It simply does not make sense," another female voice added, only this one didn't sound as petulant. "She is quite lovely, after all. I don't understand why most gentlemen barely give her a passing glance."

Charlotte wondered as well. It wasn't as if she made herself unappealing. And she'd heard from many others, including her mother, about her pleasing appearance. Some even went so far as to tell her she would be the belle of the ball. But so far, that had never proven true. What about her repelled eligible gentlemen?

"My dear, do you not know?" Amelia asked. "Charlotte owns a bookshop. That puts her in with the working class." Distaste dripped from her words. "We all know we are supposed to master the fine art of managing a household and learning our place in society. Working and owning a business does not fit with that plan."

Charlotte wanted to walk away, but morbid curiosity kept her feet planted where she stood. If nothing else, she wanted to determine the identity of the other two ladies keeping company with Amelia. Perhaps she'd discover something important if she allowed their conversation to play out.

"But I have known other young women who have married, and they also worked," a third voice said. "Why should Charlotte be any different?"

"Are you referring to Genevieve Chatterton or Margaret Howard?" A dismissing huff punctuated Amelia's words. "Or perhaps I should say Lady Margaret instead." Sarcasm laced every word.

"Yes," the second voice replied. "Margaret is a baroness now, and she spent a great deal of time working in her father's factory in Wilmington."

"Look at her tonight," the third lady added. "She appears every bit the refined lady, befitting her title."

"You can dress the part easily, but your garments cannot hide what lies underneath. And it's only a matter of time before Margaret's real identity shows itself."

Amelia should heed her own words. Charlotte didn't dare peer around the corner, but Amelia no doubt looked the part of the demure and charming lady. Yet hidden inside was a bitter soul. Charlotte might feel sorry for her if Amelia's biting remarks hadn't been directed at both Margaret and her. Perhaps Amelia was one of those people Margaret had mentioned moments ago. The ones who delivered malicious remarks.

"Still," the third voice continued, "I cannot see Charlotte being considered less than worthy in any way. She has always seemed generous, kind, and almost amiable to a fault."

"But she keeps her nose buried in her books and her bookshop," the second countered. "And that is no way to meet a potential suitor."

Charlotte almost smiled. If only they knew how much inaccuracy their estimations contained. Spending time in her bookshop had brought a very eligible bachelor into her life. Richard might not be an actual suitor, but he certainly possessed all the qualities of one.

"I must disagree with you on that point. The bookshop is not deterring eligible gentlemen. Charlotte has a great deal to offer a potential beau. They merely have to spend a bit more time getting to know her first."

Charlotte gasped. Bethany! Why was she associating with ladies of that sort? Her own sister was standing there, allowing the other three ladies to discredit her name? And she waited until now to defend Charlotte's honor?

"You are only saying that because she is your sister," Amelia replied. "Mark my words. Charlotte Pringle will likely never marry. She will become a spinster, sequestered among the musty, lonely confines of her bookshop with nary a prospect for a secure future."

The room suddenly grew quite constricting. Charlotte had trouble catching her breath. Unbidden tears pooled in her eyes. She withdrew a handkerchief from her reticule and touched it to her nose. She had to get out of here.

But the only exit necessitated walking directly past the hallway where those ladies stood. She could return to the veranda, but far too many people were already out there. She couldn't stay here or the tears would surely fall. Someone was bound to take notice.

Throwing caution to the wind, she kept the handkerchief in front of her face and faked a sneeze. Then she ducked her head and made a dash for the main door leading toward the front of the manor.

"Charlotte!"

Her sister's cry barely registered. She had to keep going, lest she lose her bravado and break down in front of an audience.

She rushed ahead, not taking time to look at the handful of people she passed on her way out.

"Charlotte, wait!"

Bethany's voice sounded stronger. She must be rather determined to chase after her in such a way. And Charlotte didn't want to think about the scene the two of them made.

Just as she made it to the front of the manor, a staff member opened the heavy oak door, allowing access over the final hurdle in her escape. She stepped onto the porch and inhaled a breath of fresh air. A moment later, a hand grabbed her arm and spun her around.

"Charlotte, I know you must have heard me," Bethany said. "Why did you not stop and wait for me?"

Charlotte looked through a blurry haze at her sister's concerned face. "Because I did not wish to make a scene in front of everyone in the ballroom."

Bethany gave a soft smile. "And you did not consider that running from the room with me attempting to catch you would cause a stir among our peers?"

Charlotte sniffed. "I didn't believe you'd come chasing after me."

Her sister took her hands and led her to a bench on the far side of the porch. Once seated, she leveled a compassionate gaze at Charlotte. "I am truly sorry you had to overhear the cruel remarks Amelia made, and any bit of that conversation with Amelia, Clara, and Alice."

Charlotte dabbed at her eyes and sniffled. "I simply don't understand why they would say such things. What have I ever done to warrant their spite or bitterness?"

Her sister squeezed her hands. "Nothing. Nothing at all. Some ladies make it a practice to lash out at others to make themselves feel better. I don't believe I've ever heard Amelia speak kindly of anyone."

"And why were you there with them?" Her sister wasn't known for gossiping, and those young women weren't her friends.

"Believe me. It happened completely by accident." Bethany's eyes revealed nothing but sincerity. "I was speaking with Alice when Amelia and Clara approached. Since we stood at the end of the hallway, they had us pinned in the corner. . .literally." A faint smile appeared on her lips. "I was pleased to see you run away when you did, as it gave me a reason to escape, as well."

Charlotte should have known her sister wouldn't align herself with the likes of Amelia. "But the cruel things they said about Margaret and me. They have no reason to hurl such insults."

"No," Bethany said, sympathy in her voice. "But that does not mean they will change their ways."

Charlotte dabbed again at her eyes then blinked several times to clear her vision. "They accuse me of remaining sequestered in my bookshop. Why ever would I wish to leave the safety of those four walls when I end up encountering ladies like them?" Tucking her handkerchief back into her reticule, she called the faces of Richard and Grace to mind. "I'd much rather face unassuming individuals like Mr. Baxton and his niece, Grace. They are so different from many who attend parties such as this one."

"And perhaps that is why you have your bookshop, sister dear." Bethany shifted on the bench and clasped Charlotte's hands tighter. "You do not belong within these social circles to find a beau."

A hollow laugh escaped from Charlotte. "Try persuading Mother of that."

Bethany nodded her understanding. "We shall have to address Mother some other time." A measured level of wisdom and concern filled Bethany's eyes. "For the time being, you need to remember God has a plan in all of this. Do not allow the words of those bitter women to upset you so. You have far more in your favor than they ever will. Focus on that, and the pain of their insults will fade into distant memory."

Wasn't she usually the one giving advice to Bethany and Anastasia? Yet here the two of them sat, the younger counseling the older. Charlotte pulled her hands free and embraced her sister. "Thank you."

Bethany returned the hug. "You are quite welcome." Leaning back, she again fixed an intent look upon her sister. "Now are we ready to return to the merriment? You cannot leave and allow those ladies to think they've achieved any measure of triumph at your expense."

A restorative laugh bubbled up from inside. "You are absolutely right."

Arm in arm, they went back inside and rejoined the revelry. But their conversation left Charlotte wondering one thing: Just when had her sister become so wise?

Chapter 9

Charlotte forgot Richard had offered to send one of his carriages, and she asked her own driver to prepare the horses then returned to the front hall to wait with her sister. A minute later, a knock came to the door, and when their butler opened it, there stood one of the Baxton carriages, ready and waiting to take her and Anastasia to Ashbourne Hills. How thoughtful of Richard to remember.

They rode together in silence with Anastasia staring out the window. That suited Charlotte just fine. She could center her thoughts on Richard. It hadn't been easy persuading Mother and Father to allow her to attend the party, but when she explained Anastasia was also invited, they had acquiesced. Perhaps they thought her sister would be more than willing to report back on all that transpired. Not that anything would. Far too many guests would be gathered for Charlotte to have any time alone with Richard. But she knew Mother and Father were just being concerned parents, looking out for her.

In no time, they'd traveled the almost nine miles to Richard's neighborhood and stopped in front of his home. Charlotte accepted the assistance of the footman as she descended onto the sidewalk. She approached the impressive home that had once belonged to Richard's brother. What had happened to the home Richard owned? Did he live there anymore, or did he sell it? She made a mental note to ask him another time.

Standing in front of the house for the first time, Charlotte studied the classic Colonial-style architecture with a hint of Dutch influence. From Richard's clothing and the way he carried himself, she almost expected to see French accents as could be found in many of the major cities throughout America, or even the newer Renaissance revival style with a wide, covered front porch. But instead, this home remained true to some of the original settlers in the area. And it blended well with the other homes on the street.

"Impressive, isn't it?" The footman stood next to her and shared her view. When she looked his way, he took a step back and ducked his head.

"Yes, it is stunning," she said with a smile.

He seemed surprised she had replied, so he offered a smile in return. Another carriage approached. The footman glanced at it then extended his arm toward Charlotte while signaling another footman to escort Anastasia.

But Charlotte remained on the front walk, transfixed by the beauty of the estate.

A handful of elm trees grew tall and protected the home set back about forty feet from the street. Two brick walks wound away from where she stood, one to the home and the other to the carriage house set farther back. It was near the end of June, and the wide variety of flowers planted out front blossomed in an array of colors, shapes, and sizes.

The footman cleared his throat, and Charlotte started.

"Oh! I am terribly sorry. You have other carriages that need your attention. Please forgive me for dawdling." She placed her hand in the crook of his arm and allowed him to escort her, with Anastasia and her footman close behind.

"It is quite all right, miss. Happens from time to time."

Many of the guests had likely already arrived, and she didn't wish to be tardy. They made their way down the brick path and ascended the five marble steps to the front porch where a butler swung wide the door.

"Miss Charlotte Pringle and Miss Anastasia Pringle," the footman announced. The man bowed and took his leave.

A moment later, the butler ushered them inside. After taking their wraps, he directed Charlotte into the parlor to the right, but pointed Anastasia in another direction. Her sister disappeared with hardly a word, so Charlotte stepped into the other room. A maid wove her way through the other guests and held a tray of glasses filled with punch and various other beverages.

Charlotte took a glass of punch and sipped it as she blended in with the other guests and took time to observe the furnishings of the room. The faint sound of children laughing carried from one of the adjoining rooms. No doubt the predinner fun and games for Grace's friends, Charlotte mused. That was likely where she'd find Anastasia, too. At least it seemed her sister would be having a great time. And Charlotte might too, once dinner was served. But this party wasn't for the adults. Most were likely there as chaperones or attending at Richard's request. So she again focused her attention on the decor.

The sofas and chairs were covered in crimson-and-black satin damask with their ends deeply tufted. The rosewood frames, delicately carved, had been polished until the wood gleamed. A grand piano sat in the corner where a young gentleman played soft strains of a pleasing melody. Even the satin drapes hanging from the doorway at the far end matched the crimson of the carpet under her feet. And the oval end tables were graced with sienna marble instead of the white slab her parents had.

The various decorative items placed here resembled their parlor, but the quality far outshone anything they had. Charlotte could only imagine the expense involved if the entire residence had been decorated in the same manner. The quality alone likely cost Richard's brother or father twice as much as what her parents had paid to decorate. The only aspects that seemed similar were the wallpaper patterns and the chandelier suspended from the ceiling in the center of the room.

She almost felt like an imposter. Her family had a great deal of wealth, but nothing compared to this. Yet for all the finery and obvious evidence of financial holdings, Richard and his niece remained genuine and approachable. They didn't allow their social status to affect how they treated others—one of many good points in their favor.

Still, it felt strange: recognizing that Richard's family must have spent a small fortune on these things, yet knowing he didn't have access to the money that would give his niece a much-needed operation. In many ways, it seemed unfair.

"It is sad, is it not," a woman standing next to Charlotte said, "to see such a finely decorated home and know of their struggle to settle the affairs following his brother's passing." She took a sip of her champagne and lowered her glass, the base clinking against the brooch pinned to her gown. With her left hand, she fingered the three rings on her right, each piece featuring a precious gemstone of a different color and cut. Even her finely coiffed hair was adorned with a delicate bejeweled tiara. "Why, it is almost as if they have nothing at all and are merely overseeing this home until the real owners return."

Charlotte wanted to ask why a woman like her didn't offer to donate something to Richard and his niece in order to help. But she didn't know the woman, and it would be rather impolite to pose such a question.

"Still," the woman continued. "I admire Mr. Baxton for seeing his niece receives the proper care and remains with family instead of one of those dreadful institutions in Wilmington or Philadelphia."

"Yes," Charlotte replied. "Not many would go to such great lengths. And little Grace is obviously benefiting from it."

The woman looked at Charlotte as if realizing for the first time she spoke with a stranger. "So, how did you come to meet Grace and her uncle?"

Charlotte hesitated before answering. How much should she tell to this woman? How well did *she* know the family? "I have had the good fortune of speaking with them on several occasions, but mostly Mr. Baxton. I have only spent a couple of hours with Grace."

"And what do you do, dear, that has led to your path crossing theirs?"

The woman seemed genuinely interested, and she hadn't yet given any indication that she might be less than trustworthy, so Charlotte decided to be completely honest.

"I own a bookshop in Brandywine, and Mr. Baxton has visited more than once to purchase books for Grace."

Recognition dawned in the woman's eyes. "Ah, so you're the bookshop owner I've heard so much about!" She set her near-empty glass on the tray as the maid walked by, then grabbed both of Charlotte's hands and gave them a squeeze. "I am very pleased to meet you, my dear. My name is Florence Lewis, but those who know me call me Flo." A twinkle entered her eyes as she released Charlotte's hands and leaned in close. "I used to be Richard and Elliott's nursemaid from the time they were in diapers to when they grew up on me and started their first jobs."

A woman who used to care for Richard and his brother as young lads certainly had to be honorable. "Charlotte Pringle, ma'am. I am pleased to meet you as well." But if she used to be a nursemaid, how was she now adorned with fine jewelry and able to afford an expensive gown?

"You are no doubt curious about my appearance," she said, laughing when Charlotte attempted to protest. "It is quite all right. I am often asked that very question. And the answer is that once the lads no longer needed me, I remarried and gained a rather substantial fortune." She waved her hand. "But enough about me. You say you own a bookshop in Brandywine?"

"Yes. Cobblestone Books. It is directly across from the east entrance to the park."

"I might just have to take a carriage ride out your way sometime." She gave Charlotte a conspiratorial wink. "See what all the fuss is about. Although after meeting you, I have a feeling it's about more than the books you sell."

Warmth stole into Charlotte's cheeks at the telling remark. Hearing this woman talk did make Charlotte wonder just what Richard—or possibly Grace—had said about her. She hadn't considered the possibility anyone would speak of her out here in Ashbourne Hills. Then again, why not? Any word spread would be good for business.

"Dinner is served, ladies and gentlemen," the butler announced. "Please make your way to the dining room."

Charlotte joined the flow of guests as they moved from the parlor and headed toward the dining room. If the first room had been impressive, this one was extraordinary. Several large mirrors with gilded frames flanked two of the walls. Large portraits of two rather distinguished gentlemen—who appeared to be Richard's father and grandfather—adorned the wall behind the head of the table, and three stately windows with brocade curtains were spaced a few feet apart on the fourth wall.

The polished mahogany table in the center of the room gleamed, and Charlotte could see the reflection of those already gathered around the table in its surface. More guests filtered in, but she held back. She seemed to be the only one unaccompanied.

"Miss Pringle!"

Grace's delighted voice rang out across the room, and all heads turned. Charlotte looked up to see the young girl wheeling herself in through a door opposite where she stood, her young friends trailing close behind. The adult guests followed the girl's line of focus and landed on her. Charlotte tried not to notice and kept her eyes on Grace.

"You came!" She maneuvered to the head of the table and pointed at two empty chairs to her left. "These seats are for you and Anastasia. I made a special request when I received your reply saying you would come tonight."

In the most unassuming manner she could manage, Charlotte made her way to the table and stood by her seat, making sure to put her sister directly to Grace's left. Grace beamed. Her reaction made the entire evening worthwhile. Yet she couldn't help but wonder about the other guests. How had she and Anastasia earned such a place of honor above everyone else? Surely someone like Flo or one of Grace's friends or even another family member should be sitting there. Then again, it seemed as if Grace's family occupied the seats on the other side of the table. A woman who had to be Grace's grandmother sat to Grace's right, putting Richard directly across from Charlotte. Flo was next in line. Not the order Charlotte would have expected, but who was she to be critical?

Her thoughts were once again interrupted by the arrival of their host, resplendent in dark trousers, a white ruffled shirt and black bow tie, and a dark coat with tails. Richard stood behind Grace and rested his hands on the back of her chair, then quickly scanned the faces of everyone seated at the table. When his gaze landed on Charlotte, he gave her a quick wink. She tried to keep the blush at bay, but she'd never seen him look so handsome.

"I'd like to thank everyone for coming this evening. You all know we are here to celebrate the joyous occasion of Grace's birthday." He moved his hands to his niece's shoulders. "All of you offered your support to us when we needed it most. Thanks to that support, we are able to share together a special day for a very special girl." He looked down the table, his gaze resting on each guest on both sides of the table. "I couldn't think of a better way to thank you than to invite you and your families here to enjoy a delicious meal."

"Uncle Richard?" Grace twisted her neck and looked up at Richard. "Can I say a prayer before we begin?"

He squeezed her shoulders and smiled. "Of course. Would everyone please bow their heads?"

It was more a command than a request, but every guest complied. Charlotte added another quality to the growing list of desirable traits: Richard made no attempts to hide his faith from his guests, whether they believed or not.

"Dear Jesus, thank You for all these friends who came tonight to celebrate with me. Every one of them is special to me and to You. Thank You for putting them in my life and for their help after my accident. Please bless our dinner and this entire evening. In Your name, amen."

Murmurs of agreement and other rumblings sounded all the way down the table. Grace's words had clearly touched almost everyone there. Charlotte shifted her gaze to Richard. After pulling out his chair and taking a seat, he extended his arms toward his guests.

"Let's get this dinner under way."

Several footmen attended to the ladies present, reaching for the napkins on the table and fanning them out before placing them in the ladies' laps.

In a matter of moments, the soft din of voices rose from the table. Flo pressed against the table.

"My dear, I am quite pleased at the company in which I find myself. I cannot imagine a more enjoyable dinner companion." The woman shifted her attention to her left. "Richard, you have done a fine job in assigning the seats here at this end. I had the fortune of meeting Miss Pringle in the parlor just prior to being called to dine. And now I can not only discover more about her"—she cast a glance at Charlotte—"but I can also divulge some amusing stories about when this gentleman was a boy."

Richard raised one eyebrow in Flo's direction. "Now, now, Miss Flo." His amused tone belied the warning in his words. "Don't you go telling tales and destroying my carefully constructed respectable image. I shall never forgive you."

"Oh fiddlesticks." Flo waved off his protest. "You know very well I mean no harm. It shall all be in good fun."

"And I would love to hear stories again of Uncle Richard when he was my age," Grace chimed in.

Flo gave a single succinct nod, the mass of hair atop her head wobbling with the action. "And so you shall, sweet girl. So you shall."

Salads were placed in front of them, and they halted their conversation for a few moments. After waiting for everyone to be served, the guests looked to Grace to take her first bite. She did and Richard waved his fork in the air to encourage everyone else to do the same.

After eating her first forkful, Flo picked up where she left off. "Now, where shall I begin? Should it be with the time when your uncle and father painted one of the carriage horses a healthy shade of pink? Or perhaps the story of how they managed to escape their father at the shipyard in Wilmington and wound up dousing several torches along the main street."

Charlotte pressed her lips closed against the laughter. How embarrassing it would be if she spit out some of her food before she had a chance to swallow it.

Richard swallowed his recent bite and placed his right hand on his chest, fork held between his fingers. "In my defense, the painted horse was in honor of our mother who had read us a story about colorful animals. Elliott and I decided to give her a live one." He gave Flo a mock angry glare, but the twitching at the corner of his lips gave him away. "As for the torches, just be grateful the lamps still ran on fire or gas. By this time next year, we'll likely have electric street lamps in all the major cities and towns here in Delaware."

"Electric lights? Really?" a young lad spoke up from Charlotte's left. He must be a friend of Grace's, or at least a friend of the family to be sitting in such close proximity to Grace.

"Clarence! Mind your manners. You speak only when spoken to." The petite woman who must be Clarence's mother spoke in a firm hush then looked at Richard. "I am sorry, Mr. Baxton."

He dismissed her apology with a wave of his hand. "Think nothing of it, Mrs. Fillmore. Young Clarence here is merely excited. . .as we all are, no doubt. Electric lights will bring an air of distinction to our primary city and nearby towns." He glanced at Flo. "And mischievous boys won't be able to douse them out quite so easily."

Their salads were removed and replaced by steaming bowls of french onion soup. Charlotte eagerly sampled the delicious broth. Silence fell upon the table as many took their initial fill of the second course. A few minutes later, Flo resumed the conversation.

"Yes, but electric lights might present an entirely different level of temptation."

A man Charlotte assumed to be Mr. Fillmore made quick order of his soup and laid his spoon in the empty bowl then rested his forearms on the edge of the table. "No more than the dynamite and nitroglycerin being manufactured by at least one of the Du Pont Company factories. If young lads succumb to the lure of mischief, they may be more fascinated by explosions than the buzz and hum of electric lamps."

"What do you think, Clarence?" Grace asked between sips of soup. "Would you prefer the electric lights or the dynamite?"

An impish grin played on his lips, matching perfectly with his unkempt and tousled hair. "I would definitely prefer the dynamite." He glanced across the table at his parents and composed himself like a dutiful son should. "But I would never play with something that dangerous. Besides," he said as he looked back at Grace, "there are more than enough ways to cause a little mischief right here in Ashbourne Hills."

Mr. and Mrs. Fillmore both shook their heads. Charlotte smiled down at Clarence and winked. He winked right back.

"You know," Richard spoke up. "Why don't we move Clarence here to the end of the table next to Grace." He looked at the two women who flanked his sides. "Mother? Would you ladies mind shifting down one seat to allow this young lad to be closer to the girls?"

"Not at all," Mrs. Baxton replied.

He smiled at his former nursemaid. "And Miss Flo? You could move to sit next to Charlotte."

"It would be my pleasure," Flo said with a mischievous grin as she, Clarence, Richard, and his mother played musical chairs.

"Clarence," Charlotte said once everyone was settled again, "you might consider reading *The Celebrated Jumping Frog of Calaveras County* by Mark Twain. I believe you will like it."

"Is that the same author who wrote about Tom Sawyer and Huckleberry Finn?"

"The very same." Charlotte finished her soup and patted her mouth with her napkin. "I have a copy in my bookshop in Brandywine, but you can likely find it right here in Ashbourne Hills at one of the shops in town."

Mrs. Fillmore nodded. "We shall look for it on our next shopping trip."

"And before long, even those trips will be more fun to make," Mr. Fillmore said.

"What do you mean?" Grace asked.

"Some of my colleagues serving on the state legislature have discussed bringing electric streetcars to Wilmington." He looked at his son. "With the city only two miles to the south, we should be able to ride in on them."

Grace straightened in her chair and grinned. "They sound like a lot of fun. Maybe even less bumpy than riding in a carriage."

"Just imagine," Anastasia added. "A carriage without horses. No more messy streets. And cars run by electricity. It's exciting!"

The girls' fascination with the modernized method of transportation was infectious. Charlotte had read stories and heard of reports from those who had ridden on the conveyances, but she had yet to experience it herself. Since the electric cars were rumored to replace the current horse-drawn ones, Charlotte had to admit a greater level of anticipation for what was to come.

The next part of their dinner was a refreshing serving of lime sorbet to cleanse their palates in preparation for the main course. Conversation stalled for just a moment as each of them took a small spoonful of the sweet treat.

From that point forward, talk continued to focus on the improvements being made in Wilmington and surrounding areas. Grace, Anastasia, and Clarence continued to focus on the streetcars, but the adults discussed efforts to become more like Philadelphia and everything that city had to offer. Conversation moved from the dinner table to the drawing room, where a substantial collection of wrapped gifts awaited Grace.

Charlotte was amazed at the warmth, love, and obvious support everyone showed toward Grace. It reminded her of her own family when her mother wasn't pushing her to fulfill social duties. And Grace's love of books was clearly not a secret. Nearly every gift she opened contained a book. What would that mean for visits by Richard to her shop? Would she see him less? Grace had enough books to keep her reading all summer and beyond.

"Don't worry, dear," Flo said from just behind Charlotte's shoulder. "Richard will find another excuse to travel to Brandywine."

How had Flo known the trail of her thoughts? Was Charlotte that transparent? As if he heard Flo's low-spoken words, Richard glanced up from his place next to Grace and looked directly at Charlotte. His eyes seemed to echo what Flo had just said, and again Charlotte questioned her own ability to keep her thoughts reined in.

Before she knew it, the evening had come to a close. Guests filtered out, each one extending their well wishes and congratulations to Grace on reaching the age of twelve. Charlotte could hardly believe Grace was only two years younger than Anastasia. Before long, the young girl would be looking to the social seasons and seeking a beau.

At that realization, Charlotte remembered Grace's circumstances and the chair where she sat. She had to do something to help. Perhaps an idea would come to her on the ride home. That thought made her realize it was time to depart. She and Anastasia had lingered long enough.

"Charlotte," Richard said just before she'd left the drawing room. He covered her right hand with both of his. "Thank you for coming tonight. You too, Anastasia. It meant the world to Grace."

Charlotte turned and looked up into eyes that showed his appreciation far more than his words. "It was our pleasure, Richard. We truly had a wonderful time. And I had the added bonus of meeting Flo." Charlotte grinned. "I'm happy we could be here for Grace."

"I'm happy you came as well." Sincerity and earnestness reflected in his gaze. "I look forward to seeing you again soon. And do not worry about the books Grace received tonight. I am certain she will take any opportunity to escape the confines of this house and go for a carriage ride. Perhaps next time we can take a walk by the creek."

"That sounds nice."

He raised her hand to his lips and placed a kiss on her knuckles. "Until next time." With a signal to the butler, he bowed and released her hand, never breaking his intent gaze. "I'll have my driver return you two safely home."

Charlotte could hardly breathe. Her hand tingled, and she longed for the warmth of his touch again. But that desire paled in comparison to the carefully controlled emotion she caught in his expression. A part of her wanted to remain and explore it further, but the wiser side recognized the prudence in leaving. She and her sister turned, only to almost stumble over Grace in her chair.

The girl watched Charlotte closely, a smile tugging at the corners of her mouth. "Miss Pringle, thank you again. You and Anastasia made tonight extra special." She extended her arms upward. "May I give you a hug?"

Oh, the preciousness of such a darling young lady. "Of course you may." Charlotte kneeled and embraced Grace as well, placing a kiss on her forehead as she drew away. "Have a good night, Grace." She tapped the girl's nose and smiled. "We shall see each other again soon. I promise."

Grace looked between Charlotte and her uncle, a smile almost appearing and a special light in her eyes. "Good night, Miss Pringle."

Anastasia led the way, but before Charlotte left the room, she turned again for one last glance at the two people who had become so special to her. Something about the way Grace said good night and how Richard now watched her set her heart thumping. Just what had the girl seen? And what thoughts lay hidden in Richard's mind?

A few moments later, she rested her head against the back wall of the carriage and relaxed her hands in her lap. Anastasia launched into a nonstop recounting of the evening, and Charlotte let her talk. Her sister didn't need anyone to reply, anyway. And it gave her time to get lost in her own thoughts. How did she fit into this entire experience? She firmly believed everything happened for a reason. While she might not be able to figure out that reason, she had a duty to give back out of her own abundance or bless others in need when she had something to offer. Grace had a need, and Charlotte had the resources to help. An idea started taking shape in her mind. God's Word said if she served those she encountered, she served as if unto Him. And she would do just that. Meeting remarkable people like Richard and Grace was just a bonus.

Chapter 10

"Can you believe it?" Margaret stood behind Charlotte's booth, arranging books and setting out others for a more eye-capturing display. "This must be the most successful bazaar I have ever attended. The abundance of merchants and tradesmen is simply splendid!"

Charlotte panned the area from left to right. Nearly fifty booths sat scattered on both sides of the walking path in the park. "I cannot disagree. When I circulated word of wanting to arrange this event, I had six or seven merchants respond almost immediately. They told other merchants, who told several businessmen, who also included tradesmen as well, and"—she twisted her hands around like a magician after performing a trick—"we have our bazaar in the park."

"It bears the markings of being both a rewarding and productive event." Margaret bent to retrieve a book that had fallen to the ground. She dusted it off and placed it on the table. "I should not be surprised if you achieve your goal of the full amount for Grace's surgery from this one day alone."

"Perhaps." Charlotte prayed it would happen, but she wouldn't know until the day ended. "But even if I fall short of my goal, I am both pleased and amazed at the diversity and array of options available to all passersby."

"And participating vendors as well," Margaret pointed out. "Although I would have to say the most comical booth is the one featuring the two costumed thespians acting out scenes from their latest play."

"That was one booth I eagerly welcomed when they approached me last week. I felt it an ingenious way of advertising the theatre company in Wilmington."

"It certainly brings a sense of merriment to an otherwise merchant-focused affair."

"Consider me a soft heart. The owner told me they are attempting to raise enough money to invest in a building they can own instead of being forced to make use of whatever unused stage they are able to find. Wilmington will benefit greatly from an actual playhouse where everyone can go to see the many plays being performed. How could I deny him that opportunity?"

"You can't." Margaret touched Charlotte's shoulder and smiled. "And I applaud you for allowing them to participate. An excellent decision."

Charlotte looked down at the table and picked up her ledger recording the day's sales. She knit her brows. "Forgive me for changing the subject so abruptly, but did we sell the copy of *Gulliver's Travels*? I do not see it here, and I know it is not marked in my ledger." She glanced at Margaret. "Do you recall if you sold it earlier today?"

Margaret bit her lower lip. "Yes, I did. And I forgot to write it down. Three other customers stood ready to make purchases, and I am afraid it slipped my mind."

"It's all right. As long as between the two of us we remember." Charlotte grinned. "But if it happens again, I shall subtract some of your wages."

Her friend raised one eyebrow. "A difficult feat to accomplish considering you are not compensating me." Margaret came ready to work in a simple walking dress, but even the quality of the cotton material gave evidence to her fairly recent rise in station. "However, I am going to make it a point to pay a visit to several booths should you permit me a period of rest from my work."

Charlotte sniggered but attempted to compose herself. She leveled her best reprimanding glance. "And what, pray tell, makes you believe you have earned a rest?" She made a sweeping gesture with her right arm. "We have only reached the halfway point of this event. And I might be called upon to see to other details. That would leave my booth unattended. We cannot have that happen, now can we?"

Margaret picked up on her jesting. "Oh, of course not. But should you be called away, I cannot promise that I will not find a random passerby to oversee the booth in my absence."

"So long as there is someone here at all times." Charlotte shrugged. "Who am I to be particular about the identity of that person?" She smiled and moved to straighten a stack of books. "Besides, far be it from me to tell a baroness she is not permitted to have a well-deserved rest. I wouldn't wish to risk the wrath of Baron Edward James Heddington of Sutherland. He might have me tarred and feathered."

With surprising speed, Margaret whipped out her fan and smacked Charlotte on the upper arm. "You are positively irredeemable. To think, my husband ever ordering such barbaric punishment." She tapped her fan to her chin. "Although I cannot guarantee the whipping post or pillory would be out of the question."

The two women dissolved into a fit of laughter at the absurdity of their conversation. At least the day would pass by more quickly than if Charlotte had been working the table by herself.

A lady with two well-dressed children approached their booth, so

Charlotte quickly composed herself. "Good afternoon, ma'am. How may we help you?"

The lady nodded and her daughter curtsied while her son bowed. Children with impeccable manners! Charlotte didn't often see that in the park.

"Good afternoon," the lady replied. She glanced at Charlotte, then at Margaret, and jerked her head back to look again. "Oh! Good afternoon, Baroness. I had no idea you would be in attendance today."

Margaret regarded the lady and pursed her lips. "Do forgive me, but are we acquainted from another event, or might we have been introduced else-where? If so, I cannot seem to recall your name."

Charlotte raised her eyebrows at her friend, who didn't seem to notice. Where had the jovial woman who had only moments before been making light of whipping post punishments gone? In her place was a dignified, proper lady with a rather refined manner of speech. Charlotte was amazed at the quick transformation.

The lady waved her hand in dismissal. "No apology is necessary, Baroness. In fact, I would be quite surprised if you recalled me at all." Margaret remained confused, so the lady rushed ahead. "My name is Elizabeth Frederick, and I was in attendance at your wedding to the Baron a few months past. You see, my cousin is the nephew of your husband's uncle."

Understanding dawned on Margaret's face. Charlotte, on the other hand, tried to make the connection. So, this lady's cousin was also a cousin of Margaret's husband.

The lady continued. "We are here from Philadelphia visiting my sister, and she mentioned this bazaar." She placed one hand on each of her children's shoulders in loving affection as she glanced down at them. "I told William and Louise here we would take some time to come. They were quite impressed with the theater pair. But I saw this booth with books and felt compelled to stop." She smiled at Margaret. "Now, I am rather delighted I did."

Margaret smiled in return. "I shall be certain to tell the baron of our meeting here today. He will no doubt be pleased to hear of it." She switched personas and became a saleswoman. "Now, is there something in particular you are seeking, or would you like me to make a suggestion?"

Charlotte chose that opportunity to leave and start her rounds. Her booth was in capable hands, and she'd likely have a sizable sale upon her return. Time to check the rest of the vendors and how their sales had gone so far.

A little over an hour later, Charlotte finished with the final vendor and tallied the results. A broad smile formed on her lips. Praise the Lord! Her goal had been reached. And the day hadn't yet concluded. Who knew how much there'd be by day's end. So many generous merchants and craftsmen. Without prodding, each one of them had agreed to donate half of their proceeds to Grace's need. They had simply heard of her plan and volunteered to be involved. A successful bazaar indeed. Just as Margaret predicted. Now Grace could have her operation.

Charlotte could hardly wait to tell Richard and Grace.

❧

"Uncle Richard, look!" Grace pointed across the creek to a red-crowned crane wading about thirty feet away. "A crane. I cannot believe I saw a crane."

"Excellent observation, Grace." Richard walked behind her, pushing the wheeled chair over the dirt path along the creek's edge.

They had met Charlotte at her bookshop about twenty minutes ago and made their way down through the tulip poplars, giving them a great deal of shade on this sunny afternoon. From the moment he saw Charlotte, he'd noticed a certain light in her eyes and extra bounce to her step. What had happened since Grace's birthday party to make her so cheerful? She must have received good news of some kind. Perhaps another rare book she treasured. Or maybe higher sales than expected at her bookshop. He hoped she'd tell them today.

"You should have your notepad and pencil with you, Grace, so you can write down the different species you see today. Then you could write a special report to include with your daily studies. Your tutor would be quite impressed."

"I don't need paper." Grace tapped her head near her right temple. "I remember it all up here."

Richard glanced at Charlotte as she walked next to them. "Says the girl who had difficulty recalling the name of the substantial land purchase President Jefferson made earlier in the century. Right about the time the du Pont family emigrated here and had heavy influence with Jefferson and France." Grace usually demonstrated a rather keen intelligence when it came to history. Something else must be on her mind. Much like Charlotte. He still wanted to know when she'd say something.

"Do you mean the Louisiana Purchase?" Charlotte asked.

Obviously not now. And he wasn't about to initiate the discussion. He'd leave it up to her.

"One and the same." Richard patted Grace's head. "This one thought it was the Lewis and Clark Territory."

"Well, they *were* the ones to explore the land and report back with their maps, notes, and charts. It could easily be an honest mistake."

Grace turned and gave a broad smile, showing her appreciation for

Charlotte defending her. She then stuck her chin in the air and harrumphed. The corners of Charlotte's lips turned down as she attempted to hide her grin. Somehow, Richard felt like the odd man out in this trio. For the moment, Charlotte was the champion and he the accuser.

"All right," he continued, forcing a teasing tone into his voice. "What about the name of the man who was responsible for claiming Delaware for the British?"

Grace folded her arms and looked straight ahead. He could imagine the frown on her face, or even the pout. With a quick bend at the waist, he leaned forward and peered over her shoulder. Sure enough, the frown and pout were both there.

"Grace," Charlotte chided, "you couldn't recall William Penn?"

"I only remembered him for founding Pennsylvania." She twisted in her chair as best she could and wrinkled her nose up at Richard. "At least I remembered Lord de la Warr."

Richard took a step closer to Charlotte and lowered his voice. "She isn't very good at accepting constructive criticism or correction when she makes mistakes."

Charlotte pressed her lips together, showing one dimple where the corner of her mouth crooked, and raised her eyebrows as if shrugging. "Do you know anyone who is?"

He made a quick jab, mimicking a parry with a sword. "Touché."

She grinned. "I believe Grace is perfectly justified in her indignation when someone chides her about those mistakes. Just remember all the facts she gets right and allow her a slip or two now and then."

"All right. I see your point." He probably shouldn't have teased his niece in front of Charlotte. But it wasn't easy remembering her young and impressionable age all the time. She seemed so much older in most instances and conversed with him, often better than many adults he knew. Again, he lowered his voice, placing one of his hands over his chest. "I promise I shall endeavor to be more lenient to my niece when the situation warrants it."

His antics caused Charlotte to laugh as she shook her head. "And I thought Grace was the impish one among us."

He shrugged. "Let us just say she comes by it honestly."

Charlotte took a deep breath then opened her mouth to say something, but Grace spoke first.

"Miss Pringle, what is on the other side of the creek?"

Yet another missed opportunity. Richard sighed. How long would they have to wait? At least Charlotte's eyes hadn't lost their excitement. But now he was getting anxious.

Charlotte turned her head in the direction Grace pointed. Several identical barns sat side by side not too far from the main house. "Oh, that's a dairy farm owned by the du Pont family. They only recently built these stone walls you see wending their way across the rolling hills."

"There are more cows than I can count. I guess that means they get a lot of milk every day."

Now it was Richard's turn to laugh, and Charlotte looked over at him with an amused expression. "She *is* quite astute, as you pointed out a few moments ago."

"Yes," Richard replied. "She is that. I am not certain how I will ever keep up with her if she continues to excel at this rate."

"Well, keeping up with her might be more of a challenge than you imagine."

"Pardon me?"

Charlotte looked out across the creek, silent for several moments. When would she share her news with them? A few more moments passed, but she didn't say anything.

"Charlotte?"

She shook her head as if to clear it. "Why don't we rest for a bit and sit on the bench over there?"

"That sounds like an excellent idea." Richard tried not to sound too enthusiastic, but it seemed whatever Charlotte was about to tell them was quite important. And he wanted to know right now.

Once seated, she turned to face him and Grace, who sat between them in front of the bench. His niece's face also showed a keen interest in the conversation.

"I wanted to tell you both as soon as you arrived at the shop. But it didn't seem like the right time. I've been plagued by your predicament for quite some time."

Charlotte fidgeted with her hands, her eyes going from Richard to Grace to her lap and back again. Her eyes lacked the light they'd had for most of their walk. Instead, he saw only uncertainty and hesitation in them.

"I suppose there is only one way to tell you, and that's straight out."

She reached into a hidden pocket of her skirts and withdrew a long envelope. Richard glanced down to see his name and Grace's on the front. He looked up at Charlotte and knit his brows. Predicament? Did she mean Grace's operation? Surely this wasn't a loan. If it was, he would refuse.

She held up the envelope, just out of his reach. "Now before you say anything, this isn't a loan. It is a collection of sorts."

"A collection?"

Once again, her face brightened, and the spark of excitement returned. "Yes. After Grace's birthday party, an idea came to me on the carriage ride home. I set to work right away, and before I knew it, I had managed to coordinate one of the largest bazaar's this area of town has ever seen."

"What's a bazaar?" Grace asked.

Charlotte smiled. "It is a gathering of local merchants, tradesmen, and other professionals who set up booths and sell or showcase something related to their line of work."

Richard pointed at the envelope. "And this bazaar is how you managed to take up the collection?"

"Well, partially." She covered the envelope with her other hand. "Only half the proceeds from the vendors is in this envelope. The rest they retained for their time and their trade." A substantial look of satisfaction reflected in her eyes as she handed the envelope to Richard. "And I want you and Grace to have it. There is more than enough money inside to cover the surgery and any additional expenses incurred as a result."

Grace watched the exchange and looked back and forth between her uncle and Charlotte. "Miss Pringle, why are you giving us money?"

Richard remained silent, overwhelmed. He could only stare at the envelope. Tucked inside was the answer to weeks and months of prayer. How in the world could he ever thank her?

Charlotte leaned forward and took Grace's hands in hers. "Because, sweetheart, I want you to be able to have that operation."

"Really? Do you truly mean it? The money is for me?"

Charlotte laughed. "Yes, dear one. Now nothing stands in your way."

Richard looked at his niece. Tears of joy pooled in her eyes and fell to her cheeks. She leaned forward and pulled Charlotte into an emotional embrace.

"Thank you! Thank you, thank you, thank you. This is the best surprise you could ever give us."

"Yes," Richard croaked. Just great. Where had his voice gone? Emotion tightened the muscles in his neck. He coughed and cleared his throat several times before continuing. "Grace is correct. This gift is quite amazing."

Charlotte leaned back from Grace and met his gaze. As he stared at her, he couldn't think of anything else to say. Words hardly seemed enough in a situation like this. What he wanted to do, he couldn't. Not only was Grace present, but he hadn't made his intentions known to Charlotte, and he wasn't about to overstep the bounds of propriety. Waiting until after something was official would be too late. He had to do something now.

Throwing caution to the wind, he reached for Charlotte's hands and placed a single kiss on the knuckles of each. Then, with a slight tug, he pulled her toward him and kissed her smooth cheek. When he leaned back and gauged her reaction, all he wanted to do was draw her into his arms. From the look in her eyes, her thoughts were close to his. But they had a rather impressionable audience. Grace was already too keen for her own good, and who knew what she'd make of this little exchange? At his first opportunity, he was going to arrange to speak to Charlotte's father.

Charlotte reached up and touched her cheek where he'd kissed it. She smiled at him.

He grinned. "I suppose saying thank you now is a rather moot point."

"Yes, but this other method is equally effective." Her sense of humor had returned.

"It appears Grace and I have some plans to make." He stood and pivoted Grace in her chair. Charlotte stood beside them. They started off in silence and walked several hundred feet. It was all so overwhelming. What could he say or do to get the conversation going again? Ah yes. Richard thought of something.

"All right, Grace. What do you remember so far from what you saw along the path and even in or near the creek?"

"Hmm. I remember the crane and the white-tailed deer." She tilted her head and looked up to the right. "Oh, and then there was the snapping turtle, the dragonflies, and the beautiful red-tailed hawk. I look forward to drawing him."

"Excellent." Richard squeezed both of her shoulders. "You should be aptly prepared to impress your tutor in grand fashion."

Grace chattered on about the wildlife as Richard pushed her chair along. Charlotte remained silent. He wished he could reach out and take her hand, but he needed both of his to steer and push Grace. So, he did the next best thing. . .put her hand on one of the handles and placed his hand on top.

She startled and looked up at him, but she didn't resist. Instead, she smiled, never breaking her stride. As they reached the cobblestone street in front of the bookshop, Grace stopped the wheels and brought the three of them to a halt.

"Miss Pringle, you will be there, won't you? At the hospital when I have my operation?"

"Of course I will. I would not want to miss that day for anything in the world."

Grace gave a succinct nod. "Good."

Richard continued to lead them to the bookshop. This day had turned out far better than he ever could have imagined. Charlotte hadn't backed away from his affectionate overtures. He and Grace had immediate access to the funds they needed for her operation. Grace just might walk again. And he would be speaking with Charlotte's father within the fortnight. How could things be any better?

Chapter 11

Charlotte sat on the same bench in the park where she had sat with Richard not so long ago. A colorful array of wildflowers grew all around, providing a rainbow's splash to the otherwise green landscape. She glanced down at the letter in her hand for at least the tenth or eleventh time. Life for Richard and Grace had been extremely hectic since their walk by the creek.

Three weeks had passed, and she had three letters from them updating her on the countdown to the day of the operation. This latest one, though, was her favorite.

It began in the obvious hand of Richard, although she could see Grace's influence as well:

Dearest Charlotte,

We are only one week away from the scheduled surgery. And we would not have been able to get this far were it not for you. I realize we have expressed our gratitude many times over, but our hearts remain forever thankful for the time and effort you invested in order for us to receive the bountiful blessing God provided through your service.

Your treasured gift was a distinct answer to prayer, and it helped us remember that God has not forgotten about us. I confess our faith had wavered several times following the accident. Now, however, we are relying on our Lord's strength, and with dear friends such as yourself, we have everything we need.

Then the writing changed to Grace's:

I am a little frightened about the operation, but Uncle Richard has said he will be there the entire time. You will too, I hope. It will help if I can hold your hand and see your face, even though you cannot be in the room with me until the doctor is all done. This is going to be one of the best days of my life, and I want to share it with both you and Uncle Richard. Only one week until I see you again. I hope the days pass quickly.

The letter concluded with Richard's parting words.

This week may very well be difficult, but thinking of you will aid in its quick passing. Before we know it, we shall be awaiting the outcome from the doctor, and I am confident we shall rejoice with a successful operation. Please continue your prayers for us and for the doctor, as well as the attending nurses. Come Thursday, my carriage will be waiting to bring you to us. Until then, we remain your friends.

Sincerely,
Richard & Grace

Only one more week. As promised, she would continue to pray for all involved. Beyond that, however, Charlotte prayed she could be what they both needed on what was sure to be a difficult day. For Grace to want her by her side meant more than words could say.

A warm breeze rustled through the tulip poplars towering above the path. It whispered through the waist-high rushes along the creek banks. Charlotte closed her eyes and soaked in the sounds of nature. From the trills of the various songbirds to the splash of the trout and bluegill, to the crickets hiding in the grass and the occasional high-pitched cry of the red-tailed hawk, the musical symphony bore clear evidence of God's handiwork. It again reminded Charlotte the Lord was with her, and He'd be with Grace throughout her procedure.

❧

The soft murmur of voices traveled into the front hallway as Charlotte made her way toward the sitting room. Father had left word with their butler, asking to speak with her. From the sounds coming out of the room, Mother was present as well. It must be something significant for her to be summoned immediately upon arriving home. Whatever they had to say, she prayed it wouldn't be something she didn't want to hear. Before she stepped into view, she took a deep breath and willed her heart to settle down to a more even pace.

"Ah good," Mother announced as soon as Charlotte walked into the room. "Please, dear, come take a seat and join us."

Charlotte's feet sank into the woven carpet as she headed straight for her favorite settee. Her parents waited in the wingback chairs opposite her and presented the image of relaxation. Father leaned back in his chair and rested his hands on the arms. Mother tucked her legs underneath her, with her hands folded in her lap. When neither of them said anything, Charlotte swallowed and wet her lips.

Finally, Father spoke. "Before we get to the primary reason for asking to speak with you, your mother and I want to say how proud we are of the success you've had with your bookshop."

"Yes," Mother added, though Charlotte could tell her agreement came with resignation. "We have heard glowing reports from many of our friends, saying how much they love to visit your shop."

Charlotte didn't know how to respond. Complimenting her obviously wasn't the purpose of this conversation. She appreciated them making a point to begin with that though. Still, anticipating what might come next made her heart race.

Father again resumed control. "Now, for the matter at hand."

There was a matter? Charlotte crossed her right ankle over her left. She slowly smoothed her hands on the folds of her skirt. It helped absorb the dampness of her palms as she awaited Father's next words.

"Charlotte, you know your mother and I only want the best for you. But before we present a possible opportunity to you, there is something we must know."

Father leaned forward and clasped his hands together, resting his forearms on his knees. "We know you have been spending additional leisure time with a certain gentleman who has been frequenting your bookshop. And you have already told us of the forthcoming operation for the gentleman's niece." He met her gaze, but she couldn't read his expression. "Mr. Baxton has paid me a visit recently, and we had an enlightening chat."

Richard had been here? And he hadn't told her? This must have happened last week when she was attending the Ridenour Cotillion. Charlotte was surprised he'd accepted her mother's invitation to dinner without her knowing. She wished her parents had said something earlier.

"With that in mind," Father continued, "we'd appreciate your honest answer to the following question."

She knew what was coming. Even so, she didn't think she could provide an answer that would satisfy her parents. At least not with certainty.

Her father pinned her with an unwavering stare. "What are your feelings regarding Mr. Baxton?"

There it was. The question she knew they would ask. Charlotte opened her mouth to speak, but no words came out. She swallowed twice and tried to gather her thoughts. Considering Richard more than a friend had only recently occupied her thoughts. Now her parents expected her to make sense of her feelings and put them into words?

"Charlotte, dear," Mother interjected, breaking the silence. She peered into her daughter's face. "Do you simply not know how you feel?"

Clearing her throat, Charlotte tried again. "Father, Mother, I must confess. Up until a couple of weeks ago, Mr. Baxton and I were nothing more than friends. Other than attending the birthday party for his niece and our recent walk by the creek, nearly every one of our conversations has centered on Grace, his niece."

"And now?" Father pressed.

"Now?" She wet her lips again. "Now I don't know. I admit he has several appealing qualities about him, and I *am* attracted. Any more than that, I don't believe I can say for certain."

There. She might not have given them the response they sought, but she had been honest.

Father angled his body toward Mother and raised his eyebrows. Mother nodded in response. Charlotte sat in silence, awaiting what felt like a sentencing, even if that was a rather substantial exaggeration.

Finally, Father returned to his original position. "We appreciate your honesty, especially when you could have misled us or given us an answer merely to pacify us." His expression brightened, and he again sat back in his seat. "With that matter settled, we're faced with the issue of the time you spend with eligible men."

Did that mean they didn't consider Richard eligible because of his current state of affairs? Her heart fell, and her shoulders dropped. Were the social engagements not enough? She couldn't be faulted for the men not taking an interest in her. On the heels of asking her about Richard, though, it was clear where her parents stood.

Mother sat up straighter, eagerness replacing the previous concern. "We have been speaking with several of our friends and believe we've found one gentleman we'd like you to meet. He is poised to assume solid positions both in his father's footsteps and in a venture he's begun on his own."

So they *did* consider this gentleman more eligible than Richard. She wished she could muster up a bit more excitement in response to this announcement. Although she couldn't say for certain where she and Richard stood, she wasn't eager to pursue a possible romantic entanglement with someone else. Nevertheless, her parents had gone to some trouble on her behalf, and as their daughter, she owed them her respect and cooperation.

Father tilted his head in her direction. "Is there anything you'd like to say?"

Charlotte took a deep breath. "I must confess this comes as a surprise. I am sure you have my best interests at heart," she added with a soft smile. Best to do what she could to set them at ease. "I'm well aware my friends are all married or engaged. And I'm grateful you have been more patient regarding my arrangements."

"We're well aware of what can come of wanting to force certain outcomes," Mother replied. "Our family has a history of somewhat meddlesome parents. Even though the pairings worked out for the best, we agreed we didn't want to do the same to you."

"I appreciate that, Mother. But I suppose it *is* time for me to take the matter of my future more seriously." She looked at them before continuing. "You've both given me so much. How could I not honor your wishes?" Maybe with this shift in her priorities, she could continue to explore the possibilities with Richard, as well.

"Where Mr. Baxton is concerned," Father said, "we must caution you. He comes from a well-established family with a solid and successful business. But at present, there is no guarantee his situation will work out to his benefit. And we do not wish to see you hurt."

What? Just when she thought her parents were providing the perfect opportunity for her to discover the answers to all her questions about Richard, Father warned her against him?

"But, Father, it isn't like that at all." She unclasped her hands and extended them in a placating gesture. "I already said he is only a friend." At the moment, that much was true in reality. "Are you saying I can no longer spend any time with him or his niece?"

Father pressed his lips into a thin line. "What I am saying is prolonged interactions with him on a social level might prevent you from seeing possibilities with the other gentlemen you meet."

He hadn't set Richard apart from the class of a gentleman. That had to be something. Perhaps she could discover more about why he was facing such difficulty with his business and if he knew when it would all be resolved.

Mother nodded and pursed her lips. "I do not see any cause to end your associations with Mr. Baxton, Charlotte, dear. But I agree with your father. There are more than enough young men right here in the Brandywine area who I'm sure will provide a suitable distraction."

Mother didn't come right out and say it, but Charlotte could read between the lines. It wasn't that Richard might distract her from the other men. It was where he lived and his unknown financial status. Well, at least they hadn't forbidden any association with him. They were only expressing their desire for her to be careful. That she could do.

"Thank you, Mother. Father." She regarded them each in turn and dipped her head in acknowledgment, maintaining a polite exterior. "I promise as soon as Grace's operation is over next week, I will devote appropriate attention to the potential suitor you have mentioned. We can discuss this further then, and you can arrange an introduction."

Her parents both stood, seeming pleased with Charlotte's promise.

"That is all we ask, dear," Mother said.

"Now let's adjourn to the dining room where I'm sure Laura has an appetizing meal ready."

Charlotte allowed her parents to precede her from the sitting room. That conversation hadn't gone as she preferred. It could have been much worse though. At least she was still permitted to spend time with Richard. But she only had a little more than a week. If anything more was to happen with Richard, God would have to work a miracle. She had to trust Him and leave it at that.

❧

"Charlotte!" Richard's anxious voice greeted her as soon as she stepped through the swinging double doors. "I'm glad you are here." He took a firm hold of her arm and started to pull her in the opposite direction.

She resisted, and he paused. "Wait a moment. Why is there such a sense of urgency?" Her right hand went to her chest. "Has something happened to Grace? Is she all right?"

"Grace is fine. But the surgeon arrived early this morning, and he wants to begin right now. I told him he couldn't until you arrived. Grace wants to see you before they wheel her into the other room." Richard resumed his tug on her arm. "Now, come with me."

They entered a stark white room almost identical to the rest of the hospital, except this room was furnished with two rose-hued chairs and a colorful patchwork quilt on the bed. Someone had thought ahead. A splash of color always brightened the spirit.

"Miss Pringle, you're here!" Grace's smile lit up the room. She tried to sit up, but the exertion took too much effort.

Charlotte rushed forward. "No, no. Please, Grace. Rest."

A nurse in starched uniform stood on the other side of the bed. "We have only just sedated her with chloroform, but it should be taking effect any minute. If you have something you wish to say to her, you should do it quickly. Otherwise, she will not be able to respond."

Grace extended a hand toward Charlotte. "Miss Pringle, will you pray with me?"

Tears welled in Charlotte's eyes. "Of course I will, dear." She looked over her shoulder at Richard, and he nodded, stepping with her to Grace's bedside.

The young girl reached first for her uncle's hand and then for Charlotte's. She waited and looked back and forth between them both. Before Charlotte could figure out why Grace hesitated, Richard's fingers brushed hers in a silent request to take her hand. Ah, so that was it. Grace wanted their prayer circle to be complete. How could she deny the precious girl such an honest request?

As soon as Charlotte moved her fingers, Richard's hand enveloped hers, the warmth of his grasp traveling up her arm and straight to her heart. They all bowed their heads.

"Dear Jesus, thank You for bringing Miss Pringle here today, and thank You for the doctor who will be working to help me walk again. Thank You for the nurse to help the doctor and for Your blessing on us. Be with all of us, Lord, through everything that will happen today, and keep us safe. No matter what happens, we love You, and we know You love us. Amen."

Grace's words softened as her prayer drew to a close, and her grip loosened. She managed to open her eyes, though, and look right at Charlotte.

"I am happy you came," she said, sounding sluggish.

The nurse stepped forward as another attendant entered the room. "We need to take her now."

As the bed on wheels passed by Charlotte, Grace reached out again and touched her hand.

"I love you," she murmured.

Charlotte's eyes widened. Had she heard correctly? She looked at Grace, at the soft smile on the girl's lips. Yes, she must have. A warm hand touched her right shoulder, and Charlotte turned to see Richard with affection reflecting in his gaze. Quick. She had to do or say something in response to Grace. She touched two fingers to her lips and touched them to Grace's forehead.

"I love you, too, Grace."

The girl didn't respond, but her smile remained. At least Charlotte could send Grace into surgery knowing her love was returned. Now they just had to wait.

&

Charlotte stood to stretch. Four hours. And in all that time, they had spoken only twice—when a nurse came to provide updates on the procedure. Other than that, they had been left alone in an alcove outfitted with two sets of benches opposite each other. There had been plenty of time for Charlotte to tell Richard about her recent conversation with her parents. She wanted him to know she knew about his visit to her father as well. But the moment wasn't right. Several times she started to open her mouth only to close it and remain silent.

Richard paced from one end of the benches to the other. In between paces, he cast a worried glance down the hall toward the operating room.

"Richard," Charlotte said, keeping her voice soft and free of chastisement. "The nurse was here only twenty minutes ago, and she reported everything being good. I know this isn't easy, but we have to have faith and trust God to be with Grace and the doctor now."

He halted his pacing and stared at her. Then his eyes closed, and a deep sigh escaped his lips. "You are right. My walking back and forth or looking down the hall isn't going to make the doctor finish any faster." He sat on the bench again, and Charlotte joined him. Running his fingers through his hair, he slumped and rested his forearms on his thighs. "I just feel so incredibly helpless. I wish I could do something."

Compassion filled Charlotte. She started to reach out and touch his hand but retracted. What would he think of her? Would he consider her too forward? He had always initiated the gestures of physical touch. But he was in no frame of mind right now to do so. Charlotte swallowed and tried to calm her rapidly beating heart. What could it hurt?

Slowly, she shifted the few inches to her right to close the distance between them. Then she eased her hand toward him and covered his folded hands hanging at his knees. He didn't react.

"There is something we can do," she said. "We can continue to pray. That is the best help we can give to the doctor, to ourselves, and to Grace."

Richard looked up, his face bearing evidence of the strain. But as he gazed into her eyes, his expression changed. His mouth relaxed, his eyebrows smoothed, and a light entered his eyes. He withdrew one of his hands and clasped hers between his.

"You are absolutely right. Thank you. I could use the reminder."

"Sometimes we all can."

Together, they bowed their heads and prayed silently. Charlotte had no idea how long they remained that way, but she didn't care. She was there for Richard when he needed her most.

"Ahem."

Charlotte and Richard both looked up at the sound of a man clearing his throat. The doctor! Could that mean. . . ? Richard squeezed her hands.

"Mr. Baxton, I have finished with your niece's procedure. I believe the operation was a success." He held up his hands as if to stop someone from rushing forward. "Now obviously we won't know for certain until she wakes, and there will be a substantial amount of time for recovery. She has been without the use of her legs for several months. Her muscles are going to need to be strengthened, and she is going to have to learn how to use them all over again. It is going to be a difficult road for her. . .and you. And there remains a possibility the operation won't create a permanent cure. But we will be certain Grace receives the highest level of care for the duration of time she is with us."

Charlotte appreciated the doctor speaking to them in terms they could understand. At least she could follow this report.

Richard stood and extended a hand to the doctor. "Thank you, Doctor," Richard said. "We owe you a lot, regardless of the results."

The doctor shook his hand and offered a weary smile. "It was my pleasure. If I can help young Grace recover even part of the sensation in her limbs, I will consider this operation a success. But we are hoping for much more." The man looked back down the hall. "Now, if you will excuse me, I need to return to the operating room and tidy up a few things. We will speak with you soon about the next steps."

As soon as the doctor departed, Richard turned to face Charlotte, excitement spread across his entire face. Charlotte shared his enthusiasm. She wanted to shout out and rejoice. But Richard beat her to it.

He smiled and spread his arms wide. "He did it!"

"Yes. The operation was a success!" Without thinking, Charlotte threw her arms around Richard's neck. He wrapped his arms around her back and swung her in a circle then set her down. Almost immediately, Charlotte realized what they had done. Heat warmed her face, and she attempted to step away. But Richard held fast. She looked up at him, and his eyes darkened with an emotion that both compelled her and frightened her. He wanted to kiss her. And she wanted him to do it.

His hands tightened around her waist, and he lowered his head. Charlotte held her breath as his lips touched hers, lightly at first, then with more pressure. She slid her hands to his shoulders and moved the fingers of her right hand up to touch his stubbly cheek. Several moments later, Richard pulled back and inhaled a deep, shuddering breath. Charlotte pressed her lips together, savoring the kiss.

"I. . .uh. . ." Richard was the first to attempt to speak.

"Mr. Baxton?"

Charlotte and Richard stepped apart and turned to face a courier who held a message. Would there be no end to the interruptions this afternoon? And if a courier came all the way to the hospital to find Richard, it must be important. Charlotte silently prayed it wasn't bad news.

"Yes?" Richard replied.

"I have a message from the lawyer who serves your father's business, sir."

The man handed over the note.

From a lawyer? This *was* serious.

Richard unfolded the single piece of paper and read it. Concern immediately creased his brow. A moment later, he reached into his vest pocket and handed a coin to the courier. "Thank you," he said. The courier left without a word.

Charlotte waited. What had the note said? And why did Richard appear so distraught?

Richard withdrew his pocket watch and flipped it open then snapped it shut in haste and shoved it into his pocket. "Charlotte, I am sorry." He turned to face her, remorse reflecting in his eyes. "But I must leave on a trip to take care of an urgent family business matter. There is a train scheduled to depart immediately, and I must be on it. I do not know how long I will be gone, but I must see to this straightaway."

Charlotte nodded, even though she wanted to protest. "I understand. And I hope the matter is resolved quickly."

The ghost of a smile appeared on his face. "As do I. There is still so much here that needs to be done."

Did he mean in regard to Grace and her recovery or something pertaining to their relationship? He didn't elaborate. Instead, he took her hands in his.

"I do not wish to impose, but Mother should be here in about two hours. Until then, would you mind remaining here until Grace awakens from the anesthetic? I will be certain to leave instructions stating you are permitted to be with Grace. It isn't the ideal situation, but when she realizes I am not here, she will want to see a familiar face."

"Of course." How could she not stay? "I would be happy to see to it that Grace is both reassured and notified of your departure. You have no worries here."

"Thank you." Raising both her hands to his lips, he placed a kiss on each. "I promise to contact you as soon as I return."

With that, he was gone.

Charlotte watched as Richard stopped a nurse in the hall and spoke to her for a moment or two. The woman glanced at Charlotte then returned her attention to Richard, nodded, and appeared to reassure him. After responding to her, he gave Charlotte a final wave and disappeared through the double doors. The nurse went back to her work, and Charlotte stood in the alcove. What should she do now? The doctor or another staff member would get her once Grace awakened, or at least when they felt it was safe to move her to a bed in the children's ward where she'd reside until she was deemed healed enough to make the arduous journey home. Charlotte wanted to sit by the girl's bedside and hold her hand. At least that would give her something to occupy her time and mind.

The ending of this day had not gone how she planned. Of course the kiss wasn't in her plan either. But she hadn't minded that at all. Now she had two things she needed to discuss with Richard. But he was gone, and she had no idea when he'd return. Left with no alternative, Charlotte again sat down on the bench. If she remembered correctly from her father's surgery a few years back, it shouldn't be long before the chloroform wore off and an attendant came to get her.

At least she had a few moments to herself to relax...*if* she could avoid dwelling on the memory of Richard's lips and the warmth of his embrace. That wouldn't be easy. She reached up and touched her fingers to her mouth, still feeling the tingle of his touch. His kiss had changed many things. Charlotte only prayed the change would be for the better.

Chapter 12

Charlotte stood in the front hall as their butler closed the door behind her. Thomas Frederick Lyndhurst had just escorted her home after their sixth outing together in three weeks. As had been true of all their other outings, he'd been charming, engaging, and humorous. Charlotte managed a smile. Thomas certainly had his appealing characteristics. And his compelling cerulean eyes only enhanced his otherwise handsome features. But try as she might, she couldn't get Richard out of her thoughts.

She missed Grace as well. It had been three days since she'd penned a letter to the young girl, inquiring after her health and recovery status. A reply should be forthcoming any day.

"Oh good. You *have* returned." Bethany stood in the doorway of the parlor, stitching in hand. "Come, join Anastasia and me in here. We wish to hear all the details."

Sharing about her latest day out with Thomas didn't exactly occupy the top spot on Charlotte's list of things she would like to do, but talking with her sisters might help put her mind at ease. When she entered the room behind Bethany, she perched on the arm of the settee closest to the door. Picking up her needlework didn't appeal to her in the least, and she had no desire to remain in the parlor any longer than necessary.

"All right, tell us everything. And do not attempt to leave out any details." Anastasia pointed her long needle in Charlotte's direction, trying to appear stern but failing miserably.

Yes, Charlotte definitely needed this.

"Very well." She sighed. "I know you two will not give me a moment's rest until I appease your curiosity, so I may as well surrender now."

"Good." Bethany spoke up from her seat opposite Charlotte. "It would be futile to resist anyway. Anastasia and I always get what we want."

"Yes, I know." Charlotte pursed her lips. "And I am reminded of that nearly every time I hear Mother speak of her daughters."

Bethany waved off her defense. "Oh, that is only because Mother is more focused on seeing you happily married with a secure future. Once you are, her efforts will turn to me." She cast a glance at her other sister. "Then Anastasia will be the favorite."

"What do you mean 'will be'?" Anastasia narrowed her eyes at Bethany. "I already am. And as I am the youngest, I likely always will."

Bethany dropped her stitching to her lap and held up her hands in mock surrender. "All right. All right. You win. You are Mother and Father's favorite. And no one can take that away from you." She gave Anastasia a pointed glance. "Now, shall we return to the reason for this conversation?"

"There truly isn't much to tell," Charlotte replied. "It was a day much like the others I've spent with him. We took a walk along the creek, and he asked me how the bookshop was faring. Then he explained some about his work in textile manufacturing. He made a point to tell me he was poised to assume control in less than three years."

"And he will likely want to have his family already established before that occurs." Bethany raised one eyebrow in her sister's direction. "A point, I am certain, not lost on either Mr. Lyndhurst or Mother and Father."

Bethany had that right. From the moment Mother and Father mentioned Thomas to her a month ago, she knew how pleased they would be to see a successful match made. And as promised, she had been giving him a fair chance. But that might not be enough.

"Yes," Charlotte replied. "While Mr. Lyndhurst has not been so forward as to intimate that point, it is clear in the selected topics of conversation and in his mannerisms that he sees our time together as pursuing a purpose." She looked up at the floral pattern of the wallpaper opposite her. It reminded her of the room where Grace had received her presents at her birthday party. "However, try as I might," she continued, bringing her focus back to the subject at hand, "I am not certain I am being fair to him."

Anastasia nodded. "And you cannot help but make comparisons between Mr. Lyndhurst and Mr. Baxton. Correct?"

Charlotte sighed. Why did she even attempt to hide it? Yes, her sisters knew her better than anyone. But even the average passerby would be able to observe her behavior when in Thomas's company and see her heart wasn't in it. Maybe she just needed more time. Or perhaps she needed to allow her heart and mind to be open to the possibilities.

"Have you received any word at all since his departure?" Bethany asked, her face reflecting compassion and understanding.

"Not even a quickly scrawled note letting me know everything is all right." Charlotte glanced down at her hands.

"And what about Grace?" Anastasia asked. "Have you heard anything from her or seen her since the operation?"

"Yes. We have written, and I have paid her one brief visit thus far. I did write to her again just a few days ago. I expect I'll receive a reply very soon."

At least, Charlotte hoped Grace would again reply. She didn't see any reason why the girl wouldn't. Grace had responded promptly to the other two missives Charlotte sent. Unlike Richard. Just thinking about the situation sent her into a melancholic state. Why couldn't she have things back the way they were just before Grace's operation? Life had been so simple, so unencumbered. Then there was the operation, the special kiss she shared with Richard, and him being called away on urgent business. Charlotte didn't know what to do anymore.

"That's it," Anastasia spoke out. "I simply cannot sit here and abide this any longer."

Bethany and Charlotte both stared at their younger sister.

"Abide what?" Bethany asked.

Anastasia aimlessly waved her hand in Charlotte's direction, gesturing up and down. "This. . .this downhearted and dismal state our sister is in." She stowed her needlepoint material and supplies in the basket next to her then hopped to her feet, making a beeline for Charlotte. "Come on," she said without preamble, grabbing Charlotte's hand and pulling her toward the door. "We are leaving." She glanced over her shoulder. "Are you coming, Bethany?"

Charlotte planted her feet and halted their progress. "Where are we going?"

Bethany stood, not appearing in any great hurry to join them. "Yes. Where *are* we going?"

Anastasia looked as if someone had delivered a personal insult to her. "I cannot believe you two are not following my thought process." She held up Charlotte's hand and pointed at it. "Our dear sister here is in dire need of something to take her mind off her current worrisome problems. There is no better place than down at the beaver pond." She smiled in triumph, like a barn cat proud to bring his latest catch. "The antics of the beaver pups always put us in a more jovial frame of mind. I *would* suggest a visit to the marketplace and a tour through the dress shops." She cast a sly smile at Charlotte. "But that will never do. Nature has always been your area of interest."

Charlotte glanced at Bethany, who shrugged. Their sister was right. What could it hurt to have a change of scenery and do something different for a change? At the very least, it would be an enjoyable afternoon with her sisters, and they'd be back in time for dinner.

"Well?" Anastasia tapped her slippered foot. "Are we going or not?"

❧

Dear Miss Pringle,

I received your note yesterday and did not want to wait another moment to reply. Recovery continues to go well, and I am increasing my movement every day. The doctor says I am his best patient, but I think he only says that so I will try harder. I have not heard much from Uncle Richard, but he sent word to say he misses me and had to go to New York. I guess that means he will be gone a little longer still. I miss him and pray he is not too lonely wherever he is. It would make me very happy if you could come see me again. Please come soon. It is hard being here with only Grandmother, the house staff, and the nurse who is taking care of me. I look forward to you coming.

Yours sincerely,
Grace

Charlotte pressed the folded note to her chest, closed her eyes, and took a deep breath. Grace wanted to see her again! And she wanted it to be as soon as possible.

"Is that a letter from Grace?" Anastasia approached from the side hallway, licking her fingers free of what appeared to be chocolate icing. "What does she say?"

"She's doing quite well in her recovery, but she's lonely." Charlotte tapped the note against her lips.

"So, why don't we go see her? I would welcome the excuse for a little journey away from the house. Summer sometimes is the most difficult season."

Charlotte stared at her sister. Could they do it? Would Mother and Father allow them to go? The first visit had been to check on Grace right after the surgery. This would be a purely social visit to the home of the very man against which her parents had cautioned her.

"Perhaps you should ask Mother and Father," Charlotte suggested to her sister. "You will likely have far greater success than if I mentioned it."

Anastasia shrugged. "Very well. I do not mind." She bounded off in search of their parents.

A little over an hour later, the two sisters were ready to depart. Already eager to make the journey to Ashbourne Hills, Charlotte had the butler arrange for a carriage to be brought around front. No sense dawdling and keeping young Grace waiting.

They didn't have to worry about arriving at an inconvenient time. As soon as the Baxton's butler stood in the doorway to the drawing room and announced Charlotte and Anastasia's arrival, Grace squealed. Charlotte waited for the man to step around her before she and her sister entered to see Grace sitting upright on a sofa. A quick glance around the room revealed a makeshift cot that no doubt served as a bed, a pair of crutches propped against the sofa, and a rather substantial pile of books on the table near Grace.

"Miss Pringle! Anastasia! You came!" Grace placed both hands on either side of her legs and bounced up and down. As her note said, she seemed to be doing rather well. "I had hoped you would get my note and come straightaway. And you did."

Charlotte smiled. "Of course I did. You didn't think I could stay away any longer, now did you? And I brought Anastasia as an added bonus." She walked toward the sofa and dropped down to be at eye level with Grace. "Besides. You are not the only one who is missing someone these days."

Grace extended her arms, and Charlotte shifted to her knees to give the girl a hug. Oh, it was so good to be with her again and to see her in such a cheerful state. Despite her circumstances and what had to be a rather painful set of exercises set up as an aid to her full recovery, Grace remained positive and buoyant. Perhaps Charlotte should take lessons from the young girl.

After pulling back, Charlotte peered into Grace's face. "Your letter said the doctor considered you his best patient. I take it that means your recovery is going well?"

"Yes." Grace smiled. "Do you want to see what I can do already?"

The girl seemed so eager, but was it wise for her to exert herself so much? "I don't know, Grace. I do not wish you to harm yourself by attempting to do more than you're able at this point."

"Yes," Anastasia added, looking from the crutches to the wheeled chair to Grace and back again, appearing uncertain. "You should take it easy."

"I promise I will take it slow." She turned and looked over her shoulder. "Laura, could you come help me please?"

The nursemaid approached, looking more like a lady's maid than a trained nurse. But if she accomplished what Grace's doctor wanted, that was the important part. Laura handed Grace the crutches, and Charlotte backed out of the way. Laura then reached for Grace's arms to help bring her to her feet. At that point, Grace placed the crutches under her arms and slowly bore all her weight on her legs.

Charlotte watched with baited breath. Amazing. This girl had gone from being confined to a wheeled chair to standing in just five weeks. When Grace started to take a step, Charlotte inhaled sharply. "Grace, be careful!"

"It is quite all right, Miss Pringle," Laura replied with a reassuring smile. "Grace has mastered this several times already."

The warning came out automatically. She should have known Laura wouldn't let Grace do anything the doctor hadn't instructed her to do. But

Charlotte couldn't help it. The protective instinct seemed so natural. And in a way, she felt responsible for Grace. Richard might not have left her fully in charge, but his parting words had been to ask her to be there when Grace awoke. So in a small way, she served as his proxy in his absence. Not that Grace's grandmother couldn't perform that role. Charlotte merely felt she owed it to Grace.

With a deep breath to calm her nerves, Charlotte stepped back again and took a seat in the nearest chair. She bit her lip to keep from calling out any more words of caution. Laura had things well under control, and Grace didn't appear to be overexerting herself or to be in any kind of pain. Before she knew it, Grace changed directions and headed her way. In no time at all, she stood in front of Charlotte, grinning from ear to ear.

"I did it! I did it!" the girl cried. "I actually walked."

"Wow!" Anastasia stared, clearly impressed.

Charlotte cupped Grace's face between her hands and placed a kiss on the girl's forehead. "Yes you did. And you are looking quite well, too. I don't think your doctor jested when he called you his best patient. I believe you are. You should be proud of all you've accomplished."

"All right, Grace," Laura admonished. "It's time for you to rest. I shall be sure to make note of your progress so the doctor can adjust the next schedule of exercises if necessary."

Laura helped Grace back to the sofa and returned the crutches to their resting place. She poured a glass of water and handed it to Grace.

"Thank you very much, Laura," Grace replied. She took a sip and swallowed. "Now, if you do not mind, could you leave Miss Pringle, her sister, and me to talk privately? I have something I wish to ask."

"Very well, Miss Grace." Laura made her way to the door, turning as she reached it. "I shall be just outside should you need me."

Charlotte raised her eyebrows as the door clicked shut behind the nursemaid. Grace had something she wanted to discuss? What could it be? The girl looked so serious.

"So," Grace began, folding her hands in her lap. "You said when you arrived I wasn't the only one who had been missing someone lately."

Had she really said that? Surely it was in reference to missing Grace. Wasn't it? She didn't know if she wanted to acknowledge anything else right now. But Grace wasn't about to let her get off so easily, not if that look in her eyes was any indication.

"Are you saying you have been missing someone other than me?"

The girl's piercing gaze seemed to see right through her. Charlotte shifted in her seat. Oh, how easy it would be to refute that question. But that meant Charlotte would have to lie.

"Of course she is," Anastasia burst out.

"I knew it!" Grace snapped her fingers and grinned. "You *do* miss Uncle Richard. I can see it in your eyes."

There was no point in denying it now. "Yes." Charlotte sighed. "I do." She brightened. "But I believe I missed you more."

Grace giggled. "I don't think so." Again, the intent gaze returned. "Do you love him?"

Charlotte's breath hitched. She tried to swallow past the lump in her throat. "Pardon me?" Her voice came out sounding more like a croak. She cleared her throat. "What did you ask?"

"I asked if you love Uncle Richard. He talks about you all the time, so I know he cares about you."

"I. . .uh. . .that is. . .I'm not certain I have an answer to that." Wonderful. A twelve-year-old girl asks her about her feelings, and she stumbles through a reply. She couldn't even come up with a viable answer. And the answer she *did* give was even more revealing.

"It doesn't usually take a lot of thought. Either you love someone or you don't. That should be easy enough to know."

"Actually, Grace, it's not that simple." If only it were. "There is far more involved with loving someone than simply admitting it or knowing it. And right now, I do not know for certain."

"And he hasn't written to Charlotte." Anastasia jutted her chin in the air. "You would think if Charlotte was so special and if he cared about her, he would keep in touch."

"I am sure he would write if he could," Grace said in her uncle's defense. "But he is probably very busy and cannot find the time."

Ah, the innocence. Charlotte wished she could believe as Grace did or even trust for that matter. Things were left so unsettled between her and Richard, though. They didn't have time to discuss the kiss they shared or what that meant to their relationship. How could she begin to sort through the confusing haze of her feelings? But she needed to come up with some sort of answer for Grace.

Charlotte knelt in front of Grace again and took the girl's hands in hers. "Grace, I appreciate your reassurance. I *do* care for your uncle. You both are very special to me. But so many other factors are at play in this situation." Not the least of which was her relationship with Thomas Lyndhurst. Grace didn't need to know about that, but she did deserve an honest response to her statement about Richard's reasons for not writing. "And your uncle's notes home or lack thereof are only a small part of the situation. Please understand me when I say I wish there was a simple solution. For now, let us leave it at you both being a very important part of my life. Anything other than that, we shall have to wait and see."

Grace nodded. "I do understand, Miss Pringle. But I also am certain it will all work out. Have faith."

Faith. Grace made it sound so simple. But another month had passed and still no word from Richard. Grace wrote to say he was now in Boston and would be home as soon as he could. The news didn't make Charlotte feel any better, though. And if he could write to Grace, why hadn't he taken an extra moment or two to write to her? True, he didn't owe her an explanation, and neither one of them had declared any intentions toward the other.

Still, it was hard not feeling neglected and forgotten in everything. Two months, and she didn't know any more now than she did when Richard left that day at the hospital. So each time Thomas came to call, she had no good reason to turn away his suit.

One evening in early September, they sat together on a bench in the park. Charlotte kept her hands folded in her lap as she looked out across the small acreage. The silence pounded against her ears. Why had Thomas been so quiet tonight? Normally by now he'd have delivered several jokes or shared a few tidbits on his daily work. But not tonight.

"Miss Pringle. . .uh. . .Charlotte," he said softly.

Charlotte leaned closer to hear better. "Yes, Mr. Lyndhurst. . .I mean. . . Thomas."

He avoided looking at her and stared straight ahead. "What I have to say tonight is not easy, but I ask that you hear me out fully before you say anything."

She nodded, wishing she could see his eyes. He turned her way, and she wished he hadn't. Resignation and pain danced with a certain dismal determination.

"I am no fool. I have known for quite some time that your heart is not fully engaged in our courtship."

Charlotte's shoulders fell. He stated it so plainly, without any rancor or condemnation. Yet she felt the sting of his words just as deeply.

"That does not change the fact that our families would like to see a union forged between us. And I must say, I cannot see any reason why that shouldn't occur. You possess a great deal of intelligence, and your ability to manage your bookshop will aid you in the managing of a household." He reached for her hands and held them loosely in his own, centering his focus on her in an unwavering gaze. "I know I am not saying this in the best manner possible, but I have grown quite fond of you in our time together the past two months. And I believe given more time, our relationship will become much dearer."

He reached into his vest pocket, and a moment later the moonlight glinted off the gemstones of a beautiful amethyst, sapphire, and emerald ring. Charlotte gasped. Could he really be doing this? Right here? Right now?

"Forgive me for not presenting this with more preamble. But I feel any further delays are unnecessary." He cleared his throat. "I would like to ask you to be my wife, with all the affection and honor I hold for you. Everything I have will be yours, and our alliance will secure the future for us both."

Well, it certainly wasn't the romantic proposal she'd envisioned. *Practical* seemed to be the best word Charlotte could find to describe it. But Thomas was sincere. And he was right. Further delays wouldn't change anything other than to delay the inevitable. She would be twenty-one next month. A spinster by anyone's determination. Her parents were eager to see her wed, and she needed to make a decision. As much as it pained her to admit it, she needed to face the facts. Richard didn't care for her as she thought he might. Otherwise, he would have found a way to notify her by now. Marriage to Thomas was a good match. She could certainly do much worse.

A resigned sigh escaped her lips as she regarded the ring Thomas held out in front of her. Charlotte really didn't have much choice. She mustered up her best attempt at a smile and extended her right hand toward him. "I should like a week to ponder this before I give you my answer. Until then, I trust you will not be offended if I ask you to keep this ring in your possession."

Thomas returned the ring to his vest pocket then leaned forward and placed a chaste kiss on her cheek. "I promise I will do everything in my power to make you happy. Please notify me as soon as you come to a decision. If your answer is a positive one, I'd like to announce this as soon as possible."

Charlotte didn't trust her voice. She nodded instead.

Thomas rose and drew her up with him. "Come, let us seek out your parents and tell them the good news. They are going to be quite pleased, I am sure."

Yes, they would. But Charlotte was certain it would be some time before she would share in that pleasure.

❧

Richard ran his hands through his hair. He didn't care if the ends stood out. All he wanted was a conclusion to this entire ordeal. It had stretched on long enough. And he didn't appreciate being dragged to New York as well as Boston in order to settle his brother's affairs pertaining to their shipping business. Richard had always been in charge of the building part of the company. Elliott was the businessman. But now Richard was left to clean up the mess.

Two entire months. It should have been settled in one week or less. When he left, he thought that was all it would take. Then he could return to Charlotte and pick up where they'd left off. Now, he wasn't so sure. He'd been gone a long time. He'd written, but she had yet to reply in any way. And he'd been sure to leave a valid address where he could be reached should a response be sent. He had walked out on her after sharing a kiss. Although his notes had expressed how much he'd missed her and looked forward to seeing her again, the words felt superficial. But oh, the memory of her upturned face and the soft feel of her lips. It was enough to distract a man for days. And he'd had two months to dwell on it. Months that allowed him to realize what he needed to do.

As he stepped on the train at the New York and New England terminal in Boston, Richard prayed the ride would pass quickly. Where Charlotte was concerned, he also prayed he wasn't too late.

Chapter 13

No! No, it couldn't be. Richard closed his eyes and opened them again, as if doing so would erase the dreadful tidings that greeted him in black and white upon his arrival home. But the *Gazette* didn't lie. He had been reading the paper in the carriage and only just reached the society section. What he read caused his heart to drop. Charlotte had been seen repeatedly on the arm of a Mr. Thomas Frederick Lyndhurst, and rumors had it an engagement might be forthcoming.

He was too late.

Richard silently cursed the timing of his trip. Had he been home when he thought, he could have straightened everything out, and Charlotte wouldn't be seeing this other man now. He was certain of it. Now what was he going to do?

"Uncle Richard! You're back!" Grace called out across the front hall.

Richard turned to see his niece using only a single crutch for support. "Grace! You're walking!" Knowing of her progress from the letters he'd received during his absence paled in comparison to seeing the reality right before his eyes. He really *had* been gone too long. He'd missed so much, and he'd never get that time back. After laying the evening edition on the hall table, he opened his arms wide and waited for Grace to jump into them. Oh, it felt so good to have his niece back.

Grace kissed his cheek then looked over his shoulder. "I see you have read the newspaper."

Richard angled his head back and sighed. "Yes. And it came as quite a surprise, I must say."

"I only heard about it two days ago, and I still can't believe it."

"Well, it's right there." He lowered his niece to the floor. "Her family has allowed the information to be printed in the society column, so it must be true."

Grace took up her crutch again and leaned on it. "But how could she do this to you? She loves you."

Obviously not or she wouldn't have rushed off to be courted by another man. He wasn't about to share that spiteful remark with his niece, though. "Miss Pringle must have decided otherwise, Grace," he said instead. "There is nothing I can do about it now."

"Yes there is," Grace protested. "You can go find her and tell her you love her, too. Then she can cease spending time with this other gentleman and the two of you can get married, the way it's supposed to be."

If only he *could* do that. Richard slipped off his coat and hat and allowed the butler to take his things. "I'm sorry, but it's too late. I cannot and will not interfere in her happiness or the choice she's made."

"It's not too late." Grace stamped her foot. "And she can't possibly be happy if she isn't with you." She grabbed hold of his arm and compelled him to look down at her. "I know she isn't, Uncle Richard. She told me so."

Richard widened his eyes. "What?"

"Miss Pringle came to visit me while you were away, and I asked her if she loved you."

"Grace," he scolded. "It wasn't your place to ask her something like that. I am rather displeased to hear you did so." Although he wanted to hear Charlotte's answer.

Grace dipped her chin. "I am sorry, Uncle Richard, but she spoke of missing both of us and said she had come to care for us a great deal."

That was a start. But it wasn't exactly what he wanted to hear. Richard drew his niece to one of two chairs next to each other. Once they were both seated, he replied. "Caring for someone is not the same as loving them."

"I know." She nodded. "But Miss Pringle said a lot of other factors were involved and that we both were very special to her." Grace pressed her lips into a thin line and gave him a rather determined stare. "I am telling you, Uncle Richard. She loves you. And it's not too late if she's not yet engaged. You still have time. But not if you don't believe."

His niece was nothing if not adamant when she set her mind on something. "Believe what?" he asked, drawing his eyebrows together.

"Believe God knows best, and He is watching over both of you," she replied. "Believe He wants you both to be happy and that won't happen if you're not together. And believe He brought you home at just the right time to do something about it."

Richard shook his head. He had to admit, Grace made a valid point. Were she a young lad, he might envision her growing up to become a lawyer one day. For now, though, she turned her argumentative prowess on him. And he wasn't sure he could come up with a valid rebuttal.

A chuckle escaped his lips, and he held up his hands. "All right. All right. You win," he said with a smile. After tousling her hair, he stood and called for the butler. "I cannot guarantee the outcome will be as you or I hope, but I will promise to try."

"You can do it, Uncle Richard," Grace said with triumphant certainty. "I know it will all work out."

＆

Richard paused just outside the door to Mr. Pringle's study. The butler had directed him down the hall and said Mr. Pringle was expecting him. Of course he was. Richard had penned a formal missive and requested this meeting almost immediately after arriving home and reading that dreadful news in the *Gazette*. Now that he was here, his stomach clenched and tension rippled across his shoulders.

With a quick prayer for strength, he took a deep breath and raised his hand to deliver two short knocks to the closed door.

"Come in!" came the immediate response.

He turned the knob and pushed the door open, stepping into the darkened interior and immediately removing his hat. His eyes searched the room and found Mr. Pringle standing next to his desk. The man's expression was too difficult to read from this distance, though.

"Mr. Pringle," Richard plunged forward. "Thank you for seeing me on such short notice."

"It is my pleasure, Mr. Baxton."

Charlotte's father didn't make any attempt to move from where he stood, so Richard approached him instead.

"I know you probably have a lot of business to attend to, so I won't take up too much of your time. I wanted to come here today to speak to you in person about your daughter Charlotte."

"When I received your note, I had a distinct feeling what this meeting would be about." The man brushed his fingers across his clean-shaven chin. "Quite frankly, I am surprised it has taken you so long to see me again."

"Yes. I was called away unexpectedly on business that kept me away longer than I thought it might. I had to make two additional journeys to New York and Boston and only arrived home yesterday."

"And what exactly was that business?"

Richard tilted his head. "As you know from our earlier conversation, sir, my family has been involved in the ship-building business for three generations. We have financial holdings in almost all of the major ports along the Atlantic Coast. The trouble began when my brother was killed in a carriage accident many months back."

"I was sorry to hear of your loss, son." His voice showed his sincerity.

"Thank you." Richard took a breath. "In short, I was left everything, but there was a seize on the profits and a delay in the ownership transfer. While our lawyer sorted through the mounds of paperwork and legal barriers, I was here caring for my niece and doing what I could to keep everything running. This recent journey finally resolved all the issues and the full transfer is now complete."

"I am sure that brings you a sense of relief."

"Yes, it does. But that pales in comparison to the surprise that awaited me in the evening edition of the *Wilmington Gazette* upon my return. I didn't wish to waste any more time than I had already lost, so I requested this meeting straightaway."

"I'm glad you did come, son, in spite of the current circumstances. It says much about you and your level of devotion to my daughter."

Richard licked his lips and shifted from one foot to the other, turning his hat in his hands. Mr. Pringle's approval meant so much. He'd dealt with industry and manufacturing magnates without missing a breath, but standing before this man put him on edge.

"I won't deny that I've been aware of Charlotte's feelings for you for quite some time now, even when she attempted to say otherwise. And I won't make you any more uncomfortable than you are by asking your intentions toward my daughter. I am certain they are honorable."

"Yes sir."

Mr. Pringle nodded. "Very well. Then, the only other issue at hand is the present status of my daughter's affections. As you are aware, she has been courted by Mr. Lyndhurst of Greenville these recent weeks." He held up a hand, palm outward. "I might have given my consent to the union, but the ultimate decision lies with Charlotte." The hint of a grin tugged at the corners of the man's mouth. "And if I know my daughter, I have a feeling a more personal conversation with her will be forthcoming rather soon."

Richard swallowed and nodded, unable to speak beyond the tightness in his throat. Did this mean the man was giving his consent for Richard to call on Charlotte as well and offer his proposal?

"You will find my daughter at the bookshop, son."

Obviously, he was.

"And if you do not wish to miss your chance, I would suggest you depart here immediately."

Richard straightened. "Oh! Yes. I will."

"Good. We will leave the rest of the details for a later time. Now if you'll excuse me, I do have some rather important matters that require my attention before dinner." He winked. "And I don't wish to upset Mrs. Pringle by being late."

"No, sir!" Richard grinned, grateful he'd again found his voice.

"I trust you don't mind seeing yourself out?"

"Not at all, sir." Richard turned toward the door then glanced over his shoulder. "Thank you again, Mr. Pringle."

"You're quite welcome."

≈

Richard peered in through the windows. The bookshop looked empty. He didn't see Charlotte anywhere. Perfect. She wouldn't see him come in. But she *would* hear him. Slowly, he opened the door, praying he wouldn't trigger the bell. So far, so good. He made it inside without announcing his presence. Now he had to find Charlotte.

That didn't take long. She stood on a stool at the far end of the first aisle, reaching to the top shelf but falling just short. Richard moved in silence and came up behind her, retrieving the book she sought and putting it in her hand.

She didn't even turn around. "Thank you."

"You're welcome." His voice cracked, and the two words came out in a combination cough and squeak. Richard cleared his throat, and tried again. "You're welcome."

Charlotte spun around. "Richard!"

She almost lost her balance, but he put his hands to her waist to steady her. As soon as she righted herself, he dropped his hands to his sides. Of course, he wanted to keep them there. Wanted to lift her down from the stool and into his arms. But he didn't have that right. She was almost engaged to another. And until that situation was rectified, he had to keep his distance. Or at least try.

"I'm surprised to see you here." Her voice had a hardened edge to it, and her eyes held a mixture of remorse and regret. "Did you not have other business to attend to?"

Ouch. But he deserved that. He had all but abandoned her, and now, two months later, he expected a warm welcome? What had he been thinking? He had written but never received a reply, so there was no guarantee his letters had even been received. He intended to find out.

Richard looked up at her. "Could you please come down off the stool? I would much rather speak with you on a more even level."

She did as he asked, but her entire demeanor remained cool, reserved. If she *had* received his letters, would she still be acting this way?

"Charlotte, I know my appearance here is unexpected and possibly unwanted. I probably shouldn't have come at all." Despite having told himself many times that he'd done what he had to do, Richard couldn't keep the self-condemnation from his voice.

Charlotte closed her eyes. The soft sounds of her breathing accompanied the faint *clip-clop* of horses' hooves and carriage wheels on the cobblestones outside. When her eyelids opened again, the same doubt, uncertainty, and fear he felt reflected back at him.

"Richard, we shouldn't be—"

"Shh." He cut her off and touched two fingers to her lips then removed his hand. She stared at him with doe-like innocence. "Let me go first."

An almost imperceptible nod followed his entreaty. All right. He had her undivided attention. Now what should he say?

"Charlotte, I repeated in my mind what I would say to you during the ride over here. And I owe you an apology." There, that wasn't such a bad start. "I left you standing in the hospital with a promise to contact you as soon as I returned home. But a trip I believed would take me just a week ended up taking me two months. In all that time, although I sent a handful of letters to let you know what was happening, I never received a response. Still, the letters did not come close to conveying how I truly felt, and you deserved more than that." He implored her with his gaze. "Can you forgive me?"

It hadn't come out the way he'd rehearsed it in his head, but it could still work. He hoped it would.

"You wrote to me?" Surprise and tender awe blended on her face as her eyes shimmered with unshed tears. "I never received a single note."

Well, that explained a lot. "I feared that might be the case," he said instead. "Nevertheless, I stand before you now, asking your forgiveness."

Charlotte took several moments before responding. "Of course I forgive you."

It wasn't much, but it was a start. "Thank you." Richard clenched his fists at his side, wanting more than anything to take Charlotte's hands in his. But not yet. "I know my timing is rather flawed and imperfect. But I came at the first opportunity. And while I do not hold any misconceptions that you will respond the way I would like, I could not in good conscience leave things unresolved between us." He had to get this out now, or he might lose his nerve. "There...there's one more thing."

Her eyes seemed to tell him to go on, but the words died in his throat. Perhaps making her smile would lighten the mood a bit and help him say what he came to tell her. It might not work, but he had to try *something*.

"At least I know I have a captive audience."

That worked. A slow smile tugged at her lips, even though it didn't quite meet her eyes. Yes. That's just what he needed to help him get through the next part of his confession. He braved reaching for her hands to clasp them between both of his. She didn't pull away.

"Charlotte, it took a longer-than-expected journey to make me realize just how special you are to me. I'm a fool for not seeing it sooner. That kiss we shared at the hospital shook me right to the core. I didn't know how to respond. I could dare to hope only that you felt the same as I." He sought her gaze and held it. "Maybe I didn't want to believe it. Maybe I wasn't ready. I don't know. What I do know is I don't want to lose you."

A sharp gasp followed his declaration. This was it. He had to say it now.

"Charlotte, I love you. I've probably loved you for a while now. I was just too blind to see it. And I know you are being courted by another, with rumors stating an engagement is forthcoming. But I have your father's permission to ask you—if you can find any fondness at all for me in your heart, please. I beg of you. Do not continue to accept Mr. Lyndhurst's suit."

Charlotte's hands moved beneath his, and she turned her wrist to interlace their fingers. He glanced down at their joined hands then back at her face. Tenderness replaced the uncertainty of a moment before. Her lips moved, but no sound came out. Then she seemed to find her voice.

"Before I say anything else, I want to say I was deeply hurt by your silence and the increasing time you were away. I thought I did something wrong. That I somehow caused your silence. That you were possibly ashamed for having kissed me and didn't know how to take it back. Then my parents pushed me toward Mr. Lyndhurst, and as your absence lengthened, I felt I was left with no choice." She averted her eyes. "So I agreed to allow him to court me. But I was wrong for doubting you and for believing you had intentionally abandoned me. Can *you* forgive *me?*"

He didn't hesitate. "Yes. Of course I will." How could he deny her what she'd just given him only a few moments ago?

She visibly relaxed. After a shuddering breath, she again met his gaze with tears glistening in her eyes. "Richard, I love you, too."

He grinned and slid to one knee on the floor, right there in the dusty aisle of the bookshop. But he didn't care. He reached into his coat and pulled out his grandmother's ring. A diamond-accented sapphire with lighter blue topaz around the rim. He held it up to Charlotte, all the love he felt inside ready to burst. "Then will you marry me?"

A lone tear spilled and traced a wet path down her cheek. Richard reached up with his other hand and brushed it away. Silence descended, and the seconds ticked by in slow progression.

"I say," an unfamiliar but proper voice sounded from the front of the store. "It appears I have arrived in the middle of the most unfortunate circumstances."

The gentleman paused. "At least for me."

Richard turned to look up the aisle and met the regretful gaze of a well-dressed gentleman about his age, only this man held an ornate cane in one hand and a top-quality top hat in the other. From the way Charlotte stiffened, this man could be only one person. Richard stood and raised his eyebrows. "Mr. Lyndhurst, I presume?"

"The very same," the man said with a succinct nod. He switched his cane to his left hand and extended his right. "And you must be Richard Baxton."

"Yes," Richard replied, returning the handshake.

"Well, I believe I have timed my appearance a mite too late." Lyndhurst gestured toward Charlotte and Richard and the close proximity in which the two stood. "Or perhaps I am right on time."

Charlotte started to turn toward Mr. Lyndhurst. "Thomas, I—"

But the man raised his hand that held the cane and lifted two fingers, effectively silencing whatever she'd been about to say. "Please, my dear Charlotte. You owe me no explanation." He softened his expression. "Only a fool would see the way you are looking at Mr. Baxton and not know of your fervent affection. It is not my place to interfere, nor would I consider it." Lyndhurst took two steps back and dipped his head, swinging wide the hand that held his top hat. "Now, if you will excuse me, I shall formally retract my suit and take my leave. I wish you both the utmost happiness."

Silence followed in the wake of Thomas's exit. Richard and Charlotte both stared up the aisle, as if the man hadn't really been there. Several moments later, Richard shook his head and turned again to face Charlotte. Resuming his position on bended knee, he again took her hands in his.

"I believe there is still a question waiting for an answer," he reminded her with a smile.

Charlotte startled and stared down at him. A dazed look clouded her eyes. Her mouth moved, but no words came out. It was as if she stood transfixed, held captive by the exchange that had just occurred.

"Say you will!" Grace's voice broke the spell.

Charlotte laughed, and Richard joined her. Just when had his niece snuck into the shop? And how had she done so without either of them hearing her? Then again, he had done it.

"It appears we have a curious little songbird in our midst," Charlotte said. "Bent on trilling out her own cadenza."

"Yes, she insisted upon accompanying me here. But this is a duet. At least for the moment." He cast a reproachful glance at his niece. "I instructed her to remain outside." He returned his gaze to Charlotte. "Even so, you know how

Grace feels. I, on the other hand, remain down here awaiting *your* answer."

Lyrical laughter again escaped her lips. "Yes! Yes, of course I will marry you."

Richard nearly jumped to his feet and gave her a quick peck on the mouth. He pulled back to look down into her face, seeing the same longing he felt. He placed the symbol of their promise on her ring finger. Lowering his lips again, he positioned himself for a better, deeper kiss this time.

A few moments later, he pulled back and glanced to his left. A chuckle rumbled in his chest. He shared a special look with Charlotte, emboldened by her nod and the look of love in her eyes.

"Grace, you have already heard and seen everything. And we both know what you think. Now, will you perhaps leave us alone to discuss a few more things?"

Grace obviously took that as a sign to come closer. "There will be time enough for that later. Right now I want to celebrate with you both." She wrapped one arm around each of them.

Richard pivoted to face Charlotte. Amusement danced in her eyes. He shrugged. They still had so much to discuss. And Charlotte had yet to let her parents know of her decisions.

They could and would discuss the details of their engagement and wedding another time. Right now, Grace watched and smiled as though their entire relationship—friends to lovers—had been entirely of her making. Richard smiled. It had been by God's design all along.

Epilogue

Charlotte leaned into Richard's casual yet affectionate embrace as she looked around at the friends and family gathered in her home. So much love and support. She could barely talk beyond the tightness in her throat. But talk, she must. Clearing her throat, she scanned the assemblage, searching for a certain twelve-year-old girl.

"Grace," she called out after locating her. "Would you please come join your uncle and me up front? I have something very special to present to you."

As Grace stepped out from the small crowd, Charlotte reached behind her for the carefully wrapped gift she'd prepared specifically for this day. The young girl—no, young *lady*—stood before Charlotte with an expectant smile on her face. Charlotte trailed her fingers down Grace's cheek and brushed back a few loose tendrils of hair.

"Grace, you already know how much your uncle and I love you. And we both look forward to welcoming you into our newly joined life together as soon as our wedding concludes. But for now, I would like you to have this."

She handed the gift to Grace, who took it and stared.

Charlotte nodded. "You may open it now."

Needing no further encouragement, Grace tore back the paper and withdrew the treasured book Charlotte had spent months attempting to find.

Grace looked down and read the title. "*Robinson Crusoe?*"

"Yes." Charlotte smoothed her hand over the cover. "This book once belonged to my great-grandmother's great-grandmother. It is a first edition with her dedication written inside. I acquired it just prior to meeting you and your uncle." She tilted her head to gaze up at Richard. He squeezed her waist and smiled, love shining in his eyes. Returning her attention to Grace, Charlotte smiled. "Now I would like you to have it. It will be a constant reminder of how God used books to bring us together and eventually make us a family."

Grace stared at the book, holding it in her hands like fine porcelain. A moment later, she looked up at Charlotte, then her uncle, then back to the book, and finally again at Charlotte. "You are giving this to me? To keep?"

"Yes," Charlotte replied. "Because, I believe we share something very, very special." She winked. "An insatiable appetite for good books. I spent a great deal of time locating this title, and now you can have it for your own." She tipped up the girl's chin with her forefinger. "But I have one requirement."

"What is that?"

"I only ask that you treasure it as much as I have, and when the time comes for you to start a family of your own, you keep this book as a gift for your daughter or son."

Grace pressed her lips tight, glancing again at the book. "But don't you wish to keep this for your own children?"

Charlotte's throat clenched at the forlorn quality in Grace's voice. Richard squeezed her waist again then reached out and brushed Grace's cheek. Charlotte did the same. But Richard spoke.

"You are every bit as much our daughter as any children we might have in the future. So this book belongs to you, and we know you will take excellent care of it."

Grace smiled, the sheen of tears magnifying the joy in her eyes. "Oh yes!" she said, and hugged the book to her chest. "I shall be certain to care for and keep this book in the best condition possible. And I shall treasure it always."

"Now," Richard shifted, removing his arm from around Charlotte's waist to bend to eye level with his niece. "What do you say we resume the engagement party and get things under way?"

Grace brightened then turned to face everyone else. With one hand sweeping out across the crowd, she announced, "Let the celebration commence!"

Rumbles of laughter and exclamations of delight sounded forth from family and friends. Grace skipped away, and Richard returned to Charlotte.

With a roguish grin, he winked and touched his forehead to hers. "We are going to have our hands full for the next few years."

Charlotte smiled, her face warming rapidly, as she reached to place a chaste kiss on his lips. "I wouldn't have it any other way."

STEALING
HEARTS

Dedication

As always, I owe a great deal to my family for their continued support. A special thank you to my husband, who takes our little ones while I press toward the finish line of each deadline. To my editors, Jessie F. and Becky G., and the entire team at Barbour, this book would never have reached this point without you. To Joy, for your critique and polishing of this book.

Chapter 1

Brandywine, Delaware, 1890

Richard! Come quick!"

At her aunt's shriek, Grace Baxton threw back the bedclothes and tumbled to the floor of her bedchamber with a thud, the pain of impact sending a searing burn from her left elbow to her shoulder. The faint sounds of commotion downstairs penetrated her groggy mind and sent Grace into action. She made a frantic attempt to detangle herself from the mass of sheets and coverlets, only imprisoning herself further before escaping. At twenty years of age, regaining her equilibrium turned out to be harder than she'd thought. Finally free, she jumped to her feet, grabbed her wrapper, and raced from the room, fastening the belt as she ran toward the main staircase.

She held tight to the banister, lest she stumble again, and caught sight of her uncle rushing from the direction of the drawing room, the sides of his unfastened black wool smoking jacket flapping back against his arms. Grace followed close on his heels the moment her feet touched the lower floor of their home.

"Charlotte, what happened?" Uncle Richard spoke without preamble the moment he entered the formal dining room.

"See for yourself." Aunt Charlotte extended her right arm toward the three-door vitrine cabinet with the mirrored backing. "Elise alerted me only moments ago."

Grace stood and stared, her tightened throat making it almost impossible to breathe. The blood drained from her face, and she grabbed hold of the nearest Queen Anne chair to alleviate her sudden light-headedness. Raising her other hand to her face, she wiped the sleep from her eyes, blinked several times, and fought back a yawn. Grace couldn't wrap her mind around the truth. The maidservant must be mistaken. One of their male servants always remained downstairs at night to prevent such an occurrence. Yet no manner of denial would erase the reality her eyes beheld at that moment.

How could something like this have happened? And while they all slept comfortably in their beds, completely ignorant of the intruder one floor below, making his way through several rooms and probing through their personal possessions. It made Grace's skin crawl, and a shiver traveled up her back.

Robbed.

Even just thinking the word brought a sour taste to Grace's mouth. She wet her lips and swallowed several times—as if that would make the circumstances less grave. Not exactly a desirable way to begin this cool May morning.

"Aunt Charlotte?" Grace croaked. "Your filigree China?"

"And my fine silver." A pause. "The tea set as well."

Her beloved aunt clutched an embroidered handkerchief to her lips. Her russet locks fell in soft waves down her back, evidence of a morning hair-pinning interrupted. She moved her hand away from her mouth and turned pain-filled eyes toward Grace.

"But that's not all," Charlotte added.

Grace followed her aunt's gaze toward the curio cabinet in the corner. Her right hand flew to her mouth as a gasp escaped.

"No!" She stared at the empty case, the tightening in her chest returning. "Not the books, too." Her aunt had spent a great deal of time tracking down several of those titles. And one in particular had been in the family for generations. Surely they weren't as valuable to the thief as the silver and dishes. "Why would someone steal those?" Whoever robbed them couldn't have known of their sentimental value. "They are precious to us, but to some unknown vagabond?"

"I can scarcely believe it myself." Charlotte waved her fingers and beckoned Grace to come closer. The woman who had been like a mother to her for the past eight years wrapped an arm around Grace's shoulders.

Her aunt wasn't one for verbose speech, but her unspoken actions said more than any words could. Grace draped her left arm around her aunt's waist and leaned her head onto the woman's shoulder, offering what comfort she could. Charlotte tilted her own head to rest her cheek against Grace's hair. The action made Grace self-conscious of her own state of undress and unkempt appearance. She reached up to touch her tousled caramel ringlets, grimacing at the telltale knots in desperate need of a brush. Harriet would see to that soon enough. They had more important matters at hand.

"What are we going to do?" Grace spoke to no one in particular.

Uncle Richard came to stand on Aunt Charlotte's other side and placed a hand on her shoulder, giving his wife a gentle squeeze.

"First things first, we are going to send Matthew for the constable." His voice took on a decided edge. "Then I will send out Bartholomew and Marcus to pay a visit to the area pawnbroker shops. Whoever this thief is, I cannot imagine he would have taken all of this for himself." Uncle Richard fastened his jacket. "If we act quickly, we may very well have a chance to retrieve some of these items."

"Oh, Uncle Richard, do you truly believe that's possible?" For the first time that morning, a glimmer of hope entered Grace's heart. Perhaps those precious books weren't lost forever.

"Only time will tell, Grace, but we will not leave a single stone unturned in our quest to return our possessions to their rightful place."

Aunt Charlotte pulled away from Grace and moved to stand facing her husband. Uncle Richard immediately pulled her to him and placed a lingering kiss on her forehead. "We will get through this. I promise."

"I know. It is rather disconcerting to be facing this, that's all." Her aunt closed her eyes and leaned against Uncle Richard. "Thank you for being my strength."

"Always," he replied.

Grace felt like an intruder on the private exchange. She took a step backward, intending to slip out of the room and leave them alone. A moment later, though, her aunt and uncle turned toward her and opened their arms at the same time in her direction. Grace stepped into their embrace and cherished the immediate security it offered—despite the recent breach of the place she'd always considered a safe haven.

"All right." Uncle Richard, the first to break his hold, cleared his throat. "Let me summon Matthew. Then we can finish seeing to our own preparations for the day." He offered them both a wry grin. "I daresay we would not want the constable to pay us a visit and find us in our present state of undress."

Aunt Charlotte's cheeks colored a rosy shade of pink, and she bit her lower lip as if just remembering her morning routine had been so rudely interrupted. "You are absolutely right, my dear." She turned toward her niece. "Come, Grace. We shall return upstairs, where Harriet and Marie will assist us. Then we can look in on Claire and Phillip."

Oh right. Her cousins. She had forgotten about them in all the commotion and unrest. Good thing they slept better than she did. Grace envied that in a way. There would be questions enough once the seven- and five-year-old discovered what had happened. For now, let them benefit from the blissful peace of sleep.

❧

"Very good, Mr. Baxton." The constable flipped his notepad closed and tucked it inside his dark chestnut trench coat. "I believe we have everything we need to further pursue this investigation."

Grace peered around the corner from the doorway of the sitting room, her hands clenched around the smooth wood frame. Her uncle and the constable stood near the front door, wrapping up their conversation. Any moment now, her aunt would chastise her for eavesdropping and bid her to return to her seat. But she wanted to know what would be happening next.

"We appreciate your prompt arrival, Constable." Uncle Richard reached out to shake the officer's hand. "You can very well imagine our great distress first thing this morning when we discovered this had happened."

"Yes." His voice was grim. The man adjusted his wire-rimmed spectacles and slid his hand down to his trim handlebar mustache. He stroked the well-groomed hairs with his thumb and forefinger. "This is the fourth report we've had in the past fortnight. I do not wish to speculate, but it seems clear we have a serious situation at hand."

Uncle Richard's eyebrows rose. "Do you mean we are not the only ones to have suffered from such an unwelcome intrusion?"

"No." The constable let out a frustrated sigh. "And each report is the same. The items stolen are quite valuable, but they are always from just one room in the home. Nothing else is disturbed, and there are no traces left following the burglary. Not even the slightest hint of forced entry or evidence of whether more than one individual might be involved." He scratched his chin then dropped his arm to his side and hunched his shoulders. "It is aggravating, to say the least."

Her uncle slipped his hands into the front pockets of his wool frock coat. "I have to admit I was greatly surprised, but it is even more disconcerting to know this thief has struck other residences as well."

Grace shifted her weight from her left to her right foot and back again. She wanted to rush forward and ask about the other homes that had been robbed. But it wouldn't be proper to interrupt. Chances were, they knew at least one, if not more, of the families who had become victims. Why hadn't something like this made the rounds in drawing-room conversations during the past two weeks?

"Why are we hiding from Papa?" Claire's hushed voice sounded from behind Grace's skirts.

Grace glanced down to see her seven-year-old cousin peering into the main foyer, mimicking her own stance. "We aren't hiding, Claire. We're listening."

"What is Papa saying to the policeman? And if you want to hear, why don't you go into the hall and stand there with them?"

Uncle Richard paused in his response to the constable and glanced in their direction. Grace shrank back from the doorway, gently moving Claire back with her. "You need to be quieter, Claire. We don't want to interrupt your papa's conversation."

"Grace." Her aunt's tone inserted more into that one word than an entire scolding could achieve.

"Yes, Aunt Charlotte?" She turned and assumed an air of innocence. "Do you need something?"

"Do not attempt to sugarcoat your present behavior, young lady." Her aunt pursed her lips and dipped her chin while raising one eyebrow. "You know very well how inappropriate it is to listen in on a conversation of which you are not a part. You are acting more like a schoolgirl than a lady of nineteen. And you are being a rather poor example to Claire."

Grace glanced again at her cousin, who crossed her arms and delivered an adorable smug expression. She pressed her lips into a thin line to avoid laughing at Claire's antics and returned her attention to her aunt.

"You are right, Aunt Charlotte. Forgive me." Grace placed both hands on her thighs. Her palms pressed into the smooth silk of her light coral morning gown as she bent to be eye-level with her niece. "Claire, I was wrong to eavesdrop. We should be minding our manners. I apologize for leading you astray."

Charlotte wagged her forefinger in a beckoning motion. "All right, both of you come back here right now and take your seats." Aunt Charlotte aimed a glance at her daughter. "Claire, you have your morning studies to finish. And Grace, I would like you to assist Phillip with his letters." She returned to the correspondence on the small table in front of her. "We shall know soon enough what is transpiring in the foyer. I assure you."

Grace moved to stand behind Phillip at the longer table where the children did their schooling. In the autumn Claire would begin studies at the academy in Wilmington. And in just a few more weeks, the children would shift into their lighter schedule for the summer. That meant Grace could return to her uncle's shipping office several days a week to assist with the record keeping. Usually she worked with Aunt Charlotte at Cobblestone Books, or helped Aunt Bethany with the antique collections at Treasured Keepsakes. But the shipping office at the port in Wilmington? So many people, so many ships, all coming and going. Grace could hardly wait.

As Phillip painstakingly copied the words and letters from his lead sheet, Grace alternated between watching the doorway to the sitting room and her aunt. It appeared the anxious anticipation had also bitten Aunt Charlotte. Although seemingly engrossed in the current message she wrote, her aunt also cast surreptitious glances from the corner of her eye toward the foyer. Grace quietly cleared her throat, and her aunt looked up. This time Grace raised a single eyebrow, and her aunt gave her a sheepish grin. It felt good to know she wasn't the only one with an insatiable curiosity regarding her uncle's conversation. Her aunt merely concealed it better.

Sudden commotion sounded in the entryway. The front door crashed open and banged against the stopper on the floor. Raised voices tumbled over each other in a muddled clamor of frantic tones. All four of them jerked their heads toward the din. What in the world had caused such a ruckus?

Grace looked to her aunt, who had scooted to the edge of her seat, her white-knuckled hands gripping the sides of the wingback chair. Every fiber in Grace's body wanted to rush from the room to see the source of the disturbance. And just as she took a step in that direction, Uncle Richard appeared. His eyes immediately sought out his wife.

"They've found him." Excitement fairly radiated from his face. "The thief."

So soon? Grace straightened and looked from her uncle to her aunt. They'd just discovered the stolen items a few hours ago.

"But how?" Aunt Charlotte shook her head, closed her eyes for a brief moment, then opened them again, as if wrapping her mind around the announcement. "When? Where?"

"Marcus and Bartholomew just got back with the news." He jerked a thumb in the opposite direction. "Seems the thief didn't cover his tracks very well. A few of the items were recovered at the third shop our young men visited. Since word spreads quickly among those brokers, when the guy attempted to sell a few more items at a different shop, the owner detained him and contact the authorities."

That was it? All the restlessness and turmoil of the morning ended just like that? Grace should be relieved, but somehow it all felt so anticlimactic.

Aunt Charlotte's shoulders dropped, and all tension disappeared from her body. "So, we will soon have our items returned?"

"Not all of them." Uncle Richard stepped farther into the room. "We have the tea set and the silver for certain. The rest, they haven't determined yet." He turned and gestured toward the foyer. "They are waiting for us to come to the shop and confirm our belongings. . .and to press charges."

So the crook was still there? And her aunt and uncle would come face-to-face with him? Grace wished it could be her. She knew vengeance was best left up to God, but God hadn't been wronged here. Her family had.

"Right now?" her aunt replied. "Do they need both of us present? Claire and Phillip are in the middle of their lessons."

"So, leave them in Sarah's capable care." He paused. "Or Grace could accompany me." Uncle Richard looked her way. "Since the items stolen will become hers one day, in a way, she has a vested interest in seeing them returned as well."

"Oh Richard, Grace does not need to be present at something like this."

"But, Aunt Charlotte, I want to go," Grace rushed to interject.

"Can I go, too?" Claire chimed in.

"And me?" Phillip added.

Uncle Richard chuckled and walked to the table where his children sat. He reached out and tousled Phillip's auburn hair then tapped Claire's pert nose. "Not this time, children. You heard your mother. You need to complete your lessons." He shrugged. "Besides, a dark and musty old pawnshop is no place for either one of you. And what we'll be doing wouldn't be of much interest. You would be much happier here at home."

"So, may I go?" Grace brought the conversation back to the unanswered question. "As Uncle Richard said, some of those items partly belong to me. And he might not be able to accurately identify everything anyway." She glanced at her uncle. "No offense intended, Uncle Richard."

He splayed out his hands. "None taken." Looking to his wife, he nodded. "Grace does have a point. It will be good to have one of you present to make certain everything is there."

Aunt Charlotte looked back and forth between her husband and Grace, appearing to weigh the pros and cons in silence. "Very well." She released a resigned sigh then pointed a warning finger at Grace. "But mind yourself and be careful. We *are* dealing with a thief, after all."

"I will." Grace maneuvered around the table to where her aunt sat and leaned down to place a kiss on her cheek. "Thank you."

"Excellent." Uncle Richard clapped his hands together. "Let us not waste any more time. I am sure the constable wishes to close this case and move on to other matters."

Grace wanted to get moving as well. The sooner they arrived, the sooner she could give this scoundrel a piece of her mind.

Chapter 2

Grace stepped into the shop as her uncle held the door for her. The musty smell assailed her nose at the same time the well-lit interior challenged her preconceived notions of pawnshops. Shouldn't they be dim and crowded, with acquired items in haphazard disarray on every available surface? This one bore evidence of a thorough and meticulous owner, not the smarmy sort Grace expected. At that moment, a portly fellow with a receding hairline appeared from behind a hung burlap curtain across a doorframe.

"Good day to you, sir, miss." He wiped his hands on a once-white apron and approached, extending his right hand in greeting. "The name's Bancroft. Jeremiah Bancroft. What can I do for you?"

The man seemed pleasant enough. But why would a man like him be running a shop like this? Why not something a bit more reputable?

"Good day, Mr. Bancroft." Uncle Richard shook his hand. "I am Richard Baxton, and this is my niece, Grace. We are here regarding—"

"—the stolen property from your home last night," Mr. Bancroft finished for him. "Yes. The constable alerted me to your coming arrival." He stepped toward a closed door. "We have the young man over here. Follow me."

Young man? Grace hesitated. Could the thief be a lad instead of a full-grown man? She didn't know if she could face someone younger than her and still maintain the same level of ire.

"Grace?" Her uncle touched her elbow. "Is everything all right?"

"Yes. I'm fine." Or at least she would be once they entered the next room. Then she could lay all her uncertainties to rest.

"Shall we?"

How could her uncle be so calm about all this? Grace scrutinized his face. From the well-groomed dark brows to the almost emotionless eyes, down the narrow yet prominent nose to the straight-line lips. And there it was. The miniscule tick in his left cheek. So, this imminent meeting affected her uncle more than he let on. And with good reason. Their intruder waited just beyond that door.

"Yes," she said with a self-satisfied smile. "We shall."

Bancroft nodded at seeing their readiness and placed his hand on the doorknob. With a quick turn, he pushed open the door and disappeared inside.

Grace preceded her uncle by just a step or two. By the simple furnishings and decor, this must be the owner's office. On the plain oak desk sat her aunt's tea service and the silver, as well as a selection of fine china dishes. Her eyes immediately caught sight of the constable who had been at their home earlier that morning. He silently acknowledged them both and gestured toward the man sitting hunched in a chair against the wall, his head in his hands.

Now they would come face-to-face with the man who had broken into their home and threatened their sense of peace. Ironically he didn't look all that threatening or menacing. And the quality of his clothing didn't line up with the ragamuffin lot she'd heard combed the streets, seeking out opportunities to make a quick strike. In fact, if she didn't know better, she'd almost mistake this lawbreaker for someone who walked the sidewalks outside their home on a daily basis. He lacked the vest, coat, and top hat, and perhaps a walking stick, but his tailored ivory shirt with thin stripes, walnut canvas vest, and sable cotton trousers balanced with that image. How did a man like this end up stealing from a family like theirs?

"Mr. Baxton, are these articles the ones in question?" The constable splayed his open hand toward the items collected on the desk.

Uncle Richard took two steps forward, and Grace took three. All of that definitely belonged to her aunt.

"Yes," her uncle replied. "These are them." His voice lacked obvious emotion, but Grace could hear the anger lacing his words. He glanced to his right at the man who still sat with his head hung low.

"I only see one complete place setting here of the china." Grace reached out to trace the salmon-shaded filigree pattern on the edge of one plate. "Is this all that could be recovered?" She looked up at the constable.

"That is all I had in my store," Bancroft chimed in from behind her. "Yes. But it is not uncommon for individual place settings to be sold this way instead of as a full set. Makes it easier to off-load the wares and not raise as much suspicion."

"And now that we have the pattern," the constable added, "we can search more specifically for the rest of the pieces." He captured her uncle's attention with his direct gaze. "Are we ready then? We need to move forward with the official charges."

Uncle Richard only nodded, but he inhaled a deep breath and clasped his hands behind his back as he turned toward the guilty party who was awaiting his sentencing.

"All right, Bradenton," the constable began. "Now's your chance. Stand up and face your accusers."

Accusers wouldn't have been the word Grace chose, but with what the constable faced day in and day out, it made sense. She shifted to stand alongside her uncle as the man in question rose and lifted his head. A soft gasp escaped her lips. She didn't expect this at all.

The offender couldn't be more than five or six years her senior. Not a lad at all, and not a hardened criminal. And she'd been right about his apparel. Judging from the way he held himself, just shy of her uncle's six-foot-two height, he came from some level of refinement.

But where was the smug expression? The cold, steely eyes? The haughtiness of a successful robbery executed with precision? Grace couldn't find a single shred of any of that in his contrite eyes. Instead she saw true remorse in their depths. Warm, with flecks of golden rays, like a fine glass of brandy.

And those penitent eyes held her captive.

※

Andrew should look away, should also acknowledge the older gentleman who stood beside the young lady. But something about the striking, crystal-blue eyes with a hint of gray left him motionless. With great effort, he broke the invisible connection and raised his attention to the man the constable had addressed as Mr. Baxton.

Now here stood a man with a silent command of authority. He kept most of his emotions from showing on his face. But the nonverbal cues said it all. The hands firmly clasped behind his back, the shoulders squared, and the angled chin raised just a hair communicated the man's disapproval. If Andrew didn't miss his guess, and if he could see behind the man's back, he'd also likely find Mr. Baxton tapping an index finger against his other hand with distinct precision. It reminded him of his own father, and the scene would probably play out in much the same manner once his father received word of Andrew's crime.

"Well, boy?" Constable Garrett spoke up, breaking the nonverbal standoff. "What have you got to say for yourself? Now that you can look into the faces of the fine people you robbed."

And there it was. The reminder of the criminal he'd become as a result of this hotheaded, solitary act. It had seemed like such a good idea at the time. The man who alerted him to the opportunity said it would be a sure thing. Breaking in had been quite easy. Almost too easy, now that he thought about it. If only he'd been smarter about disposing of the items he'd stolen. Maybe then he could have pocketed the money and not looked back. Andrew sighed. No sense pining for what he couldn't have. He'd been caught red-handed. And he had to confess.

Andrew squared his own shoulders. "Mr. Baxton, sir," he began, looking the man directly in the eyes. "I know you must be thinking a few things about me right now, and none of them are favorable." No, in fact, the man's thoughts probably obliterated any chance at him maintaining even a shred of good character. "But now that I stand before you, I have nothing left to say except, I am truly sorry."

Mr. Baxton didn't flinch, didn't move, didn't even blink. He remained a solid statue, carefully watching. Andrew almost cowered under the man's silent degradation. Come on, he could do better than such a lame apology. Couldn't he?

"You have every reason to consider me among the most undesirable lot. To mete out the most detrimental of punishments for what I've done." Though Andrew prayed that wouldn't be the case. "All I can ask is for your forgiveness. What I did was reprehensible, but I hope not unforgiveable." All right, time to drive the point home. "Contrary to the evidence, this is not a regular habit of mine. In fact, it is the first time in my life I have ever done such a thing."

The man and the young lady with him both reacted to that. Baxton immediately looked to the constable.

"Is that true, Garrett? This young man isn't the one who also robbed the other homes in our area?"

"As much as I would like to deny it, I can't," the constable replied. "What Mr. Bradenton says is the truth. We found no evidence he'd ever done this before, and none of the shop owners had seen him at any time prior to this."

Baxton turned back to face him. "Then why this time? Why us?"

Should he answer that honestly? Why not? He had nothing else to lose. He'd already sullied his good name and would have to stand before a judge for sentencing. At least he could be candid with everyone. It might even help his case.

"To tell you the truth, sir, I made a rash decision because of my mother." Another startled expression from the young lady. And perhaps a bit of sympathy? "She's been sick for a while now, and she's had several surgeries. The doctors aren't sure what the problem is, but while they try to figure it out, their bills continue to come. My father never spoke of it, but I could see the strain taking its toll. He's too proud to admit we can't afford it all at once like this." Andrew splayed out his fingers and shrugged. "I was only trying to help." He sighed. "But now, I've just made things worse."

"I won't disagree with you there," Baxton stated in a no-nonsense tone. "The question is, what are we going to do about it?"

"That's a question *I* can answer," Constable Garrett said. "But first, Mr. Baxton, are you going ahead with pressing formal charges?"

Baxton hesitated a fraction of a second, and in that fraction, Andrew's hope rose. But the man's next words dashed that hope.

"I do not have a choice," he answered, his tone both stern and forgiving.

Andrew noted the obvious lack of the word *we*. He looked again at the young lady who had accompanied Baxton. Since introductions hadn't been formally made, he had no idea of her relation or connection to the older man beside her. Her bare left hand bore no evidence of a wedding band, and she shared a family resemblance to Baxton, although not an overt one. He also couldn't forget the way she'd held his gaze at the onset of their meeting. That alone ruled out a wife. So who was she?

The constable stuck his thumb almost into Andrew's chest and interrupted his musings. "Well, then Bradenton here has an appointment with the judge across the street. Now that we've confirmed the stolen items, we leave it up to the judge to decide." With precise movements, Garrett grabbed hold of Andrew's upper arm and propelled him toward the door. "Let's go."

Andrew didn't know what he expected of his "trial," but the informal gathering of no one but the judge and the five of them from the broker's shop didn't even come close. In no time at all, both sides had presented their cases, and the judge had made a few notes.

The judge reached up to remove his spectacles and rubbed the bridge of his nose. "Does anyone else have anything to say before I pronounce the sentence?"

Silence answered his question.

"Very well." The judge made a final note on the paper in front of him then leveled a direct gaze at Andrew. "Mr. Bradenton, it is both my recommendation and my direct order that you serve three months in the employ of the Baxton family as restitution for your crimes."

A sharp gasp came from the young lady, now hidden from Andrew's view. Work for the family he'd robbed? Face them day in and day out with the constant reminder of how he'd wronged them? He would have gasped, too, if he hadn't been determined to maintain a stoic attitude in the judge's presence.

"The extent and duration of the work to be completed," the judge continued, "will be left to the discretion of Mr. Baxton. But you shall remain in their employ for three months, and not a day less. Only then will your sentence be complete. Do I make myself clear?"

Andrew nodded. "Yes, sir."

"Very well." The judge raised his gavel. "You are all dismissed." He brought the instrument down with a single echoing thud against the surface in front of him. "Constable? Mr. Baxton? You both can see my assistant out front for the necessary forms you'll need to sign. Thank you all for coming in."

And with that, the trial concluded. Garrett again took hold of Andrew's arm to escort him from the courtroom. As they pivoted, Andrew caught sight of the young lady. He almost stepped back and stumbled from the onslaught of her silent ire. The compelling crystal-blue had been replaced with cold-as-ice depths. What had happened to make her so angry? Back at the shop, when he'd confessed and asked for forgiveness, he could've sworn there'd been sympathy in her eyes. But not now. He hadn't said anything different in front of the judge than he had at the shop.

Perfect. Not only did he have to be reminded daily of his crime, but he had to deal with the animosity of the young lady he still had yet to meet. At least it eliminated the possibility of any distractions while he served his time. He'd complete his sentence and that would be the end of it. Nothing more, nothing less. Andrew prayed the three months would pass quickly.

Chapter 3

Andrew paused by the nearly full barrel and set down the two pails of waste from the kitchen. Almost time for a new barrel. The wagon would be by later that evening to haul away the waste, but at the rate this one got filled, they might end up with three or four before the day ended. He ran the back of his hand across his brow and wiped the sweat on the rolled-up sleeves of his shirt. It shouldn't be this hot in the middle of May. The sun beat down on him in merciless fashion from the cloudless sky.

He'd been at the Baxtons' for only four days. So far he'd been up on a ladder to wash the outsides of all the windows on the upper levels of the home, scrubbed the floors in the scullery and the kitchen, and emptied the waste pails several times a day. He'd even cleaned out the mud and grime that had collected on the carriages following the recent spring rains. After a morning like this one, though, his mere four days felt like weeks.

With a deep breath, Andrew bent and grabbed the pails then hefted them over the split-rail fence and dumped out their contents. He turned his head and coughed at the stench from a half a day's waste all gathered in one place. Oh, the things he'd learned about the inner workings of a country house in the short time he'd been here. If he had to endure this particular task much longer, he didn't know how he'd last.

Of course, it was only by God's grace that Andrew had the luxury of serving his sentence under Baxton's watch. By all rights, he should have been sent off to the penitentiary in Philadelphia. From what he'd heard, the months of solitary confinement drove some men mad. Day in and day out with no human contact whatsoever, and meals shoved through a hole in the door of the cell? Andrew shuddered at the thought. At least here he had the house staff going about their daily business. Though he rarely, if ever, spoke to one of them, their mere presence comforted him and made him grateful for the judge's favor.

As he headed back to the house, swinging empty pails by his sides, Andrew recalled the final day leading up to his arrival. His father had been incensed, as expected. But concern for his wife tempered the elder Mr. Bradenton's ire.

"How could you do something so completely reckless and foolhardy?"

The man paced back and forth in his study as Andrew stood, head bowed and hands tucked into the pockets of his trousers. Even at twenty-four, he could be reduced to a mere schoolboy by one well-placed look from his father. Father had removed his coat but not his vest, and rolled up his shirtsleeves. That didn't make him any less intimidating, though, as he continued his rant.

"You didn't stop for one moment to think of anyone else and how this rash decision would affect us. And the consequences!"

Another turn. Several long strides across the Aubusson rug. Then back to the original direction. Father halted halfway in his trek across the room and spun to face Andrew.

"You obviously see the error of your actions now that you've been caught." He gestured and Andrew would have received his father's backhand had he been standing in front of him. "But why couldn't you have thought about that *before* you went through with this impetuous scheme? Before such a black mark was made against our family? And before you broke your mother's heart when she heard the news?"

Andrew didn't have any words for his defense. Everything his father said rang true. He *had* thought only of himself. He *did* do the quickest thing that might result in immediate money. And worst of all, his actions *had* disappointed his mother.

"It is true," his father continued, his voice taking on a more forgiving tone, "the doctors' bills are accumulating. And I have been forced to withdraw funds from accounts that by all rights should be reserved strictly for you and your brother and sister."

His voice hardened again as he moved to his desk and placed both palms on the surface. He leaned forward to pin Andrew in his direct gaze.

"But that does not give *you* the right to go off half-cocked and cook up some lamebrained ploy, hoping to gain a fast sum. No." He straightened and tucked his thumbs into the pockets of his vest. "When you need money, you earn it. You don't steal to get it." His father's shoulders slumped a little. "I thought I taught you better than that."

"You did, Father." Andrew took a step forward then froze at the steely resolve in his father's eyes. "And I'm sorry. . .for everything."

Father waved off Andrew's apology and turned his back. "I do not wish to hear another word. At the moment, your confession and act of contrition is meaningless to me." He bowed his head. "I need some time to come to grips with all this. I believe it is divine providence that you will also be boarding with the Baxton servants during your sentence. It just might take me that long to set things right. And I shall have to find someone to replace you at the mill." His father dismissed him with a brushing of his hand at his side. "Now, go see your mother. We'll talk again before you leave."

That second conversation hadn't gone any better. If anything, Andrew considered that one worse on the guilt scale. He grabbed a shovel from the shed to dig and till an extension to the existing vegetable garden then headed to the plot, his mother's words replaying in his mind.

"You have brought a great deal of disgrace to our family, Andrew," she whispered. Her eyes closed, and she inhaled a ragged breath before slowly releasing it. The pain must be an almost constant companion these days. Mother reached out and patted his hand. "I know your heart was in the right place, but your head wasn't." She opened her eyes and regarded him with the severe yet tender expression only a mother could achieve. "The two must always be in alignment."

Andrew rotated his hand to clasp hers. "Mother, I know I have wronged you and Father. But worse, I have caused you greater anguish than even your physical pain. And I cannot apologize enough to make up for what I've done." He gave her hand a squeeze. "But I vow to make things right again. I promise."

Mother slowly nodded. "I know you will, son. Of that, I have complete faith." She tilted her head up just a bit. "Now, give me a kiss and be on your way. I will pray daily for you as you fulfill your obligations."

The image of his mother in bed, in pain, and dealing with the shame in the wake of his mistakes haunted him even now. But the knowledge of her daily prayers kept him going. He drew strength from them, comfort and peace. Father had also invited him to write, and Andrew would do that at week's end. At least he hadn't been cut off. Praise God for that.

A small shadow fell over the dirt Andrew tilled.

"Excuse me, Andrew?" One of the kitchen maids, Elsa, spoke up, though even at this close range, her voice could be termed meek at best. "I've been sent to tell you that when you're finished with this, Mr. Baxton wants you to clean out the stalls in the stables and polish the saddles in the side room."

Andrew's shoulders fell. Didn't he have stable hands for that? Just what were these servants doing in place of the chores he completed for them? They weren't sitting idle. But if the work he did only freed up the staff to do other tasks, maybe Baxton should hire more help.

"Thank you, Elsa. I will go straight there as soon as I'm done here."

Elsa bobbed a curtsy, either out of habit or because she knew the reason for his presence there. Servants usually did *his* bidding, instead of the other way around. What an ironic twist of fate had befallen him.

Once the maid had disappeared again into the house, Andrew put the finishing touches on the tilled ground, returned the shovel and other items to the shed, and headed across the back lawn. How long would Baxton come up with menial tasks like these before he followed through on his promise to move Andrew up to the next level?

"Now that you've met the principal house staff," Baxton had said, "and are aware of the members of my family, we'll start with the first of your assignments." Baxton led the way into the dining room and paused before the butler and steward. "Harrison and Charles will oversee the majority of your duties. Anything I'd like done will be relayed through them, or another servant. If you accomplish your tasks in a satisfactory manner, we shall discuss entrusting you with more." He pivoted to leave then paused and cast a glance over his shoulder. "As head of this household and overseer of a rather successful shipping business, trust me when I say there is an abundance of work to keep you busy for three years, let alone three months." Baxton raised one eyebrow. "Your hands will not grow idle."

That parting remark had lined up more in reference to his hands being what stole than with the day-to-day chores he now did with them. Grabbing hold of the two handles, Andrew swung open one of the doors and stepped inside the stables.

"So, the errant jailbird with deep pockets finally comes down from the high perch of the manor house to grace us with his presence." A jeering greeting came from within the surprisingly well-lit interior.

Andrew searched the stalls, nooks, and crannies for the owner of the voice. A few seconds later, a solid young man about his age stepped into view halfway down the center aisle. He wore a pullover work shirt and a pair of tan trousers with suspenders hooked up over his shoulders. The brown tweed cap over sandy-brown hair curling at his collar rounded out the image.

"Best if you know right now," the man continued, "I call the shots in here." He came to stand less than two feet from Andrew and folded his arms. "The name's Jesse, and anything that's to be done goes through me first."

Jesse had obviously forgotten about the head coachman. Andrew held his grin in check. Even standing nearly toe-to-toe, he still had Jesse by about three inches. Not much cause for concern.

Andrew shrugged off the obvious baiting. "Well, I'm only here to muck out the stalls and polish the saddles. You won't have any trouble from me."

Not that Jesse could do anything anyway. Andrew didn't give him a chance to respond. He just headed for the wheelbarrow and pitchfork and set to work, grateful Jesse didn't follow.

Halfway through the stalls, though, a commotion behind him made Andrew turn. The wheelbarrow he'd filled a moment ago sat on its side, the contents spilled. Now he had to fill it again. At least the manure remained in a pile. Shouldn't take him too long. He didn't see anyone nearby, but Jesse's sinister cackle sounded from somewhere near the front. Guess the stable hand didn't intend to leave him alone after all.

With the minor setback behind him, Andrew finished the stalls and moved to the saddles. He had three of them done when Jesse popped into the room. The stable hand walked to the far corner and randomly picked up miscellaneous pieces of tack, inspected them, and returned them to their original spot.

What did he want now? Andrew tried to ignore him and return to his work, but the man didn't make it easy.

"Be sure you hang those saddles back on their hooks. We don't want no rodents sinking their teeth into the leather, and they sure don't need to be on the ground where they'll get wet and musty."

Andrew clenched his teeth, not looking up. "Not a problem. I assure you." After wiping clean the glycerin, he poured more oil onto the cotton cloth he held and rubbed it into the leather in circular motions. Sure was a good thing he'd spent some time with Charlie, one of their stable hands back home, or Jesse might have had more chances to mock him for not knowing his way around the stables.

"By the way," Jesse added, reaching out to lift one of the saddles away from the wall. "This one's going to need to be done again."

Andrew looked at the saddle Jesse held. It had a dirt streak right across the center of the seat. He'd done that one first. No way had he missed something so glaring. If Jesse didn't stop, he might find himself at the mean end of a pitchfork before long. Or Andrew might grab one of those bits and use it for something other than placing in the horse's mouth. He didn't move though. It would be better to wait Jesse out than make another rash decision like the one that had landed him here in the first place.

After several minutes, Jesse brushed past Andrew, nudging him on his way out. Andrew swallowed several times and squeezed the cloth in his hand while rubbing far more vigorously than necessary. He was here to pay his penance. But he wouldn't sit back and take vindictive behavior like that for long.

Chapter 4

"Where are you going?" Seven-year-old Claire broke the silence of morning reading time with her rather loud voice.

Grace turned from the doorway and looked at her cousin. "I am stepping out for some fresh air, and I believe I will go for a ride."

"Can I come?"

The little girl's book fell to the floor when she scooted to the edge of her seat. Her sweet pixie-like face and eager expression coupled with how she bounced in the chair could wear down even the most stalwart of souls. But Aunt Charlotte gave an almost imperceptible shake of her head.

"Not this time, Claire," Grace replied. "Perhaps next time." She raised her index finger and waggled it at her cousin. "*If* you finish your studies."

"Oh I will!" Claire scrambled from the chair to retrieve her book, hopped back against the cushions, and flipped open the pages to where she'd left off.

Grace chuckled and shook her head. Oh, to be so young and carefree. And to have desires appeased so easily.

"You can't finish and still go with Grace." Phillip spoke up from his secluded spot in the corner. "Grace is all done. You will take too long."

Even at five, he exhibited signs of greater interest in books or solo activities than outdoor exercise. Just like his mother. Claire, on the other hand, had as much of Uncle Richard as possible. And Grace couldn't fault that. She, too, loved being outside. Every chance she had, she took it.

"Well, I am almost done," Claire said, laying her book on her lap. "I could go if I wanted." She crossed her arms, jutted her chin in the air, and closed her eyes. "But I don't want to." A peek from one eye at her brother. "Not now, anyway."

Grace exchanged a silent look with her aunt. Those two were quite a pair.

"Have a nice time on your ride, dear," Aunt Charlotte said.

"I will."

A part of Grace wanted to wait for Claire to finish. Her cousin could be a lot of fun riding horses in the nearby park. She always pointed out so many things Grace overlooked, and seeing the world through the eyes of a young girl could be quite effective in reminding her to appreciate the simple things in life. But not today. After a morning receiving an endless line of callers inquiring about Aunt Bethany's upcoming sale on some of her restored furniture, Grace had had her fill of people. Today, she wanted solitude.

It didn't make sense why they came to Aunt Charlotte to ask their questions anyway. Shouldn't they be going to Aunt Bethany? Just because Charlotte put the announcement in both *The Morning News* and *The Evening Journal* didn't mean those inquiring should come to her. But come they did, and now Grace needed some time alone. So after having Harriet assist her with changing into her riding habit, Grace headed for the stables.

She paused just outside and breathed in the scent of fresh hay and horses. As she pulled open the door to step inside, the smell of leather, lye, and oil joined the bouquet of aromas assailing her nose. Some might not find the stables appealing. In fact, they might find the ever-present odor repulsive. To Grace though, it brought a great deal of comfort, and it remained her favorite place in the world.

"Will you be needing your horse saddled, Miss Baxton?"

Grace started at the unfamiliar voice and turned to her left to see the criminal sentenced to work for them coming out of the room where they kept the saddles. It had been a little over a week since the incident. She'd all but forgotten him. Today he wore clothing more befitting a stable hand or assistant to the groundskeeper. But even these clothes bore distinct markings of specific tailoring. What was his name again? Adam? Albert? Arthur? Andrew? Andrew. That was it. Andrew Bradenton. But where was Jesse? Or Willie? They usually had her horse ready and waiting.

"Yes," she finally answered. "Yes, I will. Thank you."

Andrew returned to the room and hefted a saddle from the hook like it weighed nothing at all. Grace tried not to stare, but with no other movement anywhere, her eyes naturally followed him. While he retrieved the bridle and blanket, she walked over to Pilgrim's stall. He already had his head over the wall awaiting her approach. A whinny and a snort signaled his pleasure.

Grace reached over the wall and scratched his forelock. "So, are you ready for another jaunt in the park, boy? A good stretch of the legs?" She leaned forward and pressed her head to his, rubbing her forehead against the coarse hair between his eyes. "Yes, I know you are."

Pilgrim dipped his head farther and nuzzled the front of her clothes, vigorously moving his head up and down. Grace laughed and grabbed hold of his jowls to look him straight in the eye.

"Silly boy." She gave his forelock a good rub. "You know I will scratch your head anytime. There is no need to use my shirtfront as a post."

Andrew appeared at that moment, and Grace caught herself before she jumped at his silent approach. Without a word he unlatched the door and stepped into the stall. In no time at all, he had Pilgrim saddled and the stirrups adjusted. Grace admired how he worked with smooth precision. He obviously knew his way around a horse.

"I'll lead him out for you," he said.

His eyes met hers for a brief moment. And in that moment, Grace again saw the remorse he'd shown at the pawn shop over a week prior. This man bore none of the telltale marks of a lawbreaker without a conscience. Instead, his expression and his actions spoke only of a silent apology. She followed a respectful distance behind as Andrew led Pilgrim through the door and into the shining sun. As soon as the two stopped, Grace came alongside her horse's left, reached for the reins, and prepared to mount. Andrew again appeared without a sound. He interlocked his fingers and stooped to give her a leg up.

Grace hesitated. Had it been Jesse or Willie, she wouldn't have blinked an eye. She would have accepted their help without question. With a man who had wronged her family though, it changed things. When she didn't place her boot in his hands, he looked up at her. His eyebrow quirked, and the faintest hint of a smirk formed on his lips, as if he dared her in an unspoken challenge.

Just where did he get the audacity to grin at her that way? And how could he even think of attempting to taunt her in such a fashion? He should be acting the part of a subservient member of the household staff. Grace could accept behavior such as that from the staff she knew well, but Andrew? No. She refused to give in to his baiting and give him any sort of satisfaction.

Grabbing hold of her split skirt, she raised the hem just enough to place her boot in his hands. With surprising gentleness, Andrew helped her mount then adjusted the stirrups. As soon as he stepped back, she acknowledged him with a nod.

"Thank you."

She might not wish to engage in any form of lighthearted repartee with him, but she would never forget her manners.

"You are welcome, Miss Baxton." He glanced at the spattering of fluffy clouds in the clear blue sky before returning his gaze to her. "It's a good day for a ride. I hope you have a pleasant time."

Andrew held Grace's eyes for several moments before she broke the invisible connection and faced forward. Her heart pounded a bit faster than usual, and her breath came in shorter spurts. She had come here to take advantage of solitude. Just her and Pilgrim. Now she needed that retreat for more reasons than one.

Heading west from the manor house, Grace guided Pilgrim along the path paralleling the Brandywine River. Her horse could walk this route blindfolded if she let him have the lead, and the knowledge of that fact brought a level of reassurance to her. It allowed her to venture out and free her mind of everything, welcoming the peace that washed over her.

The screech of a red-tailed hawk sounded overhead, and to her left, a crane flew just a foot or so above the water's surface, the swoop of its wings causing ripples below. That brought to mind Andrew and how easily he'd hauled the saddle from the hook and lifted it to Pilgrim's back. His feather-light touch against her boot when he'd adjusted her stirrups still left an impression, and despite her best efforts, Grace couldn't get him out of her mind.

He'd confessed his crime as not being a normal one for him. And he'd told the judge the same thing. His speech, his mannerisms, and the cut and quality of his clothing attested that he wasn't of the working class. So, why then had he lowered himself to the point of a common thief? Surely his family had other means of securing funds for their medical bills. Another relative, investments from the bank, or even money saved for the future. A man with a background obviously closer to Grace's than the riffraff who frequent the local jails should have had multiple options available to him. So why steal? And why their house? How had he gained access anyway?

Grace mulled it in her mind over and over again as she rode. Since Pilgrim knew the trail so well, she allowed him free rein, enjoying the exhilaration of the wind in her face and the thrill of riding such a powerful steed. Far too soon, the time came to return to the stables. Aunt Charlotte would be calling her to the midday meal, and after that, she would head to the bookshop. Would Andrew also be there upon her arrival?

She didn't have to wait long to find out. From the sound of things, Jesse was somewhere inside.

"I warned you, jailbird, not to do anything without asking me first. There's an order to the way things are done here, and if you want to change it, you go through me."

Jesse's voice carried on the wind. The jeering name Jesse used gave away the recipient of the tongue lashing.

"And I know my orders come from Mr. Wyeth, the head coachman." That strong and confident voice belonged to Andrew. "He oversees everyone here in the stables. Mr. Baxton instructed me to report to him, and him alone. If you have any complaint regarding my actions, you will need to discuss it with him."

There it was again. The cultured quality to his speech. The sign that someone had taught him propriety in more ways than one. Grace walked Pilgrim into the fenced area and dismounted, giving her horse a pat on his neck. She didn't want to alert the men inside to her presence, so she tiptoed toward the open doors and continued to listen. Aunt Charlotte's reprimand for eavesdropping came to mind, but in this instance, Grace knew her aunt would likely do the same.

"Well, Mr. Wyeth isn't here right now," Jesse continued. "And that makes me next in command. You still haven't cleaned out the two stalls at the end, and there's the feed and water for the horses."

"And if I do all of that, what will that leave you to do?"

"So now you're trying to tell me what I'm supposed to be doing? You sure have some nerve. I'm tempted to report you to Mr. Baxton myself at the first chance I get."

The tone of Jesse's voice hardened, and a menacing edge laced his words. Grace had never heard Jesse talk like that. He'd always been nothing but kind to her, albeit a bit cocksure at times. But nevertheless, respectful. Why all this animosity toward Andrew?

"Do what you will, Jesse," Andrew replied with a nonchalant air. "It won't change the fact that I was not told to water and feed the horses. So, I won't be doing it."

"Guess that means I'll have to teach you a lesson my own way."

All right, enough was enough. Grace knew she needed to intervene before Jesse did something he'd regret. She'd seen Andrew, and she knew Jesse's size. Jesse didn't stand a chance. She rushed inside, not even waiting for her eyes to adjust from the bright sun.

"Jesse, you will do no such thing. And I will not have you tormenting anyone working these grounds in this manner."

"Miss Baxton!" Jesse immediately stepped back from Andrew and turned to face her. "I didn't know you had come down to the stables." He offered a forced smile. "Have you come for your normal ride?"

Grace inhaled and released a slow breath. "No, Jesse. I have just returned, and if you had been paying more attention to your regular duties instead of deriding Mr. Bradenton here, you would have realized that."

Jesse dipped his head and closed his eyes. She had purposefully used Andrew's formal name to set him apart. Jesse had noticed. Grace wanted to look at Andrew, to see how he was taking her interruption, but she refrained. He or Jesse might infer something that didn't exist, and she needed to stay on task.

"I am of a mind to speak to my uncle directly regarding your behavior a few moments ago. But if you give me your word it will not happen again, I will cease from doing so. . .this time."

"Miss Baxton, you have my word," he replied through clenched teeth. "And do forgive me. I know I was out of place."

Grace didn't bother to address the fact that him knowing his place and still acting the way he had were in direct opposition. He had apologized, and she'd leave it at that.

"Very well. Now, please return to your work, and leave Mr. Bradenton to his."

Jesse only nodded, but Grace didn't miss the narrowed eyes or the meaningful glare he gave Andrew on his way to the back of the stables. That wasn't the end of it, but at least she'd prevented it this time. After seeing Jesse disappear into one of the stalls at the far end, Grace turned to face Andrew.

"I am sorry you had to endure that. Jesse isn't usually like that, and I—"

"I would appreciate it if you would let me speak for myself," Andrew interrupted. "I am not an errant schoolboy who needs help fighting my battles." Anger fairly dripped from his words, and fire flashed in his eyes. "So please refrain from helping in the future."

With that, he pivoted on his heel and walked away. Grace stood, her mouth open, unable to come up with a response. She thought he'd appreciate her stepping in on his behalf. At the very least, it was her place. Jesse shouldn't be treating him like that, and she'd prevented an almost certain altercation. So why hadn't he been more grateful? She clenched her fists. He could have at least uttered a simple word of thanks.

Grace spun in the opposite direction. Next time she wouldn't rush to his aid. As he wished, she'd *let* him deal with his own fights.

Chapter 5

Andrew walked down the corridor from the direction of the dining room, where he'd just helped two footmen position a new buffet and service set then remove the old. He slowed his steps just before the foyer when he saw Miss Baxton enter through the front door. Harrison swung the door wider then held out his hand to take her wrap and hat as soon as she stood in the entryway.

"Thank you, Harrison." She graced him with a genuine smile and made eye contact with him.

"My pleasure, miss," Harrison replied with a nod and slight bow.

"Is my uncle in his study?" Miss Baxton removed her gloves and handed them to the butler.

"Yes, miss." Harrison stacked the gloves neatly with the hat and wrap. "He left your aunt in the parlor and went straight there about fifteen minutes ago."

"Very good." She smiled again. "I believe I shall speak with Aunt Charlotte first then go see my uncle. He will no doubt appreciate the few moments of solitude. Thank you."

The butler only nodded this time, but then he winked, and Miss Baxton chuckled softly. They obviously shared a special rapport. Not many folks of the Baxtons' class would interact with their servants in such a manner. And from the way the servants responded to the family, the admiration and respect went both ways. Andrew thought of his own servants. They performed their duties without noticeable complaint, but how did they feel about his father or mother, or even him? He didn't know. And being here made him question his own treatment of those who served him.

Miss Baxton headed straight for him and halted when she saw him. Her expression clouded and a frown marred her dainty lips. Even her eyes took on a noticeable hesitation. Well, he couldn't stand there forever in a visual stalemate.

"Good afternoon, Miss Baxton," he said with a slight bow.

"Mr. Bradenton," she replied, her words clipped.

Silence again.

A moment later she flounced away and disappeared into the parlor, sliding the doors closed behind her. Now what had he done to deserve that kind of treatment? She'd been far more cordial the other day when she'd come to the stables for a morning ride. And she had almost responded to his unspoken teasing when he offered to help her mount.

Oh, the ride!

When she'd returned, she'd stuck her nose into that disagreement he was having with Jesse. Had all but upstaged him and made him out to be a milksop who couldn't fend for himself. And that's when he'd snapped at her. Sure, it had been a rash response, but she had it coming. She shouldn't interfere in a man's affairs without his permission. Still, no wonder she'd greeted him in such a cool manner. He'd do the same thing in her shoes. . .although he hoped never to be there. The mere thought of changing clothes so often, entertaining callers, and planning menus made his lips curl in disgust. Give him the mill and manual labor any day.

On the thought of manual labor, he had another job to do. He'd best get to it.

&

"Why did you pull the doors to, Grace?" Aunt Charlotte spoke from the settee where she sat with a teacup in hand.

Grace glanced back over her shoulder, as if she could see through the panels. If she could, would Andrew still be standing there? Or would he have left as soon as she did? What did it matter? She shouldn't give him a second thought, anyway. He was paying off a debt to her family.

"Grace?"

She turned to face her aunt. "Forgive me, Aunt Charlotte. I am afraid my mind wandered a bit."

"That much is obvious," her aunt said with a grin. "Now why don't you have a seat? Join me for tea, and you can tell me all about it." She extended her arm toward the empty seat opposite her and the tray of assorted sweet breads on the table.

"Thank you. I believe I will."

Once Grace sat and poured herself a cup of tea, her aunt leaned back against the settee. "Did you have a productive morning working with Aunt Bethany?"

Grace took a bite of a fruited scone and swallowed. "Yes. We managed to separate out the items she is going to be selling at the auction, categorize the items she has yet to place in her shop, and take inventory of what remains."

Her aunt's eyes widened. "Sounds as if you two accomplished quite a lot."

"We did have a little help." Grace gave her aunt a playful grin. "Aunt 'Stasia was there, too. With George. And James arrived midmorning."

"Ah, so my mischievous little sister decided to put her talents to good use instead of lurking about, attempting to find another innocent victim for her matchmaking schemes."

"Now, Auntie, you know as well as I that Aunt 'Stasia has been quite successful with her matches over the years." Grace quirked an eyebrow and gave her aunt a meaningful look. "As I recall, she was rather instrumental in arranging the match between you and Uncle Richard."

"No, as I recall," her aunt countered with a smile, "you were the key to that pairing." She replaced her teacup on her saucer and held them in her lap. "Had it not been for your insatiable love of books and your uncle's quest to assuage that love, you might never have ventured into my bookshop."

"And aren't you glad we did?"

A twinkle lit up her aunt's eyes. "Immensely so."

Grace laughed. "Still, you have to admit, your youngest sister encouraged you to pursue a dalliance with Uncle Richard." She took another small bite. "And she made certain to have a new book for me every time we came so the two of you could have uninterrupted time to talk."

Her aunt's eyes widened. "Oh, is that why you two always seemed to disappear so quickly?"

Grace winked. "We had to do something. With all the time you spent in the bookshop, it would have been years before a suitable gentleman captured your attention."

"And it did not harm the situation any with Anastasia being only three years your elder." She pursed her lips and gave Grace a half grin. "The two of you could scheme and orchestrate to your hearts' content, and you no doubt found great pleasure in doing so."

"Well, her more so than I." Grace shrugged. "But I enjoyed her company so much, and she made me forget about being in that wheeled chair all day."

Aunt Charlotte nodded. "Yes, it is to Anastasia's credit that she treats everyone equally. And with her recent engagement, I am hoping to see her settle a bit in her impish ways."

"Aunt 'Stasia will always be a bit mischievous. But I am certain George will manage to keep her somewhat subdued from time to time." Grace grinned. "As much as is possible, that is."

"Yes." Her aunt chuckled then gave Grace a poignant glance. "Which brings me to the matter of your associations with eligible gentlemen."

Grace had wondered how long it would take her aunt to come around to that topic. Perhaps she shouldn't have mentioned George or James, Aunt Bethany's intended. It was a natural segue, considering Grace remained the only one in their family at present without a beau.

"Or lack thereof," Grace quipped.

"Yes, exactly." Her aunt took a sip of tea. "We must do something about that."

Unbidden, Grace's thoughts wandered to Andrew, and his face appeared before her mind's eye. She attempted to banish him, but his roguish grin and teasing golden eyes persisted. Why couldn't she recall his face after her ride? When he'd been incensed. Or a few moments ago when he'd been aloof and cordial? No, her traitorous memory would only focus on the appealing qualities and the moment when he'd been at his most charming.

"So, are you agreeable to that?" Her aunt's voice broke into her reflections.

"Pardon me?" Grace focused on her aunt. "I am sorry. I am afraid I wasn't listening."

"So I noticed." Aunt Charlotte narrowed her eyes and tilted her head just slightly. "Might something else. . .or perhaps someone else. . .have your attention?"

Warmth stole into Grace's cheeks and flushed her neck as well. "It is nothing."

"And that right there, young lady, is a falsehood. If you don't wish to tell me, that is fine. But do not pass it off as unimportant, when it clearly is." Her aunt's voice remained kind, yet held a distinct reprimand behind the words she spoke. "Otherwise, you would not have been so distracted as to completely miss what I said."

"You are correct, Aunt Charlotte." Grace nodded. How could she argue with such logic? "And again, I do apologize."

Her aunt brushed it off. "Never you mind. I shall find out soon enough the individual who has you slightly befuddled and not at all your usual attentive self." She paused with a wink. "In my own way."

Grace would never win that battle, so she might as well let it go. "So, what was it you said a moment ago?"

Aunt Charlotte grinned. She knew very well Grace had sidestepped the issue, but gratefully she let it drop. "I merely suggested an introduction to several young men of whom I'm aware through my association with their sisters or mothers, thanks to their patronage at the bookshop. Perhaps you would be interested in meeting them?"

"Oh! That reminds me." Grace jumped to her feet, sloshing a few drops of her tea onto the carpet. "I must go see Uncle Richard. I have a message to deliver to him."

"Grace," her aunt chided.

Grace bent to dab a cloth onto the drops to save the parlor maids the added work. "I am sorry, Aunt Charlotte," she said as she stood once more. "I promise to return, and we can continue this discussion, but I truly must speak with Uncle Richard."

"Very well." Her aunt dismissed her. "But don't forget. We must discuss this soon."

"I won't."

Grace shoved open the doors and cringed when they slammed into their cubbies. "Sorry, Aunt Charlotte!" she called as she rushed from the room. Grace turned the corner, made her way down the hall, and had her hand on the study door when it opened without her. She braced her hands on the doorframe to keep from falling into the room.

"Oh, pardon me." Andrew paused at the doorway and stepped back inside to allow her room to enter. A second later, he shifted the rather large box he held.

She straightened and stared. Why was he here? And how had he opened the door so quickly with both hands holding what appeared to be a box of books?

"Ah, Grace," her uncle greeted. "Do come in."

So, that was how. Uncle Richard had opened it for him. That still didn't explain his presence though, or the box.

"Andrew," her uncle continued, addressing the man who regarded her with a mixture of solemnity and eagerness. "Be sure that box is delivered to Charles. He will see it's delivered to my wife's bookshop tomorrow."

Only when her uncle finished did Andrew shift his gaze from her. "Right away, Mr. Baxton."

"Well, Grace? Are you going to enter and allow Andrew to see to his work, or will you stand in the doorway until supper?"

Grace shook her head. She really needed to keep her wits about her. Stepping into the room, she made sure to give Andrew a wide berth. His eyes never left hers though as he passed to leave. And that expectant, or perhaps hopeful, look never dimmed. Did he have something to say to her? Perhaps an apology for his boorish behavior the other day? Or would it be more teasing as he'd done prior to her ride?

She certainly wouldn't find out now. Instead of saying anything, Andrew disappeared, leaving her staring in his wake.

Sharp snaps near her ear a moment later drew her attention back to her uncle. When she turned to face him, his lips curled in a bemused grin, and a twinkle lit up his eyes. Grace had to stop this. That was twice now in the span of a quarter hour when she had allowed Andrew or thoughts of him to distract her. If this persisted, someone might misinterpret her behavior and form an incorrect assumption that she found him appealing in some way.

"Uncle Richard, forgive me for interrupting your afternoon, but I have a message for you from James." Her aunt's intended worked at her uncle's shipyards.

"No need to apologize. What does James have to say?"

Good. Her uncle was willing to let the matter drop. "He wanted me to tell you that the shipment you were expecting—the one with the coffee beans, flour, and other dry goods—arrived this morning, and he needed your signature in order to prepare it for delivery to the local shops."

"Splendid." Uncle Richard clasped his hands together and sighed. "We have been awaiting that shipment for two days now. It appears a storm set the ship slightly off course farther south down the coast. I'm pleased to see it has finally arrived." He took a couple of steps backward then turned toward his desk, where he made a brief notation on a piece of paper. "I shall make my way to the river at the first opportunity." He glanced up, one hand still resting on the desk surface. "Now, was there anything else?"

Now was as good a time as any. Grace took a step forward. "Uncle Richard?"

"Yes?"

"Did Mr. Bradenton share anything at all about his background with you?"

"Andrew?" Her uncle straightened. "Why would you ask?"

Grace wet her lips. She had to be careful not to appear too interested, or her uncle would start asking her probing questions. "Well, do you recall the day we went to Mr. Bancroft's shop and met Mr. Bradenton for the first time?"

She didn't know why she insisted on calling Andrew by his proper name in her uncle's presence. He referred to him as Andrew. Why shouldn't she? Distance, she told herself. She had to maintain the proper distance. And speaking his given name aloud would shatter that.

"Yes, of course," her uncle replied. "Was something amiss that day?"

"No, at least nothing beyond the obvious reason we had been called there."

She paused. How could she ask what she wanted to know without appearing inquisitive beyond cordial curiosity? In truth, she couldn't. And if she admitted it to herself, her interest extended further than mere politeness. Might as well proceed.

"I could not help but notice the clothing Mr. Bradenton wore. It did not paint him as a common thief." She gestured in the general direction of the hall. "And even now, his clothing bears distinct evidence of tailoring." Grace shrugged in an attempt to downplay her inquiry. "It does make one wonder."

Uncle Richard inhaled a deep breath and moved around his desk to perch on its edge. He folded his arms and pressed his lips into a thin line then nodded. "Yes, yes. I can see why you would ask about that. And to be honest, I don't know a lot beyond what he said to us and the judge that day. He has been quite focused on his work since his arrival."

Oh well. There went that chance to discover a bit more about the enigmatic addition to their household staff. Perhaps she should quit now and pursue it another time. He would be there for two and a half more months. Surely she'd learn more before he left.

"All right," she replied. "I was merely curious, and I thought you might be the best one to ask."

"Under normal circumstances, you are right. I would. But Andrew came to us as a result of a unique situation. His work has been far above standard, and I suggest we leave it at that. We know all we need to know for the time being. If he wishes to share anything further, that will be entirely up to him."

"Of course." Grace nodded, even if she was disappointed her uncle couldn't provide anything else. "And again, I am sorry for the interruption."

"Again, no apology is necessary, Grace. You are welcome to speak with me anytime."

She stepped back toward the hall and placed her hand on the doorknob. "Would you like this closed?"

"Yes, please. Thank you."

"All right. I shall see you at supper then," she called as she pulled the door shut with a click.

That conversation hadn't gone as planned, and it made her even more determined to discover something else about Andrew. She might just have to come out and ask him herself. It was the least he could do for invading her thoughts as often as he did. And there was still that matter of an apology owed to her. Grace intended to collect.

⁂

Andrew shrank back against the wall, grateful for the dimly lit hall outside Mr. Baxton's study. He prayed Grace wouldn't notice him. And he received an immediate answer to that prayer as she proceeded again toward the entryway without a backward glance or pause in her steps. He waited until she turned the corner before releasing the breath he held.

He shouldn't have been eavesdropping on her conversation with her uncle, but when he'd returned with a message from the steward and heard her still in Mr. Baxton's study, he couldn't resist. So she wanted to know more about his background. He grinned. That meant she didn't find him as offensive as she attempted to make him believe. His next breath came out somewhere between a laugh and a snort.

Now he only had to decide if he wanted to cooperate or not. The latter seemed to be the more preferable choice.

Chapter 6

The balmy breeze blew through the doorway to the kitchen, making Andrew glance in that direction as he lifted the two vats of waste. Another day, another trip to the garbage barrels. Make that four trips. He glanced over his shoulder at the cook and maids bustling about. It must be baking day the way they all scampered to and fro like mice scavenging for food. And the cook barked orders loud enough for their neighbors across the way to hear.

In this atmosphere, Andrew appreciated the opportunity to escape. Then again, perhaps he should linger a bit more until they put all the ingredients together to produce their first dessert or confection. That might make the heat of the kitchen somewhat bearable. But when he didn't continue on his way, he received a threatening glare from the cook. On second thought, perhaps not.

He steadied the containers and stepped outside. Pausing, he lifted his face to the sun. The warmth seeped into his skin. He took a deep breath then exhaled. Even the ever-present stench of the excess food in the pails he carried didn't diminish the fresh air and sense of freedom from the confines of the house. How those women survived working for hours on end in that kind of heat in their layers upon layers of clothing, he didn't know. It made him grateful for the diversity of his work.

All right, enough lollygagging. His chores wouldn't finish themselves. Andrew shifted the weight of the buckets and started forward once more. As he passed below the veranda, a slight movement captured his attention. Shifting his gaze upward, he caught sight of Miss Baxton, perched on a cushioned lounge, her mouth set in a slight grin, her eyes half-closed, and her entire demeanor quite peaceful. She held a book in front of her which, from her expression, he could only assume entertained her rather well.

Miss Baxton chose that moment to look up from her reading and over in his direction. As her gaze drifted downward, Andrew knew the moment she saw him. Her body language changed. A frown marred her lips, her eyes narrowed, and her shoulders stiffened. He offered as much of a congenial smile as he could muster. She only nodded then quickly averted her eyes.

At least she'd acknowledged him. She could have pretended she hadn't seen him at all. But as Andrew made his way to the fence, he had a sense of someone watching him. Since he hadn't noticed anyone else, it had to be Miss Baxton. A grin tugged at the corner of his mouth. Raising the buckets higher, he threw back his shoulders and marched toward the barrels. With practiced ease, he emptied the contents at the same time, silently thanking God the waste actually hit its target instead of spilling all over the ground. That would have been fitting for his foolhardy attempt at showing off. But God chose to spare him the embarrassment. . .this time.

Pivoting on his heel, Andrew shoved his hands into the pockets of his pants, whistled an unnamed tune, and ambled toward the veranda. He kept his gaze away from Miss Baxton as he approached, but the moment he stepped to the edge of the stone terrace, he sought her out. To the casual observer, she seemed to be absorbed in her book. But he knew better.

"Good morning, Miss Baxton."

Nothing.

Andrew cleared his throat. "Good *morning*, Miss Baxton," he repeated.

With an exaggerated sigh, she looked up from her book and made direct eye contact. "Mr. Bradenton," she replied.

She should be in the theater on stage the way she masked her interest and pretended not to notice him. Then again, he was glad she didn't sit downwind of him, or she might have to speak to him from behind a handkerchief to protect her delicate nose. He resisted the urge to take a whiff of his clothes. They couldn't possibly smell as fresh as when he'd dressed that morning. Not after that task he'd just completed. Best to keep the focus on Miss Baxton, and off of him.

Andrew nodded at the book she held. "And what is that you're reading?"

She placed a ribbon marker in the book and closed it, glancing down at the cover. "If you must know, it is Mark Twain's *The Adventures of Huckleberry Finn*."

"Ah, yes. I read his story of Tom Sawyer a few years back. Quite a tale he tells about those boys."

Her eyes widened, and her lips parted. "You have read Mark Twain?"

He stepped onto the veranda and leaned against the railing, crossing his right ankle over his left. Andrew pretended to inspect the dirt under his fingernails and shrugged. "Of course. Why do you sound so surprised?" He pinned her with a stare. "You've read his books."

"Well, yes, but my aunt owns a bookshop, and my uncle possesses an extensive library. I do not exactly have a lack when it comes to a selection of literature with which to pass the time."

"And you don't think I also have access to a variety of books?"

"I. . .uh. . .that is. . ." She floundered for an appropriate response, and he forced himself not to smile. "That is not what I meant." She managed in a huff.

"So what did you mean?"

Yes, he baited her. But he couldn't resist.

Miss Baxton stuck her chin in the air just a bit but maintained eye contact. "I merely meant that I didn't expect someone like you to find books so entertaining that you would read something written by Twain."

"Someone like me?" He folded his arms across his chest. "Do you mean a thief or a servant? Or both perhaps?"

"Neither," she said without hesitation. "But rather someone who seems to prefer being out of doors instead of cooped up inside with a book."

Andrew withdrew his right hand and gestured in her direction. "You aren't inside *or* cooped up. And you're reading. There are many places where one can enjoy books."

"Point well taken."

"So I gather books are quite special to you. I've seen you in various places around the manor, seeming to enjoy the pastime."

Miss Baxton looked down at the book she held in her lap and caressed the cover. "Yes, I treasure each and every one. Have since I was a little girl." A faraway look appeared on her face. "They allow me to forget my troubles for a time and escape into another world. When I read these books, I can be anyone and go anywhere I please without concern."

Concern? Troubles? What kind of troubles could she possibly have living in a place like this, with servants tending to her every need and an uncle and aunt who doted on her like they did to their own son and daughter? For all appearances, she had everything a young lady her age could want.

"But none of these books I have are as special as the ones you stole from us and sold."

Andrew braced himself against the railing at the instant shift in her demeanor and the vengeful tone to her voice. Silent daggers shot from her eyes, and she pressed her lips into a thin line. Now how had that happened? How could she go from a melancholic state to one of anger and resentment in the span of mere seconds? And what in the world could he say in reply to that?

Choosing defeat, Andrew lowered his head and slumped his shoulders. He inhaled and released the breath slowly. "Yes, I know. And I cannot tell you how sorry I am for the distress I have caused both you and your aunt." He dared to meet her gaze again. "I wish there were some way I could make it up to you, for I know working for your uncle at the judge's orders doesn't even come close."

"No, it does not," she replied, the hard edge remaining. A moment later, she sat up straight and pressed her hands against the book in her lap, seeming to draw energy from it. "You break into our home, take what does not belong to you, and then you attempt to sell it all without any thought to the sentimental value of the items you stole." She paused only long enough to draw in a breath before laying into him again. "I will have you know the books inside that curio cabinet had been in our family for at least six generations. One of them belonged to my aunt's great-grandmother's great-grandmother. Aunt Charlotte spent more than a year attempting to locate it after learning it had mistakenly been borrowed from her shop." She looked away. "And now it's gone again, thanks to you."

Andrew couldn't be certain, but he thought he heard a soft sniffle and could just barely see a lone tear make its way down Miss Baxton's cheek. She kept her face averted though. When she reached for a handkerchief and dabbed at her nose, he knew. Andrew groaned in silence. A woman's tears were his undoing. Why did she have to show her vulnerability? Now he'd have to do something more to repay his debt. But what? Certainly not say anything more that might only upset her further.

With certain defeat and as much remorse as possible reflecting in his eyes, Andrew sighed. "Miss Baxton, I had no idea. And you are absolutely right. I thought only of myself and my own needs when I chose to do what I did. It amazes me you can even tolerate my presence in your home, much less actually acknowledge me when our paths cross. For that, I am grateful." He pushed away from the railing and stood tall, arms hanging straight at his sides. "But I promise," he began, and Miss Baxton again looked his way, "I will make it up to you."

With that, he turned and stepped off the veranda, not even giving her a backward glance or a chance to respond. Again he felt the heat of her stare burning into his back, but he didn't turn around. No, if he had to see her tear-filled eyes a second longer, he might be tempted to do something completely inappropriate. And that would seal his fate. He was in deep enough as it was. He didn't need to complicate matters further. Distance. Distance was the key.

❦

Grace watched Andrew walk away. So many words came to mind, and she hadn't uttered a single one. Instead, she'd chastised him and laid into him like a parent scolding a child for naughty behavior. Yes, he had caused a great deal of hurt to her and her aunt, but he had apologized, and he was serving his time, attempting to make amends. She wanted to take back her words, but it was too late.

Hadn't her aunt counseled her just that morning about the tongue being worse than a two-edged sword? Well, her sword had slashed through Andrew like the finest of sharpened steel. And that verbal wound had cut deep. His reaction made that quite clear. Grace really needed to heed her aunt's wisdom more, as well as the precepts in the scriptures. Perhaps then she wouldn't hurt Andrew again the way she just had.

Chapter 7

Grace paced back and forth in the sitting room, from the small table by the door to the fireplace against the far wall. At each turn, she stopped to rearrange the items on the table or stoke the fire. Then she crossed the room again.

"You are either going to wear that rug out clean through to the floor or you're going to put out the fire and bring a chill to this room." Aunt Charlotte spoke from her seat at the long table with Claire and Phillip, causing Grace to pause in her movements. "Or both. If you do either, you will be required to rectify it."

"I am sorry, Aunt Charlotte." Grace took a step closer to the trio. "I fear my mind is not at ease this morning, and my emotions are rather distraught."

"That much is obvious." Her aunt gave her a pointed glance. "But you are distracting your cousins from their studies. They are spending more time watching you than they are on the books in front of them."

Grace looked at Claire and Phillip, who sat sideways in their seats, their legs dangling and opposite arms draped across the backs of their chairs. Their rapt attention to her might be flattering under other circumstances. But not today.

"So," her aunt continued, "why are you remaining in this room instead of seeking out Mr. Bradenton to apologize?"

Grace snapped up her head to stare at her aunt. "How did you know?"

Charlotte pressed her lips into a thin line and tilted her head to the left, raising her eyebrows slightly. "I do have ears, my dear, and I am afraid you weren't exactly careful about how far your voice carried yesterday afternoon."

"Oh." If her aunt had heard, how many of the household staff had also been privy to that conversation? And with Andrew being one of the staff at present, if they heard her speak that way to him, would they also believe she might do the same to them?

"I can see you realize the mistake made. But what's more important is what you do about it."

"I will go find him right now."

Her aunt only nodded and said, "Very good," before returning her attention to her children.

Grace slipped from the room, careful not to distract her cousins any further. But as she stood in the foyer, she looked down the corridor toward the dining room; then she looked the other way toward her uncle's study. No sound came from either of those places, or anywhere else for that matter. Where would Andrew be at this time of day?

Well, the only way to find out would be to go searching for him. The manor wasn't too expansive, and the grounds could be covered in less than thirty minutes. Surely she'd find him somewhere. Feeling like an amateur sleuth, Grace ventured into every room she passed and peered around. Any servant in the room stopped their work and looked up when she appeared, asking if she needed anything. In light of yesterday's incident, was it any wonder? Before long they stopped asking and merely stared until she left. Oh, she had to undo the damage she'd done, and fast. Otherwise her entire relationship with the staff would be irreparably changed.

After twenty minutes only the scullery remained. Andrew couldn't possibly be in there. Could he? She'd hate to not look and later learn she'd missed him though. So she went outside to the exterior entrance and pushed open the door. Just like all the other rooms, the maids paused and looked up at her arrival. But one servant didn't.

"Mr. Bradenton!" Grace said before she could stop herself.

Andrew stopped scrubbing, but he didn't look at her. A muscle twitched in his cheek, and his breaths came slow and measured. As predicted, he remained either hurt or upset. Grace couldn't determine which. It could be both.

"Mr. Bradenton," she said again, only this time with more calm and control. "I am glad to have found you."

Still he kept his eyes downcast. Didn't he wonder why she'd sought him out? The two maids also present had no qualms about showing *their* curiosity. Not Andrew though. Grace would have preferred this conversation take place in private, but since she had yet to even garner Andrew's full attention, that possibility didn't exist. Very well. She would proceed anyway.

"You no doubt do not wish to hear from me, but I could not allow this to wait any longer."

Andrew looked as if he might actually glance up. Then, a moment later, he began scrubbing again. Perfect. Not only did he refuse to grant her eye contact, but now he had returned to his work, as if her presence didn't matter at all. He had been hurt by her words. Yes. She knew that. And she had hoped to remedy some of that now. Just not like this, feeling as if she had to work twice as hard to merely be heard. He wasn't going to make this easy. Truth be told, she likely wouldn't either, if she were in his shoes. Might as well get straight to the point.

"I confess," she continued, "this does not come easy to me, but I must beg your forgiveness for my deplorable behavior yesterday."

And still he scrubbed. Grace glanced around the serviceable room. It functioned as the location for all the washing, whether it be clothes, cooking items, or upholsteries and linens. With so much soap in great abundance, why bother scrubbing at all? Come to think of it, why was Andrew the one down on the floor? Didn't one of the maids usually do that? Could this be further punishment commanded by her uncle? Surely not. Uncle Richard wouldn't do something like that. Yet it would explain Andrew's unpleasant mood. What he did now would normally be done by a maid of the lowest ranking. No wonder he didn't want to look at her. He was no doubt embarrassed to be found in such a position.

"Mr. Bradenton. . .Andrew. . .please." Grace didn't want to beg, but she'd do what she must to be certain he heard her. "I am attempting to offer a sincere apology. The least you could do is acknowledge my presence."

Andrew mumbled something under his breath and kept moving the sudsy bristle brush back and forth across the floor.

"I beg your pardon, what did you say?"

He sighed. "It was nothing."

"It certainly did not sound like nothing to me." In fact, if she were to hazard a guess, Grace thought she heard something about maintaining dignity. She understood that in regard to his current chore, but not in regard to simple eye contact. How would looking at her be a slight against pride?

"Someone like you would never understand."

"I would like to." He seemed bound and determined to be difficult and uncooperative. And she only wanted to know why. How hard could it be to accept an apology and put it all behind him?

"No. You can't."

Grace crossed her arms. All right. Enough was enough. "I might be able to if you gave me half a chance."

She waited several moments for a reply. None came. Andrew merely remained on his knees, head bowed. Silent. Before she had a chance to say anything, the scrubbing began again. In a huff, Grace spun on her heels and left the scullery, stepping into the bright sun. Not even the harsh assault on her eyes affected her as much as Andrew's stubborn behavior. That man truly was insufferable. Well, she had said what she'd come to say. Whether he accepted her apology or not would be his choice.

Since she obviously wouldn't accomplish anything further at the house, she might as well summon Harriet and head to her aunt's bookshop. At least there she could attain a measure of success with the customers. And right now, she needed that.

&

"Oh, Grace. We're so glad you're here!"

Maureen fairly pounced on Grace immediately on arrival. Her longest friend, yet she lacked just a little in the area of decorum.

"Yes," Aunt 'Stasia chimed in with a grin from her position behind the front counter, "she has been waiting nearly an hour for you to arrive and talking almost as long."

"Now, that is not true, Anastasia, and you know it," Maureen countered, stomping one dainty foot. "You are just as anxious as I to hear it from Grace herself."

Grace gave them a halfhearted smile then took her time removing her wrap and hanging it on the hook by the front door. Next came her hat and gloves. Usually her aunt and friend could coax a genuine smile out of her in little or no time at all. But not today.

"All right." She made her way to the feature table near the counter and straightened a book that had been knocked over. "Now that I'm all the way inside, would one of you mind telling me what has you both so eager to speak with me?" Grace didn't exactly want to engage in a lengthy conversation, but she couldn't be rude either. "What is it you wish to hear?"

Maureen leaned forward and rested her elbows on the shelf on the other side of the counter. "First, why the long face?"

Grace picked up a random book, dusted the cover, examined the spine, and set it back down. Best to keep her response as vague as possible. She sighed. "I attempted to apologize to someone for something I said yesterday, and I'm afraid it wasn't received as well as I had hoped."

"This someone wouldn't happen to be a 'him,' would it?" Maureen nearly tipped the bookshelf in her eagerness. "Perhaps a certain new member of your servant staff?"

She should have known. In all the years she'd known Maureen, the young woman with freckles spattered across her nose had made it clear she was enamored with anything that had to do with the male species. And Aunt Charlotte had no doubt mentioned Andrew to her sisters. She shouldn't be surprised Maureen knew, too. News like that spread fast. Although it did strike her as odd that her youngest aunt wasn't more curious. She usually pounced on details such as this like a dog with a brand-new bone. Perhaps she knew more than she let on.

Grace attempted to come up with a way to share what had happened without identifying Andrew, but it was no use.

"So come on," Maureen pressed. "Don't hold back with all the details. We want to know everything!"

"Correction." Aunt 'Stasia stretched across the counter and poked Maureen with her index finger. "*You* want to know everything. I already know the basics and would be happy with just a little more."

"Oh, all right, Miss Priss." Maureen leveled a haughty glare at Anastasia. "*You* might not want to hear about this fascinating story, but *I* do." She straightened and gripped the edge of the bookshelf, barely able to contain her excitement. Her eyes held a decided gleam. A second or two later, Maureen's knuckles turned white. "Now, do tell. How did it all happen?"

So her aunt did know a little something. Grace shook her head and chuckled in spite of herself. She might not feel much like talking this morning, and the thought of time alone sounded rather appealing. Nevertheless, spending even five minutes with these two almost always bolstered her spirits.

"You don't have to share anything with her that you do not wish to share, Grace." Aunt 'Stasia narrowed her eyes at Maureen, who glared right back.

"Oh, please don't quarrel on my behalf." Grace raised her hands in a placating gesture. "I'll be more than happy to share what I can and answer any questions. I hate to disappoint you though. There truly is not much to tell."

Maureen folded her arms across her chest and stuck her chin in the air with a triumphant grin on her face. Anastasia rolled her eyes and returned her attention to the tally sheets in front of her, which marked their sales so far that day. Her aunt might appear uninterested, but Grace knew better. This was the woman who went out of her way to make matches of people who might otherwise never meet. She prided herself on seeing potential relationships where none previously existed. Between her and Maureen, Grace didn't stand a chance.

She picked up an apple from the basket on the counter and took a bite, savoring the sweet juices. After swallowing, she shifted to lean against the table behind her and settled back to describe her encounters with Mr. Andrew Bradenton. From their first meeting to the handful of brief conversations that followed, Grace shared enough to cover the essentials and ended with the episode from earlier that morning, but kept her retelling strictly factual. No sense borrowing trouble just yet. That would come soon enough, especially with these ladies involved.

"I can scarcely fathom having someone like him working under the very same roof where I sleep at night," Maureen remarked when Grace finished. "And the times your paths have crossed. I'm amazed you haven't done everything you could to avoid him." She took a step forward and rested one arm on the counter. "I know I would."

"Well, I can't exactly make it obvious that I don't wish to be in the same room with him," Grace replied, even if her words were far from the truth.

"Still. . ." Maureen's eyes lit up again, a sure sign of trouble. "There is a certain appeal to the knowledge that this Mr. Bradenton is being forced to work for your family to repay his debt. Then there is the matter of his obvious class position and tailored clothing. From the way you talk about him, I gather he is quite handsome, too."

And her friend had returned. The fanciful, daydreaming, obsessed-with-stories-of-romance friend. She could be rather trying at times, and her constant focus on the potential for amorous associations might be bothersome to most. But Grace wouldn't have it any other way.

Aunt 'Stasia waved her hand to get Grace's attention. "So will you attempt to speak with him again? Perhaps to be sure he accepts your apology?"

"I don't know." Grace twisted the apple she held and watched the light reflect off its shiny skin. "I suppose I should, if for no other reason than to be certain any harm done is repaired."

"Oh yes," Maureen added. "Don't even consider the possibility that he might be the prince of your dreams or something remotely similar, Miss Practical." Maureen waved her hand in dismissal as she straightened and picked up a stack of books in need of shelving. "Do me a favor though. If you spoil your chances with this gentleman, please cease from informing me about it. I only wish to hear a report of your time with him if the discussions go well."

Aunt 'Stasia shuffled a few steps to her left and leaned over the counter toward Grace. "Pay her no mind. You do what you feel you have to do." She reached out and placed a reassuring hand on Grace's arm. "And regardless of whether or not Maureen wishes to hear of your future encounters with this gentleman, you can always come find me if you're in need of someone to listen."

Grace gave her aunt an appreciative smile. "Thank you. I will be certain to tell you both what happens." She glanced at the large clock on the wall. "Now, we should all get some work done before the day disappears without us."

Once settled into the routine tasks at the bookshop, Grace couldn't get her mind off Andrew. She had managed to push him somewhat to the back of her mind on the carriage ride to the shop, but thanks to Maureen's romantic fantasies, Andrew now occupied her thoughts fully. What was she going to do? Both her friend and her aunt would be sure to follow up on this presumed or potential relationship. And they would want to know more about Andrew's background. But how would she find out something like that? She couldn't just walk up to him and ask him about it.

Then again, why couldn't she?

Chapter 8

"You are coming to the shipping office and docks today, Andrew." Mr. Baxton's no-nonsense voice sounded from the other side of the door Andrew was repairing. "Meet me in the front hall at half past eight."

Andrew leaned back on his haunches to peer around the door, but Baxton had disappeared. The man didn't leave any room for a response. Then again, since he had issued a command and not a request, a reply wouldn't be necessary. At least not one he would expect, anyway.

So the shipyard would be his destination today. Andrew resumed tightening the hinges and pictured it all in his mind. He had traveled the Delaware River a handful of times on business for the mill, but most of his work ended up with him holding the reins and driving a cart or wagon full of supplies. Once in a while, he ventured to Baltimore or Philadelphia via train. But the main port in Wilmington? The grand ships, the merchant tradesmen, the sailors. So many different people coming and going. He could hardly wait to leave.

A glance over his shoulder at the clock on the wall showed he had forty minutes until the instructed meeting time. Might as well finish the door and maybe get the repairs finished on that bench in the hall. He'd have to meet Mr. Baxton there. Early would be best. And if he was there, that wouldn't be a problem.

Thirty-five minutes later, Mr. Baxton came into the front hall from his study. "Ah, good. You're here already. Excellent." He nodded to Harrison, who held out his coat and top hat. "Shall we go then?"

"I'm ready."

"I have already called for the carriage, sir," Harrison said in his drone voice. "It should be waiting outside momentarily."

"Thank you, Harrison."

Like his niece, Baxton gave the butler direct eye contact, not merely the cursory nod. It said so much about the man and his relationship with those who served him. Harrison opened the door for them both, and as Andrew passed the butler, he looked him straight in the eye.

"Thank you," Andrew said with a nod.

Harrison didn't reply, but Andrew didn't expect a response. The butler did show a minor reaction in his eyes though. Just enough for Andrew to know his actions had an effect. Technically, he ranked lower than the butler, but that wouldn't be forever. This could be a new way of handling things, and it could make quite a difference with the servants at his father's home. Yes. He would do it. He would make the effort to treat them all better, no matter their station.

Once settled inside the carriage, Andrew admired the plush seats and custom craftsmanship on the interior. In fact, it looked rather familiar. He glanced at the small plate just below the window in the door. GREGG & BOWE FINE CARRIAGES. A rather prominent Philadelphia company that had expanded down to Wilmington as well. Yes, he thought he recognized their work. His own father used the same company.

Baxton plopped his top hat on the seat beside him, flipped open the day's issue of *The Morning News*, and settled back against his seat. Andrew supposed he should do the same, but he couldn't relax. What had made Baxton change his mind all of a sudden and assign him somewhere other than the manor? And would it be the same as his work so far? Emptying waste, scrubbing, and doing minor repairs?

Andrew looked across at Baxton. Engrossed in the paper, the man didn't look like he'd be talking anytime soon. That left the passing scenery to occupy Andrew's attention as they traveled to the southeast, toward the river junctures. And that meant it would be a long ride.

Without even glancing up from whatever he read, Baxton suddenly folded the paper and tucked it under his arm. A few seconds later, the carriage slowed and came to a stop.

"We are here," was all Baxton said before stooping to exit the carriage.

How had he known if he hadn't been paying attention or watching the landmarks they'd passed as Andrew had done? Sure, he no doubt traveled this route often, but no one could know a path that well, could they? Amazing.

The faint brackish air and the smell of marshland hit Andrew's nose. Why hadn't he smelled that until now? He'd been watching out the window the entire time. They didn't live too far from the river, but the slight change of scenery from the residential and business district to the waterways was usually hard to miss. His mind was definitely somewhere else.

Left with no other choice but to follow in Baxton's wake, Andrew stepped down from the carriage and rushed along the uneven cobblestones to walk just a step behind him. A few seagulls let loose with their distinct calls, and the faint sound of water lapping at the shore reached his ears. After about a minute Baxton spoke again.

"You no doubt are wondering why I've brought you here today."

Yes, that was exactly what Andrew wanted to know.

"Well, it has been one month since you started working for us, and I figured it was about time to give you a more meaningful task." Baxton glanced over his shoulder with a pointed stare. "Mind you, I did not have to do this. You know as well as I that the judge left the specifics of your sentencing up to my discretion."

How well Andrew knew that. He had to remind himself of it almost every day, but especially when his tasks bordered on something a young page could do.

"But," Baxton continued, facing forward again and never once breaking his stride, "you have demonstrated exemplary dedication and thoroughness in everything you have done, no matter the work. Do not think it has gone unnoticed." He clasped his hands behind his back. "For that, I am grateful." Then he unclasped them and slowed his stride.

Andrew eased his pace as well, careful not to walk ahead. He didn't know where he was going anyway, so he *had* to follow Baxton.

"Mrs. Baxton and I have spoken at length about this, and she agrees with my decision. We both feel you should have the opportunity to work here at the shipyard as well. Being cooped up inside so long isn't good for a man, particularly one who is no stranger to the out-of-doors."

Well, Baxton had that part right. Andrew had spent a great deal of time working in the sun at the mill. His skin no doubt showed that. And unlike the genteel ladies around him, the telltale marks of sun weren't a definitive sign of the lower classes. Not that it mattered to Baxton. Andrew was still a servant, and who he was before he stole was inconsequential.

"With that being said"—Baxton paused and swept his left arm outward in an arc—"I give you Hannsen & Baxton Shipping."

Andrew stepped forward to be even with the brick archway covering the path where they stood. His eyes widened. Laid out before him stood an impressive sentinel of ships of varying lengths and designs. Several barques, a handful of clippers, a flyboat or two, a collier, three fishing smacks, some schooners and brigantines, a windjammer, and a trawler. Andrew clenched and unclenched his fists. He leaned forward on his toes and rocked back on his heels. His breaths came in shorter spurts.

Baxton chuckled. "I see you are a man after my own heart." He clapped Andrew on the back. "So I was not mistaken in my estimation of your interests. You will do much better here than at the manor." With a random wave of his hand, he added, "The work you've been doing is better left to the household staff anyway. You? I have far more challenging tasks in mind."

Andrew didn't know if that should excite or concern him. For now, he'd tread lightly. . .at least until he knew for certain what Baxton would have him do.

"So," Baxton said as he clapped his hands and held them together, "shall we get started?"

Andrew shrugged. "I'm at your service, sir."

"Very well. We shall begin at the main office here in port."

With that, Baxton led the way to a nondescript brick building with the company's name emblazoned on a shingle hanging over the main door. It sat just to the left of a larger three-story brick building with the same name on a large metal plate near the roof. That must be where the smaller manufacturing work took place. Once inside, the layout and overall appearance reminded Andrew of his father's mill office farther up the Brandywine. As Baxton explained the roles of each person working in the office, Andrew's mind drifted.

"You will be overseeing the staff here in the office," his father had told him the day he'd promoted him to a supervisory role. "Choose each individual carefully. It's essential to have a team whose strengths and weaknesses complement each other. Otherwise, the efficiency is at risk and so is the productivity."

And Andrew had done just that. It had meant reassigning two workers to other areas of the mill, but the end result far outweighed the brief bump in the road of adjustment to the new order of things. Now, as he listened to Baxton report on the operation of the shipping office, Andrew realized this man and his partners utilized a similar practice.

"This shipping company has been in my family for well over one hundred years. We are second only to Harlan & Hollingsworth Company, with J. A. Harris Shipyard running a close third to our industry's output. Mrs. Baxton's family has a similar lineage going back six generations. One of her great-grandfathers was in the British Royal Navy." He smiled, more to himself than at Andrew. "I, too, have direct ties to Britain. We are grateful our ancestors eventually switched their allegiance to the Patriots, or this company might not exist today."

"I can well understand that," Andrew replied. "For a company thriving on trade and industry, loyalty to the United States would have been essential, especially once the British pulled out their support. Now it's not such a significant element, but following the War for Independence, it would have been critical."

"Exactly." Baxton nodded, seemingly impressed with his response. "We merged with my wife's family company about four years ago. It's been quite the experience getting operations running smoothly and adjusting to the new branches of shipbuilding and manufacturing."

"I can imagine." So that explained how the company increased its holdings so fast. He'd heard reports but hadn't been involved in business and trade as extensively in recent months.

"It's a good thing the visions of the two companies aligned," Baxton continued, "or the merger might not have been successful."

"Yes. My father owns Diamond State Mills, and he merged with another mill not long ago to acquire the manufacturing of jute, yarns, and twine, in addition to the rifle powder and millinery supplies they specialized in up to that point." Andrew wasn't sure how much to reveal, but Baxton no doubt knew of his family at this point anyway. He didn't get to be in charge of a successful shipping company without connections and knowledge. "Stepping into unfamiliar territory is always an adjustment. You have to love what you do and respect your employees to make it work."

"Let us just say," Baxton said as they paused by a rear door, "shipping seems to be in our blood, flowing strong and vital. Even as a new era dawns with the increased appearance of steamships and iron hulls, we will remain dedicated to keeping our company thriving, no matter the cost."

Andrew didn't have anything to say to that. He didn't feel it was his place either. For some reason, Mr. Baxton had decided to provide him with a great deal of background information that didn't seem necessary. They ambled down toward the river's edge, where a flurry of activity could be seen on board several of the ships. With them docked, the normal crew wouldn't be present. But the skeleton crews who made certain the ships stayed in excellent condition would always be there. Baxton's ships stood like beacons in port, beckoning to all who gazed on them and signaling that the owners took great pride in their property.

Shouts rang out, commands floated on the air, and the few crew members on deck scrambled to heed the orders. Every man knew his duty, and he did it without complaint. In fact, they seemed to thrill to the task. Was it any wonder? Men didn't sign up to work on board a ship if they didn't love it. Andrew gazed up as they came to the river's edge. He shaded his eyes from the morning sun, now about midway in the eastern sky. Seagull screeches fused with human voices in a cacophony of sounds. The port was alive with activity, and Andrew could hardly wait to get started.

"As you can see"—Baxton again reined in Andrew's focus—"we keep most of our ships here near the mouth of the Christina. But some of them are docked across the way at Helms Cove." He pointed through the narrow view between two ships.

Although the width of the Delaware River made it impossible to see clearly to the other side, Andrew knew of the cove. He'd been on a ship once that had sailed from there farther south down the river toward the bay and ocean.

Baxton signaled to a man who had just come down off one of the ships and now headed their way. "I would like to introduce you to the man who will be overseeing your work here with the ships."

When the man stood a yard away, Baxton made the introductions.

"James Woodruff, I'd like you to meet Andrew Bradenton." Baxton turned his shoulders to include Andrew, but he didn't look at him. Instead, he kept his eyes focused on James. "Andrew, this is James. Should you have any questions at all, or should you need to report the completion of a task, you are to come see him."

James extended a hand. "Mr. Baxton has already told me about you. I'm looking forward to seeing what you can do with some of these beauties."

Andrew hesitated a fraction of a second before he took the proffered hand and gave it a firm shake. "And I'm looking forward to the challenge."

James held his gaze a moment longer than what Andrew felt necessary, and if he read it right, there was a distinct narrowing of the eyes coupled with a silent animosity, although on a minimal level. Not that he hadn't grown accustomed to looks like that in the month he'd been serving his sentence. He *was* a thief after all, and that invariably caused suspicion in anyone who met him for the first time, especially if his crime had preceded that introduction.

Still, if Baxton could trust him enough to tend to his ships, the man must have seen something worthwhile. Andrew didn't know how to deal with that though. He could handle being treated like the criminal he now was. But his benefactor had deemed him ready for something more. That alone made him determined to avoid making a mistake. . .any mistake. . .that might send him back to the manor. Then again, a rather charming young lady remained back there. And that put him in a quandary.

Accept the tasks Baxton had for him here at the shipyard and surrender the chance of crossing paths with Miss Baxton, or return to the manor and the mundane work of household staff simply to be near her. Andrew couldn't decide which held greater appeal.

Chapter 9

Grace perched on the edge of the seat cushion inside the carriage. She shifted back and forth to get a good view out the side window. The briny air coupled with the faint call of seagulls and geese started her legs bouncing and her feet tapping on the carriage's floor. Harriet sat calmly on the seat opposite her. How could she not be affected? After being confined to the manor more this past winter than at any other time of year, Grace wanted to jump out right now and run the rest of the way. But she wouldn't. Someone might see her. What would people think?

And what if Andrew happened to be here? She didn't want to admit that possibility was half of her reason for telling her aunt she'd come today. He'd been gone from the manor for less than three days, yet despite his boorish behavior when last they spoke, Grace missed seeing him. If he was somewhere visible, she didn't need to make a fool of herself.

The *clip-clop* of the horses' hooves slowed to a dirgelike pace. How much farther? Had this part of the journey always taken this long? Grace peered out the window again, attempting to determine the reason for the delay. A rather angry pair of voices reached her ears a moment later.

"This is entirely your fault," one voice stated, his words punctuated with annoyance. "And don't try to tell me otherwise."

"My fault?" the other voice replied. "This wouldn't have happened if you had been more careful with that oversized wagon of yours."

"And my wagon wouldn't have been in your way if you had taken the path meant for carts like yours." Grace saw an arm extend into her view as one of the men pointed. "Over there. On the other side of the stone wall."

"I have a right to be here, same as you or anyone else," the second man said.

"Yes," the first man replied, "but you don't have a right to protest or complain when a wagon upsets your cart because you were driving it on the path meant for larger delivery wagons."

Grace scooted closer to the door and stuck her head out the window. Her driver turned in his seat to look back at her.

"We shall be through this in just a few minutes, Miss Baxton. I am sorry for the delay."

She waved off his apology. "No worries, Matthew. You could not possibly have foreseen this happening." And unfortunately, neither could she, or she *would* have jumped out of the carriage much sooner. Now she could only wait.

"We aren't going to get anywhere arguing over who was at fault more," the second voice continued. "But could you at least help me get my cart right side up again so I can put my fruits and vegetables back in it?"

"Why should I help you? I wasn't in the wrong here."

Grace could imagine the first man standing there, arms crossed, looking down his nose at the other man. She hadn't seen the accident, but from the sounds of things, the second man shouldn't have been there. Still, the first likely could have avoided it if he had been more careful with his driving. So, in a way, they were both to blame. And that meant both should set the cart right once more.

"You're just going to stand there and watch?" the second man asked.

"Seems like a good idea to me," the first replied.

Grace had had enough. They would get nowhere at this rate. And that river beyond beckoned to her. She turned the handle to the door and pushed it open. Gathering her skirts close, she placed one foot on the step and descended from the carriage. Heedless of propriety or her uncle's standing caution to remain in the carriage until the footman deemed it safe for her, Grace marched right up to the two men. She stepped around scattered oranges, apples, broccoli spears, and heads of lettuce in her path.

The two men halted their argument when she came into view and turned to stare. They looked her up and down, and one man ran his beefy hand across the two days' growth on his jaw. A lascivious look entered his eyes. Grace forced back a shiver. Based on where he stood, that had to be the first man she'd heard, the one who refused to help in any way.

"Pardon me, but would it be possible for you two gentlemen to remedy this situation at a speedier pace? I have a message to deliver to my uncle, and my driver and I need to pass."

"Need to see your uncle, do you?" He raised his eyebrows, and his tongue snaked out to wet his lips. "Maybe we can escort you to him then. It wouldn't take long."

"Aw, come on, Jensen. Leave the lady be, will you? She's only trying to get to where she's going."

The smaller man wore an apron over his clothes, and his shirtsleeves were rolled to his elbows. His receding hairline and bushy eyebrows reminded her of the butcher near her aunt's bookshop. At least Grace didn't have to deal with two ill-mannered men.

The man called Jensen whipped around to face the other man. "You shut your mouth, Lucas." He slowly turned back to Grace. "I'm only trying to be... hospitable...to the lady."

He'd had to search for *that* word. Under normal circumstances, his attempt at more refined speech would have made Grace smile. But his uncouth behavior ruled that out.

"Well, she doesn't need your hospitality," Lucas retorted. "She needs to see her uncle. And if you would help me, we could get this mess cleaned up so she could be on her way."

"I'll even give you a hand."

Grace jumped a little at Matthew's voice coming from just over her right shoulder. She hadn't even heard him jump down from his perch in front of the carriage. The two men also regarded him with instant wariness.

"Miss Baxton," Matthew said, lightly touching her arm, "why don't you wait in the carriage. I promise we'll have this all cleared away in a jiffy."

Jensen and Lucas looked back and forth from Matthew to Grace. A small smile tugged at the corner of her lips. Jensen's demeanor had changed the second he'd noticed Matthew. And for good reason, too. Her driver wasn't exactly lacking in size, and he could present an imposing presence when he so desired. Grace turned to leave but paused when Jensen inhaled a sharp breath and his eyes widened.

"Wait a minute," he said, holding up his right hand in a staying gesture. "Did you say Baxton? As in Hannsen & Baxton Shipping right here at the river?" He swallowed slowly, his Adam's apple bobbing once. "So your uncle is Richard Baxton?"

"Yes," Grace replied. "Yes, he is."

Jensen straightened and immediately spun toward the upset cart. "I am terribly sorry, miss. Forgive us for keeping you from your business." He grabbed hold of the cart and, with Matthew's help, set it right once more. Then he reached for whatever items he could find near his feet and dumped them in the back of the cart.

Lucas stood watching, his mouth open. Matthew took a step back and waited near the horses. A few seconds later, Lucas stooped to retrieve his goods from the ground around his own feet. But Jensen worked much faster. In less than two minutes, the obstruction had been cleared and all items returned to the cart.

Jensen approached and paused in front of Grace. With a slight bow, he also lowered his head. "Again, please forgive the delay. I was on my way to Baxton's shipyard when this whole accident happened." He made direct eye contact once more, all evidence of carnal thought eradicated from his expression. In its place, only veiled respect remained. "If I can help in any other way, I will be happy to do so."

The man's instant change in demeanor surprised Grace. He obviously knew her uncle, or at least knew *of* him, enough so that the mere mention of her uncle's name sent the man into immediate obedience. It happened often, especially here at the shipyard. But that didn't make Jensen's behavior any less inappropriate, simply because he'd tried to save face the moment he'd heard the name Baxton. Nevertheless, it wasn't her place to chastise him for it.

"Thank you, Mr. Jensen." Grace held out her hand, and Jensen accepted it briefly with another bow. "But that will not be necessary. I appreciate your offer though. Thank you for resolving this state of disorder so promptly."

"My pleasure, miss," Jensen replied, taking a step back.

"Have a nice day, Miss Baxton," Lucas called, his hand raised with two fingers and a thumb up in a minor wave.

Grace nodded. "Matthew," she called over her shoulder, "I believe I'm ready to finish the drive to our destination now."

Beyond ready, actually. Grace returned to the carriage and accepted Matthew's assistance inside. If Jensen thought enough of her uncle to change his actions so abruptly, Uncle Richard should know about the incident. It might change his dealings with Jensen, or at the very least make him speak to the man.

A few short minutes later, Matthew stopped the carriage again and hopped down to help Grace out.

"Thank you," she said and waited for him to close the door. "I shouldn't be too long inside, but if that changes, I will be sure to send someone out to notify you."

"Very good, miss," Matthew replied. He moved to stand next to the horses then stretched his arms overhead and brought them down to twist to the left and right.

Grace rolled her shoulders a little, feeling the slight stiffness from the ride. She didn't have the luxury of working out the kinks though. Not here in public anyway. Perhaps the walk along the river to her uncle's office would ease the aches.

She made her way down the cobblestone path toward the brick archway that served as a gateway of sorts to the riverfront. She stood under the arch and breathed in the distinct pungent scent of the river. Grace always thrilled to the unique aroma. It didn't possess the same appeal as the salty sea air of the ocean farther south, but it held its own regardless. With the abundance of bass, herring, carp, and trout, along with the various waterfowl feeding on those fish, and the constant movement of the shipyards or merchant trade, the river never lacked for activity. Compared to life at the manor, the river teemed with excitement.

"Hey! Bradenton!" A voice boomed down a few hundred feet from where Grace stood, and she looked that direction. "Get that sail secured then come help me sift this powder and clean out the cannons."

Grace shielded her eyes and scanned the ships for sight of Andrew. Her eyes hopped from person to person working on board the ships until she finally spotted Andrew's familiar form two ships away. He had just lowered the main sail and now rolled it on top of the boom. Like all the other workers and sailors, he wore a pullover cotton shirt with dropped shoulders and full sleeves to allow for freedom of movement. The cream color suited his skin tone, and it was tucked into a pair of beige canvas trousers, held up with a set of Y-back braces. His gray wool tweed cap reminded Grace of Jesse from their stables. Andrew sure knew how to blend in with everyone. And he did it quite well.

The piercing *cheereek* of an osprey leaving its nest and taking to flight drew Grace's attention overhead. The brownish-black raptor spread its impressive wings and flew over the ships toward the river, its keen eyes scouting the water for a fresh catch. As soon as it disappeared from her sight, Grace returned her attention to the ship where Andrew worked.

Even from this distance, she took note of his broad shoulders and the way his muscles flexed as he tied the knot around the sail and boom. He cut a rather impressive figure, and warmth crept into Grace's cheeks at her scandalous appraisal. What would her aunt say if she were here to witness her niece behaving in such a manner?

"Bradenton! Let's get moving. The day won't wait forever."

That same booming voice called out, and Andrew finished securing his knot with a deft yank. He stood and stretched, much like Matthew had, only Grace found Andrew's actions far more compelling.

"On my way!" Andrew called in return. Then, as if he sensed her staring, he turned and looked right at her.

Grace startled, but she couldn't look away. Heat raced up her neck and lapped at her cheeks. Despite the expanse of space between them, his gaze held her captive. A slow smile spread across his lips. At closer proximity, Grace was certain a distinct twinkle would be in his eyes as well. She had to break the trance. Somehow. But her body refused to cooperate. Then he raised a hand to wave, and she shook free from the invisible ties.

Away. She must get away. Ah, yes. Her uncle's office. She had a message for him. The perfect excuse to flee from this embarrassing moment. With haste, she spun on her heel, stumbling and catching herself before she fell. Grace dared not look back over her shoulder for fear that Andrew might still be watching.

"Ah, Grace." Uncle Richard looked up from the desk where he leaned, going over some papers his receptionist held. "What brings you to the office today?"

Good. She didn't have to wait to see to her main purpose for this visit. Waiting would only leave her mind to wander to Andrew and the incident from a moment ago.

"I have a message from Aunt Charlotte." Grace reached into her reticule to retrieve the folded note. "She said she didn't need a response until you returned home this evening."

Her uncle reached out for the note. "Very good. Thank you."

Grace looked around the front room of the office. Nothing had changed since last autumn, not even the staff who worked there. And there was something comforting in the familiar. The familiar didn't come with any surprises, and it certainly didn't cause any embarrassing situations.

Just then the door opened and in walked Andrew. Grace averted her eyes and focused first on the sofas and chairs nearby, then on the scenic painting hanging over the waiting area. Anywhere but at the man who'd made fiery heat a consistent temperature on her face three times already that day.

"Andrew." Uncle Richard acknowledged his entrance. "Finished with the cannons already?"

"No, sir," Andrew replied, and Grace glanced at him from the corner of her eye. "We will likely be working on those most of the afternoon. Sifting the powder, too." He stepped closer. "I have a progress update from James though. He asked me to bring it directly to you." Andrew reached into the patch pocket on his shirt and handed the note to Uncle Richard.

"So," her uncle said as he took the note and read the scribbled words, "It appears you're having a rather successful day thus far. Impressive." He nodded. "I appreciate the report. Seems the good weather has been in your favor."

"Yes. The clear blue skies and minimal wind have made securing sails and airing out the gunpowder a rather simple feat." He turned his head to look in her direction. "And the view is undeniably riveting."

For a fourth time her cheeks flamed, and Grace jerked her face away from anyone who might see her. This had to stop. Someone might think she was ill with the constant flush.

"I won't argue with you there," her uncle replied, completely oblivious to

Andrew's concealed reference to her staring. "It's impressive from the ground, but from the deck of a ship? Thrilling!"

"Well, I had best get back to work or they might wonder about the delay in my return. Good day, sir." Again Grace peered at him. Andrew bowed to her uncle and turned toward her. "Miss Baxton." His voice held a hint of mirth as he tipped his cap in her direction. "Always a pleasure."

And with that he was gone. The door clicked closed behind him, leaving Grace to stare at the space he'd just occupied. She swallowed several times and wet her lips, praying her face had returned to some semblance of a normal color. Good thing Andrew hadn't engaged her beyond those few words. She likely wouldn't have been able to produce a reply. At least not one that would make any sense. And she didn't babble. Not for any reason or anyone.

"Grace," her uncle asked, "are you going to stand there and stare at the door all afternoon, or was there some other reason you've come here today?"

Grace spun to face her uncle. "No, Uncle Richard. I only came to give you Aunt Charlotte's note. I've done that. So now I believe I will take a walk along the river."

He nodded. "Just be sure Harriet remains with you at all times." Her uncle signaled to one of his clerks. "And I shall alert James to your intentions, so he can keep a watchful eye as well. You can never be too careful."

"Thank you, Uncle." Grace didn't relish the thought of having more than one chaperone, but her uncle was right. After the encounter she'd had prior to her arrival, she must remain cautious. She started to head for the door then stopped with her hand on the knob. "Oh! Uncle Richard. I almost forgot." She turned to face him again.

"Yes?"

"There was a man I met on my way here, just before Matthew dropped off Harriet and me at the walkway. Some altercation involving a wagon and a cart. But the man's name was Jensen, and he said he was on his way to meet you."

"Jensen? Yes, I know of him." Her uncle gave her his undivided attention. "What about him?"

How would she tell this without implicating herself too much? "Well, he wasn't the most mannerly of men upon first introductions. But when he learned who I was. . .or more importantly who *you* were, his entire demeanor changed." Grace shrugged. "I thought you would like to know."

Uncle Richard narrowed his eyes and peered at her for several moments, as if weighing the truth of her story. "We'll speak on this more when I return home this evening. I have a feeling there is more than you are telling me. But thank you for what you *have* said." He nodded toward the door. "Now, I believe you have a walk to take?"

Grace said her good-byes and left the office. Harriet hung back several paces, close enough to be there if needed but far enough away to give Grace some privacy. And she desperately needed it. Her thoughts had remained on Andrew the entire time she'd stood in her uncle's office. Now that she walked alone, the memory of Andrew catching her staring returned full force.

Just a few days ago, he'd been less than cordial, bordering on impolite. Today he'd had the audacity to grin like a rake at her and even make a veiled reference to the incident in her uncle's presence. Then there was the twinkle in his eye as he'd tipped his hat and left. It was enough to drive her mad. Grace inhaled the familiar scents of the river, already relishing the invigorating breaths she could take. Yes, this walk would do her a world of good toward clearing her head.

Chapter 10

G race?"
Uncle Richard called to her from his office, so she filed the current folder she held, shut the drawer, and stepped into the other room.
"Yes, sir?"

"Would you do me a favor?" He consulted a spreadsheet of sorts on the desk in front of him, but she couldn't make out the heading at the top. A second later, he looked up at her. "Would you walk down to the ships and fetch Andrew for me? Tell him I need to speak with him as soon as he's available."

"You wish Andrew to come here? Why not speak with him down at the dock?" This had to be something of great import. She hoped he hadn't done anything to upset her uncle.

"Because what I have to say to him is best said without other listening ears."

Grace tilted her head just a little to the right. Her uncle didn't give an indication if the upcoming conversation would be serious or a run-of-the-mill topic. And it wasn't her place to ask. That didn't stop the questions though. Why didn't he want anyone else to overhear him? How would here at his office be any different than his study at home? Or even in the carriage ride home, since Andrew rode with him each day? Both of those would afford him the privacy he sought. And what made him ask *her* to go find Andrew? Why not one of his clerks?

"I would like to speak with him sooner rather than later, Grace." His voice held a hint of amusement.

"Oh!" She shook her head. Best to not ruminate too much with her uncle watching. "I am sorry, Uncle Richard." She placed one hand on the doorframe. "I will go straightaway to find him for you."

"Thank you."

He returned his attention to the spreadsheet in front of him, picking up a pencil to make some additional notations. Grace turned in a slow arc. She wouldn't get anything further from her uncle at this point. Perhaps afterward he would be more inclined to answer some of her questions. . .at least the ones she'd be permitted to ask.

"Harriet, I'll only be a few minutes," she said to her maid who rose from her seat. "No need for you to join me."

Grace grabbed her satin bonnet from the coatrack by the door and looped the ties beneath her chin as she stepped outside. She squinted and blinked a few times as her eyes adjusted to the bright light of the sun. If she could, she'd be outside more often. She walked down the path toward the docks. Aunt Charlotte would never approve of so much time spent being exposed to the sun. Grace touched the chiffon ties, wishing she could have left the bonnet inside. From what her uncle told her, she'd inherited her mother's wanderlust spirit. Her father had been content to remain cooped up behind a desk. But not her mother, and not her uncle. And certainly not her.

"Afternoon, Miss Grace." One of the swabbies tipped his hat to her as she passed.

"Good afternoon, Henry." She smiled at one of the few crewmen she knew by name, a man whose wife would be delivering a new baby any day now. "Are you and Clara still praying for a little boy?"

"Yes'm, we are." He leaned on the pole end of the mop he held and grinned. "With them three girls we got, it'd be nice to have a boy to give them what for and help me keep them in line." Henry swayed a little closer to her. "And I wouldn't mind learning him a trade right here with the ships neither."

"No, I do not imagine you would." Grace nodded. "Passing on a legacy is a fine and admirable dream, Henry. You keep praying. I know the Lord is listening."

"Yes'm. I know He is, too." He straightened and assumed a more down-to-business expression. "Now, is you here for a walk, or do you gots business from Mr. Baxton?"

Ah, good. She might save some time if Henry could assist her. "Actually, Henry, I am on an errand for my uncle. He needs to speak to Mr. Bradenton as soon as possible. Might you know where I could locate him?"

"Sure do." He pointed. "He be down there on that collier yonder, about five docks down."

Grace looked in the direction he'd indicated. She couldn't make out any individual worker from this distance, but if Henry saw him there, Andrew would be there.

"Thank you, Henry. You have saved me a great deal of time."

Henry tipped his rather worn slouch hat. "My pleasure, Miss Grace."

She took a few steps toward the collier then heard Henry call out to her.

"I'll be sure and tell you bouts the baby when he or she gets here."

Grace raised one hand in acknowledgment and continued walking. She glanced up at each ship she passed. As usual, the smaller crew retained while the ships were in port all bustled about, seeing to their duties. It never ceased to amaze her that a single ship would require so much work when it wasn't even sailing. But her uncle had told her about the need for keeping the deck swabbed, the cabins below free of moisture, rats, and other vermin, and the anchor free of barnacles. Then they had to check the tackle, repair the cables, examine the rigging, and tend to any necessary repairs on board to make certain the ship continued to be seaworthy. No wonder some men could say they spent every day of the year on board a ship.

And no wonder her uncle had employed Andrew here at the shipyard rather than back at the manor. His skills seemed far more suited to this work than the everyday tasks back home. It took a lot of work to maintain her uncle's impressive fleet, and Uncle Richard no doubt capitalized on Andrew's sentence and his strength to benefit the most from both.

Grace stopped at the ship she hoped was the collier Henry had pointed out. Yes. No doubt about it. She'd found the right ship. Blackened sails from the coal dust, no ornamentation, and no figurehead. She could only imagine the travails of sailing on such a vessel. When she sailed, she primarily spent her time on board the *Amethyst*, one of her uncle's merchant ships. This ship spent most of its time sailing the Chesapeake and transporting the coal from the Virginia mines. Cleaning it would take days. And how could the crewmen ever keep from getting the dust all over them?

She looked up to the bow of the ship and had the answer. They didn't. A giggle escaped her lips, and she covered her mouth with her hand. Andrew dumped a bucket of black water over the port bow then raised one arm to swipe it across his forehead, smearing the layer of grime and dust and leaving a track where his sleeve had touched. With the sun beating down from overhead, the heat likely made the working conditions quite unpleasant. But Andrew presented such a comical image, Grace couldn't hold back the laughter.

Andrew paused midway to bringing the bucket back over the rail and looked down. When he spotted her, he grinned, his teeth standing out even more in the middle of a blackened face.

"I have a message for you," she called, raising her voice just enough to be heard but not enough to draw unwanted attention.

He signaled for her to wait, and a moment later, he made his way toward the gangplank leading from the ship to the dock. Andrew jogged down it and leaped the remaining distance when he had almost reached the end. In no time at all, he stood opposite her, coal dust covering every visible part of him.

Again laughter bubbled up from within, and she tried to stifle it. No such luck. She covered her mouth a second time, her shoulders shaking from the mirth.

"Do tell, Miss Baxton, what you find so amusing?"

He no doubt hadn't the faintest idea what he looked like. A looking glass wouldn't be of great concern on board a ship, and certainly not for the workers. But someone should tell him, and since he asked, it would have to be her.

Grace removed her hand from her mouth and lowered her arm to her side. "Please forgive me, Mr. Bradenton, but your face. And your clothes." She pressed her lips together to stave off another chuckle. "They're black."

As if it had just dawned on him how he might appear to her, Andrew ducked his head. "Oh." He reached into his back pocket and withdrew a surprisingly clean handkerchief. "I must look a sight." As much as possible, he cleaned the dirt and dust from his face, grimacing when he saw the now dark handkerchief. Meeting her gaze again, a twinkle lit his honey-colored eyes as he added, "Quite a difference from the last time you took note of me on board a ship."

Her cheeks warmed, though not the searing heat she'd experienced then. Oh, what an aggravating man to remind her of that.

"I believe I prefer the coal dust," she countered, daring him to deliver a retort.

Instead he quirked his eyebrows and regarded her with surprise, as if he couldn't believe she would say such a thing. "I believe you said you have a message for me?"

Yes. Back to business. A much safer subject than their lighthearted banter. That sent her thoughts in a direction she'd much rather not pursue.

After wetting her lips, Grace swallowed and forced a calm composure. "Uncle Richard asked me to come fetch you. He'd like to see you in his office at your earliest convenience."

Andrew furrowed his brow. "Did he happen to say what this is regarding?"

"No." She shook her head. "He only said he wished you to come to him."

"Very well." He held out his hands and inspected them, giving them and the state of his clothes a wary glance. "I will attempt to wash up and be there directly."

Grace opened her mouth to tell him she'd wait, but that would be completely inappropriate. It would also leave her standing there, thinking thoughts best left ignored. They would venture into dangerous territory, and she needed to keep a clear head. So instead she nodded.

"All right. I will inform him you're on your way."

"Thank you." And with that, he turned tail, disappearing from view around the far side of the ship.

She stood and stared at that spot for several minutes. Then she shook herself from the reverie and turned back toward her uncle's office. She'd just told herself she didn't need any distractions, and then she'd allowed Andrew to do just that. It'd be best if she went back to work and put the disturbing image of Andrew washing the grime from his clothes out of her head.

But about thirty minutes later, in walked the man who wouldn't leave her thoughts, looking as fresh as the morning dew, his hair wet and slicked back. He'd changed his shirt, too, though the one he now wore had several wet spots from the remaining water in his hair. Heading straight for her uncle's office, Andrew barely acknowledged her as he rapped three times on the closed door. A muffled voice from within beckoned him to enter. With a nod in her direction, he entered, closing the door behind him.

Grace wanted to move closer to the door to see if she could hear anything at all about what they discussed. But her uncle's receptionist would have something to say about that. So she went back to work and focused all her efforts on the filing.

After what seemed like just a few brief minutes, the door to her uncle's office opened, and Andrew stepped out. "Thank you very much, Mr. Baxton. I am grateful you agree." He touched two fingers to his forehead, where a stubborn lock of hair curled down across his brow. "Miss Baxton."

He left almost as quickly as he'd arrived. Grace turned her head from the front door to her uncle's office, where he stood in the doorway, watching her. A silent nod beckoned her to join him, and she did. With the door again closed, her uncle stepped behind his desk and took a seat, inviting her to do the same.

"I suppose you have a lot of questions," he began, steepling his fingers as he rested his elbows on his desk.

Of course she did. A meeting he'd made to sound extremely important and confidential, and it had only lasted mere minutes? Grace perched on the edge of her seat and opened her mouth, about to let loose with the slew of questions she had, when her uncle held up one hand.

"Before you ask, I will tell you that I have declared Andrew's sentence fulfilled in terms of repaying his debt."

"You did what?" Grace covered her mouth at the escaped words. She should bite her tongue and wait for her uncle to finish. "I am sorry, Uncle. That was quite ill-mannered of me. Please continue."

Her uncle cleared his throat. "Indeed. Now, as I said, Andrew no longer has to work for us, but he has asked to continue for the remainder of his assigned sentence." He shrugged. "Said he wanted to send money back to his family. He has been quite advantageous to the workload here at the docks, and I would be a fool had I denied his request."

Money for his family? Grace had been certain he came from a station very similar to her own. Perhaps not quite as affluent, but close. Why would he need to earn money? And why send it to his family instead of keeping it for his own needs?

"So he will remain working for you for another six weeks?" she asked, since her other questions would have to be answered by Andrew himself.

"Yes," her uncle replied. "At that time, we will revisit his employment and it will again be his choice to stay or leave."

Grace couldn't decide if she liked the idea of him staying or if she wanted him to leave. She'd already come to terms with him serving a sentence in working for them, but for him to be there of his own accord, and earning a wage as well? That changed things a great deal.

"Now, if you don't mind, Grace," her uncle continued. "I have work that requires my attention."

Her uncle's dismissal was clear. She took her leave and returned to the front room. Again sliding into the systematic groove of filing, Grace let her mind entertain several possible answers to her questions. At least with Andrew staying, she had the chance to probe deeper and find out more about him. That was one point in his favor. But would Andrew answer the questions she asked? Or would he remain as silent about his affairs as he'd been in response to her apology a few weeks ago? Only one way to find out.

Chapter 11

Do you enjoy making repairs such as that?"

Grace sat on a bench opposite Andrew, who perched on a crate near the brigantine where he worked that day. Dressed much like he had been for most of the days she'd seen him, at least today his clothing hadn't been ruined by coal dust. He held a heavy-cabled net in his hands as he ran his fingers over the cross-knots, checking for frays and areas that needed reinforcement.

He shrugged without looking up. "It certainly beats hauling waste to the barrels or scrubbing floors."

"But you have scrubbed the decks of some of these ships during your time working at the docks."

"That's different."

"How so?" Grace had attempted to engage Andrew in conversation several times that week. Today marked the third time in as many days, yet he hadn't been any more talkative now than the other two previous days.

"It just is."

That line of questioning clearly wasn't working. "You must have spent a lot of time around the water and various ships." Perhaps appealing to his pride by noting his obvious skills would produce better results. "You know quite a lot about them, and my uncle has remarked more than once about the asset you have been to the workers here."

"I am no stranger to ships," he replied, "but my skills don't come from extensive experience with them. Working with my hands is simply something I enjoy, no matter what the task."

That sounded a lot like her uncle. He made no attempt to hide his distaste for paperwork and being isolated in a dark office.

"Is that what you did before you—" No wait. That wouldn't do. She couldn't remind him of why he ended up working for them. He'd clam up for certain. Not that he cooperated all that much now. "Before you came to work for my uncle?" she ended up asking.

"Tasks with my hands?" He actually looked up at her with that one. "Sometimes."

And back to his work. Grace sighed. This proved harder than she thought it'd be. Either her questions needed a little refining to become more appealing to Andrew, or she needed to improve her delivery.

"You have been with us for nearly seven weeks, yet you haven't requested any time to visit your family. Do they not live near enough for you to do so?"

A tic pulsed in his cheek, and his jaw moved back and forth, almost as if he was grinding his teeth or attempting to hold back a groan.

"They are aware of my whereabouts, and as you might recall, I have been serving a judicial sentence for my crimes." His words came out through clenched teeth. "Assignments like that don't usually afford the opportunity for visits home."

Perfect. She wanted to avoid reminding him of the deed that had brought him together with her family, and now she'd gone and done just that. Maybe if she focused on his exemplary work that led to Uncle Richard forgiving his debt early.

"But you are now working for wage with my uncle. He declared your debt paid in full five days ago. Does that not change anything?"

"Nothing of consequence." Andrew took a deep breath, and his expression relaxed. "It merely means I am earning a sum for what I do instead of being forced to toil at whatever task is deemed appropriate."

"And you are free to use that money however you wish." Grace wanted to ask about him sending money home, but he didn't seem all too eager to speak of his family. "That must make a substantial difference in how you view the work you do."

"I do whatever is asked of me with the same level of devotion, whether someone is paying me to do a job or not."

Uncle Richard had said as much to her the other day. And Harriet had mentioned more than once how much the rest of the staff at the manor liked Andrew. For a man who had only been with them such a short time, he had accomplished quite a lot. His actions spoke a great deal to his impeccable character, even if he could be rather vexing at times.

"Many of our staff have noticed your dedication and have spoken of it."

"They will do that," he replied without emotion.

Back to the single-phrase replies. Either he was oblivious to her attempts at gathering information from him, or he intentionally offered the least amount possible. She leaned more toward the latter.

"So you view all of your duties equally?"

"Yes."

A spark of mischief lit inside her, and she smiled. "Even when that task involves hauling waste and dumping it in barrels?"

Finally the faintest hint of a grin formed on his lips. She might wear him down yet.

"Yes, even then."

※

Andrew peered at Grace through half-lidded eyes. For the third time that week, she had sought him out, initially claiming to need his assistance for this or that. It didn't take long though before she launched into her barrage of questions about his past. He did his best to respond without being impolite, but no matter what he said, she had another question to immediately follow.

"And what about mucking out stalls or polishing saddles with Jesse there to provoke you?"

He raised his head to look across the way at her. If he didn't know better, he'd swear she was baiting him. She wouldn't do that, would she? Then again, if her amusing attempts to coax information from him had failed, humor might prove more successful. He'd better watch himself or she might actually find a way to break down his carefully constructed barriers.

"Jesse is nothing more than a self-appointed peacock with more fluff to his tail feathers than substance." Andrew rolled his eyes. "His actions are of no concern to me."

"I must say, he isn't the same now that you're no longer there for him to antagonize. Poor Willie is back to bearing the brunt of the torment."

"If Willie is anything like I saw, he can handle himself with Jesse." And more, if Andrew didn't miss his guess. That young lad had quite a bit of spunk in him. "I'd be more concerned for Jesse than Willie."

"You do have a point."

The sound of her melodious laughter worked its way into his defenses more than he cared to admit. The way she sat on that bench, her ankles neatly tucked beneath her with her hands primly folded in her lap, made it seem as if she waited for a friend. No one would suspect she had ulterior motives.

"And you seem to know quite a lot about Jesse's type," Grace continued.

"We have a pair of stable hands much like him and Willie."

Her entire face lit up at that remark. Oh no. She'd done it. She'd managed to get him to let down his guard for just one second, and now he'd admitted to having a stable as well as servants to work there. He didn't want to keep everything about his past from her. He just didn't want anyone feeling sorry for him. So he said the least he could. Unfortunately staying quiet proved more and more difficult with Miss Baxton around.

"Oh? Do you ride? Or is that for someone else in your family? Perhaps a brother or sister?"

"I go out every once in a while," he replied.

No way would she trick him again. He'd pay much closer attention. Of course, that might have been what got him into trouble in the first place. Watching her too closely only distracted him.

And that dress. He couldn't remember a more suitable shade of blue. The same color as her often mesmerizing eyes. With at least a dozen buttons on the front of the jacket and lace trim at the neck and sleeves as well as across the middle of her skirt, Grace presented the picture of perfect femininity. Even her bonnet matched, right down to the lace ties. Charming and attractive both came to mind. And that was a very dangerous combination.

"Bradenton!"

James Woodruff's voice called out from the deck of the brigantine. Andrew looked up.

"You finished with that net yet?" Woodruff glanced from him to Grace and back again.

Andrew glanced at the item tangled in his fingers. He'd actually been finished with it for a little while now, but he'd tarried to remain with Grace. "Yes, it's done."

"Good. Come back on board. I've got another task in mind for you." Another look at Grace, and he disappeared over the starboard side.

Andrew gathered up the net in his arms and stood. Grace did the same.

"Miss Baxton, do forgive me this abrupt departure, but it appears I am needed on the ship."

Grace twisted the tip of her parasol against the ground. "No apologies necessary, Mr. Bradenton. I have taken up more than enough of your time already."

As much as he would rather sit with her, he did have a job to do. But Andrew didn't want to leave in such a brusque manner. He grinned.

"Perhaps our next conversation will result in a more successful outcome to your inquisition attempts."

She lowered her lashes and a pretty shade of pink filled her cheeks. He didn't exactly leave her with much to say in response. So he changed the subject.

"Will I see you at the festival on Saturday?"

Surprise filled her face at that. "Yes. I'll be there with my family."

Touching two fingers to the brim of his cap, he winked. "Until then, Miss Baxton."

Walking away from her proved harder than he'd thought. He wanted to turn around, to see if she watched his departure. But that might make him change his mind. He took a deep breath and forced himself to stay focused.

Just like his reasons for asking Mr. Baxton to stay on in spite of being given his freedom. Grace had factored rather heavily into them. He wasn't ready to say good-bye to her just yet. But he'd never admit it to anyone.

*

"Uncle Richard!" Grace sat up straight and pressed her arm against the side cushion of their open carriage. "I see Maureen over by the ticket booth. May I please join her?"

They had just arrived on the edge of the park a few streets north of the shipyards. What a sight to behold! There had to be hundreds of people gathered on the grassy area, and that didn't include the number in small dinghies or rowboats on the river, or even those enjoying a swim in the chilly water. It might be July, but she'd stepped in that river on the hottest day of the year, and even then she couldn't last long.

Her aunt and uncle exchanged a silent glance between them, their unspoken communication saying more than any words might say. Grace prayed they'd agree.

"Yes," Aunt Charlotte answered for him. "But mind your manners and stay away from the deeper throes of the masses."

Uncle Richard signaled to Matthew to stop the carriage long enough for Grace to accept his assistance and climb down. She released his hand and offered a reassuring smile to them both. But it was Aunt Charlotte's expression that caught her eye. She grinned and winked. Grace returned the wink and fairly skipped to join her friend. Her aunt was a true kindred spirit.

"Maureen!" Grace waved her handkerchief in the air.

Her friend looked from left to right and smiled when she saw Grace. The two clasped hands and exchanged a quick kiss on the cheek.

"I was hoping you would be here today." Maureen placed her gloved hand over her mouth to conceal a yawn. "It's been a day full of events, but I am not fond of the crowd. I even left my maid on the blanket with my family over there." She gestured a few yards away then turned an earnest gaze on Grace. "You will stay with me, right?"

"Of course." Grace nodded and drew her friend into a hug. "When I saw you, I begged my aunt and uncle to let me leave the carriage." She placed a hand across her brow and feigned the act of fainting. "I would simply swoon from the trials of enduring several hours standing amidst my family with no one my own age to share the fun."

Maureen pressed a gloved hand to her lips and laughed. "Oh, Grace, I am happy you're here to make this day much better."

Grace tucked Maureen's arm into the crook of her own. "Come then. Let us not tarry another moment." She led them closer to the center of the festivities so they could better hear what was taking place.

"Hooray!" The crowd responded in hearty agreement, the cheers drowning out the speaker's next words.

Grace stood on tiptoe to see over the heads, trying to identify the man in the middle of the group. Why could they not have chosen a spot a bit higher on a hill? If only the woman holding the parasol over her head would step a little to the left, Grace could see.

"There has to be another way."

She huffed and took a few steps toward a bench and scrambled to her task before Maureen could stop her.

"Grace!" Maureen gasped. "Someone will see you there."

"But I cannot abide not seeing who is speaking. Everyone is all in a twitter. I simply must find out."

"Well, don't include me in this scheme. I remain innocent if someone from your family or mine discovers you."

Grace grinned at Maureen's folded arms as her friend turned her back. She wasn't deterred by the antics though and focused once more on her goal.

"At last!"

Maureen's reaction belied her uninterest as she unfolded her arms and pressed against Grace, straining on tiptoe. "What is it you see?"

Grace swayed to the left and right. "Oh, it's Mayor Rhoads." She craned her neck and stretched her ear closer to the sounds booming from the central stage. She rapidly patted Maureen on the shoulder. "He just announced the arrival of electric streetcars and said they will slowly begin to replace the horse-drawn cars in Wilmington."

"Really?"

"Yes, something about the United States having forty-three states now, with Idaho just being added, and how we need to progress if we are to keep the pace with the other states."

"My father mentioned the other day that Wyoming is due to be added to the union any day now as well."

Grace looked down at her friend. "All right. Forty-four states then."

Amazing to consider how fast the country grew with each passing day. Every time she turned around, there seemed to be something new and exciting taking place. From lightbulbs, to telephones, to talking machines, and now electric streetcars.

"What is happening now?"

Her friend's voice broke into her thoughts and brought her back to the present. Grace once again pushed up on her feet, only this time, she lost her balance.

Panic struck her as she flailed her arms in an attempt to stand. She only caught a glimpse of the terror on Maureen's face before an arm snaked around her waist and held her upright. Her breath escaped in one swoosh, while her heart pounded in her chest.

"Mercy!" Grace placed one hand on her chest and turned to see who had rescued her. "I do apologize for my clumsiness, but—"

"I commend you, Miss Baxton, on your ingenious method of observing the proceedings at the park center," Andrew began with a twinkle in his warm eyes. "But I daresay there is another, safer, place where you might still be able to see."

Maureen giggled from her place beside Andrew. Were it not for the commanding way his gaze held hers, Grace would have leveled a glare at her friend for not warning her. Instead she couldn't look away.

Finally finding her voice, she parried his teasing with "You are no doubt correct, Mr. Bradenton, but I find the view from this position to be quite to my liking."

A smile tugged at his lips. "Then perhaps you should make certain you are tied to the bench in order to preserve your balance."

"And risk appearing even more foolish?"

Maureen shamelessly stood there with open amusement on her face. Mindful of their unexpected companion, Grace only silently scolded her friend, making a vow to speak with her later. She accepted Andrew's assistance and returned again to the ground.

Andrew nodded toward the crowd, where voices continued to be raised and declarations were issued from the middle of the throngs. "I gather you are in favor of these new streetcars for the city?"

"Of course!" Grace replied. "Why would I not?"

"No reason. I am merely surprised to see you so interested in developments such as this."

Grace tried not to take offense at his words. He likely didn't intend them to be an insult in any way. She might often be more interested in the people and the social aspects of the city, but Aunt Charlotte remained quite involved and informed, and she made sure Grace and her children did, too.

"As you know, I do read a lot." He should know that from his remarks about how often he caught her with books when he worked at their manor. "And I pay attention when pivotal changes are in the offing."

"Ah, so you stay abreast of the political developments taking place in this area?"

"Not as much as the social changes, but I am aware of most of them."

Andrew glanced toward the center of the crowd, his height affording him a view Grace envied. As much as she longed to again see what was happening, she didn't dare attempt to use the bench a second time. Besides, Maureen might faint away from the shock of it all. At the moment, she remained a silent observer, while providing Grace with a necessary chaperone.

"Well, do allow me to join you ladies then, and we shall enjoy the festivities as well as the forthcoming fireworks on the river."

Grace shot a silent look to her friend, and Maureen nodded. She turned back to Andrew. "I could think of nothing I would like more, Mr. Bradenton."

As he moved to stand behind them both, Grace looked at Maureen from the corner of her eye. She couldn't say anything now, but her friend would no doubt discuss this meeting in great detail once they were alone.

Chapter 12

Feeling like a waiter with the four dishes he balanced, Andrew lowered himself to his knees with great care onto the blanket beside Grace. She jumped in response. Almost as if she didn't expect him to join her. "Sorry. I didn't mean to scare you."

He held out a dish with vanilla ice cream in it and fumbled with two tin cups of water while settling his own dish in his lap.

She took the dish in one hand and waved off his comment with the other before accepting the tin cup as well. "It's all right. I must have been daydreaming." Grace avoided his eyes and instead paid close attention to her dessert.

Her voice trembled a little. She wasn't comfortable. That much was clear. But what had happened from the time they left her family to now? He assessed the spot she'd chosen before he'd gone in search of their sweet treat. Blankets of every pattern and color spread out like a patchwork quilt all across the grassy park. A handful of people weaved their way between those seated, but most of those gathered had found a place to relax while waiting for the explosive show.

Maureen sat with Grace's Aunt Anastasia on another blanket just a few feet away, but the rest of her family had found a spot somewhere else in the park. Now Andrew wondered if he'd been wrong to suggest they share a spot. She didn't need to see his hesitation though. Grace was already nervous.

"See? What did I tell you?" Andrew announced with forced pride. "This is the perfect spot."

Grace looked around them with a guarded expression. "It is a bit closer to the water than I expected. That's for certain." She hesitated a moment then nodded. "But it does appear to be a good choice. We will have an excellent view of the fireworks."

Andrew snapped his fingers and pointed at her. "Exactly."

She took a spoonful of ice cream but still looked to the left and right, as if trying to determine if anyone was watching them. He was the one who had to be on his best behavior. Having Grace's aunt and friend sitting so close, they would see every move he made for certain. With that in mind, she had nothing to worry about. So why was she so jumpy?

"Did you have to go far to get these?"

Andrew jerked his gaze back to hers and stuttered. "Oh, um, not at all." At least it didn't seem that far to him. Then again, Grace had become quite nervous from the time he'd left her to the time he'd returned. So maybe it had been farther than he'd thought.

Grace shifted her focus and regarded her dessert as if it held some special secret. "This is quite delicious. One of the best dishes I've had in quite some time."

Her voice was so soft he had to strain to hear her above the lapping of the water against the riverbanks and the noise from the crowd.

"Have you enjoyed the festival so far?"

Grace looked at him and smiled, her entire face lighting up, despite only having the torches to illuminate the park. "Immensely! It is an ideal culmination to the week."

"Well, I have to work tomorrow," he pointed out, "but the next day we have Sunday services. That's a good end. . .or start. . .to the week, depending on how you look at it."

"I agree." She took a sip of water and lowered her cup. "And what are your thoughts about tonight?"

He winked. "I believe the company I've kept this evening has made it more pleasant than had I remained where I was."

She glanced over his shoulder to where her friend and aunt sat. "Yes, even if we must endure the close inspection of watchful eyes." Grace nodded her head in their direction. "I can only imagine what they might be saying."

"Oh, you can be certain they are talking about us. . .or at least me, at any rate." He set down his cup and dish and placed his right hand flat across his chest. "But I vow to be absolutely above reproach this entire time. You won't even find a speck of dirt on my clothing." He glanced down and pretended to flick off a speck or two.

Grace giggled. "You'd better, or I'll be the one who will not hear the end of it."

Good. He'd managed to get her laughing again. And she didn't seem as nervous as when he'd first joined her. Now to keep her relaxed.

"Do you mean to say your friend wouldn't give you the benefit of the doubt where I'm concerned?" He dished up a heaping spoonful of ice cream and stuck it into his mouth.

"Not at all," she immediately countered. "In fact, Maureen would be the first to become the leader of the inquisition, followed closely behind by my Aunt 'Stasia."

After swallowing, Andrew pressed his tongue against one side of his teeth and nodded. "I believe I'm beginning to understand why your uncle agreed so readily to us not joining them. They have a built-in scout network to report back to them on every detail."

Grace slid her spoon slowly from her mouth and swallowed her ice cream. Andrew had to force himself not to focus on her lips.

"More so than that," she replied. "I believe Maureen is merely looking out for her own interests and building up material she can use against me should I catch her in a similar situation. Rumor has it there is a certain young gentleman who has been escorting her home from my aunt's bookshop." Grace smiled and took a drink from her tin cup.

Andrew waggled his eyebrows. "Ah-ha. That explains it. She's besotted."

Her lips tightened, preventing the water she'd just drunk from escaping.

He laughed and took a drink as he attempted to school his expression into one of nonchalance. It was no use. "I'm sorry," he said through barely contained chuckles. "I do thank you though, for sparing me the spray of your drink."

With a swallow and dainty clearing of her throat, Grace regained her composure. "You are most welcome," she replied, raising her cup again to her lips. "But I cannot guarantee that should a repeat occurrence take place, you will remain free from harm."

It took Andrew a moment to process what she'd just said. He narrowed his eyes at the playful, underlying threat laced between her words. She spoke with such calm, her expression devoid of any mischief. He couldn't tell if she was flirting or serious. And she likely preferred it that way. Such a unique blend of sophistication and affability.

He finished his dessert and took a sip of his own water, then turned toward a makeshift stage not too far away where a band had assembled. Almost instantly, the rousing strains of celebratory music filled the cool night air. "What do you think?"

"About your sense of humor or the music currently playing and the ambience of the festival?" She took a final spoonful of her ice cream, the corners of her lips turning up slightly as she savored the last remnants.

"My—" He paused. Wait a minute. Had she just given him a taste of his own medicine? He clenched his jaw and raised his chin a fraction of an inch. "The festival, of course."

She swallowed and washed down her dessert with another drink. "In that case, I approve. The city has truly outdone itself with the vendors, the performances on some of the other stages, the entertainment, and soon the fireworks."

He leaned back on his left elbow and regarded her through half-lidded eyes. "And here I thought the ice cream would be the climax of the evening."

Grace covered her mouth and giggled. "I am sorry, Mr. Bradenton, but even such delectable ice cream pales in comparison to fireworks and lively music."

Andrew held up his cup with his right hand and tipped it in her direction. "I am not so certain. I have had some flavors that seemed to dance in my mouth with their stimulating tastes."

After taking another sip of water, she lowered the cup and looked at him over the rim with a grin. "Ah, it seems you have an overdeveloped sweet tooth, Mr. Bradenton. First it was the candied apples. Then the sugar sticks. And finally the ice cream. It's a wonder you still have all your teeth."

He tipped his cup toward her. "I'll have you know our cook prepares delicious meals three times a day and makes sure each one of us eats some of everything she's made."

Grace paused with her cup midway to her mouth and stared, her lips parted. "So you *do* have a cook! I knew it."

Oh no! She'd done it again. Caused him to let down his guard and share more about his past. How did she manage it so easily?

"Yes, I admit it. My family employs a cook." He might as well give in this time. She'd been relentless about divining information from him, and in such a charming manner, too. So far he'd received nothing remotely close to pity for what he'd temporarily given up, so why had he been so worried about that?

She cocked her head and remained silent for several moments. Andrew could feel the heat warm his neck and creep toward his cheeks. If she started to believe he'd answer anything, there'd be no end to the long line of questions she'd ask.

"I can understand that," she finally said with a nod. "Nearly all of the families in this area have a cook to prepare their meals."

Andrew pressed his lips into a thin line. Now was the time to truly come clean. They'd enjoyed quite a bit of banter, and he couldn't remember the last time he'd been so relaxed in the company of a lady. If he continued to clam up, he'd lose everything he'd gained where Grace was concerned.

"This is true. Employing a cook is not uncommon. But my mother isn't as involved as most ladies of their homes." He tilted his head and stared up at the stars in the night sky. "She's had to endure several surgeries of late, and I'm afraid they've taken their toll on her strength. The doctors didn't know what was wrong. She's been confined to a bed for months now."

Grace yanked a stem of a dandelion weed from the ground and twirled it between her fingers. "You mentioned the surgeries the day we first met. How the doctors' bills had driven you to such extreme measures."

Andrew pushed himself to a sitting position and set aside his cup. Softening his voice, he added, "Yes, then I heard one doctor tell my father it was likely a tumor that could be cancer, and I prayed to God it wasn't true. When the doctor spoke of an operation that could potentially save her life, I formed that foolhardy plan." He sighed and mumbled as he reached for a blade of grass and twisted it back and forth. "But you couldn't possibly understand."

A pained expression flitted across her face before she had the chance to hide it. "Actually, you might be surprised. Our worlds and experiences might be more similar than you'd imagine."

Now Andrew hadn't expected that. Pity? Yes. Blame? Perhaps. Derision? Most certainly. But empathy? Not in the least. And she looked like she had a story to tell. Perhaps it would help him feel less like a man on an island in all of this. He took her dish and cup from her and set them on his other side; then he reached out and covered the hand in her lap with his own. "Tell me about it. . .please?"

&

Grace looked down at the hand covering hers, his tanned skin a stark contrast to her pale tone. She glanced behind him toward Maureen and Aunt 'Stasia. They seemed rather engrossed in their own conversation, so she returned her attention to Andrew and gave him a wary look.

"Are you certain you wish to know? It might affect the preconceived notions you've formed about my family and me."

Andrew stiffened, and Grace immediately regretted how harsh her words had sounded. But she had grown tired of his assumptions and generalizations without knowing the truth. He sighed and nodded.

"Yes, I do. I would not have asked otherwise."

She looked across the river and took a deep breath. It had been eight years, but in some ways, it felt like yesterday.

"Well, you already know I live with my aunt and uncle."

He nodded, giving her hand a squeeze. "Yes, and your uncle told me it was because of an accident that took the lives of your parents."

Moisture formed at the corners of her eyes, but she blinked it away. "An accident that also left me without the use of my legs. I was in a wheeled chair for several months."

His eyes widened at that, but he didn't say a word. So she continued.

"I, too, endured endless visits with specialists and doctors following the accident. And it came down to a single operation that could give me back the use of my legs or cripple me permanently." She sighed. "My uncle was already dealing with financial struggles, and the transfer of the assets from the shipping company was delayed. The added expense of my visits only made the situation worse." Grace stared out in the general direction of where her family sat. "I must admit, seeing my young cousins with my aunt and uncle just a bit ago started me thinking. They have given up so much for me. Sometimes it makes me feel guilty for the burden I was at the time." She mumbled under her breath. "And in some ways still am."

He snapped his fingers. "I knew something had happened."

She shook her head and turned to face him. "What do you mean?"

Andrew pulled back and rested his forearms on his knees. Grace immediately felt the loss of warmth from his withdrawn hand, but his nearness still offered a great deal of comfort in its place.

"I noticed when I first sat down here tonight that you seemed a bit distracted. And you weren't yourself. That easygoing manner of yours was missing."

Grace ducked her chin. "Oh." And she had hoped her teasing remarks and smiles might cover up her pensive thoughts. Obviously it hadn't. Andrew had seen right through her unsuccessful attempts.

She saw his hand before his fingers touched her chin as he raised her head to meet his gaze. "Hey," he said softly, "I am every bit as guilty of lumping far too much weight on my own shoulders. It would be wrong of me to blame you for doing the same."

He moved his index finger back and forth on the underside of her chin. She quelled the shiver that started somewhere near the base of her spine. Instead she got lost in the caramel-colored depths of his caring eyes.

As if he had read her mind, he jerked his hand back and put some distance between them.

"Sorry about that." He averted his gaze for a brief second then released a short sigh. "It's clear the operation was a success." He gestured toward her legs. "I mean, you are obviously walking, and I don't recall noticing a limp of any kind."

Grace blinked a few times. The operation? Oh, right. She'd better get a handle on her emotions. And fast.

"Yes, thanks to my aunt and a bazaar she'd organized, we received a generous donation that allowed us to make an appointment with one of the best surgeons in his field."

A dimple in his right cheek appeared, accompanying his grin. "Well, I am grateful it was a success. Otherwise I'd have had to brush up on my skills at pushing a wheeled chair through the grass." He wiggled his eyebrows. "And you would be decidedly taller than me sitting on this blanket."

Grace smiled at his antics. How good it felt to laugh and share a common bond. They had definitely reached a new level in their relationship, whatever it was at the moment. She started to respond when his face turned serious again.

"Thank you, Miss Baxton, for sharing what you did. And I apologize for my wrong assumptions where you're concerned. I'll try not to make the same mistake again."

"You're quite welcome, Mr. Bradenton." She nearly stumbled over his formal name. In all her thoughts, she called him Andrew. It grew increasingly harder to remind herself not to call him such verbally.

As if he'd read her mind, he cleared his throat. "Yes, about that." He once again held her gaze. "Might I have your permission to call you by your given name? After tonight, addressing you as 'Miss Baxton' does not feel right anymore." He held up his index finger. "But only if you will also agree to call me Andrew."

Relieved he'd been the one to suggest it, Grace nodded. "Yes, you may. And I agree."

"Excellent. Glad that's settled." Andrew looked toward the river then back at her. "Now, it looks like the fireworks are about to start." He lowered his left arm and silently invited her to move closer. "Are you ready?"

She didn't know if he referred to the Independence Day celebration or where their relationship was headed. Or both. Either way, she could answer in the affirmative. With a glance behind his back at Maureen and Aunt 'Stasia, who both grinned and nodded their encouragement, Grace shifted closer to Andrew and allowed him to rest his arm around her back.

As the night sky lit up with a blaze of flashing color and exploding fire, a nagging reminder flitted through her head. At least she could show her appreciation for the enjoyable evening they'd shared.

"In case I forget to tell you later," she said without looking at him, "thank you for joining me tonight. And for listening."

He turned his head toward her, making her acutely aware of how close they sat. "You're quite welcome," he said. "We should do it again."

"Perhaps." She grinned. "Next year around this time."

She felt rather than saw his surprise in the way his arm flexed against her back, and Grace realized what she'd just said. One year from now? She didn't even know if he'd be there five *weeks* from now, let alone a full year. But just as she was about to retract what she'd said, he jumped in with a reply.

"You can count on it."

Chapter 13

Andrew stepped outside the Wise & Weldon Lumberyard and looked up and down the street. He didn't get to that area of Market Street often. Since the proprietor informed him it would take about an hour to collect the order Mr. Baxton had placed three weeks ago, he had plenty of time to do a little detective work.

It had been three days since Grace shared about her own surgery and all her aunt had done to help. Not only had he misjudged Grace and her family, but his thievery had cost them precious items. Mr. Baxton might have declared his debt paid through the work he'd done, but what they'd lost couldn't be replaced with mere money or time served. He had to do something.

Glancing around the various business establishments on both sides of the street, Andrew's eyes alighted on a sign positioned on the third floor of a brick building just a few hundred feet away, C. F. THOMAS AND COMPANY. The ample display of books and stationery in the storefront windows gave him an idea.

"Perfect!" he said out loud to himself.

After he looked up and down the street, Andrew crossed to the other side, whistling as he walked. This should get him started in the right direction.

The bell above the door jingled as he entered, and he stepped into the musty yet clean shop. In the far corner, an impressive printing press stood like a sentinel announcing its prominent function. He looked straight back where a man wearing an apron soiled with ink stood in front of another machine Andrew didn't recognize.

"I shall be with you momentarily," the man called out, peering to the front of the shop through the parts of the machine he operated.

"I'm in no rush," Andrew called back.

He stepped closer to a rack advertising used books. Quite a collection the proprietor had amassed. And their condition nearly rivaled that of the brand-new books on the next rack. If only he could remember the name of the ones he'd taken from the Baxton manor. But even reading the ones on the shelf didn't jog his memory.

"My apologies, sir," the man with the apron said as he approached the counter. "But my assistant is not in today, and I fear I am forced to do the work of two people." He wiped his hands on his apron. "Charles Thomas, at your service. How may I assist you?"

"Andrew Bradenton," Andrew replied. "I work for Hannsen & Baxton Shipping."

"Ah yes." Thomas nodded. "A notable and well-respected company."

"From what I've heard and seen, yes." He gestured around the expansive storeroom. "You have quite an impressive establishment here as well."

Mr. Thomas raised his chin an inch or two and stuck out his chest. "Yes, we recently expanded to double our previous space. It has been excellent for business." He raised his eyebrows then puffed out his cheeks as he blew out air. "But it has meant an increased demand in the personnel required to keep the shop running."

"I can well imagine that." Andrew pointed toward the machine in the back. "What is that you were working on a moment ago?"

Thomas's eyes lit up and he returned to the machine, setting his hand on top like he would a son or even a valued employee. "This? This is the J. L. Morrison Cast-Iron Book Binding Machine, straight from New York." His hand slid across the top almost in a caress. "One of our recent acquisitions for the expansion, and my pride and joy."

Andrew smiled. "That I can see."

The man cleared his throat. "Yes, well, the patented spring-feed gear gives automatic adjustment to any size wire for the wire stitching. It will greatly improve my output for our pamphlets and blank books, another part of our increased development." Thomas moved back behind the counter and regarded Andrew with a quizzical eye. "Now, enough about me. What is it that brought you here this fine morning, and how may I be of assistance?"

Ah yes. Business. It would be so easy to peruse the various product out-puts in the shop, connecting the merchandise with the paper milled at one of his father's mills. Quite the experience seeing things from this end of the manufacturing line. But his hour of free time was disappearing with each pass-ing minute.

"To be honest," Andrew began, "I am not certain where to start."

"Usually at the beginning," Thomas said with a grin.

Andrew chuckled. The man was likable. No doubt about it. "Yes. But I'm afraid that will take too long to tell. Suffice it to say, I am in search of some rare and valuable books that were recently lost to a family in Brandywine."

"What are the titles?"

"Unfortunately I don't know them offhand." Andrew sighed. "I hadn't intended to come here today, but I had some additional time come available to me, so I decided it might be worthwhile." He held up his index finger. "I can get the titles from a member of the family though."

Thomas rubbed his thumb and forefinger across his smooth chin then adjusted the wire-rimmed spectacles resting on his nose. "Hmm. I cannot say for certain, but my best advice would be to inquire with Joseph and William Adams. They operate Adams & Brother General Variety Store, and they have four stories of commodities of all shapes and sizes. If there have been any valuable books circulating at any point throughout this city or area, they would know about it."

"Splendid!" Andrew stretched his arm across the counter. "Thank you. This has helped a great deal."

Thomas accepted the handshake. "My pleasure, young man. If I can be of any further assistance, if you have any print or binding needs, do come back and see me again."

Andrew touched the brim of his cap. "I will do that. Good day to you, sir."

"And a good day to you," the man replied.

With a spring in his step, Andrew headed outside to the sidewalk once more. He withdrew his pocket watch and flipped it open. Thirty-five minutes left. Just enough time to stop by the bank. After patting his back pocket and feeling the slight bump from the bills he'd placed there, he turned to the left and walked the two blocks north.

He paused outside the ornate SaVille Building at the corner of Sixth and Market Streets and closed his eyes. He opened them again and glanced across the street to SaVille Wines & Liquors. A part of him was tempted to go there and pay a visit to Alexander SaVille. See what new stock he had. At one time, it would have been quite easy, but not anymore. After inhaling and exhaling two deep breaths, Andrew placed his hand on the door to the bank and pushed it open, praying this visit would go well.

"Well, well, well," a jeering voice greeted him. "If it isn't the prodigal son of the mill owner, finally deciding to grace our bank with his presence again."

Andrew forced a grin to his lips and turned to face Henry Johnston, one of the proprietors of the bank. If he didn't keep his voice down, Alfred Elliott would come out to greet him as well.

"So, Mr. Bradenton has decided to return."

Too late.

The other proprietor stepped out of his office and leaned against the doorframe, folding his arms across his chest. "To what do we owe this pleasure?"

He should have known he wouldn't be able to set foot inside this building without Al and Henry seeing him. They'd been friends for a good many years. His absence of late wouldn't change that. Andrew nodded to each man in turn.

"Good morning, Henry, Al."

"Why so formal and distant, Drew?" Henry asked. Stepping forward, he added, "It's good to see you again." He pulled him into a quick hug, giving Andrew's back three firm thumps before backing away.

"Yes," Andrew replied. "And I'm sorry I haven't been here in a while." He glanced around the open area of the bank's lobby. "I can't stay long, but some things have happened that have kept me away."

Henry gestured for Al to join them and extended his arm toward his private office. It looked the same as it always did. Papers stacked in several piles on his desk and ledgers open on every available surface. A stark contrast to Al's office, which made everyone wonder if anyone actually worked in there. Neat and tidy, with every shelf along the one wall alphabetized in exact precision. The two made a dynamic team though.

Once all three of them had taken a seat in the leather chairs in front of Henry's desk, Al was the first to speak.

"Everything *is* all right, isn't it?" He leaned forward and rested his forearms on his thighs, concern evident in his eyes. "I mean, the weekly deposits for your father's mill have still been made on schedule, but it's been done by some man named Billingsly."

"And he's been rather tight-lipped about the goings-on with you or the mill," Henry added. "I haven't been able to get a thing out of him." He smirked and leaned back in his chair, once again crossing his arms. "And believe me, I've tried."

So predictable. Andrew likely could have anticipated the entire conversation before it even happened. Henry, with his comical outlook on life, and Al, with his level-headed approach. Andrew fell somewhere in between.

"All right," Henry continued. "Let's have it." He narrowed his eyes. "You haven't met a fair maiden, have you? Because if you have, we want to know all about it."

Andrew's thoughts immediately went to Grace. No. He'd best not go there yet. There'd be plenty of time for that later. Better stick to business for now.

"Well, you know about my mother's health," Andrew began. Both men nodded. "And the rising bills from the doctors." He closed his eyes. *Just say it and get it over with*, he told himself. After taking a deep breath, he plunged right in. "I made a rather foolish mistake that put me in front of a judge who sentenced me to three months working for the family I'd wronged."

Henry opened his mouth to respond, but Al stayed his response with a hand. "We'd heard something along those lines but didn't want to believe it," Al said, his eyes reflecting a sincere sympathy.

"So, how did you make it here today?" Henry wanted to know. "If I count right, it's only been eight weeks."

"Well, Mr. Baxton forgave my debt a little over a week ago," Andrew replied, "but I asked to stay on and work so I could give my father the money I'd earn."

"You're working at Hannsen & Baxton?" Henry whistled long and low. "That's an impressive operation they've got going down there. You're lucky the judge didn't issue a harsher penalty."

"You don't have to tell me twice." Andrew sighed. He didn't want to dwell on the past. He reached into his back pocket to retrieve the thin stack of folded bills. "It won't undo what I did, but it will at least help a little."

Al gestured with his head toward the money. "Is that what you'd like to deposit into your father's account?"

Andrew held out the small amount. "Yes. And if you could see that Billingsly receives a note upon his next visit stating the deposit, I'd appreciate it."

"Of course." Al reached into his breast pocket and withdrew a tablet and flipped it open. After grabbing a pencil from Henry's desk, he took the money from Andrew, counted it, and made a notation in the tablet. He tucked the money into his vest pocket and returned the tablet to his coat. He set the pencil back on the desk then leveled a direct gaze at Andrew. "Is that the only reason you came in today?"

Andrew nodded and looked back and forth between the two. "That, and because I knew it was time I came by to explain what had happened." His shoulders drooped. "I really am sorry for not coming in sooner or even scribbling out a quick note to you both."

"Ah, think nothing of it," Henry replied with a wave of his hand. "We all make mistakes. And if you'd been in bigger trouble, we would have known about it." A somber expression crossed his face, so opposite of his normal affable self. "We're just glad everything is all right." He glanced at his partner and clapped him on the back. "Aren't we, Al?"

Al jerked forward from the thump and cleared his throat. "Yes. Yes, we are." He stood, and the other two followed. "Now, I am certain you have other tasks to attend to this morning. We don't wish to keep you or make you late returning." He led the way out of Henry's office and paused just outside the door, extending his hand. "Come back and see us anytime. I mean it."

Andrew shook his friend's hand. "Thank you." A moment later, the expected clap on his back came from Henry.

"Next time you can tell us all about Baxton's lovely niece." Henry leaned in between the two of them with a knowing grin and winked. "I hear she comes to the shipyard a few days every week to work for her uncle. We want to hear more about her."

Regarding them both, and seeing the undisguised interest on Henry's face coupled with the single raised eyebrow on Al's, Andrew grinned. "We shall see."

And with that, Andrew turned heel and left. A chuckle rumbled from his stomach and made his shoulders shake as he ventured outside once more. That meeting had gone better than he'd thought it would. But he shouldn't be surprised. Andrew inhaled an invigorating and cleansing breath. Just one more stop before returning to the lumberyard and then back to the docks.

≈

"Uncle Richard?" Grace stood in the doorway to her uncle's front office, clutch and parasol in hand. "I am about to take a carriage up to Market Street to drop off Aunt Charlotte's necklace for repair. Is there anything you need while I'm out?"

Her uncle quirked his mouth and looked up before returning his eyes to her. "Umm, would you mind stopping by Diamond State Insurance for me?" He searched on his desk for something then produced a handwritten note from under one stack. "They have some rather sensitive documents for me, and I won't be able to leave here today to retrieve them."

She stepped forward to take the slip of paper from him. "Of course." Grace glanced down at the paper. "Shall I return them here or would you like them taken home where you can have them in your study there?"

"Here, please," he said without hesitation. "I have a meeting tomorrow to discuss them."

"Very well." Grace didn't question further. The partners and investors usually met monthly. Relieved she didn't have to take part in any of that, she signaled to Harriet to accompany her and left the office.

As soon as she reached the carriage Matthew had waiting, her name sounded from somewhere behind her.

"Grace!"

She turned around to see Andrew jogging toward her from the docks. "Matthew, I shall just be a minute," Grace called up to the driver then turned to her maid. "Harriet, you may go ahead and step inside the carriage."

After Matthew hopped down to assist Harriet, Grace walked toward Andrew and met him about halfway. "Andrew? Is there something you needed?"

He paused and bent to regain his breath, despite it being only minimally labored. "Yes," he replied once he stood straight again. "I see you're about to depart somewhere?"

Grace glanced back over her shoulder at the carriage. "I am. I have some business on Market Street for my aunt and uncle."

"Might I accompany you?"

She thought about the errand for her uncle. She could always request a binder in which she could transport the papers.

"I only ask," Andrew rushed to add, likely seeing her hesitation, "because there is one place I would like to go, and I would like you to join me."

Now that she didn't expect. He wanted her to come with him somewhere? She pressed one side of her lips together and narrowed her eyes as she regarded him. His expression didn't give away any hint of what he had in mind. Just what was he up to?

"Very well." Grace didn't know if she should trust him or not. His actions had become quite irregular all of a sudden. "I am certain Matthew will not mind taking an extra passenger. And there is more than enough room for the three of us inside."

Andrew glanced up the walkway, his brows drawn together. "The three of us?" Then he looked back at her. "Is someone else going?"

"My maid, Harriet," Grace replied. "It wouldn't be proper for me to travel alone unchaperoned." A spark of mischief lit inside. She grinned and spun on her heels. "Especially with you," she added, not giving him a chance to respond as she made her way back to the carriage.

A few seconds later, his rapid footfalls sounded behind her as he rushed to catch up with her. Placing a hand at the small of her back, he didn't say a word. She peeked at him from the corner of her eye and saw the grin tugging at his lips. At least the afternoon showed the promise of being enjoyable, and perhaps a bit entertaining.

Chapter 14

So, what is our next destination?"

With one hand Andrew held open the door for Grace and assisted her into the carriage with his other. Harriet remained just where they'd left her, the same as with the other three stops they'd made. Sometimes he wondered about the purpose of a lady's maid, especially when they spent so much time merely accompanying their lady.

"Actually I'm done with everything I had to do this afternoon." Grace patted the satchel between her and Harriet and drew it closer to her then gave him a sly smile. "That only leaves the mysterious place you mentioned earlier."

Andrew pulled the door closed and took his seat opposite the two ladies then thumped on the roof of the carriage. A second later, Matthew slapped the reins as he called to the horses, and the carriage lurched forward.

"Mysterious?" Andrew asked once they were moving. "There isn't anything mysterious about where I'd like to go."

"Well, you were being rather vague earlier when you mentioned it." She brushed her knuckles against each other as she fiddled with them in her lap. "And I could not determine anything from your expression."

Ah, so her curiosity *had* been piqued. Andrew grinned. "That's only because I wanted it to be a surprise."

"Well Matthew might appreciate knowing where we're going, even if you insist on not telling me."

Andrew almost laughed at the affronted set of her chin and shoulders. Grace might pretend not to be interested, but by asking him to convey their destination to Matthew, she clearly hoped to gain her information that way. He pressed his lips together to suppress a chuckle and leaned back against the seat cushion.

"Matthew already knows. I informed him before entering the carriage."

Grace opened her mouth to respond then clamped it shut. She was making this far too amusing.

"You shall just have to be patient and wait until we arrive." He glanced out the side window and scanned the street corner for the signs. "And we only have two more blocks to go." Andrew quirked one eyebrow. "Surely, you can wait that long, can't you?"

"Of course I can." She squared her shoulders and jutted her chin up an inch or two. "I am not a child."

No, she definitely wasn't that. As soon as she shifted her attention out the window, Andrew took that opportunity to observe her at greater length. Dressed in a simple, yet elegant striped blouse of pale blue with skirt to match and a wide, black velvet belt, she appeared every bit the lady he knew her to be, all the way up to her charming yet jaunty hat. To him, it seemed a bit overdone with all that lace, netting, flowers, and feathers, but the colors matched quite nicely. And it set off her eyes to perfection. Eyes that could drive him to his knees or give him strength to conquer any obstacle in his path.

He touched his own wool tweed then glanced at his plain pullover work shirt and trousers, and his grin became a frown. Why would she be willing to be seen in public with him, let alone even speak with him? No longer sporting his pinstripe trousers, wingtip shirt, vest, and coat, Andrew felt like an imposter in workman's clothes. He lowered his hand to where his silk puff tie normally graced his neck. Gone, too.

The carriage slowed to a stop, and Andrew looked out the window. "We're here," he announced and immediately exited to the sidewalk.

Andrew gripped the handle to the door and closed his eyes. He might not look the part, but he could still conduct himself as the gentleman his parents had raised him to be. Grace at least deserved that, and so much more.

"Andrew?"

Grace's concerned voice stirred him from his thoughts. He looked up at her and forced a brightness he didn't feel.

"I'm sorry," he said, offering her his hand.

She took it and stepped down in one fluid motion, bestowing a demure smile on him as she paused for him to close the door.

"Well?" Andrew swung his arm wide, gesturing toward the shop in front of them.

She looked at the windows first then raised her gaze to the sign above. "Adams Variety Store?" Grace returned her eyes to him. "This is the place you wanted to bring me? But why?"

Andrew had practiced what he'd say over and over in his head until he'd perfected his response. But now that he was standing in front of the store with her, words failed him.

"I. . .uh. . ."

Perfect. She stood there waiting for a reply, and he could only stutter. He had to pull himself together.

"I made a stop earlier today," he finally managed. "And I spoke to a gentleman who recommended we come here to search for those treasured books you lost." Andrew looked down and mumbled, "Thanks to me."

But she didn't seem to notice that last part. Instead her eyes widened and her entire visage brightened. She looked from him to the store to him and back to the store again. Like a young girl who'd just been presented with a brand-new pony for her birthday, Grace's excitement was almost tangible.

She covered his hands with hers. "Oh, Andrew, really?"

Andrew wanted to look down at their hands, but she might realize what she'd done and remove them. So instead, he shrugged. "This place is known for their diverse collection of goods of all kinds. Everything and anything a person might need. Dry goods, boots and shoes, carpets, window shades, books, furniture, and an endless variety of games and toys for children. If they don't have them, they are sure to at least know where else we might search."

"Thank you!" Grace leaned in so fast to place a kiss on his cheek, he didn't have time to react. She pulled away almost before he even realized what had happened. "This is perfect."

Before he could catch himself, Andrew glanced down at their hands, and Grace immediately did the same. Uh-oh. Just what he didn't want to do. She started to pull away, but he flipped his hands around to swap places with hers. Her head snapped up, and surprise registered in her eyes.

"You are quite welcome," he said softly, giving her hands a slight squeeze. "It is the least I can do after the loss I caused both you and your aunt."

A passerby looked at the two of them and then at their joined hands before continuing on his way. Grace noticed and her appreciation for Andrew's thoughtful gesture changed to wariness. They *were* standing on a busy and rather public city street. He'd best not draw any further attention to them than he already had. He released his hold and put a few extra inches between them. She quickly reached for her belt and gave it a tug then smoothed down her already wrinkle-free blouse.

"I would apologize for any untoward behavior on my part," he began then smirked. "But I rather liked the show of gratitude," he added with a wink.

Grace ducked her head as a shade of pink rivaling one of the prize roses in his mother's garden crept into her cheeks. Andrew probably shouldn't tease her, but he couldn't resist. And she made it so easy. Still, he didn't want to push beyond her comfort level. Extending an arm out toward the front doors, he offered the most encouraging smile he could muster.

"Shall we?"

She slowly raised her head and regarded first him then the store. With a nod, she took a step in the right direction. "I believe we shall."

Andrew placed his hand at the small of her back and guided her inside. Let the tongues wag and the whispers float on the air at the mismatched pair they made. He had the good fortune to be escorting a beautiful young lady, and her trust in him made him believe he *had* donned his finest attire. He had no reason to feel inferior.

❧

After a disappointing visit to the Adams' store, they spent the remainder of the afternoon following one recommendation after another, combing the other bookshops in town, asking with all the broker establishments, and even checking with one or two specialty stores who had regular dealings with frequent merchandise providers. All to no avail.

Andrew had to clench his fists each time the hope in Grace's eyes turned to dejection with the negative response of a proprietor or broker. Every fiber in him itched to pull her close and ease her despair, but he couldn't. He just didn't like seeing that look in her eyes.

As they returned to the carriage following yet another dead end, Grace paused before stepping inside. "One moment," she said.

His hand remained in midair, waiting for her to accept his help into the carriage. She had one laced-up boot on the step but turned partway toward him.

"I cannot do this anymore." The words came out so quiet, Andrew had to strain to hear. "I know we still have some valuable advice on where else to search, but I'm not sure I can continue." Her shoulders slumped. "My aunt did this for over a year, and I can barely last one afternoon."

Again, the temptation to reassure her almost made his arms shake. But since he couldn't touch her, he could use words.

"I have an idea." He waited for her to look him in the eyes to be certain he had her attention. "Let's return to the shipyard, and you can deliver those papers to your uncle. I'll check with some of the merchants and tradesmen at the docks. They see a passel of goods come and go in their daily activities. I'll see if they know anything that might be helpful."

Grace chewed on her lower lip. Her eyes had lost that spark he'd come to expect, and the way she stood showed her weariness. Still, she managed to perk up a bit and give him a wan smile.

"Very well. If you believe it will be beneficial, I am willing to accept anything."

Taking his proffered hand, she again moved to enter the carriage. After she joined Harriet on the one side, Andrew climbed in and sat opposite her. Everyone remained silent for the entire ride, but that suited him just fine.

Grace might not wish to continue the search, but he would. And maybe it would be better if he only notified her on the solid leads, instead of the loose trails that led them nowhere.

He glanced across the small space between them. She sat with her hands folded primly in her lap, the satchel she'd retrieved from the insurance company securely under her clasp. Perhaps a new topic of conversation would help.

"What is it your uncle had you fetch for him? I gather by the way you keep it close it's some rather important papers."

Grace looked up, somewhat startled by his sudden question, but also seeming a little relieved. "He has a meeting with the partners and investors tomorrow, and he needs these papers for that." She shrugged. "I don't know anything more."

No doubt a reassessment of their capital and where best to utilize the insurance coverage so it remained over the most valuable aspects of the business. Andrew had been privy to several conversations along those lines with his own father and their mill. Never a fun meeting, but a necessary one.

"Well, then we best get them to him as soon as we can." With a grin he added, "He no doubt already believes we've gotten lost somewhere."

Grace answered with a small smile of her own. "This might be the last time he sends me on an errand for him. We've been gone all afternoon."

"If he is cross in any way, let me explain. I've already been on the wrong side once." He straightened and assumed a tough and confident air. "I can handle it."

A giggle escaped her lips. "Better you than me."

In no time at all, they had arrived back at the shipyard. Matthew hopped down to assist Grace and Harriet, so Andrew merely descended after them. Grace glanced up the hill toward her uncle's office and said a few words to Harriet, who immediately headed toward the brick building. A moment later, Grace faced him.

"I wanted to thank you again for accompanying me today and for leading me on this impromptu expedition." She sighed. "Even if our efforts weren't successful, I do believe some progress was made."

"Yes. We now know where *not* to go next time."

He intended the remark to be lighthearted, but she didn't take it that way.

"A venture you shall be making alone, I am afraid." She closed her eyes for a few seconds and shook her head before her eyes opened again. "I need a rest from it for now."

Andrew reached out and tipped up her chin with his forefinger. "Hey," he said almost in a whisper, "I know today was difficult for you, but I'm not going to give up." He placed his thumb just below her mouth, fighting hard not to brush her lower lip. "I will not quit until those books are returned. I promise."

Her lower lip trembled, and she pulled it between her teeth. "Thank you," she managed with a shuddering breath.

His eyes drifted to her mouth. He swallowed twice. "My pleasure," he ground out before releasing her chin and stepping back. Distance. He needed distance.

Grace hesitated, her eyes taking on a sad and vulnerable expression. No, please. If she didn't leave right now, he might follow through on his desire to sample the soft enticement of her lips. A moment later she sighed and slowly turned toward the path. He almost reached out and spun her back around to face him, but he held himself in check.

Andrew marched away from her and down toward the docks. He'd inquire with the merchant sailors and tradesmen as he'd promised. And then maybe he'd take a cool dip in the river.

Chapter 15

G ood afternoon. My name is Montgomery T. Wentworth. Is Mr. Baxton by any chance available?"

The unfamiliar voice at the front door caught Grace's attention as she tucked the latest issue of *Lippincott's Monthly Magazine* under her arm and crossed the foyer on her way upstairs to fetch a shawl. An unknown caller on Saturday? They didn't often have them. She paused with one hand on the banister and attempted to peer around Harrison to catch a glimpse of the gentleman who'd come to call.

"I do apologize," the visitor continued, "for not announcing my arrival beforehand, but I have a matter of great import to discuss with him."

"I shall inform the master of your request," Harrison replied in his predictable monotone manner. "You may wait in the sitting room."

Harrison swung the door wide and in stepped a very well-dressed gentleman with impeccable taste in clothing. Grace stepped back and pressed herself against the railing. His satin-trimmed, dapper gray coat fastened with polished buttons over a bluebird jacquard vest complemented his dark gray pinstriped pants, which fell over shiny black lace-up boots. Sliding her gaze upward again, she noticed his finely folded silk puff tie held down with what appeared to be a pearly tie tack. And the view only improved from there.

She should duck back into the hallway to avoid being seen, but the man arrested her attention. She couldn't move. About Andrew's age, or perhaps a little older, his angled jawline gave way to smooth cheekbones and somewhat thin lips. He handed his silver-plated cane to Harrison and removed his felt derby hat, revealing a wavy head of russet walnut hair, trimmed with precision around his ears and allowed to grow slightly long at his nape. That left the dark, brooding eyes that held just a hint of arrogance.

And those eyes now turned on her.

With a slow and partial bow, his gaze never leaving hers, the gentleman's thin lips turned into a smile. "Good day to you, Miss. . . ?"

Harrison's face registered annoyance, and with a stony expression, he supplied, "This is Miss Grace Baxton, the master's niece, sir. Miss Grace, this is Mr. Montgomery Wentworth." With a stiff nod, Harrison went in search of his employer.

Mr. Wentworth reached for her hand, bowing as he raised it nearly to his mouth. "Miss Baxton, the pleasure is all mine, I assure you."

His warm breath fanned her knuckles. Grace's left arm went slack at the smooth tone of his cultured voice. The magazine she held slipped with a rustling of pages and slapped against the floor. As she bent to retrieve it, the gentleman stayed her with a gold-ringed hand and released her fingers.

"Allow me, please."

Still shaken, Grace took note of his finely manicured hands as he retrieved and dusted off her magazine. Now this was a gentleman. She admired the tailored fit of his coat and the high-stand collar of his dress shirt under his vest.

Straightening, Mr. Wentworth flashed a disarming smile and glanced down at the magazine before handing it to her.

"Ah, *Lippincott's*." He nodded toward the cover story. "And *The Picture of Dorian Gray*. A rather scintillating tale of the craving for personal satisfaction and a decadent lifestyle." His eyebrows arched. "I am surprised a lady such as yourself would find this story to your liking."

It wasn't the first time someone questioned her choice of literature, and it wouldn't be the last. Grace pressed the magazine against her chest and hitched her chin to look him straight in the eye.

The story hadn't ranked among her favorites, but it presented a unique perspective. "If I limit my reading, I limit my ability to form my own opinions, and therefore deprive myself of an experience that might broaden my horizons."

Wentworth placed a conciliatory hand across his coat lapels. "I consider myself duly chastised." He dipped his head. "Forgive my presumption. I am afraid my lapse of good manners has offended you. I am sorry."

Lapse? He'd been nothing short of flawless in his demeanor. His commanding presence and self-assured air differed from the other pompous gentlemen she met who dressed in similar fashion. On the contrary, Mr. Wentworth seemed every bit the type of gentleman she respected.

"So, is your business with my uncle of a personal or professional nature?"

"Why don't we allow Mr. Wentworth to address the answer of that question to me?" Uncle Richard announced from behind Grace.

She spun to face her uncle. How long had Harrison been gone? Had Mr. Wentworth distracted her that much?

Uncle Richard extended his hand in greeting as soon as he reached them. "Richard Baxton," he said, drawing his eyebrows together. "And Montgomery Wentworth, is it?"

"Yes. An honor, sir." Wentworth shook her uncle's hand. "Reports of your business acumen have spread far and wide in this area. It is a distinct privilege to make your acquaintance."

"I am sorry, Uncle." Grace spoke low and dipped her head. "I didn't mean to pry."

Her uncle brushed a knuckle down her cheek and smiled. "I know you didn't, Grace." He turned toward their guest. "But I am curious about the purpose of your visit, Mr. Wentworth. Would you like to accompany me to my study? Or would the parlor perhaps be a more suitable room?"

"Actually. . ." Wentworth glanced at Grace. "My purpose involves your charming niece and the lady of the house as well."

"Now you *do* have me intrigued." Her uncle tapped his finger to his chin. "Please proceed."

"Perhaps showing you would be better than trying to explain." He reached inside his coat pocket and retrieved a rectangular package wrapped in simple brown paper tied with twine. "I do believe this belongs to you, Miss Baxton," he said, handing the item to her.

Grace looked to her uncle, who nodded. She accepted the package, furrowing her brow as she touched the string. What could this gentleman have that belonged to her, and that made him come to their home to deliver it? She inhaled a sharp breath and widened her eyes. Oh! No, it couldn't be. Could it?

"If you open the package, Miss Baxton," Wentworth continued with a self-satisfied smile, "I believe all your questions will be answered."

Had he read her thoughts? Grace dropped her magazine onto the stairs next to her, yanked on the twine around the package, and peeled back the paper. She gasped. Yes! Oh, she couldn't believe it. The paper fell to the floor as she hugged the treasured book to her chest. The first edition copy of *Robinson Crusoe* had come home again. Grace lowered the book and flipped open the cover. There, in slightly faded ink sat the familiar words of her aunt's grandmother, five generations back.

"This book has produced the reaction I imagined it would," Wentworth said, his grin evident in his words.

Oh! Her manners! She'd forgotten them. Taking her eyes off the book for a moment, she looked up at their guest.

"Mr. Wentworth, thank you. This means more to me than words can say." She bestowed a bright smile upon him. "How did you find this? Where did you find this? And how did you know it belonged to us?"

Uncle Richard laughed. "One question at a time, Grace. I know you are overjoyed, but do allow our guest the opportunity to explain everything on his own before you belabor him with questions." Her uncle shifted his attention to Wentworth. "Before you do though, I would like to sincerely thank you for returning this item to us. My wife will be extremely pleased as well."

Wentworth clasped his hands behind him and rocked back and forth on his heels. "You are more than welcome, sir. It was a fortuitous circumstance that brought this book to my attention. As I said upon our introduction, sir, you are quite well-known in Wilmington and nearby towns." He scowled. "Your unfortunate experience with the reprobate, swindling thief became known in certain circles, as did the items you lost."

Grace bristled at the callous reference to Andrew. But of course, Mr. Wentworth didn't know him. Their guest's impression could only be based on hearsay. Had she been in his shoes, she might view the situation in a similar fashion. Truth be told, she *had* viewed things that way. . .at first.

"I believe there are three other titles which belong to you as well," Wentworth continued. "But I do not have them with me." His expression grew slightly smug. "I did take the liberty of asking the proprietor who has them for sale to hold them for me until I could speak with you. At my first opportunity, I shall return there and bring those books to you."

A nagging thought flitted through Grace's mind at the apparent convenience of Mr. Wentworth's story, but she brushed it away. She had her beloved book back. And it had been delivered by a rather charming and handsome gentleman. Nothing else mattered.

"Well, Mr. Wentworth," her uncle replied, "we are in your debt."

Wentworth waved off Uncle Richard's gratitude. "Think nothing of it. I would however like to discuss another business matter with you." He pulled one hand from behind his back and held it out in front of him. "But only if you can spare the time. If need be, I can leave my calling card, and you can get in touch with me at your earliest convenience."

So smooth. So refined. And with such manners. Grace became more impressed by the minute.

"Nonsense," Uncle Richard replied. "Come, come. Join me in my study, and we can discuss whatever you would like."

"If you don't mind, sir, I shall join you posthaste." He offered a kind smile to Grace before returning his attention to her uncle. "I should like to speak with your niece for a brief moment first."

Her uncle nodded. "Very well. But don't take long. I have an errand in about one hour."

The look her uncle gave Wentworth just before departing said quite a lot. Grace would have giggled had the silent warning not been so serious. Their guest better be on his best behavior.

"Miss Baxton," the gentleman began, "I am pleased to see you so delighted to hold that book in your hands once more."

"You have done me and my family a great service by bringing this book to me and letting us know the others will soon be back in their rightful place as well." She smiled. "As my uncle said, we are in your debt."

"And again, it is my pleasure." One side of his mouth curled up. "Although in your case, if I may be so bold, I might decide to collect on that debt in the form of a walk in the park."

Movement behind Wentworth's shoulder made her look in that direction. Just as quickly as her smile toward Wentworth had formed, it faltered. Andrew approached from the opposite corridor with a dark and brooding countenance that made her heart jump.

Had something happened below-stairs with another one of their servants? She tried to catch his eye, but he didn't even notice.

No. His attention was focused on Wentworth. The unconcealed contempt in his eyes could have wilted a flower. Could he possibly know something untoward about Mr. Wentworth? She prayed not. At last Andrew looked in her direction, seeming to struggle in his attempt to soften his expression. A lost cause.

"Grace," he said between clenched teeth, causing Wentworth to turn around in surprise, "if you're ready, Matthew has the carriage waiting. We can be on our way." He extended his hand and silently invited her to step toward him.

"Good day," Wentworth spoke up, offering his hand. "The name is Montgomery T. Wentworth. And you are...?"

Usually cordial and considerate, Andrew stared sullenly at Wentworth's extended hand as though it were leprous. That sort of oafish behavior would be more than welcome with the likes of some of the dock workers, but not with someone like Mr. Wentworth.

Grace reached out and lightly touched her guest's sleeve, eager to make amends. "Mr. Wentworth, please forgive me. I fear my excitement over the treasure you have returned has addled my wits. Allow me to introduce one of my uncle's employees, Mr. Andrew Bradenton."

"Mr. Bradenton," Wentworth repeated and extended his hand once more, a trace of smugness in his tone.

To Grace's embarrassment, Andrew still hesitated a fraction of a second before accepting the handshake, long enough for Grace to know he only did it out of deference to her. "Mr. Wentworth," he said, stepping in front of Grace as if drawing boundaries. And he was marking her clearly off limits.

Men!

Grace stepped around Andrew, eager to move away before he made a further buffoon of himself. "It was a pleasure to make your acquaintance, Mr. Wentworth. Perhaps we'll meet again sometime." She bent to retrieve her magazine from the stairs as Andrew reached for her arm.

"I believe I am ready, Andrew," she announced, holding the book and magazine close and stepping away.

"Perhaps I can invite you out for that walk Wednesday next?" Wentworth called after her.

To be seen on the arm of such a dashing gentleman? How could she say no? Grace turned to answer. "Why, yes. I would like that very much." The muscles in Andrew's arm flexed against her fingers, but she ignored it. "Please come for me around half past ten. I shall be waiting."

Mr. Wentworth touched his thumb and forefinger to his forehead and bowed again. "Then, I shall see you Wednesday. It was a pleasure to meet you both. Good day."

No sooner had Wentworth stepped down the hall leading to her uncle's study when Andrew tugged her toward the front door as though hounds nipped at his heels. Gathering her skirts with her free hand, she nearly stumbled into him.

He remained silent all the way to the door and outside as they descended the front steps to the paved walk. He'd been given the day off because her uncle worked from home that day. And he'd invited her to a speech in the park. But now she wasn't sure she wanted to go.

"And just what was the meaning of that ill-mannered exchange?" she demanded, breathless in her attempt to keep up with his pace.

He slowed momentarily, but didn't stop. "I don't wish to talk about it. You wouldn't understand."

"I wouldn't—"

Andrew stopped and spun to face her, heading off her impending outburst. "Grace, please." His words were minced through his even white teeth. "Trust me." With that, he whirled again and pulled her along toward the waiting carriage.

Trust him? How could she trust someone she didn't understand. . .especially after he'd behaved in such an oafish manner? And now he wouldn't even give her the courtesy of explaining himself? But, why would he—

As soon as they stopped, a single answer entered her mind. No, that wasn't possible. Was it? Grace took a deep breath, her thoughts staggering as fast as her heartbeat. Could he have been. . .jealous? Upset at Mr. Wentworth's attention? He hadn't acted that way toward anyone else she'd met. Why Wentworth?

She tried to see his face, to look into his telling eyes, but he kept his gaze averted and his head turned away. If she could be face-to-face with him, she'd know.

Only last night, Grace had started to see Andrew in a new light, especially considering his willingness to go to such great lengths in locating the books she'd lost. Now he didn't have to search anymore. She wanted to share the great news with him, but now didn't seem to be the best time. Could he possibly return some of those same feelings she'd only just started to experience? That might explain some of his actions.

Her head swam in confusion as Andrew assisted her into the carriage in cold silence. Just when she thought she was beginning to understand, his actions contradicted what she'd reasoned in her mind.

Would she ever figure out Andrew and his intentions?

Chapter 16

Andrew could have sworn that man looked familiar. But he couldn't place him. Not even the name registered as anyone he might know. Something about his swarthy appearance and slick talk nagged at Andrew though. The man was just too smooth. In both his story about finding the book and the way he'd conducted himself in front of Grace and her uncle. And that book.

The one no one in any shop in Wilmington had seen. Not even the merchant sailors and tradesmen at the docks could tell him much of anything. Yet in walked this stranger, brandishing not only the one missing book, but saying he had located all four of them. Then to request a private audience with Mr. Baxton? It didn't add up.

No, he shouldn't have eavesdropped on their entire conversation. And Grace would be quite disappointed if she knew. Ah yes, Grace. The young woman he'd invited to the park now sat opposite him, glowering. He had been quite the cad. He really should apologize.

"Grace?"

Nothing. Not even a twitch indicating she'd heard him.

"Grace, please," Andrew tried again.

If things between them were different, he'd move to the seat beside her and take her hands in his. But that would likely earn him a menacing glare and a firm strike on the arm at this point. Besides, she'd introduced him to Wentworth as nothing more than one of her uncle's employees. Not even as a friend. No, he'd be safer if he remained where he sat, holding his felt hat in his lap to prevent his hands from doing anything they shouldn't. And he'd try one more time. Third time lucky?

"Grace, I would like to apologize. . .if you will allow me to do so." More silence as she continued to stare out the window. "And the apology would go much smoother if you would at least look in my direction." He made an attempt at humor, hoping that might break through her silent wall. "I would prefer not to speak to the seat cushions, despite their charm."

That did it. Finally a spark of a reaction. Andrew schooled his facial features into a somber and contrite expression. If she caught him grinning, it'd all be over.

Slowly Grace shifted in her seat and angled toward him. She slowly turned her head and opened her heavily lidded eyes to regard him. Andrew flinched. Maybe he should have left her staring out the window. It would have been better than the contempt he read in her eyes at that moment. But he'd already started this. He couldn't back down now.

"I really am sorry," he began. "And you were right. My manners were deplorable. I don't know what came over me, except that Wentworth fellow grated on my nerves. Something doesn't seem quite right with him." He leaned forward and implored, "Forgive me? Please?"

Andrew sat like a statue, waiting for her reply. He held his breath and fought hard to keep his leg from bouncing or his foot from tapping. Let her say something soon.

"Very well," she finally said.

His breath came out in a whoosh, and his shoulders relaxed.

"But this doesn't repair all the damage you've done," she warned. "It is a good thing my uncle wasn't standing there to witness your behavior, or he might have had some choice words to say to you." The look she gave him next reminded him of the schoolteacher he'd had at the academy nearly fifteen years ago. "But I suppose I can keep this between us for now. . .as long as you promise it won't happen again."

"Thank you," he replied. "And I promise."

Well, that had gone far better than he'd imagined. Good thing she didn't seem to be one to hold grudges or their time together would be nothing but stilted. At least now he could look forward to attending the public speech with her and being seen accompanying such a lovely young lady.

"Now, perhaps you will allow me to compliment you on the fetching gown you've chosen this afternoon?" He sighed and gave her a sheepish grin. "I had intended to say so before, but well, you saw how that played out."

A trace of a grin played at her rosy mouth—a mouth that shouldn't be distracting him at the moment. He forced his gaze upward to meet her eyes and smiled at the glinting amusement he saw there.

"Thank you, Andrew." Grace smoothed one hand across the ruffled lace bordering her blouse buttons then fluffed out her skirt a bit. "Aunt Charlotte helped me select this ensemble. I had a more simple walking dress in mind."

"Then I shall be certain to thank your aunt the next time I see her." Perhaps for more reasons than one. If her aunt had encouraged Grace to change her mind, Mrs. Baxton might be encouraging something else between him and her niece. Only time would tell.

Andrew stretched his long legs, angling them off to the side, and leaned back against the cushions. Interlocking his fingers behind his head, he regarded Grace through narrowed eyes.

"Now, tell me more about this recent treasure you've acquired," he said with a grin and a wink as he nodded toward the book on the seat next to her.

Grace brightened considerably at this. "How did you know?"

He shrugged. "Never let it be said that I don't pay attention."

"Or eavesdrop," she retorted with a giggle.

"That, too." He smiled. "What's the story behind this book? You're going to have to start at the beginning."

She launched into the tale of the book that had become a precious commodity to her and her family, and Andrew settled in against the seat. Her face reflected her joy, and her demeanor bubbled with enthusiasm. He didn't want to think it was due to Wentworth and the part he'd played in returning the book. Even that couldn't dampen his enjoyment of the moment. Sitting opposite her, free of a shadowing lady's maid for the first time, Andrew looked forward to what was yet to come.

This made it all worthwhile.

≈

Wentworth again.

That was the third time in the past week the man had come to the shipyards to escort Grace on a walk. Andrew seethed and clenched his teeth as Wentworth placed a hand at the small of Grace's back and urged her forward. If only Grace didn't respond to him with such enthusiasm, it might make seeing them together a bit more bearable. But no. She graced him with a beaming smile and dropped everything in order to accompany him the moment he asked. Andrew leaned over the railing of the ship, trying to get a better view of the pair.

"What's the matter, Bradenton?" James clapped him on the shoulder, startling him from his irritated thoughts and nearly causing him to drop his hammer in the river. "Got yourself a case of the green sickness?"

"No." The last thing he needed was someone else noticing his jealousy. He attempted to brush off his interest in Grace and Wentworth with a shrug. "What makes you say that?"

"Oh. . .just that I called your name four times before I had to walk over here and find out what had your attention." He paused to take a breath. "Since it obviously isn't your work."

Andrew jerked his head around. "I'm sorry. I'll focus."

"See that you do." James nodded in the direction Grace and Wentworth had gone. "And do your spying on your own time from now on."

Andrew growled at himself. He had to pull it together. Grace could take walks with whomever she pleased. Andrew had no claim on her. Not an official one anyway. Anything between them clearly only existed in his mind. So why did Wentworth aggravate him so much? It was right there in front of him. Andrew knew it. Right there for the taking, and he couldn't put his finger on it.

Then it hit him.

Yes! That was it. Andrew straightened. He knew where he'd seen the man before. But wait. If that were true, then Wentworth's presence meant more than merely preventing Grace from spending time with Andrew. The blackguard was up to something else far more sinister. But how could he prove it?

૨૦

"Miss Baxton, your company this afternoon made the walk doubly enjoyable." Wentworth bowed over Grace's hand and placed a chaste kiss on her knuckles. "I appreciate your willingness to accept my invitation without my notifying you beforehand."

Andrew clenched his fists and swallowed at the smooth-as-honey tone of the man's voice. If he didn't release Grace's hand, he might find it shoved away. But Grace withdrew her own hand and reached into her reticule for a fan, which she snapped open and waved in front of her face. Andrew couldn't tell if she was warding off the early-August heat or being coquettish. Or both. He hoped it was the former.

"Mr. Wentworth, you make each and every walk most pleasurable."

"Then, might I invite you to accompany me to Sunday services three days hence?"

Grace nodded and continued to fan herself rapidly. "You may. And I accept."

"I shall call for you around nine."

"Very good," she replied. "I look forward to it."

Another bow. "Not as much as I."

Andrew waited for Grace to disappear inside the brick building. When Wentworth was a decent distance away from the shipyard office, Andrew approached.

"I'd like a word with you, Wentworth."

The man paused and turned in a slow arc, his expression one of annoyed tolerance. "I beg your pardon. . .Bradenton, is it?"

"Don't play that game with me." Andrew held back a groan. "You know very well who I am and how I came to be here. Don't act like our supposed introduction two weeks ago was genuine."

Wentworth sighed. His eyes registered disinterest, and his thin lips were pressed into a nonchalant line. "I see you finally put two and two together," he replied with grating arrogance. "I had wondered if you would recognize me or if you had even seen me that night your foolish decision led you down this dreadfully unfortunate path."

Andrew wanted to punch that self-righteous smirk off the man's face. But what good would that do except make him feel better? No, he wouldn't give Wentworth the satisfaction of seeing him lose control. He was here for Grace's sake, and for her family as well. He had to keep reminding himself of that.

"I did see you, and while I didn't recognize you right away, I do now." Andrew took one step closer to Wentworth and looked him in the eye. "And I'm warning you," he ground out. "Stay away from Grace and stay away from Hannsen & Baxton Shipping."

"Or what?" The man laughed. "Don't tell me you'll seek me out to enact whatever form of revenge you might concoct. Because if that's the case, I believe I have no reason to be concerned."

How could the man be so conceited as to think he actually stood a chance should Andrew decide to let go of his restraint? He might stand a whole inch taller, but what he had in height, he lacked in build. Something in Wentworth's eyes told Andrew not to press though. And he didn't.

"If anything happens to Grace or her family, if you hurt her in any way. . ." Andrew clenched his fists again. "I'll expose you for the scoundrel you are."

Wentworth shrugged. "Be my guest," he replied. "Tell Miss Baxton of your suppositions. Or better yet, inform Mr. Baxton himself. Neither of them will believe you. Of that, I'm certain." He sighed and raised his right hand to inspect his nails, as if the conversation bored him. "Now, if you are finished, I shall return to more important matters that require my attention."

Andrew wanted to say more, but now was not the time or the place. He couldn't leave Wentworth with the last word though.

"I'll be watching you," he said with as much menace as he could muster.

Another grating laugh. "I wouldn't have it any other way," Wentworth retorted and walked away.

Andrew almost ran after him to give him the pummeling he deserved. But he didn't. That pent-up anger had to come out though. With a feral growl he swung and punched the storage shack to his left. The wood cracked and splintered and searing pain turned his knuckles to fire. Ouch! Not the wisest move.

"What was that all about?"

Andrew stiffened at Grace's voice behind him.

"Grace!"

Had she heard what he and Wentworth had said? He certainly hoped not.

"How long have you been standing there?"

"Long enough to see you enter into a boxing match with an innocent shed," she replied. "Would you care to tell me what's wrong?"

Andrew massaged his throbbing hand and turned to face her, forcing his anger to some faraway spot. She didn't deserve to be the recipient of his repressed hostility. In all honesty, she hadn't done anything wrong. But how was he going to tell her that?

"Wentworth and I had a few things to discuss. And the conversation didn't go exactly as I had planned." At least that wasn't a lie.

Grace narrowed her eyes, clearly not convinced by his explanation. She peered over his shoulder in the direction Wentworth had gone then returned her gaze to him. She reached for his injured hand and raised it for her inspection. "A conversation that led you to punch a shack?" She pressed her lips into a thin line and sighed. "Somehow I find that rather difficult to believe." Releasing his hand, she quirked an eyebrow. "Care to tell me the truth?"

With one look in her eyes, he couldn't lie. Andrew closed his eyes and prayed for strength.

"I discovered something about Mr. Wentworth and warned him to stay away from you."

She chuckled. "Whyever would you do that?" She waved her hand idly in the air. "Mr. Wentworth poses no threat."

That's what she thought. "Don't be so certain," he countered. "The man is up to no good." Andrew reached for her hands and compelled her to focus on him. "I promise you, Grace. You need to be careful around him."

Grace pulled her hands free and laughed off his warning. "Don't be silly, Andrew. You are merely imagining things that aren't there. And what's worse, you're acting like a jealous schoolboy."

He groaned. Why wouldn't she listen to reason? "I am not jealous," he retorted, hearing the anger in his own words. "I have no reason to be." And *there* was the lie.

Grace stepped back as though he'd struck her. The carefree expression on her face turned to one of distress and hurt. Moisture welled in her eyes, and her lower lip trembled. But she stood resolute. A moment later, she whirled away from him and disappeared around the side of the building.

Andrew wanted to kick himself. He'd intended to caution her, to make her aware of Wentworth's schemes. But he'd only succeeded in wounding her. . . far deeper than if he'd physically lashed out at her. She definitely wouldn't listen to him now. He could only pray she'd reconsider what he'd said *before* his outburst. Otherwise, he'd have to be there to pick up the pieces.

Chapter 17

Andrew shut the door behind him and crossed the lower courtyard to the stairs leading up to the back lawn. Maybe a breath of fresh air would help him clear his head and get his thoughts flowing in the right direction. Although the sun had set, the heat from the mid-August day remained.

Taking his lantern in one hand, Andrew reached into his shirt pocket for the match he'd stowed there on his way out the door. With a scratch against the stone, the match sizzled, and he lit the wick that ran down into the oil.

There had to be a way to prove Wentworth's underhanded involvement in everything. He'd tried to make a few inquiries on his own, but he'd come up dry. Maybe if he could figure out who employed the man, or what his intentions were regarding Mr. Baxton and the shipping business. If he could get a shred of evidence, he could take it to Mr. Baxton and encourage him to investigate further.

But how?

A branch snapped to Andrew's right. He froze. The hairs on the back of his neck stood up.

"Hello?" His voice sounded thin, even to his own ears. He cleared his throat. "Is somebody out there?"

Andrew turned toward a slight rustling in the bushes. He held up the lantern, but the light didn't extend far enough.

"Hello?" he tried again.

Only silence. Eerie silence.

Andrew took two more steps, but before he could take his third, the lantern was yanked from his hand and snuffed out. The sudden darkness set his nerves even more on edge. Of all the nights for a new moon, why'd it have to be tonight?

Scuffling boots on grass and dirt sounded around and behind him. He spun to the left and right. Whoever was there avoided his vision with adept agility. A second later two sets of beefy hands grabbed hold of his arms. Andrew fought against them, digging in his heels as they dragged him toward the stables.

Great. Maybe Jesse or Willie would be there and wake up. He prayed it'd be Jesse, although he'd take anyone at this point. Or did the two hands sleep in the house with the other servants?

Finally the two men stopped and a lone figure stepped out from the shadows.

"Wentworth," Andrew hissed. He pulled against his human restraints and got nowhere.

"Yes. I see you still remember my name," the man's taunting voice replied. "Although that doesn't come as a surprise, considering the many times you've mentioned me lately."

Andrew could see Wentworth's silver-plated cane, held about waist-high in the man's hands.

"It seems you've been asking about me quite a lot during the past couple weeks." Wentworth paced a short span back and forth in front of Andrew, tapping his cane into the palm of his left hand. "Tell me, did you find out what you wanted to know?"

Andrew wasn't going to play this man's game. He clenched his teeth to keep from hurling a few choice curse words in his direction.

Wentworth leaned closer and cupped his fingers to his right ear. "What's that? I don't believe I caught your reply."

Andrew writhed back and forth. But his assailants held tight, their grips never loosening.

A menacing laugh split the night air. "I wouldn't bother attempting to break free. My men here are the best at what they do. And you won't be escaping from them anytime soon."

The best at what they do? Andrew didn't even want to think about what Wentworth meant by that.

"See"—the man resumed his pacing across the small patch—"I have spent a great deal of time planning out my strategy where Baxton, his niece, and his shipping business are concerned. Your dire need a few months back played right into my plans, providing me with a stooge to incriminate and set my plan into action." He waved his left hand in the air. "And the other thefts in the same neighborhood only assured my anonymity."

Heat burned in Andrew's chest, and face. He couldn't believe he'd been a pawn in this man's schemes all along.

"But we can't have you poking your nose in places it doesn't belong. You might stumble on to something important. Something that might bring to light all of my careful strategies." He tapped his cane. "So I brought along some insurance tonight. If you hadn't come outside when you did, I would've found a way to entice you outdoors." Wentworth paused in front of Andrew and bent toward him. "And now, I shall leave my men to deliver a final message to you to cease with your interference. I believe it will be most effective."

Before he realized what the two men had planned, a fist smashed squarely into the ridge of bone over Andrew's eye. White light flashed, and Andrew blinked. He'd been freed from his confines, but he could only stumble in the dark. His vision cleared just as one of the men came at him again.

Andrew charged and swung, but his adversary dodged him. Blood pounding in his temples, Andrew plowed into one of the men, and once again, the thug danced away. But not before delivering a stabbing kidney punch. Ignoring what felt like a steel blade twisting in his back, Andrew spun on the man with a powerful hook, only to have it deflected and his arm wrenched behind his back as he was driven to the ground.

That hadn't gone well.

⅔

Andrew didn't know if he'd blacked out or if he'd blocked out the full extent of the attack. Either way, only pain registered to his brain. It didn't feel like anything was broken, but with everything in a fog, he couldn't know for sure.

"Harlan ain't gonna like that we had to resort to this..."

The words of one of the thugs trailed off as his attackers disappeared into the night. Andrew's head rolled around on his neck. He stuck out his tongue and tasted blood. He should press his handkerchief to the cut, but his arms lacked the strength to pull the folded square of cotton from his pocket. The solid wall of support behind him meant he must be propped up against the side of the stables.

That was when the parting words of his assailant registered. Harlan. As in Harlan & Hollingsworth. At last! He had his shred of evidence.

Andrew's eyes drifted shut. He'd close his eyes for just a few minutes to regain his strength. Then he'd take his proof to Mr. Baxton.

⅔

"Andrew?"

Hesitant hands pressed against his chest and rocked him back and forth a little. He recognized that voice. It belonged to Bart, one of the footmen at the Baxton manor.

"Andrew, get up," Bart encouraged. "You have to get up. Mr. Baxton wants to see you in his study right away."

"Uhhh," Andrew moaned. Where was he? And how had he gotten from the stables to here? He turned his head toward the light coming in through the window and opened his eyes a slit. Daytime. But which day? Saturday or Sunday? Had one or two days passed? He had no idea.

"We did the best we could with your wounds," Matthew said. "But if anything's hurting that we can't see, there wasn't much we could do about it."

"And really, you don't look all that bad, all things considered," Marcus added.

Two footmen and the carriage driver. Who else knew about his unfortunate encounter that night?

"Relax," Marcus continued. "No one else knows you're up here but the three of us."

Andrew forced one eye fully open and squinted. The three other men stood like guardians at the foot and sides of the bed that had been his for the past three months. He had somehow been carried inside and up three flights of stairs without anyone else noticing? Amazing. With their help Andrew managed to swing his legs over the side of the bed and place his feet on the floor. His vision began to clear enough to focus on the room and the men around him. He gained strength with each deep breath he took.

The men had also given him a fresh change of clothes and washed away what he could only assume was dried blood. Mr. Baxton wanted to see him downstairs immediately? Maybe word had reached him of the attack on his property, and he wanted to see the proof for himself. But Marcus had just said no one else knew.

What could Mr. Baxton want with him? Only one way to find out.

Tapping into whatever strength reserves he could find, Andrew pushed himself to his feet and stumbled toward the door. He flexed as he walked, using the wood railing along the wall for support. Maybe his injuries weren't so bad after all. He touched a finger to his temple and winced. Rolling his shoulders produced the same result. Then again, maybe not. He wished he had a looking glass handy, so he could see if he looked as bad as he felt. No time for that though. He had to get downstairs.

A few minutes later, Andrew walked down the corridor toward the study. The hum of voices greeted him before he reached the door.

"No, I cannot believe it." Grace's voice reached him first. "Andrew would never do a thing like that."

"But he has stolen before." Mrs. Baxton's calm voice pointed out, reminding him that he might never escape that branding.

"That was a solitary incident," Grace again protested. "He's changed."

Andrew had no idea what had happened, but hearing Grace defend him bolstered his spirits and gave him strength to face whatever lay behind that door. With one hand on the smooth surface, Andrew pushed it open. The creak of the hinges announced his arrival.

All heads turned toward him. Grace gasped and Mrs. Baxton covered her mouth with her hand. Well, that answered one question. He obviously *did* look as bad as he felt.

"Jupiter, man!" Mr. Baxton was the first to respond. "What in the world happened to you?"

Andrew offered a rueful grin. "I fell into a couple of men's fists and came out on the losing end." He took a quick glance around the room to find the constable who'd been present at his sentencing and one other staff member standing back from the other four people gathered. "What's this all about?"

Mr. Baxton inhaled a long breath and released it slowly. His hands went behind his back. Uh-oh. That wasn't a good sign. "Andrew, there have been some rather important papers and some money that have gone missing from my safe here in this study."

A safe? He'd never seen one. Then again, this was only the second time he'd been in this room. Andrew furrowed his brow. "And what does that have to do with me?"

Something told him he already knew. He wouldn't have been called down here and the constable wouldn't be in this room if the answer were anything different than he supposed.

"The money was found stuffed in a drawer next to your bed," Mr. Baxton replied. "And one page of the papers was found at the bottom of your wardrobe. The rest of the papers are still missing."

Andrew sighed. Yet again. The victim of a carefully thought-out plan. Wentworth's words came back to him. He'd said this warning would stick. And so it had.

"Who found the items in question?" He likely didn't want to know, but he had to ask anyway. Call it morbid curiosity.

"That would be Sebastian, here," Baxton answered.

Andrew leaned to the right to get a look at the man Baxton indicated. "Him!" Andrew pointed at the footman who'd just been identified. "He was here the night I first came to this house. He's the one who unlocked the rear door and granted me access."

Yet one more piece to the confusing puzzle his life had become of late.

"That's ridiculous," the young man protested. "It wasn't even my night to take watch on the main level."

"We've got no witnesses to your intrusion," the constable chimed in. "But that's all in the past. You've served your time for that mistake." He smoothed his fingers down his mustache. "Now there's substantial proof to incriminate you yet again. And I'm afraid we're going to have to take you to the jail until this can all be worked out."

Jail? For a crime he hadn't committed. Not a chance! That was just the first stop toward the penitentiary in Philadelphia. He'd avoided that place once. He didn't intend to tempt fate a second time.

"But I didn't do it! Surely you cannot believe I'd repay your generous trust in me with this kind of treachery, can you?"

Andrew searched the faces of everyone in the room. Sebastian certainly wouldn't be of any help. And neither would the constable. That left only Mr. Baxton, Mrs. Baxton, and Grace. He let his gaze fall on the latter. She'd been defending him when he'd first arrived. Why was she remaining silent now?

"Please, Grace, you must believe me." Touching what he knew was a visible bruise on his face and then the cuts around his mouth, he continued. "Look at me. Why would I have been so brutally attacked and left to rot for the most part if I had stolen these things?"

"Maybe you were on your way out the door when someone caught you in the act," Sebastian chimed in.

"That is enough, Sebastian." Baxton's stern reprimand effectively silenced the lad.

"But if I was on my way out, why would I have stashed the items in my room where they could be found? Why did I not have them on me?"

His plight was likely a lost cause, but he had to try.

"Look." The constable adjusted his wire-rimmed spectacles and tugged at his overcoat lapels. "None of us here are saying it's an open-and-shut case. But we have to act on what we've found." The man's face turned grim. "And that means we have to take you in for further questioning. At least until we can get to the bottom of things."

The constable withdrew a pair of silver handcuffs. "I'm sorry to have to do this, son, but it's the law."

For a brief moment, Andrew thought of resisting, but in his present state, he wouldn't get far. No. Fighting would only lend credence to his presumed guilt. If he cooperated, maybe things wouldn't be so bad. But he wasn't about to stick out his hands willingly. He spotted a tablet of paper and a pencil on a round table near one of the wingback chairs. He snatched a single piece and the pencil and wrote down a few words before folding the paper into his palm.

After he returned the pencil to its previous spot, he caught Grace watching him with a question in her eyes. The constable stepped toward him, and Andrew tensed. No time to explain.

"Grace, please. Look into this with an objective eye. Persuade your aunt and uncle to take on a further investigation," he pleaded and silently rejoiced when a bit of resolute strength shined back at him. "You said yourself you don't believe I did this. Now prove it. Please. That's all I ask."

"Hold out your hands please, Bradenton."

Andrew did as the constable asked, taking care to keep the note tucked under his fingers. When the handcuffs snapped around his wrists, he cringed. At least the last time he hadn't been led away in shackles. Somehow the bindings made the situation seem that much more hopeless.

"All right," the officer stated, "let's go."

When the constable moved to Andrew's other side and swung him around toward the door, he stepped near Mr. Baxton.

Andrew pleaded with his eyes for the man to understand. "I'm sorry," he said.

At first only a wall of disappointment reflected back at him from the dark depths. Then a spark of trust appeared. Perfect! A tiny morsel of hope. He didn't need anything more.

He tried to extend his hands closer to Baxton. Feigning a stumble, Andrew managed to take a step or two toward him. The man registered his surprise, but Andrew quickly shoved the paper into his hands before the constable could pull him away.

He prayed Baxton. . .and Grace, too. . .would investigate further.

Chapter 18

It couldn't be true. It just couldn't.

Grace had repeated those words to herself countless times over the past five days. Yet, no further evidence had come forth to prove otherwise. She folded her arms and rested them on the table. The veranda afforded her privacy while also allowing her to gaze out on the back lawn of her uncle's manor.

The groundskeeper and gardeners kept the plants, roads, paths, buildings, and orchard in pristine condition. From the plants lining the garden path to the berry patches and the peach, apple, and pear orchards at the rear of the property, every piece of the manor's grounds seemed to be laid out in perfect order.

Not everything *was* as it should be though. Andrew sat alone, awaiting his sentencing for a second time. Only this time, he'd spent almost a full week in a jail cell. A cold, lonely, barren jail cell. She had to do something. But what?

"Excuse me, Miss Grace?"

Grace searched the veranda for the owner of the meek voice. Finally her eyes fell on a young chambermaid who stood partially hidden by the stone wall and the rather substantial shrub at the opening to the lawn.

"You may approach, Ella."

The girl took a few shuffling steps before her entire body could be seen. Even then she refused to let go of the ornate planter that came nearly up to her waist.

"Ella, you have no reason to be afraid." Grace beckoned to her. "Please. Come and tell me what's on your mind."

Grace's encouragement seemed to work. Ella released her hold on the planter and closed the distance to where Grace sat, but she still maintained a respectful distance. Her eyes remained downcast, and she buried her fingers in the folds of her apron.

Would the maid ever get the gumption to speak? Grace didn't want to scare her off, but at this rate, it would be dinnertime before the girl managed to share her concerns. All of a sudden, Ella snapped up her head and inhaled a deep breath.

"I beg your pardon, Miss Grace, but I couldn't remain silent any longer," she said in a single breath.

"Silent, Ella?" Grace drew her eyebrows together. "Silent about what?"

"About Andrew, Miss Grace."

Andrew? Ella knew something about Andrew? Grace almost jumped up from her seat to beg Ella to continue. But at any moment the girl could bolt. And then Grace would have no idea what she'd come to say.

Calming both her breathing and her heartbeat, Grace offered a reassuring smile to the girl. "Ella, please proceed when you're ready."

That minor boost must have given Ella the courage she needed. Her bowed posture straightened, and her averted gaze became direct.

"Miss Grace, I'm sorry I didn't come to you or Mrs. Baxton sooner, but I was worried Sebastian might find out and snitch on me, and then I might end up like Andrew."

"Snitch, Ella? To whom?"

"To Mr. Wentworth, miss. He was the one behind this whole thing. Sebastian knew I knew, and he threatened to report me to Mr. Wentworth if I said anything. So I kept my mouth shut." She took a bold step closer. "But I like Andrew, Miss Grace. And it isn't right to see him stuck in that jail when he's done nothing wrong."

Grace closed her eyes and took several calming breaths. She'd prayed every day that week for an answer, and now she had it. With a smile she opened her eyes and reached out toward the maid.

"Ella, please come and sit and tell me everything. I am certain my uncle will be quite interested in all that you have to say."

❧

"Uncle Richard?"

Grace pushed on the partially open door and peeked inside the darker room.

"Come in, Grace, come in," her uncle replied.

She stepped all the way into the study and went straight to her uncle's desk. He stood behind it, sifting through some papers.

"Uncle Richard, we were wrong," she announced without preamble. They'd wasted more than enough time already.

Her uncle grabbed the stack and tapped it against the desk's surface, setting the papers in alignment. "Yes, Grace, we were."

Her eyes widened. "You knew?"

"I only discovered it earlier this morning." He raised the stack he held and flicked the top page with his fingers. "Thanks to this report...or rather answers to some of the inquiries I made this week."

"So you believed Andrew, too, didn't you?"

Grace didn't know why she'd doubted that. It was her uncle, after all, who forgave Andrew halfway through his sentence. And her uncle had trusted Andrew enough to employ him at the shipyards. Why wouldn't he believe Andrew?

"You remember that note Andrew scribbled right before the constable escorted him out?"

How could she forget? He'd seemed so intent about it, so determined to get it done. "Of course." Grace nodded.

"Well, he'd written the name of Harlan & Hollingsworth on it."

The shipping business just two blocks away from Hannsen & Baxton? "What did he mean by it? Or mean for you to find?"

"Turns out our Mr. Wentworth works for them, and he's been the key manipulator in a scheme to steal the blueprints for our newest iron-hulled ship." Her uncle set down the report on his desk again. "The bound stack of bills in the safe at the time were merely a bonus. And only part of it was planted in Andrew's room."

"Oh, Uncle, we have made such a grave mistake."

He sighed. "I know." Planting both palms flat on his desk, her uncle captured her in his direct gaze. "And I believe it's high time we set things right."

She smiled. "I couldn't agree more."

"But first. . ." He glanced over her shoulder and beckoned to someone who'd just arrived. He moved around his desk to stand next to Grace. "I believe we should pray for guidance on how to proceed and ask God's forgiveness for not doing right by Andrew."

Aunt Charlotte joined them, taking hold of both her husband's and Grace's hands. "I think that is a truly splendid idea."

❧

The constable slammed the door closed on the jail wagon with a self-satisfied smirk. He touched two fingers to his double-brimmed hat and saluted before climbing into the driver's seat and setting off for the jail.

Grace watched the wagon disappear behind one of the many industrial buildings along the river. She shouldn't be happy to see someone sent to prison, but Wentworth had received his due comeuppance. Stepping an inch or two closer to Andrew, Grace nudged him. He nudged her in return, and she cast a sly smile up at him from the corner of her eye.

"Well, well, well," Uncle Richard announced, a bit louder than necessary. "Now that we have all that sorted out, there are just two things that need to be settled."

Her uncle exchanged a private look with her aunt, and they both smiled.

"Uncle Richard?" Just what were those two up to?

Richard reached behind his vest and withdrew an envelope. He tapped it against his left hand and pressed his lips into a thin line as he addressed Andrew. Andrew squared his shoulders and distanced himself just slightly from Grace.

"Andrew, my boy, you have more than proven yourself at least three times over and endured far more than any man should have to endure in your shoes." He glanced again at his wife, who nodded and gave his arm a squeeze. "With that being said, Mrs. Baxton and I agreed we owed you more than just our words of gratitude."

"Sir, you don't need to—"

"Please don't attempt to dissuade me, my boy," Uncle Richard interrupted. "We have made up our minds, and"—he handed the envelope to Andrew—"this is yours."

Andrew didn't immediately reach for it, so Uncle Richard shook it in front of him.

"Don't force me to tuck it into your pocket as well," he threatened with a half grin.

"Andrew, he means what he says," Grace chimed in. "He'll do it, too."

With a sigh, Andrew accepted the gift. "Very well, but know that I do this under coercion from two very persuasive people."

Uncle Richard laughed. "I wouldn't have it any other way." He leveled a frank look at Andrew. "You be sure and put that to good use." Empathy entered his eyes. "Maybe even help pay for a surgery or two."

Andrew inhaled a shuddering breath. "I will, sir. Thank you."

Grace tucked her hand into the crook of Andrew's arm and leaned against him. She couldn't love her aunt and uncle more than at that very moment.

"And now about that other matter," her uncle said with a slight chuckle. "I wanted to tell you both that I give my permission for you, Andrew, to court my niece."

What? Grace straightened, looking from her uncle to her aunt to Andrew and back to her uncle again. Court her? Had Andrew somehow managed to speak to her uncle without her knowing?

Uncle Richard held up his hand. "Now, before you both start speculating or asking a lot of questions, let me assure you no one has spoken to me or made any intentions verbally known." He clasped his wife's hand in his and placed his free arm around her waist, pulling her close. "I do however have eyes, and I know undisguised interest when I see it. So I'll save you both the trouble and grant my permission right from the start." He narrowed his eyes. "You treat her right, my boy."

Andrew reached out and shook her uncle's hand. "I will, sir. I promise."

Her aunt and uncle stepped close and each placed a kiss on Grace's cheek before they left her standing alone with Andrew. Moisture suddenly formed in Grace's palms, and she wiped them on her skirt. Andrew turned to face her, taking her now dry hands in his. He opened his mouth once, then twice, then shut it. Good to know she wasn't the only one having trouble coming up with something to say.

Finally he shrugged. "Guess your uncle pretty much said it all, huh?"

Oh, he wasn't going to get away that easily. And she intended to have her say as well. Giving him another sly smile, she allowed her delight at the recent turn of events to travel all the way to her eyes. "Not exactly," she replied with a wink.

He narrowed his eyes. "And just what is that supposed to mean?"

"Well." She drew out the word. "For starters, it means I still have to apologize to you for not believing you when you tried to warn me about Wentworth. I knew you weren't guilty of stealing those papers and money from the safe, but if I had listened to you from the start"—she reached up and caressed the bruise above his eye—"you might not have had to suffer to such a great extent." Returning her hand to his grasp, she raised her eyebrows. "Forgive me?"

Andrew gave her hands a squeeze. "Of course. You didn't even need to ask." He shrugged. "We all make mistakes. Who am I to judge?" He grinned. "Even if you did have the wool pulled over your eyes by a dapper, yet devious, rake."

Heat stole into her cheeks, and she dipped her head. He immediately reached to tilt her chin with his forefinger so she again met his gaze.

"Besides, after all that's been forgiven of me, how could I not in turn forgive you?" Andrew grinned. "I had a lot of time to think these past few days, sitting in that jail cell. And I talked a lot to God, too."

"What did you discuss?"

"God and I? We had some real quality one-on-one time." He gave her a rueful grin and ran his hand through his hair, making several of the thick strands stand on end. "And He set me straight on a few things, too."

Grace reached up to smooth out some of the haphazard locks, and when she lowered her hand, Andrew captured it again in his.

"Namely how carelessly I'd treated our friendship, and that I hadn't made it clear how I feel about you." His thumbs started making lazy circles on the backs of her hands. "But not anymore." He gave her hands another squeeze and pinned her in his earnest gaze. "Miss Grace Baxton," he heralded with great fanfare, "will you do me the honor of allowing me to come calling at your earliest convenience?"

A giggle started in her stomach, traveled up past her ribcage, and escaped through her lips. "Of course I will. And I've come to care a great deal for you as well. It took a scheming libertine to set your path on a direct interception with mine, but it took an ever-watchful God to make certain that juncture turned into a parallel journey."

"Guess we both got caught in the tide's strong flow."

"I know one thing though," Grace said with a bright smile. "I look forward to all He has in store for us farther down the line."

"I agree." His eyes darkened, and a telltale gleam entered into them. "And now, with your permission, I'd like to show you just how grateful I am our paths did converge and that our course is set together from this day forward."

Grace licked her lips, her palms again growing sweaty, despite Andrew's firm hold on them. Her breath caught in her throat at his earnest gaze. Unable to voice her agreement, she merely nodded.

Andrew freed one of his hands to cradle her chin. Drawing closer to her, he lowered his lips toward hers. As his mouth touched hers, he conveyed his deepest emotions to her. His kiss captured her lips as well as the rest of her heart.

ANTIQUE DREAMS

Dedication

Thank you to my husband for your support, especially when I'm on a deadline. Thank you to my editing team and everyone at both Barbour and Harlequin who made this book happen. Thank you especially to Joy, for pulling all-nighters with me to get this book in tip-top shape. I owe you some chocolate.

Chapter 1

Delaware, 1912

H old on, friend. Hold on. Help is on the way."
Aaron Stone pressed his bloodied coat to the deep gash on Conrad Bradenton's leg. He stared past the faces of the others in their lifeboat. Strangers, save their present shared experience. His gaze traveled across the frigid waters into the almost black night, a darkness interrupted only by the sight of the sinking wreckage that had been their ship.

"Soooo cooold," Conrad mumbled. He clutched the blanket around his shoulders and closed his eyes.

"Don't you give up, Conrad." Aaron glanced down at his friend. He applied more pressure to the wound, but the blood flow showed no signs of lessening. "Don't you die on me."

A wan smile found its way to Conrad's pale lips, and he opened his eyes to mere slits. "Not exactly the turn of events we were expecting, is it?" he managed to say, his voice strained and weak.

Aaron could only muster derision at Conrad's words. That was an understatement if he ever heard one. "*The ship is unsinkable,*" they'd touted. Unsinkable. Right. Tell that to the over two thousand passengers and crew who had either already lost their lives or were fighting at that moment to keep them. The churning waters of the icy Atlantic bubbled around the remains of the *Titanic*, as the ship sank farther and farther beneath the ocean's surface. What were those engineers saying now after learning the news? They'd likely think twice before making such audacious claims again.

If only Conrad hadn't insisted they secure their passage from London on this particular vessel. But his friend had gotten caught up in the prestige and excitement that came with being a first-class passenger, and he wouldn't be dissuaded. Look where that got him, though—where his hasty decision had gotten them both.

A raspy, shuddering breath drew Aaron's attention back to Conrad. His friend's face had taken on a deathly pallor, and blue tinged his lips. No. This couldn't be the end. Why did the ship's pitch have to shove that trunk into Conrad and send him flying? And why had he landed on that large shard of mirrored glass? Just when their escape had been within their grasp. Yet, despite Conrad's almost useless right leg, they'd clawed their way to safety and snagged a spot on one of the lifeboats. They'd gotten away from the danger of the sinking ship.

And now this.

"Please," Conrad whispered.

Aaron leaned down, putting his ear close to Conrad's mouth. His friend's words were barely discernible above the lapping waters against their boat and the roaring groan of bending metal as the greedy fingers of the Atlantic pulled the ship deeper into its clutches.

"Please," Conrad repeated, the veins in his neck popping from the strain of speaking.

"Shh," Aaron cautioned. "Save your strength. You're going to pull through this."

Where was that rescue ship? The *Carpathia*? The one that had telegraphed to say it was en route to their location, no doubt with extra boats and medical care. Aaron would make sure they saw to Conrad first.

"No. Must. Tell. Sister," Conrad continued.

Each word slipped through his friend's lips on a gravelly breath. Aaron leaned as close as he could to save his friend the effort. Whatever it was he wanted to say obviously couldn't wait.

"What is it, friend? What must you tell your sister?"

Conrad managed to raise his right arm enough to hold up a well-worn book. Now, where had he been keeping that? And how had Aaron not noticed it before now?

"You." Conrad's eyes opened all the way, and his earnest gaze sought Aaron's. "You take care of her." He wet his lips with his tongue. "For me," he finished in a whisper.

The book fell into Aaron's lap, and Conrad's arm dropped to the base of the boat. His eyes drifted closed, and his chest rose and fell one final time. In slow motion, the life that had infused Conrad for over two decades left his body.

"He's gone," one of the other passengers said.

"If we bury him here, we can make room for two or three more in the boat," another voice spoke.

Aaron's ears heard their words, and his brain processed the wisdom of it all, but at his core, he couldn't accept the truth. They were right, though. Nothing could be done to save Conrad now. He barely managed a nod, never taking his eyes off his friend. Immobilized, he watched as the others dumped

Conrad's lifeless body over the side. Aaron shut his eyes tight. The body made a muffled splash as it slipped away with no fanfare. Or was that only what he heard? A near silent testament of a life so full of unrealized potential. No man should have a burial like this.

Even when the boat rocked as they took on new survivors, Aaron didn't look. Instead, he ducked his head and opened his eyes to look at the book in his lap. If he acknowledged the other passengers, they'd only remind him of the place where his friend had just lain. Running his hand across the faded cover, he moved his fingers to the edge, caressing the fine leather binding.

How in the world could he make good on Conrad's request? He didn't even know where his friend's family lived, let alone any of their names beyond the surname of Bradenton. They had briefly talked of heading south once they docked in New York to some area south of Philadelphia, but for the life of him, he couldn't recall the town. Aaron slid his fingers to the edge of the cover and opened the book.

There, scrawled in blotted ink was what looked like it could be an address, but in the darkness, he couldn't make out the words. He could only see a few numbers and possibly a town name. All right, so maybe he had the where. Now, he just needed the how and the what once he arrived...if he arrived. They hadn't been rescued yet. And until that happened, Aaron had no guarantees of anything. But he couldn't lose hope.

After closing the book, he placed his right hand on the cover and raised his eyes to the midnight sky. "I promise, friend," he spoke to the heavens. "I'll find your family. If it's the last thing I do."

೩

Aaron trudged along the road on a Saturday afternoon as he ventured into a more affluent area to the northwest of Wilmington, Delaware. He could barely recall the past three and a half weeks. Everything since the ship sank blended together in a muddied blur. Even the train ride down from that New York station failed to produce any significant details. He'd just been going through the motions, putting one foot in front of the other, trying to make it through each day without letting the gloom of grief overpower him. Nothing stood out, save one fact. Conrad was dead. And he'd been left behind to pick up the pieces.

One of those pieces had brought him here to Greenville. The trolley system in downtown Wilmington had been out of the question, but the concierge at the newly opened Hotel DuPont had secured him a driver the moment he'd made his needs known. After being dropped off at the edge of the main road, the sudden quiet in the wake of the departing motorcar made a world of difference. Since he didn't know how long he'd be, he couldn't in good conscience ask the driver to wait. A telephone call to the hotel when he was ready would take care of that. Right now, he needed this time to rehearse what he would say when he came face-to-face with Conrad's family.

"I can't believe I'm actually doing this," he muttered.

Aaron raised his head and glanced down the street, lined on both sides with full poplar trees in perfect symmetry. A lot like the street where he'd lived outside of London before his Mum and Dad had passed. Only there, they'd been sycamores. The effect was the same, though. Inviting, peaceful, and attractive to those who viewed it.

But enough of this dillydallying. He'd made a promise, and he had a task to complete. Flipping open the worn book Conrad had left him, Aaron glanced down at the now familiar scrawl on the inside cover—3047 Ashview. Another look at the homes. Several acres separated each home. He should have had the driver bring him a little closer. Oh well. One step at a time brought him to the Bradenton manor. His journey was almost complete. At least the traveling part. Something told him this meeting would only be the beginning.

As Aaron stood at the end of the circular drive leading to the impressive brick colonial, he took in the well-groomed lawn and protective copse of trees to the right and rear of the home, affording a decent level of privacy. He wet his lips and swallowed then made his way to the front door, stepping in between the twin white columns and onto the porch. A family like this would either close the door in his face or welcome him inside. Only one way to find out.

"Here goes nothing," he said to himself.

Aaron raised his arm and rapped three firm times on the oak door then stepped back to wait. He had taken great care with his grooming that morning and wore what some might consider his Sunday best, yet he still felt shabby and insignificant. It didn't matter that he looked like he belonged. Inside he didn't feel it. If only he could have had someone else accompany him. It might have made the purpose of his visit easier to handle. At least that way he could share the weight of the load he carried.

But no. He was here alone. And alone he would do it.

The lock to the door clicked, and Aaron straightened. Best make a good impression right from the start. At least he'd sent a message ahead announcing his pending visit. The door swung open, and a butler greeted him.

"May I help you, sir?"

"Yes," Aaron rasped. He cleared his throat. "Yes," he said again, this time stronger. "My name is Aaron Stone. I believe Mr. Bradenton is expecting me."

The butler's eyebrows rose.

Aaron smiled. "My accent is a bit of a shock, is it not?" Aaron nodded. "You likely do not encounter many around here who sound like me."

"Do come in, sir," was the butler's only response as he swung the door wider.

Aaron expected nothing less. He stepped over the threshold onto the marble floor of the foyer. After handing his top hat and cane to the butler, he took in his first view of the inside of the manor. Two sets of columns much like the ones out front flanked both sides of the entryway, leading to a sitting room on the left and an informal dining room on the right. A wide curving staircase sat to the right and rose to the second level. A hallway straight back past two more rooms and continuing under the stairs led to where Aaron assumed the kitchen would be.

"Will you wait here, sir, or would you like to have a seat in the parlor?"

"Here will do just fine," Aaron replied. "Thank you."

"Very well, sir. I shall fetch Mr. Bradenton immediately."

The butler disappeared down the hall and under the stairs toward what appeared to be a corridor to another section of the home. Aaron tucked the book under his right arm, brushed back the left side of his frock coat, and slid his hand into his trouser pocket then rocked back on his heels. The staff kept the home remarkably clean, an earmark of respect and pride.

A door opened down the hall, and out stepped a young lady, garbed completely in black. With her head bowed, she walked in his direction but showed no signs of seeing him. Should he alert her to his presence or allow her to continue uninterrupted? Aaron couldn't see her clearly, but her veil had been pushed back from her face, revealing carefully styled blond hair, pinned with a decorative comb. Her demeanor and clothing confirmed what he'd wondered from the moment he'd arrived in Wilmington. They had been notified of Conrad's passing.

Was this the sister he was supposed to find? Or perhaps another family member? She placed a hand on the knob at the bottom of the banister. A loud smack echoed in the foyer, and the lady immediately stopped. Aaron looked down at the book that had slipped from under his arm then back up at the lady. The resemblance to Conrad was uncanny. No doubt about it. This had to be his sister.

"Do forgive me, miss." He withdrew his hand from his pocket and bent to retrieve the book then straightened again. "I did not mean to startle you."

"Oh! You're British," the young lady said without preamble.

Aaron gave her a rueful grin. "Guilty."

"Are you here to see my father?"

"I believe so, yes." He quirked an eyebrow. "But that all depends on your identity."

Despite the somber dress and her obvious state of mourning, a light pink colored her cheeks.

"Oh, I'm sorry." She raised her right hand to her cheek then clasped her hands in front of her. "My name is Lillian Bradenton. Andrew Bradenton is my father."

Under normal circumstances, a cordial smile might grace her lips, but not today. Sadness made her brown eyes dark, and a slight frown pushed her mouth into a straight line. Aaron wanted to approach for a formal introduction, but he didn't want to make her uncomfortable.

"Miss Bradenton, my name is Aaron Stone. It is a pleasure to make your acquaintance." He nodded. "And yes, I am here to speak with your father."

"I am sure he will be here shortly."

"Actually, I am already here," a man spoke from behind Miss Bradenton. She turned, and Aaron swayed to the left to peer past her shoulders.

"Mr. Stone, I presume?" Mr. Bradenton approached, aided by a polished beech-wood cane with a brass handle. His slicked-back, silver-lined hair and tailored black suit befitted the owner of such a manor. He paused to touch his daughter's cheek before standing directly in front of Aaron and extending his hand.

Aaron accepted it. "Yes, sir. Aaron Stone, sir." He released the man's hand and put his own in his pocket, holding the book close. "I sent a message ahead to alert you to my coming arrival."

Mr. Bradenton nodded. "Yes. I received it." He turned to his daughter. "Lillian. Would you please fetch your mother then join us in the parlor?"

"Yes, Father." Miss Bradenton nodded at Aaron before again resuming her path toward the stairs.

This time, she ascended them with grace and dignity, her head held high, and the smooth slope of her shoulders erect. The lone lock of blond hair curled into a tight ringlet had fallen across her back and now bounced with each step she took on her way to the second floor.

Mr. Bradenton cleared his throat, and Aaron shifted his eyes back to the man in front of him, who regarded him with a slightly amused expression.

"You wouldn't be the first gentleman to be taken by my daughter's quiet charm, Mr. Stone. I'm only sorry this meeting isn't under better circumstances."

"As am I," Aaron replied.

"Please." Mr. Bradenton swung his right arm wide. "Would you join me in the sitting room? As your message stated you had a matter of great importance to discuss, I have invited my wife and eldest daughter to join us, and we can wait for them there."

A dozen scenarios played out in Aaron's head about how he'd begin what he'd come to say as he walked ahead of Mr. Bradenton. He only hoped the one he'd rehearsed was the right one. Moving to the farthest seat available, he settled into an upholstered accent chair adjacent to the white stone fireplace with a dark stone hearth. Bradenton chose a wingback chair to Aaron's left, and the two waited in silence.

A few minutes later, the sound of shoes clicking on the marble floor in the entry preceded the ladies' arrival. Both men stood as Mrs. and Miss Bradenton entered, the mother dressed in a similar fashion to her daughter. Mr. Bradenton reached for his wife's hand and drew her to his side, turning almost simultaneously to face Aaron.

"Mr. Stone. I'd like you to meet my wife, Grace. And sweetheart, this is Mr. Stone, the gentleman I mentioned would be paying us a visit today."

Mrs. Bradenton smiled. "Mr. Stone. It's a pleasure."

"Our daughter, you have already met," Mr. Bradenton announced. "So, let us all take our seats, and we shall see to this important matter."

Aaron didn't settle into his seat. Instead, he perched on the edge. It would help him to not get too relaxed. After all, he didn't know how long he'd be staying. That all depended on how the family received what he'd come here to say.

"Mr. Stone, if you please."

All right. The day of reckoning had come.

Aaron took a deep breath, pressed both hands on top of the book Conrad had given him, and wet his lips. Time to recall the speech he'd committed to memory.

"I would like to thank you for seeing me. As has been established, my name is Aaron Stone." He paused a second or two, regarding each family member in turn. "And I have come at Conrad's request."

Mr. Bradenton stiffened. Mrs. Bradenton bit her bottom lip as the sheen of tears brightened her eyes. And Conrad's sister gasped, clutching a handkerchief as she raised her hand to her mouth. None of them offered any verbal response. His speech hinged on that. What was he going to say now?

Chapter 2

Your son. . .and brother," he amended, with a glance at Miss Bradenton, "asked me to come just before his life passed from him. And do allow me to say," Aaron added, placing his hand upon his chest, "I am deeply sorry for your loss." Best to dive right in and skip testing the waters. "I, too, was on the *Titanic*, and I was with Conrad right up to the end." Aaron sighed. "He handed me this book and asked that I come find you." After opening the cover, he leaned forward and passed the book to Mr. Bradenton. "Your address was written on the inside."

Well, all right. So, that was only half the truth. But he wasn't about to tell them Conrad's exact words. Aaron glanced at Miss Bradenton, who watched her father most intently. *"Take care of her for me,"* Conrad had said. With parents who loved her, and a home full of servants, no doubt even a personal lady's maid, she had plenty of people to look after her. Why in the world had Conrad made such a request?

As if his thoughts beckoned her, Miss Bradenton glanced over at Aaron. But instead of immediately looking away as most ladies would have done, she held his gaze. A great deal of sadness and loss reflected back at him. She and Conrad must have been close. The shadowed circles under her eyes, and the weary slump to her shoulders gave evidence to her recent lack of sleep.

"This is Conrad's writing," Mr. Bradenton spoke. "No doubt about that." He passed the book to his wife, who hugged it to her chest. "We only recently received word of our son's fate, so I am surprised to see you make it here so soon."

"I saw to a handful of matters directly, once we had reached solid ground again in New York." He pushed what he hoped was an earnest expression into his eyes. "The moment I had completed my affairs, I set forth to locating you and your family. I knew how important this would be. It might have taken me a bit longer than anticipated, but I came as soon as I could."

"So, tell me," Bradenton replied. "How did you come to be acquainted with our son?"

Mrs. Bradenton scooted forward on the settee and reached for a silver bell on the table in front of her. "I believe I shall have some tea brought in. It sounds as though we shall need it."

The tinkling of the bell was almost immediately followed by the appearance of a chambermaid, who curtsied upon appearing in the doorway.

"Phoebe, please prepare tea for us and our guest, and bring some of Mrs. Fletcher's biscuits as well."

"Yes, ma'am," the maid replied, curtseying again before beating a hasty retreat to see to her mistress's wishes.

Aaron didn't know if he should wait until the tea had been delivered, or if he should go ahead and answer Bradenton's question. The man saved him the trouble.

"Now, please, Mr. Stone. Start from the beginning."

"Well, Conrad and I met in London not too long ago. As you are no doubt aware, he had come to town to meet with who I learned were a handful of your business investors on the other side of the Atlantic."

"Yes." Bradenton nodded. "It was his first solo venture over there, and he was excited at the possibilities." He dipped his chin and sighed. "If only I had accompanied him. He might still be with us."

Mrs. Bradenton reached across and placed her hand on her husband's arm. "Or you might have been lost along with him," she pointed out softly. With a quick glance at Aaron, she returned her attention to her husband and continued. "But now, thanks to Mr. Stone, we have the privilege of learning more about the time our son spent over there."

The elder man covered his wife's hand with his own and gave her a partial smile. "You are absolutely right, my dear." He looked again at Aaron. "Forgive me, Mr. Stone."

Aaron held up one hand. "No need to apologize on my account. I completely understand your logic. In fact, I have repeated similar words in my mind several times since arriving here in America. There have been at least a half dozen 'if only' thoughts plaguing me for weeks. Not a single one has brought me any comfort." He paused, allowing his gaze to rest on each one of them in turn. "I can only imagine the questions you have asked yourselves."

"Far too many," Miss Bradenton mumbled. It was the first she'd spoken since entering the room. All eyes turned her way. "I only wish Conrad had been able to get in touch with us one last time."

"Well, perhaps what I share today will help."

❧

Lillian observed Mr. Stone's calm assurance, but she also detected a great deal of uncertainty in his demeanor. The way he worried the material of his left trouser leg, and the attempts at being subtle as he shifted his position on the upholstered seat. He no doubt knew the risk of his story not being believed, yet he came anyway. An admirable decision. The way he carried himself, and the tailored cut of his clothing, showed he came from an affluent family in London. So, he wasn't a vagabond or drifter by any means. But his eyes appealed to Lillian the most. He'd held her captive in his midnight blue gaze more than once in his short time there.

"Please." Father's voice shook her from her reverie. "Tell us more." He leaned back into his chair, extending one long leg out in front of him, while tucking the other back. His right hand rested on his ever-present cane.

Mr. Stone cleared his throat. "It was during one of those meetings that I happened to be present. You see, my uncle is a merchant trader, and he secures investors from ports all over in order to continue his business. My father had been a partner before influenza claimed both his and my mum's lives nearly fifteen years ago."

"My condolences."

"Oh, I'm so sorry."

Father and Mother responded immediately. Lillian didn't know if she should say anything or not.

"Thank you," Mr. Stone replied. "My aunt and uncle took me in and raised me. And time has gone far toward healing the ache."

Mother nodded. "My uncle did the same for me after I lost my own parents when I was ten."

Obviously, no one expected Lillian to respond. And that suited her just fine. But, Mr. Stone had no parents? What about any siblings? Had he been the only child at the time? It certainly sounded that way, since he didn't mention anyone else. He couldn't have been more than eight or nine, if she gauged his current age correctly. How sad to have been left all alone.

"In any event," Mr. Stone continued, "Conrad and I struck a fast accord and friendship. When he discovered my experience with merchant trading, he took me into his confidence and invited me to join him in business. He said I had what he called an 'impressive and endless mental ledger for remembering details.'"

Lillian concealed a soft giggle. That was Conrad, all right. It sounded exactly like something he would say. . .only without the charming British accent. And it was the first time she'd come close to smiling in over a week since they'd first learned Conrad wouldn't be returning.

Mr. Stone caught her eye and smiled. One corner of her mouth upturned. Perhaps this meeting wouldn't be so difficult after all. That made twice in as many minutes where a hint of mirth was felt. She still sensed Mr. Stone was withholding something, but she couldn't determine if it was important or not. If it was, he'd no doubt share it. So she brushed that thought aside and focused again on his story.

"Conrad never was one for details," Father supplied. "But he could persuade a merchant with overflowing shelves of the need for more inventory if he set his mind to it."

Mr. Stone chuckled. "Indeed. Conrad did have quite the flair and affinity for the interpersonal relations. I am afraid he far surpassed me in that area."

Lillian had to clamp her lips shut to avoid a verbal reply to Mr. Stone's self-deprecating remark. How could he think he lacked anything when it came to social interactions? He'd been doing admirably well so far today. By Mother and Father's expressions, they felt the same. But Mr. Stone left no chance for a response from anyone.

"Nevertheless, Conrad spent some time familiarizing me with your family's business in antiques, and I must say, I am impressed."

"It all began with my Aunt Bethany," Mother replied. "She was the first in the family to venture into antiques dealings, but it didn't take long for the rest of us to be involved as well."

Mr. Stone focused on Mother. "And I understand your uncle has a successful shipping venture here as well, does he not? Hanssen-Baxton Shipping, I believe?"

Mother nodded. "He runs a warehouse and has charge of several dozen ships at the yard near the mouths of the Brandywine and Christina Rivers."

"Yes, I am familiar with them," Mr. Stone replied. "And that venture intrigues me far more than the antiques. As you can imagine, I have been involved in merchant trading most of my life. My uncle has even delivered merchandise via some of the Baxton ships before."

"And you, Mr. Stone," Father interjected, "do you work in your uncle's employ, or have you ventured into a lucrative pursuit of your own?"

Mr. Stone shifted again, only this time, he made no attempts at hiding it. "Actually, up until about three months ago, I *was* employed by my uncle." A mixture of bitterness and hurt reflected in his eyes. "But, that was before he decided to disown me in favor of the full share of his wealth going to his blood offspring. He informed me I was welcome to continue under his employ, but an employee was all I would ever be to him in regard to his financial affairs."

"But that's not fair!" Lillian blurted then immediately covered her mouth with a gloved hand when Father gave her a silent reprimand. "Oh, I am sorry. That was uncalled for. Forgive me."

Mr. Stone was gracious, though. "Apology accepted, Miss Bradenton. And I said that very thing many times following my uncle's pronouncement. But then I met your brother, and my once-dismal prospects began to take a decided turn for the better." He sighed. "That is, until the great loss suffered in the crossing from London to America."

At that moment, Phoebe returned with the tea service. The four of them drifted into silence as the maid poured and served each one in turn, setting out the plate of biscuits and positioning the teapot closest to Mother before again leaving.

Mother raised her cup and took a sip then set it on the saucer. "So many of our acquaintances and friends either lost someone themselves or directly know someone who did."

"With nearly two thousand registered passengers and several hundred crew members," Mr. Stone added, reaching for his own cup, "and probably hundreds more who weren't officially registered, I cannot say that fact surprises me." He added a single spoonful of sugar and just a dash of cream before resuming his perch.

"Our family has suffered the great loss of Conrad," Father intoned, "but others have suffered far more, losing entire families with the sinking of that ship."

Lillian had barely even begun accepting the fact that she'd never see Conrad again on this side of eternity. She could hardly fathom losing her entire family. Sympathy filled her as she again looked at Mr. Stone. With his uncle disowning him, his parents gone, and no brothers or sisters, he might as well have lost everyone. Yet, he still found a way to journey all the way here from New York to fulfill a promise. She didn't know if she'd do the same in his shoes.

"This tragedy has far-reaching effects all around the world," Mr. Stone continued. "And I have no doubt those effects will be felt for years to come."

Father held his saucer in one hand and teacup in the other. After taking a sip, he inhaled deeply. "Now, I must ask the question we are all no doubt wanting to ask." He paused again, and his shoulders drooped just a little. "What happened out there?"

Mr. Stone hesitated. "Sir," he said with a glance at both Mother and Lillian before looking again at Father. "Are you certain you wish me to answer that in present company?"

Lillian leaned forward on the settee she shared with Mother, silently pleading with Father. Of course Mr. Stone should continue. They didn't need to know all the details, but she certainly wanted more. Father looked at Mother first, who gave a demure nod. Then he looked at Lillian. Yes, he understood. When he turned back to Mr. Stone, Lillian released the breath she'd been holding and slowly resumed her previous perch.

"I believe my wife and daughter are as anxious as I to learn about Conrad's last moments." Father raised his teacup and nodded toward Mr. Stone. "So, please continue."

"Very well," Mr. Stone replied. "As long as you are all in accord."

He leaned forward to set his saucer and cup on the table then straightened. His eyes darted up and the corners of his mouth turned down, as that same sadness crossed his face again. He wet his lips several times and opened his mouth to speak twice before closing it, as if he couldn't decide where to begin.

"As you can imagine, once we figured out what had happened, we ran with the other passengers to the nearest doorway, which would lead us to the lifeboats. Conrad and I had just gained our footing in one of the dining saloons when the ship pitched violently. A random trunk came barreling toward Conrad, and he had no time to react. The impact caused him to fall, and a large shard of glass from one of the mirrors that had been hanging on the wall lodged into his thigh."

With each detail shared, Mr. Stone's expression seemed to play back all the emotions and atrocities of the horrible experience.

"The moment I saw what had happened, I heaved Conrad to his feet and dragged him to the boat deck. We managed to reach a lifeboat just prior to its release into the churning waters." He closed his eyes, and his brow furrowed. "I did everything I could, but the rescue ship took far too long."

When Mr. Stone opened his eyes again, Lillian could almost understand everything he felt in those final moments. And she felt a strange connection to Conrad as well. The sheer reality of it all left her speechless. Father found his voice first.

"The missive we received said 'buried at sea.' Is that what happened?"

Mr. Stone nodded. "When we realized nothing more could be done, and we saw other passengers barely staying afloat above the icy waters, we had to make a decision. Or rather, the others in the boat with me made a choice. I refused to be a part of it, even though I knew it was a sound decision."

The truth of Mr. Stone's words settled over Lillian. Oh, how difficult that must have been. And yet he still took the time to venture this far south to pay them a visit. Respect for this man who had been the last to see Conrad alive grew with each passing minute.

"After that," Mr. Stone continued, "we remained afloat until the ship en route to rescue us arrived."

No one spoke for several moments. Then Mr. Stone emptied his teacup and placed it on the saucer in front of him. "Well, I believe I have taken up more than enough of your time today. I should probably see about returning to Wilmington."

He started to stand until Father's voice made him pause.

"Where are you staying?"

"I have secured a room at the Hotel DuPont on Market Street."

"And how did you get here?" Father added.

"A driver employed with the hotel delivered me here in a motorcar."

Father stroked his chin with the fingers of his left hand. "So, you don't presently have transportation back to the hotel?"

Mr. Stone replied with a rueful grin before answering. "Actually, no, sir. I do not. I had intended to ask if I might use your telephone to ring the hotel and have them send someone to retrieve me, but I as of yet had not gotten around to doing so."

Father stood and pounded his cane into the carpet once. "Then it's settled. You shall stay in one of our guest rooms. There are still a few things I'd like to discuss with you and several more questions I'd like to have answered."

Wait a moment. Mr. Stone? Stay at their manor? Under the same roof? Lillian swallowed. It was one thing to sit through a brief meeting with him. But it would be another to share the same living space and most likely several meals. The prospect both excited and concerned her.

"Oh, sir, that will not be necessary," Mr. Stone replied. "I do not wish to impose upon you or your family in any way."

Father dismissed Mr. Stone's remark with a wave of his hand. "Nonsense. You are always welcome in my home." He hooked one thumb on the pocket of his vest and rocked back on his heels. "You might not have come under the most desirable circumstances, but the mere fact that you came at all shows a great deal of character. You could have chosen to completely disregard my son's last wishes and deprive all of us of this glimpse at his final moments." Father laid his cane against his chair and extended a hand toward Mr. Stone. "I insist. And you would be doing me a great favor by accepting."

Mr. Stone took a deep breath, raised his eyebrows, and tilted his head slightly to the left. "How can I possibly refuse?" he replied, shaking Father's hand. "Thank you."

"Now, would you like me to send for your things to be brought from the hotel, or would you prefer to retrieve them yourself? I can have one of our grooms drive you there if you wish."

"I would like that." Mr. Stone nodded. "Thank you again."

Father was being rather accommodating, but that didn't stray far from normal. He seemed to have a keen insight into people, even after just meeting someone. Conrad had been the same. She wished she shared that trait. It might have saved her a few punishments as a child.

Lillian narrowed her eyes and regarded Mr. Stone with a new level of curiosity. So, what did Father see in him that led to this hasty yet insistent invitation? Not that she minded, of course. Conrad had been convinced enough to invite him into business together, and now Father approved as well. Lillian looked forward to learning more about this enigmatic British gentleman.

Chapter 3

The butler greeted Aaron at the bottom of the stairs from the second level. Retrieving his few belongings from the hotel hadn't taken any time at all. Only what he'd managed to purchase with the minimal funds he secured in New York, but he was a long way from replacing what was lost with the ship. And everything else was back home in London.

"Dinner is being served in the formal dining room, sir," the butler intoned, stepping back and indicating the direction of the room.

The man was so much like his own butler, Quimby, in both stature and appearance, right down to the almost miniscule cleft in his chin. Aaron paused in the doorway.

"Do forgive me, old chap, but we have not been properly introduced." He reached out his right hand. "I have already told you my name." He raised his eyebrows. "And you are...?"

The butler hesitated a brief moment then shook Aaron's hand. "Charles Parker, sir."

Aaron nodded. "Very good, Charles. I shall feel better knowing how to address you." He peered through the doorway into the first room. "Now, is the formal dining room through here?"

"Yes, sir." Charles gestured toward the other arched doorway. "Straight through there, sir."

"Thank you."

Just out of sight of anyone who might already be in the room, Aaron stopped and double-checked his appearance. He tucked in his puff tie, tugged on his vest, and smoothed the lapels of his coat. It was one of the two outfits he presently owned, and he hoped it would suffice. Nothing he could do about it now, though. Satisfied he'd done the best he could, Aaron proceeded into the other room.

His gaze quickly located Mr. Bradenton, who acknowledged his arrival with a nod before returning to a private conversation with another gentleman. Aaron glanced around the room. He was certain Mr. Bradenton mentioned only three other children besides Lillian and Conrad. Even counting the servants and Mrs. Bradenton, there were far more people present than he thought would be there. Obviously, he wouldn't be the only guest joining the family for dinner.

And he was clearly tardy.

One of the maids wove her way through the assemblage and held a tray of glasses filled with punch, wine, and champagne. His eyes first passed a younger version of Miss Bradenton before stopping on the young lady herself. She took a glass of champagne from the tray and raised it to her lips, smiling at something her conversation partner had just said. Clad in an olive silk gown with a fitted jacket that accentuated the slimming lines hugging her feminine curves, she presented an appealing picture. The puffed sleeves and lace around the collar gave a smooth appearance to her gently sloping shoulders. Her upswept hair had been styled to perfection with the ever-present single lock tucked gracefully against her neck.

As if sensing his perusal, Miss Bradenton glanced his way. Aaron touched one finger to his forehead and offered her a grin. An answering smile teased the corners of her lips as her head dipped ever so slightly in his direction. A second or two later, she returned to her conversation.

"Ah, Mr. Stone, it is good of you to join us." Bradenton approached from Aaron's left and clapped a hand on his back while shaking with his right.

"Sir, please forgive me. Had I been aware the arrival time differed from what I was originally told, I would have been more careful about my tardiness."

"Nonsense," the man countered. "You aren't late at all. The other guests here merely arrived early. They are very close friends from down the street." He cleared his throat. "Excuse me, everyone." His voice rose to a booming level, and the room immediately quieted. "Grace and Lillian have already met our guest, but I should like to introduce him to the rest of you." He dropped a hand on Aaron's left shoulder. "This is Aaron Stone. He and Conrad met in London not too long ago, and Mr. Stone traveled on the *Titanic* with him."

An almost audible collective gasp rose as the others realized he was one of the few survivors from the ship. Mr. Bradenton didn't pause, but his hand squeezed Aaron's shoulder slightly.

"Mr. Stone, these are our good friends and neighbors." He started to their left and pointed to the man he'd been talking to when Aaron arrived. "First are Edward Duncan and his wife, Maureen, standing with my wife." His finger moved around in an arc to a group of young lads. "Then, there is Pearson, Daniel, and Alexander, their three sons, along with Geoffrey and Theodore, my two youngest." He indicated the young lady standing with Lillian next. "Arabella is their daughter, and Chloe is mine."

Aaron attempted to repeat the names in his mind, relying on his proven technique of familiar association for recalling important details. Some were easy, such as Pearson having dark, piercing eyes with an obvious wandering gaze in

Lillian's direction, or Theodore's plump, round face reminding him of a stuffed teddy bear. He remembered that cartoon from the *Washington Post*, and the image definitely fit. The others would likely require a bit more time before he could determine something that worked. But he was up for the challenge.

Charles approached right then and spoke low in Bradenton's ear before stepping back toward the wall.

"It appears I completed introductions just in time," Bradenton said. "Charles has informed me that dinner is ready to be served." He made a sweeping gesture over the perfectly set table in front of them. "If everyone will take your seats, we shall prepare to enjoy Mrs. Fletcher's delicious meal." He started to move to his seat then stopped and turned to Aaron. "Mr. Stone, your seat is next to Mr. Duncan."

As everyone moved to their respective seats, Aaron did a quick cursory review of the room. The chairs were covered in crimson and black. The finely carved wood visible beyond the upholstery had a gentle artisan's curve. What could be seen of the polished mahogany table gleamed beneath the place settings. Aaron caught a blurry reflection of himself as he sat. Several large mirrors with gilded frames flanked one of the three walls. A large portrait of a man who resembled Bradenton adorned the wall behind the head of the table, and three stately windows with brocade curtains were spaced a few feet apart on the opposite wall. Even the drapes that framed the doorway where he'd entered matched the crimson of the carpet under his feet. And the chandelier hung overhead illuminated everything with just the right amount of light.

"Impressive, isn't it?" Mr. Duncan leaned close and spoke low.

"Yes." Aaron nodded. "Quite."

The room resembled the one in his uncle's home, but the quality far outshone anything they had. The antiques and shipping businesses had obviously been generous to this family. Aaron could only imagine the expense involved if the entire home had been decorated in the same manner. Yet nothing felt overly pretentious or appeared as if the Bradenton's were boasting in any way.

"I've often asked Andrew to divulge the name of his decorator to me," Duncan continued, "but he always says she's not for hire."

Bradenton gave Duncan a tolerant yet amiable smirk. "You know very well why, too, Edward." He reached for his wife's hand and raised it to his lips.

Duncan grinned and waggled his eyebrows. "He just doesn't want his wife making my home better than his." He glanced across the table at his wife with a fond smile. Aaron followed his gaze. "Though I'll contend my wife's gardens are the envy of Greenville."

Maureen Duncan beamed under her husband's praise. The two couples showed obvious affection and a long-standing love for each other. Just like his parents, or what he remembered of them. Of their own accord, his eyes traveled slightly to the right and met Lillian's gaze. She colored prettily when he caught her looking at him, and she dipped her chin. With the example of her parents set before her, she had an excellent chance of finding the kind of love they shared. And the man who married her would be extremely lucky.

A man like the one he'd been before his recent loss.

Considering his present circumstances, Aaron felt almost like an imposter. It seemed wrong somehow to be sitting in a room this ornate when he had recently been deprived of his own wealth and inheritance. The entire experience, from his uncle's pronouncement to the moment he'd arrived in New York following the ship's demise, made him begin to view so many things in a different light.

His thoughts were once again interrupted, this time by their host. Bradenton pushed back his chair and moved to stand behind it, resting his hands on the high back.

"I'd like to thank everyone for coming this evening. In light of recent events, it is good to enjoy the company of family and friends at a time like this." He looked down the table, his gaze resting on each guest on both sides of the table. "I couldn't think of a better way to thank you for your support than to invite you to join together and enjoy a delicious meal."

After resuming his seat, he extended his arms out toward his guests.

"Now, let's get this dinner under way."

Several servants assisted the ladies present then reached for the napkins on the table, fanning them out before placing them in the ladies' laps.

In a matter of moments, the soft din of voices rose from the table. Mrs. Duncan leaned close to Lillian.

"My dear, I am as always pleased at the company in which I find myself. I cannot imagine a more compassionate or industrious family than your own. There aren't many here in Wilmington who have suffered the loss your family has, yet you've stepped up to offer your support and assistance any way you can." The woman turned to smile at Lillian's mother. "Grace, you have set a fine example for both of your daughters, and it's wonderful to see them following in your footsteps." She winked. "Should aid well I would think in them finding suitable matches."

So, the integrity Aaron had seen in Conrad stemmed directly from his parents. Not that the fact surprised him. But hearing about Lillian's compassion in the midst of her own grief spoke volumes in favor of her own character.

Bradenton winked from his seat, while his wife nodded at Mrs. Duncan.

"Thank you, Maureen," she said, pride reflecting on her face. "I am honored to have two such dutiful daughters, as well as two sons showing such promise. And all so willing to help wherever there is a need."

Salads were placed in front of them, and they halted their conversation for a few moments. After waiting for everyone to be served, they looked to Bradenton to take his first bite. He did and waved his fork in the air to encourage everyone else to do the same.

After eating her first forkful, Mrs. Duncan picked up where they'd left off. "I do know for a fact that the visit you paid to the Holmsteads, Lillian, meant a great deal to them."

"Well, I can't take all of the credit," Lillian stated. "Chloe and Mother also accompanied me."

"Yes," Mrs. Duncan replied. "And the three of you have made a remarkable impression."

Lillian glanced across the table to find Mr. Stone watching her with unmasked admiration. The heat of a blush crept up her neck and filled her cheeks. Yet again, her fair skin betrayed her. Were she more coquettish, she might carry a fan with her to flip open in front of her face in situations like this. At least she could hide the blush.

Arabella leaned close. "I believe you have caught the attention of a certain handsome gentleman," she whispered.

"Shh," Lillian replied, giving her best friend a stern look.

"At least he's impressed with your compassion for others," Arabella mumbled from the corner of her mouth. "That has to count for something."

Father took that moment to speak up as well. "It has been difficult since learning about Conrad, but the good Lord has given us His strength to keep going."

"Comforting others," Mother added, "in a way, has brought comfort to us." She raised her finger and caught a lone tear that had collected at the corner of her eye. "We've been able to step outside ourselves and our grief and realize how blessed we are in spite of the great loss."

"Blessed is an excellent way of looking at it," Mr. Duncan replied. "Conrad might no longer be with us, but he has left his mark and substantial shoes to fill."

"I might only have known him for a short while," Mr. Stone spoke up, "but I observed the same qualities in him that I now see in all of you. It is an admirable trait, and I am certain Conrad's memory will survive well through those who loved him most."

Moisture collected at the corners of Lillian's eyes. She wouldn't cry. Not again. And especially not in front of their guests.

"I couldn't have said it better myself, Mr. Stone," Mr. Duncan said.

Lillian sniffed once, but quietly. Why did Mr. Stone have to say something so endearing? It sounded exactly like what Conrad might have said. But Mr. Stone was nothing like her older brother. Where Conrad had been blithe and carefree, Mr. Stone appeared focused and determined. Conrad was always about the people. Mr. Stone seemed to be all about business. Of course, she'd only been privy to that one conversation in the parlor. Mother would chastise her for rushing to such hasty conclusions.

Sniffing again and blinking away the tears, Lillian set her attention on her salad. She was about to look away when she caught Mr. Stone's eye. His gaze held hers for a moment. Arabella nudged Lillian's foot with her own, but Lillian ignored it. There it was again. That indeterminate look she'd seen when he'd told them about Conrad's last request. Before she could ponder it further, Father cleared his throat.

"All right. I believe it's time we shifted the focus of this dinner conversation away from our recent losses."

Lillian inhaled and released a long breath. Yes. Anything but adding to the constant reminder she'd never see Conrad again. Never have her beloved older brother to watch out for her. She looked upon the faces of those nearest her, but no one seemed to have a topic at the ready. The blur of something passed through her peripheral field of vision, and Lillian turned to the left to see what it was.

"Alexander!"

"Theodore!"

The dual chastisement came from both Mrs. Duncan and Mother at the same time. The youngest boys were seated across from each other, flanked by their older brothers and sister, but that hadn't stopped them from mischief.

"Teddy, if I see that happen again," Mother warned, "you and your father will be taking a walk to the woodshed by the carriage house. Do I make myself clear?"

Teddy ducked his head, appearing duly chastised and contrite. "Yes, ma'am," came the meek reply.

"And the same goes for you, Alexander," Mrs. Duncan echoed. I am certain that woodshed is plenty large enough for a suitable punishment."

Again, the ducked head. "Yes, ma'am," Alex replied.

Soon the salads were removed and replaced with steaming bowls of french onion soup. It might be early May, but a chill in the air still remained in the evenings, and hot soup was Lillian's favorite. She eagerly dug into the delicious broth.

Silence fell upon the table as many took their initial fill of the second course. But a few minutes later, Father resumed the conversation.

"So, what has anyone heard regarding the recent march along Fifth Avenue up in New York City?"

Mr. Duncan had made quick order of his soup and laid his spoon in the empty bowl then rested his forearms on the edge of the table. "Do you mean the thousands of women and some men who were speaking up about women getting the right to vote?"

"One and the same," Father replied.

"I think it's a splendid thing happening," Mother added.

"And an admirable one at that," came from Mrs. Duncan.

" 'Tis a pity it likely won't lead to much," Mr. Duncan added.

"Oh, I wouldn't be too sure about that," Mrs. Duncan countered. "That many women together in one place can have a significant impact."

Arabella sat up straighter in her chair. "Really? Thousands marching in the city? And all supporting women's suffrage?"

"It must have been an incredible sight to see," Lillian added.

"Nothing like that ever happens here or in Wilmington." Arabella's disappointment almost made her sound like a pouting child.

Lillian couldn't help but smile. "But what about the hundreds of people who assembled in the city square to plant that one cherry tree back in March? They all gathered to support the bigger ceremony in Washington led by the First Lady and the viscountess." She winked at her friend after taking a final spoonful of her soup. "Doesn't that count as something exciting?"

Arabella shoved into Lillian with her shoulder. "Now you're just teasing me."

"Well," Pearson spoke up from across the table with a smile, "we now have forty-eight states in the Union. If life here in Delaware isn't exciting enough, you could always find another state that suits you better."

"All right, all right," Mr. Duncan interrupted. "Let's not pester Arabella anymore."

"That's right." Arabella jutted her chin out and stuck her nose in the air. "When women get the right to vote, you won't be poking fun at the march or anything else like it."

Mother tapped her fingertips together. "I suppose we'll have to wait and see."

The next part of their dinner was a refreshing serving of lime sorbet to cleanse their palates in preparation for the main course. Conversation stalled for just a moment as each of them took a small spoonful of the sweet treat.

"One thing that might surprise a lot of people," Lillian said as soon as her mouth was clear, "is just how involved women and young ladies are in the everyday development of things." She set her spoon on the plate under her sorbet dish and folded her hands in her lap. "Earlier in March, a woman by the name of Juliette Gordon Low organized Girl Guides down in Savannah, Georgia. Seems girls wanted to join the boys in the scouting activities, and now they can."

"If a woman can fly solo across the English Channel like Harriet Quimby did," Arabella added, still obviously on her soapbox, "and the Girl Guides can join the Boy Scouts in taking on constructive roles in society, it's only a matter of time until they start making significant decisions as well."

"No one is denying the importance women and ladies have in society, girls," Father replied. "But with something like voting, a greater level of responsibility is required."

Arabella opened her mouth to speak, but Mr. Duncan held up a hand to stop her, and Father continued.

"Not that you, or any other young lady, wouldn't be prepared to accept that responsibility. However, it isn't something into which you should tread lightly, or without a great deal of consideration."

"You make a valid point, Father," Lillian replied.

"And I'm certain," Mother added, "the ladies present at this table this evening will do just that."

From that point forward, talk shifted away from advances for women and young ladies and centered on a variety of different topics. Lillian couldn't keep track of the smaller conversations that took place, though she managed to interject a comment or two. Before she knew it, the evening had come to a close, and Charles shut the door behind the Duncans after everyone had said their good-byes.

Father leaned on his cane and moved it around in a circular motion as he stood next to Mother in the foyer. Chloe stood next to Lillian, and their brothers had already been taken upstairs by Mrs. Fairchild. But where had Mr. Stone gone? He wouldn't have been there to bid farewell to the Duncans, but he couldn't have retired to his room already, could he?

"Well, I must say I enjoyed the evening immensely," Father said.

"Yes," Mother added. "And I believe it was an evening we all needed."

Father raised one eyebrow and grinned at Lillian. "I never knew you and Arabella were so well informed about current events."

Lillian shrugged. "We try to stay abreast of the important matters."

"Well, you did admirably well this evening. I was suitably impressed."

Father exchanged a silent look with Mother, who nodded.

"Lillian, Chloe," she said, "let us adjourn to the drawing room and work on some of our knitting for the Ladies' Aid. I believe your father has some business to discuss with Mr. Stone."

Lillian started at this. So, he *was* still present. She almost looked over her shoulder to see if she could locate him but decided against it. Her mind already thought of him far too often. And he'd only been with them for less than a day. But he'd been equally affected by the loss of Conrad, perhaps even more, since he'd been right there by his side at her brother's final breath.

What exactly drove him to make the long journey south to come calling on her family? Why did he not simply walk away from it all and return to his own life?

As she, Chloe, and Mother turned to leave, Mr. Stone approached from the shadows by the wall. His gaze caught hers for a brief moment. Again, the admiration was present, but there was also something more. Sadness and even weariness mixed with a hint of worry. It all made sense. So much had happened to him in the past few weeks alone, and now to be entangled in their family as well? Stranded on the other side of the ocean from everything he'd always known?

Lillian had to force herself to break eye contact with Mr. Stone. She watched from the corner of her eye, though. He nodded at Mother and Chloe before stepping forward to join Father as the two headed for his study. Just how had God decided which families would suffer and which wouldn't? The reports claimed more than half the passengers didn't survive. Why their family? Why Conrad? And why had Mr. Stone been spared instead?

That started another line of thought. . .the purpose in everything. Lillian firmly believed everything happened for a reason. While she might not be able to figure out that reason, she still had a duty to take what had happened and find the strength to keep going. If that meant blessing others in need when she had something to give to them, or serving from her abundance, she would do it. Mr. Stone had no one and nothing here. God's Word said if she served even the least of those she encountered, she served as if unto Him. Meeting someone like Mr. Stone was merely a bonus.

Chapter 4

P lease, take a seat, Mr. Stone."
Bradenton closed the door to his study and gestured toward one of two high-back, upholstered chairs opposite the impressive dark cherry desk occupying more than a quarter of the room. He leaned his cane against the desk and continued toward the far side of the room. Aaron took note of the rich Aubusson rug covering most of the floor and the heavy velvet drapes at the windows. This was without a doubt a gentleman's domain. A lone gas lamp on the desk illuminated the otherwise dark room, but light immediately flooded the room when Bradenton turned on an electric lamp near the window.

Aaron blinked a few times at the sudden brightness.

"My apologies, Mr. Stone. I should have warned you."

"No worries." Aaron waved off the apology.

As soon as his eyes adjusted, his gaze landed on what had to be portraits of the family patriarchs lining the wall to his right. Some might view those and feel as if they stared down in condescension, their expectations high for the present occupant to not destroy the legacy they'd established. But Aaron had a feeling Bradenton, and likely Conrad as well, were encouraged and strengthened by their presence. His own father's study had been decorated in a similar fashion, though only one portrait hung on the wall. That of his great-grandfather, who'd earned a medal of valued service during the battle against Napoleon. The rest of the portraits hung in the hall outside the formal dining room, where they could look down upon all who passed by.

On the other side of the room, custom-built, floor-to-ceiling shelves held a wide selection of books, references, and even small photographs in quality frames. Just like the fine craftsmanship of the dining room table and chairs, these shelves bore evidence of quality care and design.

"I commissioned the man myself," Bradenton answered, even though Aaron hadn't posed a question. "Robert Gillis is his name. Governor Pennewill sang his praises when I last visited his home in Dover, and I decided to seek out the craftsman myself."

"Was Mr. Gillis the one who built your dining furniture as well?"

"Yes, he was." Admiration sounded in his tone, and Aaron turned to see

Bradenton's eyebrows raised. "How very astute of you."

Aaron reached up and tapped his temple with one finger. "It's that attention-to-detail skill I possess, sir. It usually comes to my rescue in substantial ways."

"Ah yes," Bradenton replied. "The skill my son noticed as well."

Aaron chuckled. Conrad hadn't called it a skill. He'd accused Aaron of having a ledger for a brain instead. "Yes, sir. And it aided Conrad and me in the handful of business dealings we had prior to boarding the ship. I could recall specific features or particular pieces of information about certain individuals then tell them to Conrad when he was negotiating with prospective buyers."

Bradenton nodded. "I can certainly see how that would prove to be useful. And it would give Conrad the decided edge when coupled with his skills with people."

He moved to stand behind his desk, placing his hands flat on the leather-covered surface. His fingers drummed a random rhythm, and he pressed his lips together, as if deciding how to proceed. Finally, he took a seat, the leather chair creaking under his weight as he rested his elbows on the desk and steepled his fingers.

"So, tell me," he began, touching his fingers to his lips. "We didn't have the opportunity to discuss anything further following our initial meeting. But now that we are away from the ladies, I'd like to know a bit more about my son's final moments."

This question was bound to come up sooner or later. A man like Bradenton wouldn't go long without the full disclosure of details concerning his eldest son. But could Aaron relive it yet again? Every time he closed his eyes, the nightmare assaulted his sleeping moments. He wanted nothing more than to forget. Conrad's father deserved more than that, though, and had the tables been turned, he'd have wanted Conrad to do the same for him.

With a deep breath, Aaron allowed the memories to rush in.

"It was an experience I shall never forget, sir," he began. "We felt the impact of the iceberg, though at the time we had no idea what had happened. Once everything seemed to be all right, everyone around us returned to business as usual."

Bradenton raised his head away from his hands. "Do you mean the sequence of events didn't all happen immediately?"

"No. At least not initially. In fact, it almost felt like hitting a significant rut in the road and driving on." If only that had been the worst of it. "Conrad and I were in one of the parlors, at a table with two other gentlemen who had inquired about your antiques, and after a few moments, we resumed our conversation." He leaned forward and rested his elbows on his knees. "I'm not certain how much time had passed before we noticed something amiss, but a definite unease was tangible among the passengers. Turns out it wasn't long at all. Perhaps fifteen minutes at the most." Aaron shook his head—as if doing so would erase the tragic night from memory. He could only wish. "The hour was late, I believe nearing midnight or later. Most passengers were already in their staterooms, though I am certain the impact woke a good majority of them. But when the alarms sounded, panic ensued."

A sigh sounded from across the desk. With him being illuminated by the brighter lamp from behind, Bradenton's features almost appeared dark and foreboding. Aaron had to focus closely on his face to read his emotions.

Bradenton lowered his arms and folded his hands in front of him. "I can only imagine the incredible shock of being woken from sleep, experiencing a few moments of peace then feeling as if the world were coming crashing down around you."

Aaron sat up and loosely pointed his index finger and thumb toward Bradenton. "You pegged the reactions succinctly, sir."

Bradenton's face took on a grim expression. "What happened next?" Before Aaron could reply, Bradenton held up his hand. "It's important that I know everything. My wife is experiencing a lack of ability to set this all to rest. If I could somehow provide her with enough information to set her heart at ease, I will do it."

"I completely understand, sir. And I applaud you for doing so."

"Thank you."

Aaron nodded. "What happened next is somewhat foggy, I'm afraid, but I shall endeavor to recall as much as I can."

He counted off with a slight bounce of his head each part he remembered and what he'd already divulged. Then, he stood. The retelling was far too difficult for him to remain seated. He had to pace in order to release it all.

"It all happened in haste, and we barely had enough time to determine our course of action, let alone ascertain what exactly had occurred. Conrad and I knew only that we needed to make our way to the boat deck as fast as possible. And that is exactly what we did."

Bradenton didn't need to know about the interrupted game of cards, or that his son had likely had one drink too many that night. No, some details were best left unsaid. It would do no good to tarnish Conrad's reputation now.

"Though we couldn't understand it at the time, the pitch and heaving of the boat were due to the ship basically splitting in half from the bottom up, almost in the middle. From what I recall and what I've read, key areas were flooding, and flooding fast, and the chambers filling with the frigid waters were hastening the demise of the ship."

Aaron pivoted and turned back in the other direction.

"If we had already retired to our staterooms, we might never have made it. As it was, we were on one of the upper levels. Once we reached the public rooms, we had one room to cross to the doors leading to the boat deck." Aaron stopped and looked directly at Bradenton. "And that was when fate dealt us a cruel blow. The pitch of the ship, the careening trunk, the substantial shard of glass. I didn't think twice before removing my coat to stop the bleeding."

And here is where his own blame came into play. The blame he heaped upon himself each time the events of that night repeated in his mind. If Bradenton saw fault in his actions, too, Aaron wouldn't hold it against him. He resumed his pacing, clasping his hands behind his back as he walked.

"The haphazard manner in which I tied the coat around Conrad's leg might not have stopped the flow, but it made it possible for Conrad to stand, and I half dragged, half carried him to the outside deck."

"This deck," Bradenton interjected. "This is where the lifeboats were? Where you managed to find a way to escape from the sinking ship?"

"Yes. We were the last two before the boat was released, and that alone was a feat. With the ship sinking more on one end than the other, it had begun to rise slowly out of the water. Lifeboats were released at an angle, and it's a miracle none of us landed on each other in the process."

"How long. . ." Bradenton cleared his throat. "How long after you moved free of danger did Conrad take his final breath?"

Aaron paused and looked over his shoulder. "I cannot say for certain, sir, but I would estimate it was less than thirty minutes. The row to safety wasn't a smooth one, either. Passengers in the water grabbed hold of the boat, attempting to climb in. We were already over capacity as it was. But their attempts pitched the boat to and fro, making it difficult to maintain a steady hand on the wound. And had the sinking not been such a catastrophic event, it would have been a sight to behold. The bulk of a ship completely vertical to the ocean surface while being pulled beneath the waves and absorbed into the angry clutches of the sea."

Bradenton closed his eyes. If Aaron hadn't witnessed it with Conrad, he'd never believe such a bevy of emotions could cross a face without the benefit of visual expression. Yet, there it was. The weight of the fear, anguish, suffering, and loss experienced by the passengers evident for Aaron to see. No wonder Conrad had such an easy time relating to people. He and his father both internalized what others felt and based their discernments from that.

"Sir?" Aaron paused and waited for Bradenton to again open his eyes before continuing. "I did everything I could to save him, sir. But the wound was too deep, and the conditions too unfavorable to sustain him." He hung his head. "When the others in the boat moved to lay his body to rest, I couldn't help but think how much of our attempt to escape had been in vain. If we had perhaps chosen another path or a different area of the boat deck, we might have made it to a lifeboat unscathed."

"Or you might never have made it to a lifeboat at all," Bradenton countered.

Aaron looked up, expecting to see condemnation emanating from Conrad's father, but instead, he saw only compassion and understanding—and he didn't deserve either.

"Mr. Stone, I will never fully comprehend everything you experienced that night, but I can say for certain right now that I owe you a great deal of gratitude for what you *did* do. For my son and for my family."

"But, sir—"

Bradenton held up a hand. "Please, let me finish."

Aaron nodded.

"You might not have been able to save my son, but that responsibility did not rest solely upon your shoulders that night." Bradenton moved from behind the desk and came to stand directly in front of Aaron. "It is not our place to say where or when will be someone's final breath here on this earth." He reached out and placed his left hand on Aaron's shoulder. "But you, Mr. Stone, made my son's last moments full of the knowledge that someone cared enough about him to risk his own life. And if Conrad could be with us now, I'm sure he'd say the same." He extended his other hand. "So let me say thank you for all you did that night, and for having the fortitude to travel this much farther in order to meet with us."

Aaron didn't know how to respond. After weeks of wondering what he could have done differently, and mentally berating himself for not being able to return their son to their family, he didn't expect to find such forgiveness. Well, at least he could return the man's handshake. So he did.

Steady footfalls sounded in the hallway outside the study, followed by three sharp knocks on the door.

"Enter," Bradenton called.

Grateful for the interruption to disperse the heavy emotions in the room, Aaron looked up as Charles appeared in the doorway. The man cleared his throat.

"Pardon the interruption, sir, but a missive has just arrived for you."

"Charles, please tell me it isn't another note from our lawyer." Bradenton stood and rubbed his temples with his fingers. "I might be tempted to ask you to return it without my even reading it."

Aaron tilted his head and furrowed his brow. Company lawyers? Were the Bradentons involved in some sort of legal hassle?

"No, sir. This is not from the lawyer." The butler glanced down at the envelope he held. "It is from a Mr. Pierre S. du Pont, sir." He started to turn away. "Shall I leave it on the tray in the front hall?"

Pete du Pont? Of the du Pont de Nemours powder companies? He and his uncle had conducted business with them on several occasions. Was there any industry in this state in which this family *didn't* have a connection?

"No!" Bradenton nearly toppled one of the upholstered chairs. "That is, no," he spoke more calmly. "I will take it now." He held out his hand.

Charles took several steps toward the dark cherry desk and handed the letter to Bradenton. "Will that be all, sir?"

"Thank you, Charles. Yes, that will be all. I will call upon you if a reply is necessary."

"Very good, sir."

As soon as Charles left, closing the door behind him, Bradenton returned to his place behind his desk and sat once more. He rested his arms on the edge and opened the letter he'd just received. Aaron resumed his seat and waited, drumming his fingers together and trying to give the man a little privacy. First, there was Hanssen-Baxton Shipping. Then, Valley Garden Antiques. Now, some connection to the du Pont family. That would be the powder mills throughout the area. Just how widespread *was* this family's influence?

"Excellent," Bradenton muttered.

Aaron looked up to see him slip the missive back inside the envelope and set it aside, patting it three times before again meeting Aaron's gaze.

"Good news, I presume?" Aaron asked.

"Yes. Excellent news." Bradenton pointed his thumb toward the note. "As I am certain you are not aware, my father is a partner with the du Pont family in more than one powder mill along the Brandywine River here in Delaware. Mr. Peter du Pont and his cousin were the ones who developed the first smokeless gunpowder a decade ago. They've spent the time since then developing and perfecting it, and now they wish to establish mass distribution of the powder for use in military exercises or actual battles."

"That could mean a substantial increase in more than one area of business for your family. Not only with the powder mill but also with the shipping. And that could become a lucrative investment on many levels."

"Exactly." Bradenton nodded. "With your sound logic and keen mind, you could prove to be a valuable asset to this venture as well."

Wait one moment. Had Aaron just heard Bradenton say what he thought he'd said? No, he couldn't possibly have heard correctly. He needed to be certain.

"Sir?" was all he could manage.

"You said it yourself, Mr. Stone," Bradenton said with a smile. "Your uncle has all but disowned you, and you were about to embark on a partnership with my son before his passing. And you were already on your way here, no doubt to meet me and my family." He turned his right hand faceup toward Aaron. "Why should any of those plans cease to happen now, when there isn't anything in your way?"

"Are you offering me employment, sir?"

Bradenton cleared his throat. "Let's just say I'm offering you the opportunity to make use of some of those skills you boasted of, and to prove to me that what my son saw in you is as valid as I believe it to be."

Well, it wasn't exactly an official offer, and it had been extended in a most roundabout manner. But Aaron's options at that moment were limited. What did he have to lose?

Aaron stood, and Bradenton did the same. They shook hands across the desk.

"Sir, I gladly accept. Thank you."

"It is my pleasure." Bradenton held firm to Aaron's hand. "Now, be sure you don't disappoint me." A teasing glint shone in the man's eyes as he ended the handshake.

Though he made light of the warning through his expression, there remained a grain of truth to the admonition as well. This was not a man to cross.

"I shall do my utmost best, sir," Aaron replied.

Chapter 5

Early the next morning, after Alice had helped her into her riding habit, Lillian headed to the stables for her daily ride. Motorcars might be starting to replace the horse-drawn wagons and buggies as the most common form of transportation, but it would always be a horse for her.

She walked down the brick path and made her way across the well-groomed rear lawn. Just past the carriage house, Lillian pushed open the heavy wooden door and paused at the entrance. She breathed in the scent of fresh hay and horses. Next, the smell of leather, lye, and oil joined the bouquet of aromas assailing her nose. Some might not find the stables appealing. In fact, they might find the ever-present odor repulsive. To Lillian, though, it brought a great deal of comfort, and it remained her favorite place in the world.

"I have your horse ready and waiting, Miss Bradenton."

Thomas, the older of the two stable hands, led Delmara out from her stall.

"Thank you, Thomas." Lillian bestowed a smile on him and met him halfway. "As always, I appreciate it."

He nodded, touched two fingers to his cap, and went right back to his work. Delmara nodded her head up and down and stomped her right hoof the second Lillian took hold of the reins. A whinny and a snort signaled her pleasure as Delmara shook her head, leaving her mane flopping from side to side.

Lillian reached up and scratched her forelock. "So, are you ready for another outing in the park, girl? Get that daily exercise we both enjoy?" She leaned forward and pressed her head to Delmara's, rubbing her forehead against the coarse hair between her horse's eyes. "Yes, I know you are."

Delmara dipped her head farther and nuzzled the front of Lillian's clothes, vigorously moving her head up and down. Lillian laughed and grabbed hold of Delmara's jowls to look her straight in the eye. If she didn't know better, she'd say her horse was toying with her.

"Silly girl." She gave her forelock a good rub, paying special attention to the area underneath the bridle. "If you would like a scratch, you have only to ask. There is no need to use my shirtfront as a post."

Lillian led Delmara into the bright sunshine and lifted the reins up over the horse's head. Just before she raised her foot to the stirrup, Benjamin rounded the corner of the barn. He looked up and rushed to her side.

"Oh, here, Miss Bradenton," he said as he fell to one knee and interlocked his fingers. "Let me help you."

"Thank you, Benjamin." Lillian placed her booted foot into Benjamin's hands and allowed him to give her a boost.

Without a word, Benjamin double-checked her stirrups and the cinch. "As usual, Thomas set everything just right."

Lillian smiled down at him. "Yes, he usually doesn't miss."

"One of these days, I'll figure out how he does it."

"Years of working with horses, I imagine." Lillian pushed against the valleys between her fingers to ensure her gloves had a tight fit then took up the reins. "You'll be there soon enough, Benjamin. I'm certain of it."

The young lad beamed a smile up at her, shielding his face from the eastern sun. "I aim to best him at something, Miss Bradenton, if it's the last thing I do."

Lillian laughed. "Well then, I'm certain you shall."

He glanced up at the sky devoid of clouds. "It's a real good day for a ride."

"Yes." Lillian also looked upward. "The past two months have been relatively mild, though March certainly kept me indoors more than I liked."

"All right, Benji," Thomas spoke from the doorway to the stables. "Stop carrying on with Miss Bradenton and get back to work."

Immediate red rushed to poor Benjamin's face. Lillian averted her eyes so he could avoid further embarrassment. If he were a bit younger, she might consider it sweet, but at fourteen, he was near enough to a man to make it an awkward situation.

"Thank you both for your help this morning," Lillian called as she urged Delmara forward.

At least she could get the focus back on her for now. Once she was gone, Benjamin was on his own with Thomas. He could handle it, though. She leaned forward and spoke in Delmara's left ear. The horse turned her ear at Lillian's voice.

"How do you feel about a ride across the Wilmington country club property and perhaps a visit to Hoopes Reservoir?"

Delmara tossed her head and mane and puffed air out through her nose.

"I suppose that answers my question." Lillian laughed. "If we're careful, we might not get caught. The last thing I need is one of the members reporting back to Father that we were on club property again without permission."

Delmara nodded her head vigorously, as if to say she understood the need for caution. Then again, if they didn't want anyone except members riding there, they shouldn't have made the grass so lush or the gardens on the northeast acreage so inviting. Heading west from the manor house, Lillian guided Delmara along the path paralleling the eastern edge of the country club property. Continuing up and across the narrow plot near the back end of the golf course, she and her horse picked up speed and raced through the well-placed trees and behind the club's own horse sheds. They usually ventured up and around the acreage marked off specifically for the club, and once they cleared the low fence on the other side of the property, they returned to more familiar territory.

Delmara could navigate this route blindfolded if she let her have the lead, and that knowledge brought a level of reassurance to her. It allowed her to free her mind of everything, welcoming the peace that washed over her. In no time at all, they'd reached Hoopes Reservoir. Perhaps someday they'd contain the water a little better, but for now Lillian enjoyed the unkempt appearance and seemingly wild feel to the area.

As if proving her point, the screech of a red-tailed hawk sounded overhead, and to her left, a crane flew just a foot or so above the water's surface, the swoop of its wings causing ripples below. This had always been a favorite stopping point for Conrad and her. They would race around the water's edge and sometimes go wading if the temperatures became too unbearable. Lillian's eyes sought out their favorite picnic spot. She could almost hear his laughter and voice.

"All right, Lil. Let's see who can skip their rock the most times before it sinks."

"I accept!" Lillian had squared her shoulders then set about finding the perfect smooth stone with which to best her older brother.

"Come now, we haven't got all day," he'd chided. "It doesn't take that long to find a rock."

"It does if you want to win," she parried back at him.

When he sighed loudly, she looked up. Conrad rolled his eyes. He then made a big show about reaching into his vest for his pocket watch, flipping it open then moving his index finger back and forth like an upside-down pendulum.

"Do not rush me." Lillian stood, crossed her arms, and stuck her chin into the air. "Maybe I'll decide I don't wish to play your silly game anymore."

"Aww, come on, sis." Conrad crossed the patchy grass in just a few strides of his long legs and draped an arm around her shoulders, pulling her close. "You know I didn't mean anything by it. Besides, you're the only one around who can play. The horses won't be much competition. And if you don't, I'll win by forfeit." He jabbed her in her side and tickled her ribs. "That's no fun at all."

Lillian jerked away but managed to catch Conrad just behind his ears and across the nape of his neck, one of his most ticklish spots.

"Now you're not playing fair!"

He raced toward her, and she squealed as she darted away from him. Too late, she realized she'd run too close to the water's edge when a swoop of water came hurling toward her. Unable to dodge the wet onslaught, she immediately bent to copy her brother's attack. In less than a minute, they were both soaked.

Conrad waved both arms in the air. "Truce! Truce!"

Lillian stopped, and they both fell to the grassy slope in fits of laughter.

"Mother is going to be livid when we return home in such a state."

"Not if she doesn't catch us before we can change our clothes," Conrad pointed out.

She gave him a dubious look. "That's easier said than done for me, though you could likely manage it without any trouble at all."

He shrugged and linked his fingers behind his head as he stared up at the sky. "Is it my fault you insist upon trussing yourself up in all those layers?"

"Fashion dictates my wardrobe. You know that as well as I." She sighed. "But fashion is also kinder to gentlemen than ladies."

"Well, I'm certain you'll figure out something."

And Lillian had. It wasn't the first nor the last time she and Conrad had gotten into mischief together, but that incident had been nearly seven years ago. As they got older, their antics changed, but their rapport never did. Times like this made her miss her brother more than ever. To think she'd never again skip a rock or ride a horse or even take a ride in a motorcar with him by her side. She reached up to catch a few tears falling from her eyes.

Lillian mulled that reality in her mind over and over again as she circled the reservoir. Since Delmara knew the trail so well, she allowed her free rein, enjoying the exhilaration of the wind in her face to dry her tears and the thrill of riding such a powerful animal. Far too soon, they'd reached the stables once more. Mother would likely ask that she accompany her to the antiques shop until the noonday meal. She'd best return Delmara to her stall and freshen up for the morning's work ahead.

After dismounting and leading her horse inside, she paused near the side room where they kept their saddles, harnesses, blankets, and bridles. Drawing the reins back over Delmara's head, she slid the bridle down and slipped the bit from her mouth. She hung it all on a nail in a post behind her then bent to unfasten the cinch. When she straightened again, from the corner of her eyes, she saw Mr. Stone step around one of the columns and lean back against it, crossing his arms and hooking one ankle over the other. Lillian caught herself before she jumped at his silent approach.

He certainly did cut an impressive figure. With his finely tailored burgundy cutaway coat, black vest, and camel-colored breeches that disappeared into knee-high black boots, he looked ready to go for a ride himself.

"Mr. Stone, you startled me." Lillian gestured toward his outfit. "Will you be riding this morning as well?"

He nodded over his right shoulder toward the back of the stables. "Yes. I was merely waiting for one of the stable hands to assist me with selecting the best horse. I believe I saw two hands working with the coachmen a few moments ago." He pointed at the saddle still on Delmara's back. "Would you like some assistance with that?"

"Yes, please. Thank you."

She had just been about to call for Thomas when Mr. Stone appeared. If no one had been available, she would have managed, but why put herself through the strain if she didn't have to?

He pushed away from the post and casually walked toward her horse. Then he turned and hefted the saddle from Delmara as if it weighed nothing at all. Lillian tried not to stare, but with no other movement anywhere else, her eyes naturally followed him. When he returned to retrieve the blanket and reach for the bridle, she walked over to Delmara's stall and swung open the door. Delmara eagerly walked inside, going straight for the fresh hay in her trough.

Deep, rumbling laughter sounded from behind her. "I suppose she was famished," Mr. Stone said as he came to stand next to her at the wall in front of the stall.

A halfhearted smile found its way to Lillian's face. She rested her arms on top of the wall. At any other time, she might have found Delmara's actions amusing, but right now, her emotions were far too raw.

"Miss Bradenton?" Mr. Stone peered at her with a quizzical expression. "Is anything amiss? Forgive me if I'm overstepping my bounds in any way, but you appear quite distraught at the moment."

Lillian sniffed. Why did he have to be so observant? Why couldn't he have simply helped her with the saddle and gone on his way? And for that matter, why did he have to still be here when she returned instead of already out on his ride? Thomas and Benjamin would have never asked any questions. She could have reminisced in peace, and no one would have been the wiser.

"I am all right, Mr. Stone, but I appreciate you asking." She sniffed again and kept her eyes forward. "I am merely dealing with some difficult memories at the moment."

Mr. Stone reached out and caught a lone tear with his finger. Then he withdrew a handkerchief from his coat pocket and handed it to her. She took it without saying anything, her throat too thick with emotion for any words to pass through.

"It will take some time, but the wounds *will* heal. The pain will not always feel so fresh. I know."

At that, she turned her head. His eyes met hers for a brief moment. And in that moment, Lillian again saw a hint of concern mixed with regret. Just like when he'd first come to tell them his story of being with Conrad on the ship. The regret she understood. But concern? For her? He barely knew her. She wasn't ready to question him about any of it right now, so instead, she took a deep, invigorating breath and stepped back.

"Well, I should see to Delmara's brushing and rubdown before I go." She grabbed the curry brush from the hook on the nearest post and backed away from him.

Mr. Stone looked at her with eyebrows drawn. "Isn't that a task usually completed by the stableboy?"

Lillian looked at him. "Yes, but I don't mind it, and it allows me to have a few extra moments with Delmara." She gave him a half grin. "I leave the hay raking, mucking, and cleaning to the hands."

He took two steps toward her and held out his hand. "Why don't you allow me to take care of that this morning? You no doubt have many things to do today and could likely use a few extra moments."

Mr. Stone hadn't actually stated her need to compose herself. Manners wouldn't permit it. But he had implied it.

Lillian hesitated. Had it been Thomas or Benjamin, she wouldn't have blinked an eye. She would have accepted their help without question. With a man who had already done so much for her family out of the goodness of his heart, it changed things. When she didn't immediately relinquish the curry brush to him, he quirked his eyebrow, and the faintest hint of a smirk formed on his lips, as if he dared her in an unspoken challenge.

Just where did he get the audacity to grin at her that way? And how could he even think of attempting to taunt her in such a fashion? He was acting just like Conrad used to. Using mirth to coax a smile out of her when she wasn't in the greatest of moods. Lillian could accept behavior such as that from her brother, but Mr. Stone? No. She refused to give in to his baiting and give him any sort of satisfaction.

"Very well," she said, removing any emotion from her face or voice as she handed him the brush. "Thank you."

She might not wish to engage in any form of lighthearted repartee with him, but she would never forget her manners.

"You are welcome, Miss Bradenton."

The compassion in his voice compelled her to raise her gaze to his. Aaron held Lillian's eyes again for several moments before she broke the invisible connection and spun away.

Her heart pounded a bit faster than usual, and her breath came in shorter spurts. She had come here to take advantage of solitude. Just her and Delmara. Now she needed yet another respite for an entirely different reason.

Chapter 6

A unt Bethany," Lillian called from the back corner of Valley Garden Antiques. "What would you like me to do with this mulberry coffeepot?"

The middle of her three great-aunts looked up from one of the work desks where she stood polishing a Westerwald floral stoneware jug.

"I am certain there are more pieces to that set."

She narrowed her eyes and tilted her head then tapped a finger to her lips. After a cursory glance around the main room of the shop, she pointed to the wall directly toward the front from where Lillian stood.

"So, let's have you place it with the silver tea service there on the Aspen credenza." She smiled. "When you manage to unearth the other pieces to the set, you can set them out with the coffeepot." A wry grin formed on her aunt's lips. "But I'm afraid you have a sizable task ahead of you, my dear. Those crates were delivered only yesterday, and I've barely had time to catalog the contents let alone compare the items against the inventory sheets I was provided."

Lillian had enough trouble keeping track of the sales alone on each piece she sold during her hours working at the shop. How Aunt Bethany managed to remember not only the location of the various categories of items she had but their cost and value as well was beyond her. But she could at least check off items from a list and record them in a register.

"Don't worry a moment more about it, Aunt Bethany," Lillian said. "If you tell me where I can find the inventory sheets, I will do that for you."

"Oh, would you?" Her aunt's shoulders dropped and some of the lines across her brow disappeared. "That would be a tremendous relief to me, Lil. You have no idea how much."

Lillian smiled. "Actually, I believe I do. Mother told me how many hours you've been working here the past few weeks." She winked. "Uncle James is starting to wonder if you're going to spend all day and night here before long."

Aunt Bethany gave her a rueful grin. "Yes, dear, I know. It hasn't been easy on your uncle, or your cousins. Praise the good Lord for Mrs. Turnbaum, or Caleb and Hannah would be forced to go to Charlotte or Anastasia's homes for their meals."

Lillian giggled. "And with the appetite Caleb has, Uncle Richard or Uncle

George might take an exception to that." She tagged the coffeepot and set it aside then reached into the crate to see what else she could find.

"You are exactly right." Aunt Bethany shook her head, dipping her cloth in the polish again. "I have no idea how the lad manages to eat so much yet claim he's hungry not an hour after each meal." She sighed and set to rubbing the next jug. "I'm relieved Samuel and Michael weren't that way. Gratefully, they took after their father. Otherwise, Mrs. Turnbaum might have submitted her resignation years ago."

"You *should* be grateful," Aunt Anastasia said, popping her head out from the back room. "You only have *one* who eats enough for an entire army. I was blessed with four!"

"At least they learned how to fish at an early age," Aunt Bethany countered. "And they were working at the shipyard with Richard and Andrew years before they could earn a wage from their toils."

"You do have a point." Aunt Anastasia shuddered. "If I'd had to endure all of them underfoot all day long when they weren't at the academy, I might have sent them off to boarding school."

Aunt Bethany glanced across the room at Lillian and winked. "She's merely jealous she wasn't fortunate to have three dutiful children like your aunt Charlotte."

"Well, Mother wasn't a child," Lillian pointed out. "And from what she tells me, Uncle Phillip and Aunt Claire engaged in their fair share of mischief."

Lillian smiled to herself. Like when they'd persuaded Jessie and Willie to rig the bucket of water and loosely gathered hay to dump on Father one day when he'd come to go for a ride with Mother. Or the time they'd switched the labels of the cinnamon and the cayenne pepper when Mother baked an apple pie for Father. They were devious when you least expected it. But Mother and Father never tattled on them, so Aunt Charlotte never knew.

"Yes," Aunt Anastasia replied. "But don't attempt to tell Charlotte about any of that. She'd never believe it." She rolled her eyes. "In her mind, her children are perfect little angels."

"Ana, is Chloe still back there with you?" Aunt Bethany asked.

"Of course. Do you need her?"

Lillian had almost forgotten about her sister. With them working in separate rooms all morning, it had been easy to think she and Aunt Bethany were the only ones in the shop, aside from the employees of course. Mother would've been there, too, had Father and Uncle Richard not needed her down at the shipyard office.

"Well," Aunt Bethany replied, "I think it might help the process immensely if she were to come out here and assist Lillian for a little while with the crates that arrived yesterday from the warehouse in Philadelphia."

Oh good. Lillian could use some help. She'd been doing her best, but so many pieces and so many different collections were making her head spin. She'd just started going back and checking off the inventory and hadn't even touched the register yet.

"All right. I'll go fetch her." Aunt Anastasia disappeared behind the gold brocade curtains tied back with a crimson silk cord.

Just like the rich lilac curtains tied back with a gold cord at the display window up front, her aunt's attention to detail always impressed her. From the rich fabrics used in the tablecloths under most of the merchandise displayed to the little touches like silk rose petals scattered among select items. Every aspect of the shop presented a welcoming appearance and invited customers to spend extended bits of time there. And that was always good for business.

Lillian took a moment to straighten and press her fists to her lower back. She'd been sitting on a stool and not the floor, but all that bending and twisting had taken its toll.

"Quitting already?" Chloe's teasing voice preceded her appearance just behind Lillian. She gave her sister a quick rub across her neck and shoulders.

"Mmm." Lillian tilted her head to the left and right, stretching the muscles there as well. "That feels great."

"You know, this isn't making me all that enthusiastic about coming to your aid if it's going to put me into a similar state."

Lillian peered back over her shoulder. "With you assisting me, though, it won't be as challenging." She brushed back a few strands of hair and tucked them into her loosely wrapped chignon. "Neither one of us will have to do all the bending and twisting."

Chloe moved to stand in front and lightly rested her hands on top of the nearest wooden crate. Her moiré, five-gore walking skirt and Somerset blouse nearly matched Lillian's own outfit, save the colors. Where Lillian almost always chose ivory, olive, or buttercream, Chloe went for the bolder blues and rich burgundies. It suited her darker complexion and blue eyes, though, just like their mother. Lillian had inherited more of her father's fair features, except her hazel eyes were more green than brown. She would never be able to pull off those bolder shades.

"So, where shall I begin?"

"Well, that all depends," Lillian replied. "Would you prefer to unpack and organize, or catalog and record?"

"Oh, unpack, definitely." Chloe glanced over her shoulder. "I shall leave the writing to you. I prefer much more movement."

"Very well." Lillian stood and moved her stool behind one of the side tables nearby and laid out both the inventory list and the record book Aunt Bethany kept of all her merchandise. "You tell me what you find, and I'll compare it to what the warehouse tells us they shipped then record it in the book. Then you'll attach a price tag and set it aside. Aunt Bethany will write the prices on the tags later."

Chloe shrugged and reached into the crate Lillian had recently abandoned. "Sounds simple enough."

In no time at all, the two of them settled into a nice routine. Yes, this was far better than attempting to do it all herself. Dividing up the tasks allowed her back to take a rest.

"So," Chloe stated as she dusted the straw from a fine piece of porcelain, "how was your ride this morning?"

"About the same as usual," Lillian said without thinking. She placed a check on the inventory sheet then penciled in the style and craft of the most recent item underneath the last.

"Is that a fact?"

The tone in Chloe's voice made Lillian look up from the ledger. Her single raised eyebrow and pursed lips bearing a hint of a grin gave Lillian pause. Did her sister know something she didn't? Oh! This morning! With Mr. Stone, and his happening upon her in such an emotional state. Chloe must have seen the realization dawn on Lillian's face, because she nodded.

"Yes, your ride *this* morning." She grinned. "Anything particular happen that you wish to share with me?"

"Well, something did happen, yes." Lillian pulled her bottom lip in between her teeth, allowing the impish fluttering at her core to travel all the way to her eyes. "As to whether or not I wish to share it with you is questionable."

Her sister shrugged. "Suit yourself. I already know most of it anyway," she said, turning her attention again to her task and pulling out a mulberry plate that matched the coffeepot Lillian had unearthed earlier. "Oh, this is gorgeous!"

Oh no. Chloe wasn't going to get away with changing the subject that easily. Not after leaving a teaser the way she did.

"Just what do you mean by saying you know most of it anyway?" Lillian folded her arms on the table in front of her. "How could you possibly know anything? You weren't there. In fact, no one was. Only Mr. Stone and me."

"Aha!" Chloe snapped her fingers and pointed at her sister. "So you admit to being at the stables this morning with Mr. Stone."

Lillian wasn't about to confirm or deny anything until she got a straight answer out of her sister. "And you haven't told me how you are aware of this."

Her sister examined the plate she held, tilting it this way and that. "Oh, you know how servants talk. This really is beautiful," she added, changing the subject again. "The Venus scene is stunning." Her brow furrowed. "But didn't Grandma Edith own something just like this? I believe I recall seeing it in Aunt Charlotte's home not too long ago."

Chloe could be exasperating sometimes. But if she didn't at least answer the most recent question her sister posed, she'd never get the other information she sought. Her sister could dance around a subject in such an agonizing manner.

"Yes," Lillian answered. "Grandma Edith owned several pieces in that very set, only most likely in another numbered collection. That plate goes with a coffeepot depicting a peaceful scene of a mother and child playing by a pond and bridge. Aunt Charlotte donated the pieces her mother owned to Aunt Bethany when she discovered the items coming here from the warehouse in Philadelphia." Lillian leaned forward. "Now, are you going to tell me any more about who spoke to whom regarding my brief conversation with Mr. Stone?" She narrowed her eyes at her sister just as Chloe looked up at her again. "Or am I going to have to devise other ways of divining the information?"

Chloe set down the plate and raised her hands in mock surrender, laughing. "No, no, no," she said, waving her hands in the air before returning them to her lap. "I would never invite the result of your scheming methods upon myself on purpose. I'll tell you."

Lillian squared her shoulders and leveled a triumphant grin at her sister. "I thought as much."

Her sister shook her head. "You're incorrigible, you know that?"

"Of course I do." Lillian smiled and waved her hand in a beckoning motion. "Now, let's hear it."

Chloe sighed. "Very well. But my version of it isn't nearly as compelling as I'm certain yours will be." At the warning look Lillian gave her, she held up her hands again. "All right already. Gracious." She took a deep breath and exhaled. "You might have thought you were alone, but it seems Benjamin either came into the stables or saw you departing, I'm not certain which. He told my maid, Lydia, about seeing you press a handkerchief to your eyes on your way back to the house. And of course, Lydia told me."

All right. That much made sense. At least the gossip hadn't traveled through more than two servants. . .that she knew of, anyway. One part didn't add up, though.

"But this incident occurred not long before we departed from home to come here to the shop. How could you possibly have learned all of this so quickly?"

"You may not be aware of this," she replied with a wink, "but Lydia and Benjamin are sweet on each other, so they spend as much time as they can together. They had been having a little tryst down by the terrace before she returned upstairs to help me dress." Chloe leaned forward with her hands on her knees and an eager expression on her face. "Now, will you please tell me your version before my insatiable curiosity gets the better of me?"

If only her sister knew there really wasn't much to tell. She and Mr. Stone had spoken only a few minutes. Hardly enough for any story of merit to have taken place. Yet her sister appeared so keen to discover some little tidbit, Lillian didn't have the heart to tell her otherwise.

"You are correct," she began, "that Mr. Stone and I exchanged a few words in the stables this morning. I had just returned from my daily ride on Delmara only to find Thomas and Benjamin were otherwise occupied with a project for Mr. Wyeth." Lillian again folded her arms on the table in front of her. "I proceeded with removing Delmara's bridle and had unhooked the cinch when Mr. Stone suddenly appeared nearby." She didn't want her sister reading any more into the situation than necessary, so she left off the part about how her heart had raced and her breath had caught in her throat the moment she saw him. "He offered to assist me with the saddle, and I gratefully accepted. It would have been quite a feat for me to manage that on my own."

Chloe nodded. "Yes, I can imagine. Thomas or Benjamin always assists me." Making a gathering motion with one hand, Chloe added, "Now, go on."

"Once he had freed Delmara of the saddle and blanket, I let her into her stall and leaned on the wall for a moment to collect my thoughts." Lillian sighed. "It had been a melancholic ride, remembering when I'd ridden with Conrad on many other mornings." She shared a meaningful look with Chloe.

"It isn't easy," Chloe stated, "doing things we once did with Conrad, or seeing him when he isn't really there."

"No, it isn't," Lillian replied. "I felt that significantly on my ride." Perhaps another time, she'd share more with her sister. But not today. "Mr. Stone joined me a minute later and immediately noticed my distraught state."

"Is that when he offered you his handkerchief?"

Lillian nodded. "Almost." She sniffed as the memory of the morning hit her again full force. "He first caught a tear I was unable to suppress before it fell down my cheek. Then he offered a few words of reassurance about time healing the pain, and that's when he reached for his handkerchief." She smiled.

"He even offered to rub down Delmara and brush her coat for me so I could compose myself before continuing with my morning. Of course, he didn't say that, but I appreciated the gesture just the same."

Mr. Stone truly had always been a gentleman. She recalled his thoughtfulness to reassure her with encouragement, and his courtesy regarding her composure. Even now, the memory brought a soft smile to her lips.

"It seems our esteemed guest has made a significant impression on you, dear sister."

Lillian met Chloe's gaze. There was no use in trying to hide it. Her sister knew her far too well. "Yes." She nodded. "In some ways, he reminds me of Conrad, but in others, he's completely different."

"And that is a good thing," Chloe replied. "It might be too difficult to face him were he to resemble our brother too much." She folded her arms. "The question now is, what are you going to do about it?"

"I beg your pardon?" Did her sister truly expect her to make the next move? This wasn't a chess match, for goodness' sake. "What am *I* going to do?"

Chloe pursed her lips. "Surely you realize I am not the only one to notice Mr. Stone's decided interest. Every time he is in our company, his gaze spends a lot of time centered on you."

Yes, and there was still the matter of the looks he gave her or the guarded concern she caught in his eyes when he likely thought she hadn't noticed.

"To be honest, I hadn't thought it necessary for me to do anything," Lillian replied. "I don't wish to be too forward."

"I can understand that." Chloe nodded. "But don't discourage him, either. Remember what happened with Mr. Chesterfield because he hadn't the faintest inclination of your interest until it was too late."

Lillian grimaced. "Must you remind me of that?"

"I only do so to help you not make the same mistake twice." She shrugged. "Of course, Henry does seem to be extremely happy with Emmaline Harris, so we can't exactly fault him for his choice."

"No, and it's clear a match with him would not have worked out, anyway. But I do appreciate you having my best interests at heart."

Chloe smiled. "Always."

Lillian picked up her pencil again and shuffled through the pages in front of her. "Now, what do you say we return our attention to our task at hand and cease this aimless chatter?"

Her sister only nodded and reached into the crate again, but her expression said the discussion was far from over. Maybe the next time, Lillian would be better prepared with an answer.

Chapter 7

The numbers didn't lie. And Aaron had to admit it. What he saw impressed him. He'd been managing the books for his uncle for several years, so he knew success when he saw it. And this was only dusting the surface of the true figures. Only what Mr. Bradenton had allowed Aaron to see to this point. Still, the Bradentons and Baxtons and all other family members involved had made a notable name for themselves in the Brandywine Valley.

They'd diversified their investments, distributed their assets across multiple business ventures, and saw to it a portion of their profits always went back into local charitable organizations. The principal recipient was Green Hill Presbyterian Church along the Kennett Turnpike. Those who knew the family well knew where their faith and priorities lay. His own faith more resembled the ocean during a storm than the steady, continuous flow of a creek or river. Sometimes cresting on the height of a wave and sometimes crashing down into the valleys between. He could learn a few things from this family.

"Mr. Stone?" Bradenton's voice carried from the outer office. "Are you ready?"

Aaron closed the ledger, resting his hand on top of it for a couple of seconds before reaching for his coat and shrugging it on over his vest and shirt.

"Yes, Mr. Bradenton, I'm ready," he replied as he grabbed his top hat and stepped into the other room. "Shall we proceed?"

The horn of a barge on the Delaware River sounded through the open windows. Along with it came the familiar river scent. Some might consider it an odor, but he'd lived close enough to the River Thames in London for it to bring a welcome comfort.

As he walked a step behind Bradenton and Phillip Baxton on their way out of the office and toward the warehouse, his mind drifted back to summers along the Thames. The Festival of Music to be specific. He could almost taste the succulent lobster, the exquisite array of fine wines and champagnes, and the mouthwatering desserts prepared specially each night by the resident chefs at La Scala. Pair that with the classical, opera, theater, and cabaret performances, and it made for an extraordinary evening.

Clanging chains as ships were secured for repair and the high-pitched whir of a saw slicing lumber brought Aaron's mind back to the present.

Bradenton stopped and stepped to the side, swinging his arm in a wide arc as he gestured toward a substantial collection of warehouses and ship manufacturing buildings that made up most of Hanssen-Baxton Shipping.

"Here we are," Bradenton announced. "The shipyard warehouses."

Aaron didn't mention that the sign at the top of the main warehouse or the proximity to the office negated the need to identify their location. Instead, he turned his head as close to a full circle as he could manage, taking in an industry that had to employ several hundred workers at this site alone.

"This is where all the *real* work of the shipyard is done," Bradenton added with a grin.

"Don't let my father hear you say that," Phillip intoned.

Bradenton lifted his walking cane just high enough to tap the younger Baxton against his leg. "He would likely agree with me, my boy."

Aaron let his gaze travel over the area directly on the river. "I see an extensive variety of ships in your docks, from colliers to brigantines to flatboats. About how often do you add to your arsenal? Or perhaps retire a ship that's outlived its usefulness?"

Bradenton stroked his chin with his thumb and index finger. "Well, most of our work involves maintaining the ships we have, arranging for the transport of goods, and seeing to it that the merchandise we receive is delivered in a timely manner." He pinched his thumb and forefinger closed and held his right hand in front of his face. "That being said, we probably see a new addition every year or so, whether it be from a ship we build here or one we acquire."

"And when a ship is beyond repair or no longer seaworthy," Phillip added, "it is first anchored at the docks and utilized for storage then taken into one of the warehouses and broken apart. Its pieces are then reused or tossed in the kiln."

Aaron shook his head and released a slow breath. "It is a sight to behold."

"You should have seen it twenty years ago when I first got involved." Bradenton raised and lowered his eyebrows. "It was impressive even then."

"It's only improved with time," Phillip stated.

"This I can see," Aaron replied.

"So, Stone," Bradenton began as he covered one hand with his other on top of his cane. "Now that you've seen the shipping side of our business, would you care to take a walk to the antiques shop? It's only a few blocks north to Market Street."

Wasn't that where his two daughters had gone earlier that morning? And could they still be there?

"Lead the way, sir," Aaron replied, attempting to strip his voice of any hint of eagerness.

"After that, we'll see if there is time enough to visit the powder mills farther up the Brandywine River. If not, we can save that for later."

"Andrew," Phillip spoke up. "I think I'll head down to the docks and get the coal ship back on its route again."

"Very well." Bradenton nodded. "Thank you for your assistance this morning, and for showing Mr. Stone here around the office."

Phillip dipped his head. "It was my pleasure."

And with that, he was gone, passing a young lad on the way.

"We will need to return to the office to collect my wife first." Bradenton paused as the lad approached with what looked like a merchandise order for him to sign. He scrawled his name at the bottom, nodded at the lad, and turned again to face the offices, continuing as if he hadn't been interrupted. "And her sister asked me to bring some additional ledger books for a substantial delivery she'd just received."

"Do allow me to fetch those for you," Aaron offered. "If you point me in the right direction, I can have them collected in no time at all."

"They should be on the shelf to the left of my desk as you enter my office." He looked up and to the right. "I would think three should suffice for now."

"Very good." Aaron nodded. "I shall return momentarily."

Lengthening his stride, Aaron walked briskly up the path and reentered the brick office building. He made his way to Bradenton's office, glancing again at the ledger he'd tossed on the desk. He didn't need to see any more to know this family's foundation was sound. . .in more ways than one.

With a turn to the left, Aaron located the stack of blank ledgers Bradenton mentioned. He grabbed three, knocking two other books to the floor in the process. As he bent to retrieve them, a carefully etched name embossed on the covers caught his eye.

"Cobblestone Books," he read aloud.

He really should be on his way, but curiosity got the better of him. Flipping open the top book, he noted a ledger of book titles with columns for date acquired, date sold, or date on loan, plus a fourth column for price sold. The second book was a detailed accounting of daily sales and monthly figures for what seemed to be a successful bookshop. But no one had mentioned this anywhere in their references to businesses and daily work. And the ledger just stopped in the middle of the year. No explanation written.

Upon further inspection, Aaron noticed the date at the top of the first page. *1 March 1898.* That was almost fifteen years ago. It must have belonged to the family at some point, or the ledgers wouldn't be in Bradenton's office. All the other industries had been around for much longer and still existed today. So, what had happened to the bookshop? And why didn't anyone speak of it?

A whistle sounded from far off and started Aaron from his ponderings. He'd better get back to Bradenton before the man wondered where he'd gone. But he made a mental note of the shop's name and tucked the blank ledgers under his arm. If Miss Bradenton was indeed still at the antiques shop, he intended to speak with her. She may have only been five or six years old at the time, but surely she could shed some light on the subject.

And if not? At least it gave him an excuse to talk to her again.

*

"Bethany, we have the ledgers you requested."

Bradenton didn't exactly march into the shop, but his confident stride and commanding presence could be interpreted as such. And to think, he'd been introduced to the family by way of judicial sentence after he'd stolen china, silver, and books from his wife's aunt and uncle. Aaron wouldn't have believed it if he hadn't heard it from Bradenton with his own ears. He followed behind with the ledgers still tucked under his arm.

"Oh, Andrew, thank you." Mrs. Bethany Woodruff greeted her nephew-in-law with a chaste kiss on the cheek. "And thank *you*, Mr. Stone," she added as she took the ledgers from him. Brushing back several strands of hair from her forehead, she smiled. "Andrew, you have no idea how much help these are going to be with the new inventory we've acquired."

"I believe I can hazard a guess," Bradenton replied with a knowing look around the shop.

Aaron followed the man's gaze. He widened his eyes and raised his eyebrows at the eclectic assortment of quality antiques. Of course, some of them he wouldn't look at twice, let alone give any credence to their value. Others, he might consider, but decorative accents weren't exactly his forte. Attention to detail? Yes. Knickknacks, dishes, and table accents? Certainly not.

Soft giggles sounded from an area of the shop to Aaron's left, and he turned toward the source. Ah, so Miss Bradenton *was* still present. And it appeared her sister remained with her as well. Splendid. He could find the answers to his questions about the bookshop as soon as he had hoped.

"So, have the two of you come to roll up your sleeves and offer your assistance, or will I be forced to shoo you away with a broom if you get underfoot?"

The motherly look Mrs. Woodruff leveled at him and Bradenton made Aaron want to jump right in and help out of dutiful obedience. Her eyes then darted to her right before narrowing a tad as she returned her gaze to Aaron, the hint of a grin teasing the corners of her lips.

"Point us in the right direction, and we shall be at your service," Bradenton replied.

Obviously, Aaron wasn't the only one affected. Remarkable how a single expression could reduce a man to a willing servant in mere seconds. And in this instance, make him wonder what she saw—or thought she saw—as he looked at Miss Bradenton and her sister.

Mrs. Woodruff clapped once then rubbed her hands together, eagerness in her expression as she looked around the shop.

"Andrew, I believe I will have you assist Anastasia with the crates in the back room." She pointed toward the curtain-framed doorway in the center of the back wall. "George arrived about an hour ago, but I am certain he would appreciate an extra set of hands to organize the unsorted merchandise."

"On my way," Bradenton called over his shoulder as he brushed past Mrs. Woodruff and headed straight for the back.

Aaron breathed a sigh of relief when she seemed to have brushed off his little visual detour a moment ago.

"Mr. Stone, if you don't mind, Lillian and Chloe could use your assistance fetching and opening the crates they're cataloging."

Then again, perhaps she hadn't. The merest hint of a grin was there again, and a decided twinkle lit her eyes. He'd been caught red-handed, and now she was sending him right into the middle of the two ladies who had distracted him. Feeding him to the wolves came to mind, but that felt a bit harsh. They had no idea of his interest or his intent, and they'd been nothing but cordial to him since his arrival.

"It will be my pleasure," he replied with a slight dip of his head toward Mrs. Woodruff.

"I have no doubt it will," she replied with a smile. "Forgive me if I don't escort you, but you already know the girls, and they know you. I'm certain the three of you can work out a suitable arrangement."

Aaron only nodded, and a second later Mrs. Woodruff returned to her place behind a counter, detailing delicate pieces of china that made up part of a larger set, all laid out in front of her.

As he made his way to the far corner of the shop, her parting words repeated themselves in his head like the wax cylinder of a phonograph getting stuck in its playback rotation. Exactly what did she mean by 'suitable arrangement'? He was there to work as he'd offered, though thoughts of Cobblestone Books remained foremost in his mind. Perhaps he could take whatever arrangement was established and coax the flow of conversation in this direction.

The two ladies sat, with heads bent as he approached. One with her attention on the pages in front of her, and the other focused on the pieces she pulled from a crate. They were both dressed in similar fashion, each having chosen pleasing shades to complement their features perfectly. But where the older Miss Bradenton's light hair had been styled in an elegant upsweep, the younger's dark tresses hung in tight ringlets down her back. Aaron cleared his throat as softly as he could, so as not to startle either of them. Two heads turned to face him in tandem, neither face displaying any surprise at his presence.

"Pardon me ladies," AaΩron began. "I arrived with your father a few moments ago, and your great-aunt has somehow managed to harness our presence to her benefit."

The younger Miss Bradenton giggled. "If by that, you mean Aunt Bethany tricked you into a designated assignment of free labor, she has a knack for that." She paused. "Though Aunt Anastasia is far worse."

Aaron raised his brows and grinned. "I believe that skill has traveled down the generations, too. Your brother was notorious for persuading me to do all manner of odd jobs and getting me into predicaments where I wondered when I agreed to anything in the first place."

A bittersweet expression crossed both of their faces. Aaron could have kicked himself for his thoughtless remark. He'd wanted to keep the mood light, yet the first words out of his mouth merely reminded them of their recent loss.

"Forgive me. That indelicate statement should not have been spoken."

The older sister exchanged a silent look with the younger before extending him obvious grace. "There is no reason to apologize, Mr. Stone. We know you intended no ill will in your words."

Aaron nodded. "Thank you." All right, time to resume the lightened mood. "So, are you both a victim of your aunt's hoodwinking skills as well?"

"Not exactly, Mr. Stone," the elder Miss Bradenton replied. "We help wherever we are most needed."

"Please," he interjected quickly, flattening his palm over his vest, "call me Aaron." He extended his hand toward them both but kept his eyes on the older sister. "And might I have the pleasure of addressing you less formally as well?"

"Of course," the younger sister replied in haste. "You obviously will be staying with us in our home for a while, so it seems prudent we set ourselves on more familiar terms. You may call me Chloe."

Aaron's sentiments exactly. Now, he had one sister's permission. What about the other?

The elder sister hesitated, seeming to weigh his request on invisible scales with a form of measurement he was not privy to. Aaron retracted his hand and slipped it into the pocket of his slacks. After what felt like an eternity, Miss Bradenton finally replied.

"Very well."

"Excellent." Aaron clasped his hands together and looked around their little corner. "Now, tell me where I can be of assistance."

"I am not certain why Aunt Bethany sent you over to us," Chloe said, indicating the collection of sorted and tagged items off to the side. "We have nearly finished."

"Yes, there only remains that last crate," Lillian added, pointing to the item being referenced.

Aaron jumped into action. "Well, then allow me to pop open the top so you ladies can finish without delay."

He removed his coat and draped it across a nearby table then set to work. It might seem menial to most, but he didn't mind. The little task allowed him to help the sisters while also giving him a foot in the door, so to speak. And if he played his cards right, that might lead to an informative conversation regarding the bookshop.

"So," he began as Chloe pulled out the first piece and described it to Lillian, "I gather from your remark a moment ago, Lillian, that you divide your available time between both this shop and the shipyard offices?"

She nodded without looking up. "Yes, though Chloe and I are often not working at the same place at the same time." She made a few notations in the ledger then handed her sister a price tag to attach to the current item. "It all depends on what any given member of our family requires." Lillian looked up and met his gaze then gave him a rueful grin. "As you have no doubt noticed, we are all rather close."

"I can honestly say the observation has crossed my mind." Contrary to his own uncle and cousins, who barely took the time to engage him in conversation at the dinner table—or any other time—witnessing how he always felt a family should be was refreshing. It gave him hope that he might one day restore what he had lost with his parents.

"We don't often venture out to the powder mill offices," Lillian continued, "but those remain primarily under the direction of our grandfather on our father's side."

She and Chloe launched into one story about their presence at the powder mill the last time being more distracting than beneficial to mostly male workers. Aaron could see that. And this was perfect. He couldn't have asked for a better segue into what he'd come here hoping to discover. It was now or never.

"What about Cobblestone Books?" he asked without preamble. "Whatever happened to that?"

Chapter 8

Lillian snapped her head up and stared. "Where did you hear about that?"

Aaron shrugged. "I caught sight of a ledger with the name embossed on it at your father's office. The opportunity didn't present itself for me to inquire directly of him, so I thought it might be prudent to ask of you."

He didn't seem anything other than curious, but what had he been doing in Father's office? And obviously without Father present? He hadn't officially been hired yet, so he wouldn't have been working. But why else would he have been in there?

As if he'd heard her silent musings, Aaron perched on the edge of an empty crate, clasped his hands in front of him, and continued. "Your Father sent me to fetch some ledgers for your aunt Bethany just before we walked here."

"What is Cobblestone Books?" Chloe asked. "The name sounds familiar."

Lillian made a final notation in the book in front of her and closed the ledger. She rested her hands, one over the other, on top of the book and took a deep breath, looking first at her sister.

"Cobblestone Books, Chloe, is a bookshop once owned by Aunt Charlotte. Her father loaned her the money to purchase the shop when she was eighteen years old." Lillian smiled. "It was actually how she met Uncle Richard." A soft giggle escaped before she could stop it. Her eyes naturally slid from her sister to Aaron. "In fact, more than one successful match resulted from meetings at that shop."

"Really?" Chloe's fanciful notions and interest in anything romantic lit up her eyes and forced a silly grin to her lips. "Why have I not heard anything about this before?"

Lillian shifted her gaze back to her sister. "You no doubt were too young to take part in the conversations about it, and no one has mentioned the shop in several years." She did a quick mental calculation. "Even I was a mere six years old the last time anyone spoke of it."

"But why?" Her sister almost pouted. "Seems like it would maintain a special place in Aunt Charlotte's heart."

"Yes," Aaron echoed. "A shop such as that obviously holds a great deal of importance and legacy with your family."

Melancholy fell like a blanket over Lillian, and she pressed her lips into a thin line. If only the story weren't a sad one. She volleyed her gaze between the two of them.

"Unfortunately, the financial crisis nearly twenty years ago had lasting effects on many businesses beyond just the railroad and manufacturing industries. Our family had already divided our investments, but a greater level of devotion needed to be given to those that produced a more substantial profit." She sighed again. "Aunt Charlotte did everything she could to keep the bookshop open, and did manage for about four years."

"Quite admirable, all things considered," Aaron said.

Again, her eyes met his and remained there. He'd posed the original question, so he deserved her direct attention.

"Yes, many respected her for what she'd accomplished with that shop. But customers eventually lacked the extra funds to spend on frivolous purchases. And from what Mother told me, there was a great deal of regret when they had to close the doors."

Sympathy reflected in Aaron's blue gaze. "I can well imagine." He shifted and flattened his palms against his legs. "If she spent as much time there as it seems, she might have even felt like she'd failed in some way."

That was exactly what Aunt Charlotte had told her eight or nine years ago. A silent connection crossed the space between them. He did understand.

"But wait a moment," Chloe said, breaking their visual bond. "If the shop was where Aunt Charlotte met Uncle Richard then it's also where Mother met Aunt Charlotte, too, right?"

Lillian nodded. "Yes. In fact, Mother's love of books is what led Uncle Richard there. And you know the rest of the story."

"But I do not," Aaron added. "And I would like to hear more." He stood and glanced around their immediate area. "It appears you are finished with this task, so unless your aunt has another job for you to do..." Aaron paused a second then took two steps toward her, holding her captive in his direct gaze. "Would it be improper to ask you to take a walk with me?"

Walk with Aaron? Just the two of them? A part of her thrilled at the prospect, and her rapidly beating heart already betrayed her. Before she had a chance to respond, though, he rushed to continue.

"I am certain the carriage to take you home is close by, but the one that brought your father and me here is still at the shipyard." The merest hint of a grin mixed with reassurance in his eyes. "I would see that you were returned home safely."

Of Aaron's integrity, she had no doubt. He'd never been anything but a gentleman in every sense of the word. What about the others, though? What would they say? She glanced at her sister who sat with a silly grin on her face. All right, so she'd be no help. From the corner of her eye, she caught movement in the doorway to the back room. A slight turn to her right revealed both Aunt Bethany and Aunt Anastasia standing side by side with amused expressions on their faces.

"Miss Bradenton?"

Lillian started at Aaron's return to her formal name. She slid her gaze to his once more. The slight grin remained, and he'd managed to slip on his coat when she wasn't looking. If he had noticed the other ladies in her family, he made no indication of such. In fact, it almost seemed as if his eyes remained focused solely on her the entire time. A second later, he extended his hand toward her in an unspoken invitation.

Throwing her usual caution to the wind, Lillian placed her hand in his and allowed him to raise her to her feet. Aaron's grin turned into a smile that traveled all the way to his eyes. Immediately tucking her hand into the crook of his arm, he guided her through the aisles and toward the front door. She resisted the urge for a final look at her sister or her aunts and instead kept her eyes facing forward. Her maid waited by the door, ready to accompany them as a chaperone.

"If you are hungry," Aaron said, "we can likely find a street trader along Market Street." He grabbed two apples from a basket Aunt Bethany kept near the door. "For now, these will have to do."

After a clumsy, yet successful, attempt at juggling, he let one apple roll across the back of his fingers before he flipped his hand to catch it and pass it to her. Laughter bubbled up and sounded, despite her closed mouth. She accepted the apple with a smile. What else did Mr. Aaron Stone have up his sleeve?

❧

Aaron took a bite of his apple and licked the juice from his lips. He walked alongside Lillian and listened as she shared about the first meeting of her great-aunt and great-uncle. Although she told the tale with minimal outward emotion, from all appearances, she seemed to enjoy the telling of it. But like so many other things he'd observed in the short time he knew her, Lillian maintained a steady composure. Compared to Conrad's dynamic personality, hers was quite the opposite.

And that puzzled him. Was this her normal behavior? Or could the reflective state be a direct result of losing her brother? The two were obviously close, or Conrad wouldn't have asked Aaron to take care of her with his final breath.

But why? If he paid close enough attention, he'd likely find the answer to that question. For now, though, he let his curiosity rest.

Lillian sighed. "I simply cannot understand why Aunt Charlotte never made an attempt to restore the shop in the years since, especially when things started to improve. The way she spoke of it proved how much she loved it." Frustration laced her words, and a frown marred her countenance. "I had all but forgotten about the shop, too, until you inquired about it." She sighed, brushing wisps of hair out of her eyes. "But now I have a renewed interest in discovering more."

Aaron took another bite and pointed the apple in her direction. "And you might be just the one to succeed, too."

Lillian cast a quick glance his way and smiled. "I *can* be rather persuasive when I so desire. And I always was Aunt Charlotte's favorite."

He chewed for a moment, and she fell silent beside him. "But what if the memories prove too painful for your aunt to risk resurrecting them?"

She tilted her head and pressed her lips into a thin line. A breeze stirred the loose wisps of hair at the crown of her head, and she tucked the strands she could grab behind her ear. "I hadn't thought about that. You could be right. If Aunt Charlotte decided not to reopen the shop when circumstances took a turn for the better, she must have had her reasons."

"Exactly." He bit the final piece of apple then tossed the core into a waste bucket outside Hardwell's Meat Market. "I have a question for you."

"Yes?"

"Should speaking with your aunt produce a favorable outcome, would you be willing to invest the hours needed to resurrect Cobblestone Books?"

Lillian stumbled, and he extended a hand to steady her. Her apple almost flew from her hand, but she caught it before it fell. She regained her footing and licked her lips several times. He hoped it was a crack in the sidewalk and not his question that unsettled her. He only wanted to gauge her commitment when it came to the bookshop. Why would that cause a problem?

"Are you all right?" He kept his hand on her elbow until she'd regained her balance.

"Yes, yes." Heavy breathing accompanied her reply, but she smiled in spite of it, and he released her arm. "I'm sorry. There must have been a bit of uneven sidewalk back there."

He motioned with his head over his shoulder and chuckled. "Yes, the sidewalk sometimes has a way of coming up to trip you when you least expect it. Cobblestone will do that to you."

A full-fledged smile accompanied his joke, and he once again felt at ease.

He wanted to see their friendship improve with each passing day—not give her a reason to withdraw. How else was he going to get to the bottom of Conrad's request and fulfill it as well?

"Back to your previous question," she said. "You would like to know how serious I am about this?"

Well, he hadn't phrased it that way, but that was his intent. He nodded and placed his hand at her back as they crossed Market to the other side. Heightened activity resulted from the proximity to the noon hour, and the manners ingrained in him from childhood couldn't be ignored.

"I can't say for certain, as before today it wasn't even a passing thought in my mind." She quirked her mouth to one side. "But now? I find I am actually excited at the possibilities."

Aaron looked back across the street to the left at a small grassy area some seemed to be using as a park. The immaculate lawns near his home in London and even the home where Lillian and her family lived made this area seem ramshackle and scraggly, but the young mother with her two playing children didn't seem to mind. And it was in the middle of a bustling center for businesses and trade. Adequate space didn't exist for more.

"Do you believe your aunt would even be open to the idea?"

"I honestly don't know." Lillian shook her head and frowned. "As I said, it has been years since anyone mentioned the shop, and the last I recall, any reference to it was made with a great deal of sadness." Her voice choked, but she swallowed past it. "So we will likely have to tread carefully when approaching my aunt."

It took a moment for Lillian's words to register, but when they did, he directed his full attention on her. We? Did she realize what she'd just said? And did that mean she already took the guarantee of his help for granted? The prospect of working side by side with her did sound appealing. But he'd best not get too far ahead of himself. They still had a substantial obstacle in front of them.

Too late, he realized his ponderings caused him to miss a bit of her side of the conversation.

"I do apologize, Lillian, but I'm afraid my mind wandered a bit there." He stopped and turned to face her. "Would you mind repeating what you just said?"

Her expression softened, and she offered a sweet smile. "I only pointed out that we're standing in front of what once was the bookshop."

Aaron shook his head then squeezed his eyes shut and opened them. "Do you mean to tell me Cobblestone Books is still right here on Market Street?"

Lillian played with her lower lip between her teeth as an amused light entered her eyes. "That is exactly what I said."

She gestured with an open hand to her right, indicating a boarded-up shop with two sizable storefront windows on either side of the door, set a few feet back from the sidewalk. The smudged and dirt-caked windows showed obvious signs of neglect, and the crisscrossed planks of wood nailed to the door had chips and cracks along the edges. Aaron could probably yank them free without much effort, but the shop didn't belong to him.

"Imagine that." He drew his eyebrows together and turned to look back the way they'd come. "I had no idea we'd walked that far." Aaron leveled a quizzical look in Lillian's direction. "Nor did I know you were leading us here."

A sly look crossed her face, and a twinkle lit up her hazel eyes. "It's in the opposite direction from the shipyard, but I didn't wish to reveal my intent. This way, it makes the surprise that much better."

"Come to think of it, I did seem to notice we hadn't been walking the way I came with your father from the shipyard."

Lillian shrugged. "You wanted to know about the bookshop, and I figured showing it to you would be the best response." She glanced at the abandoned storefront. "If only it wasn't in such a desolate condition."

Aaron attempted to see the shop as it was in its heyday. He could envision the featured books out front and center, and if Lillian's oldest aunt possessed any of the decorating skills her younger sister did, some well-placed fabrics in bold colors would have probably complemented the display. He peered through the dirty windows and could just make out a few dark shelves, but not much else.

"It might be a bit dismal now." Aaron glanced a bit farther down the street to what appeared to be a peaceful and inviting park. "But the location is excellent, and the potential exists for a successful rebirth, should your aunt be agreeable."

"If you truly believe it's possible, I will speak to my aunt at the earliest opportunity."

This was exactly what Aaron had dreamed of when he and Conrad had struck an accord in regard to business ventures. Of course, Conrad had mentioned antiques and shipping in his proposal, but an antique bookshop could fall under that classification. To be involved right from the start of resurrecting a once popular establishment. Fortune had certainly shone down on him. Anything to get out from under his uncle's thumb and the manipulating manner in which he controlled his family.

"Aaron?"

Lillian's soft, hesitant voice broke Aaron free from his musings. Oh. He'd done it again. Twice now in the span of several minutes. She deserved his full attention. He turned to her with what he hoped was remorse in his expression.

"I do apologize, Lillian. It appears I am guilty yet again of allowing my thoughts to wander." He gestured, palm up, and dipped his head slightly. "Please. Tell me what I missed."

"It appears you are as excited about the possibilities as I." She smiled. "And I only mentioned that we might want to make our way back to the shipyard. My father's carriage will likely be waiting to take us home."

"Ah yes. The carriage. And the shipyard." Aaron nodded. "Yes, let us not tarry here any longer. If all goes well, we shall have time enough to spend here at the shop." He glanced up and down Market Street and back at Lillian. "Now, is there a faster way other than retracing our steps, or shall we make an about-face and return the way we came?"

"From here, it is almost a square, any way we choose. But we can walk down East Eleventh to Church and East Seventh from there. Otherwise, we walk down past the opera house and take East Seventh from there."

The Grand. Aaron had glimpsed the name on the outside of that establishment as they'd walked past. A poster advertised a performance from a vaudeville circuit coming soon. Perhaps he could escort Lillian to that. And there he went again. He really needed to keep his thoughts on a tighter rein.

Aaron pivoted to face the park he'd seen a moment ago and placed his hand at the small of her back. "I believe I should like to see more of this fair city. So, let us take the course down East Eleventh, shall we?"

"Very well."

Lillian followed his lead this time, casting a glance over her right shoulder just before they fully passed the bookshop.

"I look forward to doing something worthwhile again," she muttered.

Aaron almost asked her what she meant, but he wasn't sure if she'd intended him to hear her or not. He'd have to store that statement to pursue at a later date. A time when delving into that remark further would be more prudent. For now, they had some plans to make.

Chapter 9

Lillian pulled the needle through the fabric of the cotton shift she was mending. Her mind wasn't remotely close to being focused on the task at hand. Good thing it didn't require much of her attention. She doubted she could muster up much more concentration.

"Ouch!"

She stuck her finger in her mouth and nursed the offending injury with both her teeth and tongue.

"Do be careful, Lillian dear," Aunt Bethany warned, barely looking up from the canvas she painted. "That is the fourth time in the last ten minutes you've stuck yourself with the needle. You are usually more attentive than that."

Yes, she was. But lately she had trouble keeping her mind on anything other than the bookshop and Aaron. After their walk together and conversation two weeks ago, little else had occupied her mind.

Two weeks. It had been two weeks since Lillian had last seen Aaron for any length of time. Despite him presently residing in their home and taking the evening meals with them, they had been like passing strangers. Father kept Aaron busy at the shipyard and the powder mill from sunup to sundown, it seemed. They faced each other across the dinner table, but she could do little more than shake her head at his questioning gaze. No, she hadn't spoken to her aunt yet.

Finally, a morning presented itself where Aunt Charlotte wasn't otherwise busy at the shipyard with Uncle Richard, so she'd made an unannounced visit. Aunt Bethany arrived moments later saying she needed to take the morning off from antiques. Lillian couldn't have planned it better had she tried. And she *had* tried. But two levelheaded women with a keen mind for business would be perfect for this conversation. Now, just how was she going to get things started?

"Lillian?" Mother spoke up and broke Lillian from her contemplation. She dropped a few pieces of dried cinnamon into the netting ball she held. "Is there something on your mind?"

"Yes, dear," Aunt Charlotte added from her chair near the fireplace, where she crocheted a complete set of doilies. "You have not been yourself this morning." She nodded at the shift in her niece's hands. "By now, you likely would have finished the mending on three or four items. Instead, you're still working on the one."

"I'm sorry," Lillian replied, resting her hands on top of the shift. "I cannot seem to concentrate."

Aunt Charlotte smiled at Mother. "Is it any wonder she's managed to put the needle into her finger more times than through the shift she's mending?"

"You should be thankful your aunt Anastasia isn't here as well," Aunt Bethany said with a grin.

Mother chuckled and nodded. "Or that Chloe is otherwise engaged with her daily lessons on the harp," she said with a nod to the far corner of the sitting room.

"Like Siamese twins, those two are," Aunt Charlotte added with a knowing look. "They would both ask you what gentleman has you so distracted."

Lillian glanced over her shoulder at her sister, who sat with eyes closed as she rhythmically ran her fingers across the harp strings, providing them all with soothing musical accompaniment to their various tasks. Yes, it was a good thing her sister didn't notice her present state, or she'd never hear the end of it. Chloe could be ruthless in her teasing where men were concerned.

"Well?" Mother asked. "Are you going to tell us, or will we have to coax the information from you?"

As she turned back to face Mother and her two aunts, Lillian allowed a slight grin to form on her lips. Their expressions all reflected great interest. It seemed meddling had become contagious.

"Oh bother," she replied. "Very well."

They all might expect her to talk about her involvement with Aaron, but she could redirect the topic to the bookshop easily enough. At least she had a way to work toward her questions.

"I'm afraid you might be disappointed by what I have to say."

"Why don't you allow us to be the judge of that, dear?" Aunt Bethany replied. "You can begin with the walk you and Mr. Stone took from my shop the other day."

"And what makes you believe it is Mr. Stone whom my great-niece fancies?" Aunt Charlotte asked.

"Have you lost your ability to be observant in your advanced years, dear?" Aunt Bethany returned.

Aunt Charlotte placed a hand on her chest and widened her eyes. "My advanced years? I might have lost a little of my awareness, but not my wits." She pointed at her sister. "You only trail me by three years, sister of mine. If I am suffering from the effects of my age, you would be as well."

"Not for another three years," Aunt Bethany retorted.

"Or sooner," Aunt Charlotte countered, "if you continue in this fashion."

"Might we put an end to this talk of old age, please?" Mother asked. "None of us are anywhere near suffering from ill effects due to our age."

Lillian sat and watched the three women with a smile on her face. They might technically be from separate generations, but they acted more like sisters. And with only nine years from Mother to Aunt Charlotte, they really were closer to sisters than aunts and niece.

"Besides," Mother continued, "I believe we were waiting for my daughter to share about a particular handsome gentleman, and that holds far more appeal than our present topic of conversation."

"I don't know, Mother," Lillian replied. "I find this quite entertaining."

"I'm sure you do," Aunt Bethany said. "But your mother is correct, Lillian. We are not going to let you get away that easily."

"Now," Aunt Charlotte added, "back to the walk."

Lillian shrugged. "As I said before, there isn't much to tell."

Well, actually, she could probably whet their appetite for sensational details if she chose to, but she'd better stick to the facts. Discussing the bookstore would come much faster that way.

"After Mr. Stone assisted Chloe and me with our task at the antiques shop, he asked me to accompany him on a walk. He wanted to know more about the various industrial pursuits of our family."

She avoided the specific question Aaron had asked for the moment. That would come up soon enough.

"Since it seems Father is moving forward with employing Mr. Stone as Conrad had hoped, I didn't see a reason not to answer his questions."

"Or prolong the discussion in order to spend more time with him," Aunt Bethany countered.

Lillian gave her aunt a mock glare. "And you were always the practical one, Aunt Bethany. Today, you seem more like Aunt Anastasia."

"Well, you do have to admit," Aunt Bethany replied, "Mr. Stone is both charming and attractive."

"And his manners are impeccable," Mother added.

Aaron's blue eyes, often infectious smile, and thick, wavy hair came to mind. Lillian nodded. "I will not disagree with either of you on those points. Mr. Stone is a true gentleman, and we enjoyed our walk immensely. He had many things to say about the family businesses from an educated standpoint, and he spent some time complimenting Father and Uncle Richard for all they'd accomplished." She recalled their conversation following their stop at the bookshop. "He even remarked about being impressed with the lack of pretentiousness, despite our family's obvious success."

Mother and her two aunts shared a silent look between the three of them, and Aunt Charlotte sent a wink her way.

"I would have to say this Mr. Stone has our dear Lillian besotted," Aunt Charlotte said.

"Were I a few years younger, and had I not yet found my James," Aunt Bethany added, "I might be smitten as well."

"But it is not like that at all," Lillian protested. "I merely enjoy his company and find him a pleasant conversationalist."

"There now." Mother gestured toward Lillian while addressing her two aunts. "Did I not tell you?"

So, Mother had been speaking about her to her aunts? It shouldn't come as much of a surprise. But Lillian had tried so hard to remain inconspicuous... at least up until that day she and Aaron took their walk. No way could she hide that from anyone.

"I must say, it is about time." Aunt Bethany smiled. "Our dear Lillian has finally met a man who has captured her attention. And now she wishes to make him her beau."

"I never said I wanted him for a beau," Lillian corrected.

Then again, perhaps her aunt was right. She might not know much about Aaron, but she knew what was important. That he respected others, he had a keen business sense, he stepped up and accepted responsibility when it was given to him, and he was a man of his word. She could certainly do far worse. But as of right now, their relationship was nothing more than friendship.

"No, you didn't." Aunt Charlotte nodded. "But you didn't say you *didn't* want him for a beau, either," she added with a wink. "And as self-appointed supporters to your mother, that grants us the freedom to pursue this line of questioning much further."

Lillian sighed. If she didn't put a stop to this, the conversation was going to go in a direction she'd rather avoid right now. Enough of this dancing around. Lillian slapped her hands on the arms of her chair.

"Mr. Stone and I only took the walk to discuss Cobblestone Books, and I took him to the boarded-up shop."

There. She'd said it. Not exactly how she'd planned, but she'd had enough of all the talk about romantic involvement and Aaron being a potential suitor. Not that the thought hadn't entered her mind once or twice. She didn't wish to talk about that, though.

"Cobblestone Books?" Aunt Charlotte leveled an inquisitive look her way.

"My old bookshop? Whatever led you to speak of that with Mr. Stone?"

"He actually brought up the subject to me and Chloe that day," Lillian replied. "It seems he found an old ledger in Father's office at the shipyard, and it set him to wondering."

"I am curious why he chose to ask you two first," Mother stated. "Why did he not speak with your father about it?"

"He told me the opportunity didn't present itself. They were leaving the offices there, and Mr. Stone had gone back to fetch some ledgers for Aunt Bethany. That was when he found the one for Cobblestone Books."

Aunt Charlotte tilted her head and pursed her lips. "So, pray tell, what did Mr. Stone say once you told him about the shop and showed him where it is?"

Perfect! Her aunt had given her the exact leading question she needed.

Lillian smiled. "He actually was impressed with its location and lamented about it having to close its doors." And now for the pivotal point. "Mr. Stone also suggested we attempt to resurrect the shop and breathe new life into it." She pleaded with her eyes but appealed to her aunt by raising her shoulders a little and chewing on her lower lip. "But only with your permission, Aunt Charlotte. After all, it *is* your shop."

"Yes, it is. And I am not certain reopening the shop is a feasible option at this point." Aunt Charlotte sighed. "I simply do not have the time to invest in getting the shop in shape again, and your uncle likely wouldn't want to add yet another investment to his already extensive list of responsibilities."

Aunt Charlotte tried to hide it, but deep down, she wanted to see the bookshop open again. And Lillian wanted to give that to her. She'd worked long and hard to make Cobblestone Books what it had been. She deserved to see it prospering once more.

"Oh, but Aunt Charlotte, you and Uncle Richard wouldn't need to be involved at all!"

"How do you intend to manage that, Lillian?" Mother asked. "You don't have any equity of your own to invest at this point, and you would need to speak to your father if you intend to borrow anything."

"No, no." Lillian waved her hands back and forth. "This would purely be a volunteer operation led by Mr. Stone and me. Since Aunt Charlotte still owns the building, we wouldn't need to invest anything to open it again. We'd just need to remove the wood planks on the front door."

"And it would need a thorough cleaning," Aunt Bethany stated. "It has been nearly fifteen years since anyone has set foot in the place. Goodness knows what condition the shop is in." She curled her lips in disgust. "Or what critters might be lurking about inside."

"That doesn't matter." Actually critters didn't exactly appeal to her, but that was minor in light of the overall goal. "We'll take care of whatever we need to do to restore the shop to its former glory." A second time, Lillian appealed to her aunt. "We only need your permission, Aunt Charlotte. And I promise, you wouldn't have to do a thing. . .unless you choose to help."

"She really is convincing, isn't she?" Aunt Charlotte said with a smile at her sister and Mother.

Mother shrugged, pride evident in her voice when she said, "I believe she takes after you." She smiled. "From what you told me, you had to demonstrate a similar dedication to your father when you wanted to open the bookshop in the first place."

"This is very true." Aunt Charlotte pressed her lips in a thin line, but a slight grin tugged at the corners of her mouth.

Lillian sat on the edge of her seat, trying for all she was worth not to bounce. She just knew her aunt was going to say yes. How could she not?

"So, does that mean we're going to reopen Cobblestone Books?" Aunt Bethany asked. "Oh, forgive me. That Lillian and Mr. Stone are going to reopen it?"

"It appears that way," Aunt Charlotte replied with a full smile.

"Oh, thank you, Aunt Charlotte!" Lillian rushed from her seat and threw her arms around her aunt, embracing her tightly. She pulled back. "You won't regret it, I promise."

"I'm sure I won't, my dear." Her aunt placed her hands on Lillian's arms and slid them down to clasp her wrists. "Now, tell me," she said with a twinkle in her eyes, "has this Mr. Stone asked you to call him by his first name yet? Or are you still at the stage of using formal address when you greet each other?"

"He made that request two weeks ago at your store." Lillian leaned back a little. "But as of right now, we are only friends interested in resurrecting the bookshop."

"When are you going to see him again?" Aunt Bethany asked.

"I am not sure. It has been nearly three weeks since the walk, and Father has kept him so busy during the day, we only see each other at dinner." She knew Aaron to be a man of his word. So there was no need to doubt him. He said he would be involved in the restoration project. They only needed to find the time.

"Very well." Mother assumed a nonchalant air. "I shall see to it that your father grants Mr. Stone a reprieve from whatever it is he has him doing." She smiled at Lillian. "After all, I have a feeling you're going to need him a lot to make this resurrection a success."

Lillian leaned in and kissed her aunt's cheek then stepped to Mother and did the same. "Thank you, Aunt Charlotte. Mother." She nearly twirled her way back to her seat then picked up her shift again and resumed the mending. Maybe now she could finish this one. "I shall make certain we keep you apprised of any and all work and report in on our progress after each meeting."

"That should work just fine," Aunt Charlotte said with a nod.

In the meantime, Lillian prayed she could maintain her focus, as well as her professionalism, when it came to seeing Aaron again.

Chapter 10

Aaron rushed down the walk in front of the ships at the Hanssen-Baxton shipyard. A messenger had just brought him a note from Lillian. She had urgent news for him and was waiting at the end of the brick path. Only one thing could bring her down to the docks specifically requesting to see him. That made Aaron quicken his steps even more.

He spotted her before she saw him. Dressed in a blue rivaling the sky that day and a jaunty hat to match, Lillian stared in the opposite direction, appearing to be deep in thought. Aaron couldn't decide if he should announce his presence or not. When he was within five feet of her, she turned her head, and her eyes met his. That solved *that* dilemma. A bright smile graced her lips, and she jumped to her feet.

"Aunt Charlotte said yes!"

Lillian threw her arms around his neck, and Aaron braced himself with one leg to avoid being knocked down from the impact. His arms went around her waist. An embrace? In public? Her father was on one of the ships. What would he say if he saw them right now?

Cheers, whistles, and hollers sounded from more than one ship deck behind them. "Way to go, Stone!" one sailor called out.

Lillian shoved away from him like she'd been bit or stung. Crimson stained her face from her temple down to her neck. She covered her red cheeks with her hands, her shaded eyes showing a mixture of fear and shame.

Aaron reached for her hands, but she took another step backward and bumped into the bench she'd occupied only seconds before.

"Lillian, please." Aaron spoke soft and low. "There is no need to be ashamed." He offered the slightest of grins. "In fact, I rather appreciated your show of enthusiasm."

Her hands lowered, but her wide eyes never strayed from his. She looked like a deer who had just heard the click of a rifle. He'd better do something fast, or she might bolt. It had been three weeks since they'd had any opportunity to speak with each other at length, and he didn't want to do anything that might jeopardize this moment. Aaron held her gaze and took one slow step toward her. She started to step away, but he captured her hands, preventing her escape.

The shrill of a couple of whistles again pierced the air. Lillian tugged against his hold, but he wouldn't let go.

"Please? Sit?" he asked, hoping she'd acquiesce.

When she did, he reluctantly released her hands, but only to step toward the unoccupied space on the bench. She immediately started to worry the white ribbon along the triangular edges of her tailored blouse.

"May I?" He gestured toward the available seat.

Lillian only nodded.

"Very good," Aaron said as soon as he took his seat, angling his knees and body toward her. The early-June sun cast partial shadows on them from its position in the eastern sky. He smiled. "Now, I gather from your zealous greeting that your discussion with your aunt went well?"

She glanced up at the ships anchored not twenty feet away, concern etching itself into the facets of her delicate face.

"Pay them no mind, Lillian." Aaron reached out and tapped her forearm to return her attention to him. " 'Tis a rare occurrence for a beautiful young lady to grace the area down here by the docks with her presence, and those sailors were merely demonstrating their lack of manners."

She blushed again, only this time, the pink glow came with the hint of a smile as she tucked her chin toward her chest.

"There now," he stated. "That is much more preferable to fear and uncertainty where I am concerned. And do allow me to assure you again. There was nothing untoward in your actions a moment ago. At least nothing *I* found improper in any way."

With a quick perusal, Aaron noted the lace-cuffed puffy sleeves matched the lace band around her hat, and a column of pearl-like buttons ran down the center of her top. The white ribbon that ran along the hem of her blouse also did the same for her skirt just above the ruffle. Simple, yet elegant. And the color suited her to perfection.

As if sensing his scrutiny, Lillian raised her head. The upsweep of the wide brim to her hat granted him a glimpse of first her delicate mouth, followed by her only slightly rosy cheeks, and finally her captivating eyes, looking more teal than hazel this morning.

"So, tell me about the chat you had with your aunt."

Lillian finally started to show some warmth and interest in their conversation again. If only those sailors hadn't whooped and hollered when they did. Aaron might have been able to enjoy the feel of Lillian in his arms a bit longer. But he needed to keep his mind from pursuing those thoughts. Business. This was just business.

"The conversation went better than I had planned," Lillian began. "I assured Aunt Charlotte, as well as Aunt Bethany and Mother, that they would not be required to help in any way unless they chose to do so. Once I did that, Aunt Charlotte's agreement to the request and permission for us to get right to work happened almost immediately."

"Splendid!" Aaron clasped his hands together and gave them a single, firm shake. "Now, we shouldn't dawdle on this project. We should make immediate plans and set straight to work."

"That is exactly what I anticipated," Lillian replied. She raised one arm and reached into a small reticule dangling from her wrist, pulling out a folded piece of paper. "That is why I made a preliminary list of the first tasks that will likely need our initial attention."

Industrious. And impressive as well. He held out one hand toward her. "Might I be permitted to see it?"

She handed the paper to him without hesitation. He exchanged a silent look with her and a brief smile before glancing down at her feminine script. Aaron nodded.

"I believe this covers any and all items that have come to *my* mind," he said as he handed the list back to her. "Now, we only need supplies and workers, and we can get started."

"Supplies should not be a problem," Lillian stated. "Workers?" She shrugged. "We shall simply have to do our best." She shot him a pixie-like grin. "Perhaps we can promise a hot meal in exchange for a few hours of their time."

Aaron laughed. "A hot meal served at a dusty old bookshop? Now *that* I should like to see."

She touched her fingertips to her lips and giggled. "At the very least, it will likely attract more workers than we could possibly need. But it might get the work done faster."

"Indubitably." He started to cover her hand with his, but it might make her skittish yet again. Instead, he narrowed his eyes and sighed. "Though, we might wish to be cautious not to encourage too many. Could prove more distracting than useful."

Lillian nodded. "Yes, you do have a point." She smiled. "Perhaps we should limit it to family and close friends only. And a simple refreshment of lemonade and iced water will suffice."

"I do believe we have settled on an excellent compromise." Throwing caution to the wind, Aaron risked the physical touch. She inhaled sharply and glanced down at their hands. He put the slightest pressure on her fingers, and she looked up at him once more. "And as Cobblestone Books began with your family, it is only fitting that we keep it as such."

For the next half hour or so, they planned out the details as much as possible. Without the benefit of being inside, assigning or making allowances for some tasks would have to wait. Lillian possessed a keen mind and had already thought ahead to how they would announce the reopening when the time came. He loved her ideas. If only that time were already here, so he could see them put into play. First things first, though.

Movement over Lillian's shoulder caught Aaron's attention, and he glanced up to see James Woodruff standing a respectful distance from them. He nodded behind him toward the offices, a silent indication that Aaron's presence had been requested. Aaron nodded, showing he understood. He waited for Lillian to finish her current thought; then he flattened his palms on his thighs.

"Well, I do believe you have been extremely thorough, right down to the types of books you would like to see featured in the front windows." He chuckled. "But I do believe we're getting ahead of ourselves just a bit. We don't even know the condition of the shop at this point, nor have we secured the necessary tools, or know how long this is going to take us merely to get the shop in working order again."

Lillian's face showed her disappointment. Oh no. That hadn't been his intent at all. Aaron didn't want to discourage the ideas or dampen her excitement. So he again covered her hand with his, and this time wrapped his fingers around hers.

"Not that any of those obstacles aren't easily surmounted, but I suggest we open up the shop first." He smiled. "Then we can move forward with the impressive plans you have made."

She smiled as well, the light returning to her eyes and her fingers flexing slightly beneath his.

"Now, as much as I wish I could continue making plans with you, I do have an important task your father has asked me to do. But I shall see you at dinner tonight. We can speak with your mother then about securing the key to the shop from your aunt and setting a day to begin work."

"That will likely prove to be the easiest step in this process," Lillian replied.

Aaron reached for her other hand and held them both in his. Oh, how he looked forward to working side by side with her, investing heart and soul into a project likely to produce an almost immediate return on their labor and commitment. For now, they must part ways.

"Miss Lillian," Aaron said as he raised her hands to his lips, "it has been a pleasure." He placed a quick kiss on the back of her right hand. The sudden warmth in her eyes at his actions made him want to stay right there. Aaron swallowed. "Until this evening," he forced himself to say.

She nodded. "I wish you success in completing your work for Father. Thank you for sitting with me and discussing the plans."

His fingers seemed to move across the backs of her knuckles of their own accord. And she didn't appear to be in any hurry to leave, either. But he had to put some distance between them. Now.

"Of course," he replied, drawing her up to stand with him. Aaron released her hands and reached up to touch the brim of his bowler. "Good day, Lillian."

He walked away and made it about halfway to the offices before he turned around, only to find her watching him. Oh, how he prayed the afternoon wouldn't pass slowly.

❧

"Are you ready for this?"

Aaron peered over his shoulder with eyebrows raised and as much anticipation in his expression as what bubbled inside of Lillian at that moment. Was she ready? Of course she was! She'd been waiting for this moment from the second following Aunt Charlotte's approval to resurrect the bookshop.

Cobblestone Books would soon live again. And she'd be part of the team that would make it happen. She could hardly wait to get started.

"Let's get the door opened," she replied.

Aaron planted his feet then grabbed hold of the top board and yanked. Freed from his outer coat, the fabric of his work shirt strained against his back and broad shoulders. He cut an impressive figure, from the top of his light camel derby right down to the stylish cut of his brown and taupe leather spats. Warmth crept into Lillian's cheeks at her scandalous appraisal. How fortunate Aaron had his back turned to her, or she might be forced to explain the blush. Mother would chastise her if she were here to witness her daughter behaving in such a manner.

A loud crack sounded as the wooden plank broke free from the nails binding it to the exterior doorframe. Aaron stumbled backward several steps, board in hand, and bumped into Lillian. Another glance over his shoulder and a sheepish grin made her smile.

"Well, it appears that board is now free." He winked.

"So it seems," she replied.

"Just one more to go!" Aaron stepped forward then paused. "Um, you might want to take a step or two back or move to the side a bit." He placed his hands on the board. "We wouldn't want a repeat of what happened with the first, now would we?"

Lillian did as he suggested, but she couldn't tell if he truly intended to protect her, or if he wanted to avoid contact with her for other reasons. His voice sounded strange to her. Like a unique blend of teasing and wistfulness.

Another crack, and the second board came loose. Again, Aaron took two steps before regaining his balance. He set the board down next to the first and brushed his hands together.

"All set," he announced, turning to face her once more. He reached into the small pocket of his vest and withdrew the key to the shop. As he held it out to her, he smiled. "If you step forward, Miss Lillian, I do believe this honor is all yours."

That was the second time he'd called her that. First at the shipyard, and now here. A sign of respect or a way to distance himself, she couldn't tell. She drew near and took the key from his outstretched hand. Their fingers brushed in the transfer, and Lillian looked up to find his gaze on her. If the look in his eyes indicated anything, he didn't wish to distance himself in any way from her.

All of a sudden, the little space in the inset in front of the shop had become rather stifling. Lillian spun toward the door and jammed the key into the lock, giving it a quick turn. She pushed on the door, but it wouldn't budge. Aaron pressed against her right side and braced his hand against the door. Lillian breathed in his heady, musky cologne, noticing the distinct scent of sandalwood, oakmoss, and caraway. Similar to the one Conrad had always worn, only with a stronger herbal content. She closed her eyes and let the fragrance wash over her.

"Are we going to actually heave our combined weight against this door or remain outside looking in?"

Lillian started, opening her eyes and staring through the grime-covered glass on the front door. She didn't dare turn her head to look up at Aaron. The amused tone to his voice said it all. He'd caught her daydreaming. She should know better, especially standing in such close proximity to a man as charming and attractive as Aaron.

Without a word, Lillian again braced herself, and Aaron did the same. Together, they shoved, not once, but twice, and the door finally gave way. Aaron's quick reflexes saved her from tumbling into the shop, and once she had regained her footing, he released her arm. A chill from the loss of warmth where his hand had been brought on a slight shudder.

Aaron stepped back and allowed her to enter first. The scurrying of little feet sounded somewhere to her left. A mouse, or even a family of mice, no doubt. But what other critters had made their home in this abandoned shop over the years? And what further surprises awaited them?

"It is obvious no one has set foot inside this place since they closed the shop."

Lillian approached the front counter and stepped behind it. Oh, the stories she'd heard as a little girl. This is where Aunt Charlotte had spent many hours and many years greeting customers, loaning or selling books to them, and sharing the joys of reading with all who crossed the threshold of her shop. Her aunt had also met her uncle and mother here. Lillian traced her finger through the layer of dust on the countertop. How difficult it must have been to walk outside the day it closed and know she might never return.

"Well, it is certainly not as dull and dreary as I imagined it might be." Aaron stepped to a bookcase on his right, picked up a misplaced shelf piece, and blew the dust from its surface.

The particles floated toward Lillian and tickled her nose.

"Achoo!"

The sneeze escaped before she had a chance to cover her mouth. More dust puffed into the air around her.

"That was entirely my fault," Aaron said as he walked toward her, holding out a handkerchief.

"Thank you," she replied, taking it from him.

"All right." Aaron clapped his hands and looked around the shop. "First order of business is to open up every available door and window in the shop."

"Yes." Lillian nodded and tucked his handkerchief into the cuff of her sleeve. "Then we will need a bucket of water, a broom, and as many rags or old pieces of cloth as we can find. We'll have to bring the lemon oil another time, once the bookcases and shelves have been thoroughly cleaned."

Aaron moved to explore the shop, disappearing down one of the aisles and coming up another before disappearing again. From her other cuff, Lillian withdrew a scarf and slipped it underneath her hair, tying the ends up top and sliding the knot around to the bottom. She opened one of the interior doors and found the bucket and broom in a closet. After grabbing the handles of both, she turned to exit, but some knife carvings just to the right of the doorframe caught her eye. Squinting her eyes, she could just make out the letters.

"R.B. & C.P.," she read aloud. And not too far below that one had been carved another. "A.B. & G.B." Both had been circled by jagged and uneven hearts. Lillian smiled. Her aunt and uncle, and her parents. Immediately, her mind conjured up several possible scenarios that would have led these couples to etch their names in the wood. Two generations had been memorialized here. Would her name eventually be the third?

"Well, would you look at this!"

Aaron's voice sounded from somewhere off to the right and toward the back of the shop. The initials would have to wait for another time. Lillian stepped out into the main room of the shop and searched for Aaron.

"There are several chairs and tables back here, right by the windows." His voice grew louder, and Lillian turned toward the sound just as Aaron appeared at the start of the farthest aisle. "Lillian, you really should. . ."

He froze and stared.

"What?" Lillian furrowed her brow. "What is it? Is something the matter?"

"No. No." Aaron shook his head and blinked a couple times. "But your hair. And the scarf." He pointed. "Momentarily took me by surprise, that's all."

Lillian reached up and touched the smooth silk covering her hair. "Oh, this. I figured it might come in handy this afternoon."

"You certainly came prepared."

"Of course." She smiled. "Now, what is it you wished to show me?"

"Oh, yes." He beckoned with his hand. "Come with me."

She obeyed and walked with him down that last aisle. He stopped in front of an alcove of sorts filled with furniture covered by several white sheets. Beams of filtered sunlight streamed through the windows. These must be the chairs and tables he'd discovered a few moments ago.

"See this here?" He stepped close to the wall and pointed at the edge. "The lines don't match the structure and style of the original building. Your aunt must have had someone push this wall back to extend this part of the shop into the courtyard and create this nook." Aaron grabbed hold of the nearest sheet. "If we tear these old sheets into pieces, we have our old cloths." He waggled his eyebrows. "Shall we?"

Lillian set down the bucket and broom then grabbed a sheet as well, and together they uncovered an assortment of matched pairs of upholstered William and Mary, Hepplewhite, and Chippendale chairs, along with several Federal-style tables in between.

"Amazing," Aaron remarked. "Their condition is excellent."

"These probably came from my aunt's antiques shop at some point."

"And they only add to the overall appeal of this little shop." Aaron glanced around. "Although, I must admit. From the outside, I expected everything to go straight back from the front. But your aunt made creative use of the primary space and the space from the real estate next door. With the aisles going width-wise and the counter to the right side, it affords one an uninterrupted view of the entire shop." He pressed his lips together and nodded. "Impressive."

All right. Enough dawdling. They had a lot of work to do.

Lillian retrieved the bucket and held it up. "Aaron, if you don't mind stepping outside to the pump to fill this up, I shall get started on the sweeping."

He stared at the bucket then at Lillian, and shook his head. "Oh, right. The cleaning," he said, taking the bucket from her. "We've got years of dirt and dust to eradicate."

Aaron returned a few minutes later, sloshing bucket in hand. After coming to stand in front of her, he bent in an exaggerated bow. "Your floor bathing solution awaits, m'lady."

Lillian giggled as he set down the bucket. She immediately dunked her hand in the icy water and scooped up a handful, flinging her arm out and sending the droplets flying.

"I thought you said we were going to clean the floors." Aaron gestured toward the drops scattered about. "You certainly can't expect to clean with that little bit of water."

"No, but we need to sweep the dirt away first. Sprinkling water on the floor helps keep the dirt on the floor and not in the air."

He nodded. "I see." Pivoting on his heel, he headed toward the far aisle again. "I believe I'll get started on ripping the sheets then see if I can find a hammer and nails for any repairs that need to be made to the shelves." He paused just before disappearing behind a bookshelf and glanced over his shoulder. "I have a distinct feeling this is going to be a rather revealing restoration project."

Lillian thought about the initials carved inside the closet near the front. Yes. It certainly would be.

Chapter 11

So, tell me," Lillian began as she poured ammonia on a cloth and cleaned the glass countertop near the cash register. She looked across the counter at Aaron, her gaze direct. "And if I am meddling too much, say so."

Lillian? Meddle? He had yet to witness that.

"What made you ultimately decide to partner with my brother and cross an entire ocean to start fresh instead of striking out on your own right there in London?"

Direct and straight to the point, as usual. One of the many things Aaron admired about her. He never had to doubt where he stood with her, though he might have to read a bit more into her mannerisms and words to discern it. When he didn't immediately respond, she continued.

"You told my family about the insensitive decision your uncle made regarding the division of his assets, but why here? And why my brother?"

Aaron knelt and ran the sanding strip back and forth across the shelves of the small bookcase in front of him. Just one more pass and the shelf should be ready for staining. But Lillian had asked him a question.

"To be honest, I am not certain," he replied, moving the strip into one corner to ensure a smooth surface all around. "I only know my time with my uncle had long outlived its welcome. He proved that by his untimely announcement regarding his estate." Aaron clenched his teeth and tried to keep the bitterness from his voice. Lillian had played no part in any of it, so she didn't deserve to be the recipient of his anger.

"I can only imagine how you felt," she replied, her voice full of sympathy. "To have spent a great deal of your life with a close member of your family only to have him turn a cold shoulder to you just when it matters most."

Aaron looked up. The expression in Lillian's eyes matched the concern in her voice. "And the worst bit of it? I haven't the faintest idea what caused such a drastic change of mind in my uncle."

"I believe you said up until that point he had treated you like a son?"

"Yes." He went back to sanding. "Then one day, he called me into his office and lowered the boom on me."

Lillian chewed on her bottom lip, and her eyebrows dipped toward the bridge of her nose. "And you hadn't done anything that he might have viewed as grounds to punish you in such a drastic manner?"

"Not a thing. In fact, I believe my performance and work for his merchant trading company was above exemplary. He had never lodged a complaint with me before."

"I am curious what might have happened to cause him to be so cruel."

He shook his head. "I have been over it again and again in my mind. Even before I came of age, he employed me to work the numbers and figures." Aaron moved the sanding strip back and forth, the rhythmic motion soothing him as much as talking out his frustrations did. At least with someone who seemed to care, anyway. "Naturally, that progressed to handling the books on a regular basis. I did that for nigh onto seven years before I was forced to pursue other options." He again looked up at Lillian. "And that led me to your brother."

She smiled. "Some might consider that a divine appointment."

"When I first met Conrad, he didn't strike me as someone with a sound mind for business." Aaron winced. "Forgive me for saying that. I didn't intend to speak ill of him."

Lillian waved off his apology. "You are not saying anything that surprises me." She resumed cleaning. "As Father mentioned that first day you came, Conrad usually focused on the people and left the business side of things to Father, Uncle Richard, or even our mother's cousin Phillip."

"Yes, I can certainly see that to be the case." He turned the bookcase on its side and ran his fingers across the smooth surface, searching for any nicks or scratches he might have missed. "Perhaps that is why your brother made such a hasty offer to me not long after we met. He knew I had a mind for business, and he knew I was in the market for a change."

"Well, that," Lillian spoke up, "plus, his uncanny ability to perceive the true character of a person from nothing more than an exchange of a few words."

Aaron grinned. "Oh, is that what you call it?"

Lillian popped open the cash register then peered over the top of it at him with a smile. "Much like your 'impressive and endless mental ledger for remembering details,'" she quoted.

He raised his eyebrows. She'd repeated the phrase verbatim from the day he'd arrived. "So, you were listening."

"Of course." She returned her attention to the exterior surface of the cash register, using her cloth to polish each individual component. "Every word."

If she was this honest with him, how much more so would she be with potential suitors? Being that forthright could often put her in delicate situations. No wonder Conrad had asked him to watch out for her. Of course, he likely hadn't intended for the two of them to spend so much time together. Aaron paused at that thought. Or had he?

"Well, this bookcase is done." Aaron stood and toted the wooden piece to the front of the shop, where he set it with the three others he'd done that morning. He then stepped over to the counter where Lillian stood, leaned on his elbow, and cocked his head to watch her work. "Day six, and we've managed to complete nearly half the tasks on our list."

"Yes, we have accomplished a lot," she replied, never taking her eyes off the register.

Aaron reached out to run his fingers across the fine etching at the top, just below the window that showed the total sale. "You know, we should probably look into trading out this relic for a register with an electric motor. That inventor with the National Cash Register Company designed one a handful of years ago. I'm certain we could locate one fairly easily."

Lillian regarded him with mouth open, eyebrows drawn, and brow furrowed. "Get rid of this beautiful machine?" She caressed the top of it. "This was my aunt's very first cash register. How could you suggest we do away with it?"

He straightened and held up his hands in mock surrender. "Now, now, don't misunderstand me, Lillian. I didn't intend for the current register to be tossed out with the garbage." Aaron flattened his right hand against his chest. "Sentimentality runs deep in my bones." He laid his hand on the counter. "No, I merely meant if we're going to reopen the shop, we should do so with the most current accessories."

She tilted her head to regard the item in question then cast a sideways glance at him. "I suppose you're right. And this register could always go to Aunt Bethany to be used in her store." Lillian turned a mock pout on him. "Though it's such a beautiful piece of craftsmanship. I would hate to see it not put to use right here in the bookshop." Her fingers trailed down the side of the register.

"I know exactly what you mean," he replied, reaching out to cover her hand with his. "But an electric one will make the transactions much smoother and faster. And it isn't as if the register would be going far away. It would merely be a few blocks down Market Street."

Aaron rubbed his fingers back and forth across hers, and she froze, staring at their hands. A second or two later, she shivered. Perhaps now would be a good time to ask her about the Fourth of July festival in two weeks.

"Lillian, I—"

The front door swung open and hit the stopper nailed into the floor. Chloe stepped into the shop, followed by an entourage of others.

"Is this a private party, or can anyone join the fun?"

Aaron yanked his hand back as if he'd gotten too close to a fire and didn't want to get burned; then he put immediate distance between him and Lillian. No need to give anyone potential gossip to spread. Bad enough, they'd spent the greater portion of the morning alone together inside the shop. Granted, the back door stood open, and Lillian's maid sat at a table outside, in full view of them both. But the presence of maids didn't always cease the tongues from wagging.

"Chloe!"

Lillian rushed around the counter, seemingly unfazed by their recent conversation and his touch. That is, until she misjudged the length of the counter by a few inches and stumbled around it. Then her steps faltered, and she had to grab hold of the cash register to steady herself. This brought her within two feet of him again, and she looked up. A light pink stained her cheeks. Her tongue snaked out to wet her lips, and she swallowed a bit deeper than normal. Aaron grinned and sent her a wink. Yes, she was affected, even though she tried to hide it.

"We have come, ready to work," Lillian's friend announced.

Aaron couldn't remember her name, but she had been at that first dinner several weeks ago. Daughter to the neighbors down the street and longtime family friends. So, Chloe and the friend had come. Did that mean—

"Wow. This is a nice shop," remarked the tall and lanky young man who entered next.

Right. The older brother. What was his name? As soon as Aaron caught sight of his eyes, he knew. Pearson. The one who'd had a hard time keeping those eyes off Lillian throughout the entire dinner that night.

"Lillian," Pearson said, stepping close to her and resting his hand on her shoulder. "If this place was anything like what I heard, you have done great work here."

He stood a bit too close for Aaron's liking. They might be family friends, but the assumed familiarity felt a little odd. Lillian smiled up at him, but it didn't reach her eyes. Perhaps she didn't like his nearness either.

"All right, Pearson," the friend and younger sister chastised, "don't monopolize Lillian right from the start. She needs to give us directions, so we can get right to work." The young lady sidled up next to Lillian's other side. "Isn't that right?"

Lillian pulled away from Pearson and leaned against her friend, but Pearson stepped close again and kept his hand in place. Lillian didn't react, only smiled at her friend. "Arabella, I am so glad you're here."

Arabella. That was her name. A unique one, for certain. Aaron wouldn't be forgetting it anytime soon.

"Tick tock, Lil," Chloe interjected. "If you don't find something for us to do, I might just rescind our offer to help," she added with a grin.

Pearson hadn't removed his hand from Lillian's shoulder, despite Lillian's obvious nonverbal cue in stepping away. Now the man cut Aaron a direct gaze, his eyes almost seeming to declare territorial rights or something like that. But that was ridiculous. If anything existed between Lillian and Pearson, he would have known by now. And they would have been spending far more time together.

"I have a suggestion," Aaron spoke up. All eyes turned toward him. "Why don't you three ladies work on the features and displays at the front, getting them ready for the books to be brought in. I'll take Pearson to the back, and he can help me reinforce the bookcases."

Anything to keep him away from Lillian, especially when she clearly didn't relish his nearness. That realization at least offered Aaron some reassurance.

The three ladies looked at each other and shrugged. Lillian shot him a look of appreciation, and he responded with an almost imperceptible nod. Pearson narrowed his eyes but didn't voice any opposition. When no one said anything, Aaron clapped his hands together.

"Splendid. Let's get to work."

As Aaron passed Lillian, he gave her another wink. And just before the trio disappeared from his field of vision, Arabella and Chloe both nudged her. He grinned. Oh, to be a fly on the wall around the ladies in a few minutes.

❧

"Oh, Lillian. We must talk."

Arabella fairly pounced on Lillian immediately on arrival. Her best friend, yet she lacked a little in the area of decorum.

"Yes," Chloe chimed in with a grin. "She has been talking nonstop the entire carriage ride here."

"Now, that is not true, Chloe, and you know it," Arabella countered, stomping one dainty foot. "You are just as anxious as I to hear it from Lillian herself."

Lillian gave them both a halfhearted smile then spun around and walked back to the counter. She kneeled down, picked up the cloth again, and attacked a smear on the glass display case. Usually, an interruption from Arabella or Chloe would be desirable. But not today. Not after being forced to cut her conversation with Aaron short. And just when he'd been about to say something important.

"All right." She pressed hard on the glass, removing the smear one section at a time. "Now that you both are here, why don't you each pick up a cloth and make yourselves useful. Then you can tell me what has you both so eager to speak with me." Lillian didn't exactly want to engage in a lengthy conversation, but she wouldn't be rude either. "What is it you wish to hear?"

Arabella made her way around the counter then leaned forward and rested her elbows on top, peering over it. "First, why the long face?"

Lillian paused in her task and sighed. Best to keep her response as vague as possible. She resumed the cleaning. "A recent conversation I had with someone had been going rather well, but it didn't conclude the way I had hoped."

"This someone wouldn't happen to be a 'him,' would it? Perhaps a certain new addition to your family's employ?" At this, Lillian looked up. Arabella waggled her eyebrows and grinned big. "And was it the little scene we interrupted a few moments ago?"

She should have known. Arabella had been her friend since they wore pinafores and diapers. All that time, she had been enamored with anything relating to the male species, even drifting toward little boys when she was a child. Just like her mother before her. Chloe had no doubt told Arabella about the workdays with Aaron this week. Lillian had mentioned something, too, but only said she'd be unavailable most of the time. But Arabella could put two and two together. News like who Lillian spent most of her days with spread fast. And her dearest friend usually pounced on details such as this like an eagle diving down to snatch a fish from a lake.

"So come on," Arabella pressed. "Don't hold back with the details. We want to know everything!"

"Correction." Chloe stretched across the side counter and poked Arabella with her index finger. "*You* want to know everything. I already know the basics and would be happy with just a bit more."

Her sister knew the basics? The basics of what? Chloe hadn't been with her on any of the walks with Aaron, and so much had happened so fast the past couple of weeks, Lillian didn't have the chance to bring her sister up to speed. It looked like she'd be doing that now, though. Did she even *know* enough for certain to give them what they wanted to know?

"Oh, all right, Miss Priss." Arabella tilted her head and leveled a haughty glare at Chloe. "You might not want to hear about this fascinating story, but I do." She gripped the edge of the counter, her knuckles turning white. Her sideways glance held a decided gleam. "Now, do tell. How did all of this happen?"

So her best friend *did* know a little something. Lillian shook her head and chuckled in spite of herself. She might not feel much like talking this morning, and the thought of continuing her conversation with Aaron sounded much more appealing. Nevertheless, spending even five minutes with these two almost always bolstered her spirits.

"You don't have to share anything with her that you don't wish to share, Lillian." Chloe shot daggers at Arabella, who glared right back.

"Oh, please don't quarrel on my behalf." Lillian raised her hands in a placating gesture. "I'll be more than happy to share what I can and answer any questions. I hate to disappoint you both, though. There truly isn't much to tell."

At least not that she could say for certain. Aaron had only just started to hint at something more when the interruption occurred.

Arabella folded her arms across her chest and stuck her chin in the air with a triumphant grin on her face. Chloe rolled her eyes and returned her attention to the display table in front of her. A table that needed some book blocks for elevation and some price cards. They'd have to get those later. Her sister might appear disinterested, but Lillian knew better. This was the girl who had followed in her aunt's footsteps when it came to making matches. She prided herself on seeing potential relationships where none previously existed. Between Chloe and Arabella, Lillian didn't stand a chance.

"We're waiting," Arabella said in a singsong voice.

She sat back on her feet and gave the display case a final swipe. Might as well get this over with. While observing her transparent reflection in the glass, she described her encounters with Aaron following their walk. From that initial idea-planting moment to the longer working days, Lillian shared enough to cover the essentials and ended with the conversation of a few minutes ago, but she kept her retelling strictly factual. No sense borrowing trouble just yet. That would come soon enough, especially with these ladies involved.

"I can scarcely fathom having someone like him residing under the very same roof where I sleep at night," Arabella remarked when Lillian finished. "And then you tell us you've been spending hours upon hours working with Mr. Stone in close proximity while getting this bookshop ready to open. I'm amazed you don't have anything further to share with us." She straightened and narrowed her eyes. "Or do you?"

"Well, I can't say for certain. We haven't exactly had the time to discuss anything without interruptions," Lillian replied with a pointed glance at her friend.

"No time?" Chloe looked up from the table she was setting. "Now, that I find difficult to believe." She planted a fist on her hip. "I was going to allow Arabella to do most of the talking, but now I must say something. You have had ample time to talk. What else have you been doing with all those hours?"

"Working." Lillian extended her arms out in a semicircle. "Look around you. This shop didn't get this way all by itself. Most of our conversations have been centered around repairs and ideas for how to best set up the shop."

"All right, I will concede on that point," Chloe replied.

"Still. . ." Arabella's eyes lit up again. A sure sign of trouble. "There is a certain appeal to the knowledge that this Mr. Stone was handpicked by your brother. Conrad always did have a knack for judging good character. Then there is the matter of Mr. Stone's obvious interest in spending time with you. Why else would he have suggested his idea to you?" She glanced in the general area of the bookcases. "He *is* quite handsome, too."

And her friend had returned. The fanciful, daydreaming, obsessed-with-stories-of-romance friend. Arabella could be rather trying at times, and her constant focus on the potential for amorous associations might be bothersome to most. But Lillian wouldn't have it any other way.

Chloe waved her hand to get Lillian's attention. "So, what if Arabella and I take care of the work up here, and you attempt through subtle hints to convince Aaron to give Pearson a project alone. Do you think he might continue your conversation where he left off?"

"I don't know." Lillian passed the cloth she held from one hand to the other. "I am not certain he wishes to have an audience present, no matter how otherwise occupied they might be."

"There is always the courtyard," Chloe pointed out.

"Still with the likelihood of being overheard," Lillian replied.

"Oh, of course," Arabella added. "Don't even consider the possibility that he might be the prince of your dreams, Miss Practical." Arabella waved her hand in dismissal as she brushed invisible dust from the countertop. "Do something for me, though. If you spoil your chances with Mr. Stone because you failed to hint of the interest Chloe and I both know you have in him, please don't tell me about it. I only wish to hear if the end result of further time with him is promising."

Chloe shuffled a few steps to her left and leaned around the counter toward Lillian. "Pay her no mind, Lil. You do what you feel you have to do." She reached out and placed a reassuring hand on Lillian's arm. "And regardless of whether or not Arabella wishes to hear of your future time with Aaron, you know I will always listen."

Lillian gave her sister an appreciative smile. "Thank you. I will be certain to tell you both what happens, if anything." She glanced at the large clock on the wall. "Now, we should finish the work up front before the day disappears without us."

Once settled into marking off additional tasks from her checklist, Lillian couldn't get her mind off Aaron. Before the arrival of Chloe, Arabella, and Pearson, Aaron was about to ask her something important. She knew it. Now, thanks to Arabella's fanciful notions, thoughts of what he might have asked fully occupied her mind. What was she going to do? Both her friend and her sister would be sure to follow up on this presumed or even potential relationship. And they would want to know more about the conversation they'd interrupted. But how would she find out something like that? She couldn't just walk up to Aaron and ask him what he'd been going to say.

Then again, why couldn't she?

Chapter 12

How is the restoration project coming along, dear?"

Mother stopped Lillian in the foyer on her way to the hall table to retrieve the mail that had been delivered earlier.

Lillian placed her hand on the banister and turned, leaving her left foot on the bottom step. "Far better than we had planned. If everything continues as it has been, we will be ready for the books from Aunt Charlotte's attic in two days."

"Sounds wonderful." Mother tapped the stack of mail against her left palm. "I suppose I should speak with my aunt about arranging for transportation of all those boxes. By the time the shop was forced to close, she had amassed a substantial collection."

"Mother?" Lillian brought her one foot down to join the other. "What happened? To the bookshop, I mean. Why did Aunt Charlotte not return to open it again when the economic situation improved?"

Mother wet her lips then pulled her lower one between her teeth. "I believe that is something you are going to have to ask her yourself, my dear." She sighed. "It is not my place to answer in her stead."

"But can you not tell me anything about the circumstances other than how sad she was to see it close?"

"Lillian, please do not ask." Melancholy overtook Mother's expression. It pained her to not be able to speak freely. Lillian could see it. "You will need to speak to your aunt on your own. I am not at liberty to discuss it any further."

"Very well. And I'm sorry for pressing."

Mother smiled. "You wouldn't be *you* if you didn't." She glanced down at the stack in her hands, sifting through the handful of envelopes. "Oh!" She paused at the last piece of mail, before looking up at Lillian. "This one is addressed to Mr. Stone." After crossing the distance to the staircase, she handed the envelope to her daughter. "I believe you shall see him before any of the rest of us. Maybe you could deliver it to him?"

"Of course." Lillian took the envelope from her mother and looked down at it. "There is a postmark and return address from London!" She flipped it over and examined both sides then shook her head. As if staring at it would divulge its contents. "I hope it isn't anything critical."

"If it were, I am certain the sender would have noted something to that effect, or notified Mr. Stone of its pending arrival."

"I wonder why the sender didn't transmit a telegram instead. It would have been much faster."

"Perhaps the contents of the letter are private," Mother suggested, "and the sender did not wish for anyone else to be privy to the information inside."

"That is a logical explanation." Lillian held tight to the envelope. "I shall see Aaron receives this directly. It has already spent enough time traveling across the ocean, and it doesn't need any further delay."

Lillian turned to resume her upward trek to the second floor but stopped as her mother spoke again.

"No," Mother agreed. "And Mr. Stone will no doubt appreciate *you* delivering it."

The slight grin on Mother's lips as she looked down at the mail gave Lillian pause. What appeared to be a full smile tugged at Mother's mouth. She clearly didn't say everything on her mind. What did she mean by Aaron appreciating something as simple as a basic courtesy? Anyone else would do the same in her place.

Lillian shrugged and began making her way up the stairs. About halfway up, she stopped. Wait a moment. Mother didn't mean Aaron might *show* his appreciation in some way, did she? Warmth crept into her cheeks at the thought. She glanced down over her shoulder to find Mother watching her. The amused expression said it all. Without a word, Lillian raced the rest of the way to the second floor and down the hall to her room.

She closed the door and leaned back against it then stared up at the ceiling. How could Mother suggest such a thing?

Pressure against the door accompanied by the knob turning made Lillian step away. Chloe came stumbling into the room and cast a look back at the door as if wondering why it had been stuck. She smoothed her hands down the front of her rose silk day gown and stared at Lillian.

"I saw this blur rush past my room a minute ago." Her sister pointed toward the hall. "Then your door closed louder than usual." Chloe searched Lillian's eyes, her face, her entire body. "Are you all right?"

Lillian closed her eyes and took one or two calming breaths. If she said she was all right, her sister would ask her why she'd run down the hall. If she said she wasn't, though, Chloe would want to know the problem.

"I . . ."

How in the world could she explain this when she didn't even know if a problem existed? For all she knew, it could merely be her overactive imagination making a bigger deal out of something than necessary.

Chloe stepped to the door and shut it. Then she turned on her sister and crossed her arms. "All right, Lil. Tell me." She gave her sister a motherly look, one eyebrow raised and her mouth quirked at one corner. "You won't leave this room until you do."

In spite of her mental bewilderment, an answering grin found its way to her lips. "Chloe, I love you."

"I know." Her sister nodded. "How could you not?" she asked with a smile and a shrug. "Now, tell me what had you running down the hall as if an angry dog nipped at your heels."

Before she answered, Lillian pivoted on her heel and walked toward the settee on the other side of her four-poster bed. She sat and patted the cushion next to her. Chloe followed and perched on the other end, facing her sister.

"It's Mother," Lillian finally said.

"Mother?" Chloe wrinkled her brow. "Did she scold you or—or was she cross with you or something?"

That would be the first thing to come to mind under normal circumstances. Lillian waved off her sister's questions. "No, no. Nothing like that." She sighed. "It *was* something she said, though. Or rather what she didn't say."

Chloe blew out a long sigh, her breath disturbing the carefully styled bangs at her forehead. "Now you aren't making any sense at all, Lil. How could something Mother *didn't* say cause you to be in such a state?"

"Well, that's just it, Chloe. I'm not certain I'm even *in* a state, as you put it. This all could be nothing more than my imagination."

"What could?"

"My reaction to what Mother said."

"But I thought you said she didn't say anything."

"She didn't. Not exactly."

"Ugh!" Chloe reached out and grabbed hold of Lillian's hands. She squeezed them as she looked directly into her sister's eyes. "Will you please tell me what all of this is about before I leave you to your Ferris wheel of emotions and seek out Mother myself?"

Oh no! Not that. She didn't need her sister talking to their mother about this. "A letter arrived in the mail today," she began. "It was addressed to Aaron, and it had a postmark from London on it."

Chloe shrugged. "He used to live in London. Why would that cause such a problem?"

"It wasn't the letter, Chloe. It was Mother asking me to deliver it to Aaron and saying he would probably appreciate it very much." Lillian swallowed.

"And she grinned a little when she said it."

Almost immediately, Chloe grinned as well then nodded. "Ah, now I see."

Not Chloe, too. "You see what?"

"Mother suggested Aaron might show his appreciation for you delivering his letter to him, and you got all agitated and flustered by the thought of him saying 'thank you' with more than just words." A full smile appeared. "No wonder you fled the way you did. Though if it were me, I might have gone the other way to see if Mother's hypothesis would come true."

"Chloe!"

Her sister's expression turned innocent. "What? There is no harm in fanciful daydreaming or even taking a couple steps toward a desirable outcome." She raised her chin just slightly. "Am I to be blamed for doing what any normal young lady would do in such a situation?"

Normal? Did her sister not consider her normal?

"But what if the gentleman in question had shown no indication that such a result might even be possible?"

Chloe gave her a doubtful look. "We *are* still taking about Aaron, are we not?"

"Of course." Who else could it be?

Her sister nodded. "Then, it's possible."

"But how do you know?"

"Has Aaron ever stood within inches of you, or sat close to you, or touched your hand, or even placed his own hand at your back when you've walked together?"

"Yes. . .to all of those." But what did that have to do with anything?

"Then he's made obvious indications of his interest on more than one occasion." Chloe rolled her eyes. "Honestly, Lil. Sometimes I wonder how you and I can be related." She sighed. "And you're the big sister. You're supposed to be giving *me* the advice."

Lillian gave her sister a sheepish grin. "What can I say? It seems I take after Aunt Charlotte the same way you take after Aunt 'Stasia."

"The question is, what are you going to do about it?"

Do? Why did she have to do anything? Lillian stood and walked away from her sister. She toyed with her fingers, lightly clasped in front of her. Wasn't it usually the gentleman who made the first advance? Then again, according to Chloe, Aaron already had. So, would that make it her turn now?

"There is no guarantee Aaron will do anything more than speak his thanks."

"And there is a chance he might."

Lillian sighed. "Then, I suppose I should make my way to the bookshop to deliver Aaron's letter to him."

"Wonderful!" Chloe clapped once, and her skirts rustled as she hopped to her feet. A second later, she rushed past Lillian to the door and threw it open. "I shall notify Lydia and Alice of our pending departure."

"Our?" Lillian raised her eyebrows at her sister's back.

Chloe paused halfway out the door and turned. "Of course. You can't possibly venture to the bookshop unchaperoned. And I would never miss an opportunity such as this."

Lillian shook her head. How in the world could she say no to that logic? "Very well. Go inform our maids we will depart immediately."

⁂

Aaron stooped and got a firm hold on the bookshelf. He leaned to the left to look around one edge at Pearson Duncan, who held tight to the other end.

"I have to say, Pearson, I do appreciate you coming down here to the shop to help again. If not for you, I might have had to ask one of the coachmen or even a footman at the Bradenton home to assist."

"My pleasure," Pearson replied. "My father didn't need me this morning, so I thought coming here might be a viable alternative to pass the time."

Pass the time? Well, at least he didn't stand idly by while Aaron did all the work. That put one mark in his favor anyway. Though, the remark about not being needed sounded suspicious. How could the eldest son in a family not be needed in the family business? Aaron shrugged it off. It wasn't his affair.

"Ready?"

Pearson secured his grip and nodded. "Ready."

Together, they shuffled toward the back wall and repositioned the bookshelf between two of the windows. Lillian had said she thought a more open layout might better appeal to customers. Aaron cast a glance around the shop. She was right. Already, the space looked twice as big.

"There. That looks good."

"I agree," Pearson replied. "Shall we move the last two shelves and call it a day?"

Well, two hours of time didn't usually constitute a full day, but perhaps in Pearson's logic, it did. And he *had* been a great deal of help.

"Yes." Aaron moved toward the first of the shelves. "Once we finish, the only thing that remains is the merchandise. And I believe Lillian's aunt has made arrangements for the boxes to be brought by cart."

The two positioned themselves around the shelf. "Hard to believe all this," Pearson remarked. "Lillian is really going to run the bookshop like her aunt before her."

"So it seems."

Again they lifted the bookshelf and moved it to the empty space along the side. The shorter shelves had been placed in the center, where the taller ones had been.

"Last one," Aaron said as he planted his feet and secured his grip.

Pearson lifted with him, and in no time at all, the final shelf had been maneuvered into its new location. Aaron gave the new layout a frank appraisal. Lillian would definitely be pleased. He then dusted off his hands and brushed at his pants.

"Well, that's done." He pulled out his pocket watch and flipped it open. "Before midday, too." Aaron headed for the front. "Now, I believe I'll have myself some lunch."

And maybe some time alone before Lillian arrived. . .if Pearson took the hint. She said to expect her a little after noon.

"Have you spoken with Lillian lately?" Pearson followed Aaron and stopped just shy of the main counter. "Do you know when she might be coming to the bookshop this afternoon?"

All right. So maybe Pearson didn't notice the hint. Either that, or he ignored it on purpose. Aaron figured the latter.

"Yes, I spoke to her yesterday," Aaron replied. Now, how would he be able to answer Pearson's second question without confirming Lillian's pending arrival? "And I do not know for certain."

At least he hadn't told a lie. Since Lillian didn't give him an exact time, he couldn't share that with Pearson. Not that he would if he *did* know. The man obviously had a reason for coming. It seemed he was determined to speak with Lillian.

"Well, I believe I shall have myself a seat and wait."

He chose a stool near the front door, propped his feet on the bar, and rested his arms on his legs. His eyes locked on the left display window, and he turned his back to Aaron. It looked like lunch would have to wait.

So that offer to help with the shelves had been nothing more than a pretense. A way to prolong his visit in the hopes of being present when Lillian arrived. And Aaron could do nothing about it. Maybe he could find something else to do to occupy his thoughts and pass the time more quickly. He certainly didn't intend to sit with Pearson and strike up aimless conversation. That window near the back needed to be unjammed. He could at least work on that for a bit.

About twenty minutes later, with the window opened and the lock repaired, Aaron walked to the storage closet and stepped inside just as the front door opened with a loud creak. He'd have to remember to get some oil on those hinges. Dumping his tools on the nearest shelf, Aaron backed out and turned to face the front of the shop.

"Oh, Lillian," Pearson greeted her the moment she walked through the door. "I am glad you are here. There's something I've been wanting to ask you."

She barely acknowledged him, though. Instead, her eyes scanned the shop and lit up when they finally rested on Aaron. Lillian started to walk toward him, but Pearson reached out to stay her with his hand.

"Lillian? Did you hear me? I said I have something I wish to ask you." His voice sounded impatient. "And I've been waiting for several hours for you to arrive."

At that, Lillian stopped and directed her attention toward Pearson. Chloe and their two maids walked in behind her and headed for the courtyard behind the shop. As her sister passed by him, she acknowledged him with a nod, but her eyes held a decided gleam. Aaron followed Chloe's progress. Now, what was that all about?

He didn't have time to ponder it. Lillian's voice drew his attention back to the front.

"Pearson, I don't wish to be impolite," she said, her voice sounding slightly annoyed, "but I have an important letter for Mr. Stone, and I need to see that it's delivered immediately."

A letter? For him? She started to step away again, but Pearson's hand held fast.

"But what I wish to ask you will only take a moment. I want to know if you would accompany me to the Fourth of July festival next weekend."

The festival? No. Aaron had intended to ask Lillian about that himself today. Pearson couldn't possibly have edged forward and stolen the lead so easily. Like a shot across the bows of a ship. Aaron took heed. He needed to make his own intentions known. And fast.

"Pearson, this truly isn't a good time," Lillian replied.

"Please tell me you will at least consider my invitation."

Did the man's persistence know no bounds? What had him so tenacious all of a sudden? Like he'd come out of the woodwork, ready to woo. Lillian didn't appear too happy with him at the moment, though. A point in Aaron's favor, for sure.

She sighed. "Yes, Pearson. I promise to consider it. Now, please excuse me." Barely giving him a final glance, Lillian escaped and headed straight for Aaron.

He tried not to appear too eager or allow his seeming triumph over

Pearson to show. But the way she had eyes only for him made it difficult.

"Aaron, as you no doubt heard, I have a letter for you." She handed the envelope to him. "It arrived with today's mail with a postmark from London. I thought you might want it right away."

London? Aaron took the letter and glanced down at the front. He didn't recognize the address, but the name he did. Flipping it over, he slid his thumb under the flap and broke the seal.

"It's from my father's lawyer."

"Your father?" Lillian said. "But I thought—"

"Yes, he's gone," Aaron finished for her. "And I haven't heard from this man in almost as many years."

Aaron unfolded the single piece of paper and started to read. He'd no sooner gotten to the third line when the space around him started spinning. He grabbed hold of the nearest shelf, praying he wouldn't fall to his knees in front of Lillian.

"It's not bad news, is it?"

Her voice barely penetrated the pounding in his ears from his thumping heartbeat. His uncle couldn't do that, could he? How long ago had the letter been sent? Aaron searched for a date and looked at the postmark. More than a month. Was he already too late? Could anything be done at this point?

"Aaron?"

He glanced up to see sincere concern in Lillian's eyes. Impulse struck. He might regret this later, but right now, he didn't care. They were in too close quarters. He needed some fresh air. After tucking the letter into his vest, Aaron grabbed hold of her hand and tugged.

"Walk with me."

Chapter 13

Lillian didn't hesitate. Aaron hadn't asked or commanded. He merely spoke his request as a statement. With her hand held firmly in his, she had no recourse but to follow. But what about propriety and a chaperone?

She barely managed to catch Chloe's eye as Aaron tugged her along with him through the courtyard and toward the gate leading out to King Street near Twelfth. He kept a steady pace for the entire two-block walk to Brandywine Park and didn't slow until they'd reached Market Street Bridge. After releasing her hand, he pressed up against the wall, his palms flat against the stone top as he stared off into the distance.

Lillian leaned against the wall and rested her left elbow on the cool stone then placed her right hand on top of her left as she turned to face him. A dozen questions floated through her mind, but Aaron had been the one to receive the letter. And the letter had obviously contained distressing news. He would speak when he was ready.

She glanced over the wall down to the Brandywine River, tripping over itself below. A colorful array of wildflowers grew on either side of the river and all around, providing a rainbow's splash to the otherwise green landscape. A warm breeze rustled through the tulip poplars towering to their left and right. It whispered through the waist-high rushes along the creek banks.

Lillian closed her eyes and soaked in the sounds of nature. From the trills of the various songbirds to the splash of the trout and bluegill, to the chirping crickets hiding in the grass, and the distant high-pitched cry of the red-tailed hawk as the screech slurred downward. The musical symphony bore clear evidence of God's handiwork. And a God who had created all this would not leave Aaron alone in his inner turmoil. That same God was right there with them both. Lillian breathed a quick prayer for peace and for wisdom to know what to say when the time came.

Sensing he needed some reassurance, Lillian reached out and touched Aaron's forearm. He started and jerked his head to look at her. For several seconds, he stood and stared. She watched uncertainty, anger, hurt, and unrest play across his features. Finally, his tongue snaked out to wet his lips. He inhaled and exhaled then swallowed once.

"Thank you." He angled his body toward her and covered her hand with his own. "The way I whisked you out of the shop and dragged you along to this park, well, I wouldn't have blamed you if you had dug in your heels and refused to follow."

"I didn't want you to be alone."

Intense emotion darkened his blue eyes to near black, and he caressed her hand beneath his.

"You obviously received distressing news in the letter I gave to you, and you need someone to talk to." She smiled. "I'm just glad you chose me."

A ghost of a smile appeared. Aaron raised her hand to his lips and placed a chaste kiss on her knuckles. Lillian swallowed at the tingling sensation and the way her heartbeat increased at the intensity in his gaze.

"Are you"—she hesitated and swallowed again—"ready to talk about it?"

He nodded. "I believe so, yes."

Aaron again released her hand, and she immediately felt the loss of warmth from his touch. He reached behind his vest and retrieved the letter then held it out to her. Lillian skimmed the brief note as Aaron gave his own retelling of its contents.

"It seems my uncle is attempting to have me declared dead in order to seize the assets from my father's side of the business." He clenched his teeth, and his mouth curled in disgust. "Along with my inheritance."

Lillian lowered her hand to her side, allowing the letter to dangle there. "Can he do that?"

"I don't know. It seems he has already started the process, and that's why my father's lawyer felt the need to contact me."

"But how could he declare you dead if you were among those reported as survivors from the *Titanic*'s demise?"

He sighed. "I'm not sure. I wrote to my uncle and sent a telegram to another one of my cousins telling them both I had survived." Aaron furrowed his brow. "Maybe they never received them."

"Or maybe they are disregarding them," Lillian countered. "Maybe even burned them to prevent them from being evidence."

"In light of all my uncle has done recently, I wouldn't be surprised."

The tall oaks and poplars formed a canopy overhead, and the lacy effect of the postbud leaves fanned out throughout the copse of trees, lending a sense of privacy to their conversation.

Lillian shook her head. "Does the man's cruelty know no bounds? Isn't it enough he's basically disowned you? Now he wants your portion of the assets and your inheritance as well?"

Aaron turned and rested his elbows on the bridge wall. "I suppose now that I've attained my twenty-fifth birthday, my uncle wanted to leave me high and dry by stealing what rightfully belongs to me." He touched his fingers to the bridge of his nose. "I never believed he could lower himself to this level."

Lillian could only imagine the ups and downs he'd endured the past couple of months. And now this? Aaron's life had been horribly interrupted, his predictable patterns shattered. Yet, through it all, he'd managed to persevere and keep pressing toward his goal of remaining involved in business endeavors.

"So, what are you going to do?"

Aaron leaned forward and dropped his head into his hands as he ran his fingers from his forehead down to his chin. "The only thing I can do, I'm afraid." He moaned. "Book passage on a vessel headed back across the Atlantic so I can show by physical presence that I am very much alive."

He was leaving? And not just the immediate area but the entire continent. He'd be thousands of miles away in a matter of weeks.

"I only hope and pray I can accomplish that without mishap or delay."

"You should speak with my father or Uncle Richard. They have ships departing all the time from the ports, and the merchant ships travel between England and here quite frequently."

She might not be in favor of Aaron having to leave, but she could at least be helpful to him in making his plans.

He nodded. "That would make the passage more familiar, but it wouldn't guarantee safety any more than any other vessel."

Lillian heard the concern and even fear in his voice. Was it any wonder? Look what had happened the last time he'd crossed the ocean. Aaron likely would be happy if he never had to make that journey again. But that didn't appear to be an option.

Aaron didn't have to say anything more. The anguish on his face only made the situation more hopeless. Compassion filled Lillian.

She wished she could do something. But what?

"And there isn't a way for you to prove you're alive without traveling all the way across the ocean?" Lillian ran through possible scenarios in her mind. "I would think a telegram would suffice. At least for now. Then you could take more time if necessary to plan your journey back to London without rushing." *And maybe even stay in Delaware long enough to see the reopening of Cobblestone Books first.* As soon as the thought entered her mind, Lillian silently scolded herself. Pure selfishness. That's all it was. No other way to describe it.

As if to prove her point, Aaron pushed away from the wall and began pacing back and forth in roughly a ten-foot length parallel to the wall. The apprehension of the entire situation forced his eyebrows down toward his eyes and his mouth into a crooked line.

"Aaron, I'm sorry," she said aloud.

He halted his pacing and stared at her. "For what?"

"For attempting to suggest you rearrange your plans to suit me." She gave him a rueful look. "I had rather hoped you would remain here long enough to help reopen the bookshop, but you have much greater things at stake."

Not offering up any argument to her remark, Aaron resumed his pacing. A few seconds later, Lillian raised one eyebrow and regarded his back-and-forth activity.

"And those things won't get solved by you putting a rut in the concrete the width of your feet."

At her attempt at a joke, Aaron stopped again. Then his eyes closed, and a deep sigh escaped his lips. "You are right. My walking back and forth isn't going to make the situation any less grim." He stepped up to the wall again, and Lillian joined him. Running his fingers through his hair, he let out a low growl then slumped with his forearms resting on the stone and his hands dangling over the side. "I just feel so incredibly helpless standing here while my uncle attempts to destroy everything I've ever owned. I wish there was something I could do right now."

Aaron's plaintive confession reached in deep and massaged Lillian's heart. Slowly, she shuffled the foot or so to her right to close the distance between them. Then she eased her hand toward him and covered his folded hands. He didn't even flinch.

"There is something we can do," she said. "We can pray. Ask God to intervene on your behalf until you can be there in person. That is the best thing we can do at the moment."

Aaron looked up, his face bearing evidence of the stress and strain. But as he gazed into her face, his expression changed. His mouth relaxed, his eyebrows smoothed, and a light entered his eyes. After a moment or two, he withdrew one of his hands and clasped hers between his.

"You are absolutely right. Thank you. I could use the reminder."

"Sometimes, we all can."

Together, they bowed their heads and prayed silently. Lillian had no idea how long they remained that way, but she didn't care. She was there for Aaron when he needed her most.

It was easy to believe everything would turn out just as they wished, but just how long would that take? Aaron didn't even know what awaited him once he set foot in London again.

Beyond that, though, she prayed for strength to endure his forthcoming long absence. What he had to do wouldn't likely be solved within minutes of him setting foot in London. And factoring in the travel time to and back, it would be at least two months, maybe more, before she would see him again.

As if that thought had entered his mind as well, Aaron moved beside her, and Lillian opened her eyes to find him watching her. He opened and closed his mouth at least three times before looking away and staring up the river. All of a sudden, he withdrew his pocket watch and flipped it open then snapped it shut in haste and shoved it into his pocket.

"Lillian, I am sorry." He turned to face her, remorse reflecting in his eyes. "But I must get to the shipyard if I am to book passage on the next ship leaving port. As much as I wish I didn't have to, I must see to this straightaway."

Lillian nodded, even though she wanted to protest. "I understand." She sniffed. No. She wouldn't cry. She wouldn't. "I hope the matter is resolved quickly, and you can return very soon."

The ghost of a smile appeared on his face. "As do I. There is still so much here that needs to be done."

Did he mean in regard to the bookshop or something pertaining to their relationship? He didn't elaborate. Instead, he took her hands in his again.

"Thank you." Raising both hands to his lips, he placed a kiss on each. "I promise to contact you as soon as I am able."

He hesitated, as if he wanted to say something more. Then he groaned low in his throat, spun on his heel, and headed in the direction of the shipyard. After about fifteen feet, he stopped. Lillian stared at his back. What now? His arms hung at his sides, and his hands formed fists then relaxed several times.

Finally, he swung around and closed the distance between them in just five long strides. Then his hands framed her face, and his mouth covered hers. Lillian didn't have time to react. She held her breath as his lips moved over hers, lightly at first then with more pressure. Of their own accord, her hands slid to his shoulders, and she moved the fingers of her right hand up to touch his smooth cheek. Several moments later, Aaron pulled back and inhaled a deep, shuddering breath. Lillian pressed her mouth closed, savoring the kiss.

"I. . .uh. . ." Aaron was the first to attempt to speak. He gave her a roguish grin. "I believe now I can leave bolstered with far more fortitude."

And with that, he was gone. . .this time, without pause.

Lillian again watched him depart until he turned southeast down Twelfth Street and she could no longer see him.

This day had not gone how she planned. Of course, the kiss wasn't in her plan, either. But that was one thing she didn't mind at all. Chloe would never believe this.

At least Lillian had a few moments to herself to relax. . .if she could avoid dwelling on the memory of Aaron's lips and the warmth of his touch. That wouldn't be easy. She reached up and pressed her fingers to her mouth, still feeling the tingle of his touch. His kiss had changed a lot. Lillian only prayed the change would be for the better.

≈

"Well, it's about time!" Chloe nearly pounced on her sister the moment Lillian reentered the courtyard. "I have been waiting for nearly two hours for the two of you to return. Pearson left in a huff not long after Aaron dragged you away. He looked none too pleased with how the events played out earlier. He obviously does not like the idea of being upstaged by Aaron." She peered over Lillian's shoulder. "Speaking of which, where *is* Aaron?"

Lillian sighed. "Gone."

"Gone? Gone where?" Chloe planted her hands on her hips. "What did you say to him?"

In light of what had just happened, Lillian might have wished for solitude. But her emotions swirled all around and needed release. Chloe would help with that.

With a deep breath to calm her nerves, Lillian moved to sit at the nearest table. Her sister immediately joined her. She looked so serious, Lillian almost laughed. But when Chloe scowled at her, she sobered.

"So," Chloe began, folding her hands and resting her arms on the table's surface, "are you going to tell me or am I going to have to guess?"

Her sister's piercing gaze seemed to see right through her. Lillian shifted in her seat.

"Aaron had to leave," she finally said. "The letter? It informed him his uncle was attempting to declare him dead in order to get his hands on Aaron's money, so Aaron had to book passage on the next ship leaving from Hanssen-Baxton's ports in order to travel there and appear in person to refute whatever evidence his uncle might have collected against him."

Chloe narrowed her eyes. "So, he just left? Without so much as a good-bye?"

Lillian sighed. "Not exactly."

"I knew it!" Chloe snapped her fingers and grinned. "You kissed, didn't you? I can see it in your eyes."

There was no point in denying it now. "Yes." Lillian inhaled a shuddering breath and touched her lips again. "We did."

Chloe giggled. "I thought so. And. . ." Again, the intent gaze returned. "Do you love him?"

Lillian's breath hitched. She tried to swallow past the lump in her throat. "Pardon me?" Her voice came out sounding more like a croak. She cleared her throat. "What did you ask?"

"I asked if you love Aaron. The two of you have spent ample time together the past few weeks, and you were the one he grabbed to walk with him when he needed to process the contents of that letter." She leaned forward. "So. . .do. . .you. . .love him?"

"I. . .uh. . .that is. . .I'm not certain I have an answer to that." Wonderful. Her sixteen-year-old sister asks about her feelings, and she stumbles through a reply. She couldn't even come up with a viable answer. And just like not answering, the answer she *did* give was even more revealing.

"It doesn't usually take a lot of thought. Either you love someone or you don't. That should be easy enough to know."

"Actually, Chloe, it's not that simple." If only it were. "There is far more involved with loving someone than simply admitting it or knowing it. And right now, I do not know for certain."

Her sister sat back in her chair. "Well, when you figure it out, be sure and tell me." She crossed her arms. "Although I'm fairly certain I know what your answer is going to be."

Lillian wished she could have the confidence her sister had. Things had just been left so unsettled between her and Aaron, though. They didn't even have time to discuss the kiss they shared or what that meant to their relationship. How could she even begin to sort through the confusing haze of her feelings? She couldn't. But she really should come up with some sort of answer for Chloe.

"Chloe, I do care for Aaron. But there are so many other factors at play in this situation." Not the least of which were the length of time he would be gone and everything that would be taking place between now and then. "Please understand me when I say I wish there was a simple answer. For now, let us leave it at Aaron being a very important part of my life. Anything other than that, we shall have to wait and see."

Chloe nodded then relaxed her folded arms. "I understand, all right, Lil. But I also know you. And I am certain it will all work out." She reached across the table to squeeze her sister's hands. "Have faith."

Faith? That was all Lillian *would* have until she saw Aaron once more.

Chapter 14

Aaron ran his hands through his hair. He didn't care if the ends stood out or not. All he wanted was a conclusion to this entire ordeal. And he didn't appreciate being dragged clear across the ocean to London in order to settle his own affairs. He prayed this misunderstanding could be absolved quickly, so he could return to America posthaste.

Eight days. The passage by ship had taken eight full days with nary a mishap. He thanked God for that. And every day his mind ran through that final scene with Lillian on the bridge. He wanted more than anything to be back with her and free to pick up where they'd left off. Oh, the memory of her upturned face and kiss-swollen lips. It was enough to distract a man for days. And he'd had over a week of solitude to dwell on it.

As he waited outside the judge's private chambers at the courthouse, Aaron listened for the cue his father's lawyer had shared with him.

"Mr. Stone, Mrs. Stone," the lawyer began, "I do appreciate your thorough attention to detail, and again, allow me to extend my condolences to you both. There is just one small matter I believe needs to be addressed. Your Honor, if you will indulge me, I believe what I have to share will be of great import to your ruling on this case."

"Please proceed, Mr. Merriweather." That voice must belong to the judge.

"Thank you," the lawyer replied. A shuffling of papers followed. "Now, as we're all aware, the facts have been presented, and Mr. and Mrs. Stone merely wish to see a conclusion drawn so they might receive closure on this case. I do not wish to cause any further sorrow, but earlier this morning, I had a surprise visitor at my office, one who can put to rest this entire hearing."

Surprise? He wasn't a surprise. Merriweather had been expecting him. Ah, but of course. He couldn't tell them that. The lawyer had planned it all out from the moment Aaron had walked into his office. It would be a shame to see his careful strategy thwarted at this stage in the game.

"And who might that be?" came the snarling voice of his uncle.

That was his cue.

Aaron shoved through the double doors. "Perhaps it would be better if I announced myself."

Four pairs of eyes fell on him. His aunt gasped, and his uncle stiffened.

Merriweather wore a smug expression. And the judge? The man didn't seem nearly as intimidating in his private chambers as he did high up in a courtroom, but he still wore the customary powdered wig.

"And who might you be, young man?"

"My name is Aaron Stone. I believe my uncle and aunt here are attempting to have me declared dead so they might assume control of my inheritance and all custodial funds set to be given to me upon my twenty-fifth birthday, which I recently attained."

Oh, the gall his uncle had. Coming here today, dressed in black, and appearing to be mourning the loss of a nephew he'd disowned nine months ago. How could he sit there and attempt to maintain such a farce? And not only him, but his aunt, too? She actually held a tissue clutched tightly in her hand, as if she'd been crying recently. They might as well have brought their three children with them as well to tip the scales in their favor.

"Did you say Aaron Stone?" the judged asked. He looked from Aaron to the couple facing him, to Merriweather, and back to Aaron again. "Is this some sort of ruse, son? According to this fine couple before me"—the judge gestured toward his aunt and uncle—"Aaron Stone is dead. He perished along with hundreds of others when the *Titanic* went down a few months ago."

"It is no ruse, Your Honor." Aaron took a step forward. "And I assure you, I am very much alive."

"Then, why have you not shown yourself before today?"

"Forgive me, Your Honor, but I was not aware of any of this. I have been in America the past few months immediately following the *Titanic*'s voyage." Aaron glanced out of the corner of his eye at his uncle, who avoided his gaze. He brought his head back around to face the judge. "I was only notified of these proceedings by letter from Mr. Merriweather, here, a little over a week ago, and I came as fast as I could."

The judge stroked the hairs on his bearded chin. "You wouldn't happen to have any proof to substantiate your claim, would you, Mr. Stone?" He pointed at Aaron's uncle. "This gentleman here submitted a list of known survivors as well as a supplemental list of those who had been reported as perishing. Forgive me if I have doubts regarding your claims."

Aaron waved his right hand. "No apology necessary, Your Honor. As Mr. Merriweather has informed me, my uncle has been quite thorough." But obviously, not thorough enough. "However, I believe those lists have been falsified in some way and the truth of them exaggerated. I have nothing but my word that I am who I say I am." He caught the lawyer's eye and the encouraging nod the man gave. Time to drive the point home. Aaron reached into his coat pocket and withdrew an envelope. "Oh, and this, Your Honor." He stepped to the desk and handed the envelope to the judge.

"What is this?" the judge asked as he took the papers.

"It is the last will and testament, Your Honor, of my father, Mr. Walter Douglass Stone."

Aaron felt more than saw his uncle shrink back under the penetrating stare of the judge. The tension in the room could rival a foggy London morning any day of the week. Aaron would have preferred to have settled this matter outside the courthouse, but by the time he arrived, Merriweather informed him the proceedings were in their final stages. Truth be told, though, his uncle deserved this.

Merriweather stepped forward. "I have verified that document myself, Your Honor. You already know I served Mr. Walter Stone for many years before his untimely death. And those pages are valid."

Silence ensued as the judge reviewed the papers in front of him. Aaron resisted the urge to look over his shoulder at his uncle and tried hard to control the anger that burned inside at the man's actions. But he heard his uncle swallow several times above his shallow breathing.

Finally, the judge cleared his throat and laid the pages flat on his desk. He leveled a direct gaze at the couple seated opposite him. "Mr. Stone, would you stand, please?"

Aaron's uncle complied.

"It is clear," the judge continued, "that you have tampered with the veracity of official reports and replaced another name with that of your nephew." The judge ran his tongue across his upper teeth. "Now, I do not abide deception in any form, but especially from someone with a position of such high esteem in this city."

Unable to resist any longer, Aaron turned to look at his uncle. His face had paled considerably, and beads of sweat appeared on his forehead.

"You were getting too close," his uncle burst out. "I had hired you to handle my books, and you did such a thorough job, I panicked. It was only a matter of time before you discovered how I'd been funneling some of the profits into my private accounts. So you see? I had to do something." He glared at Merriweather. "I made a mistake, though, in not keeping the details away from your father's lawyer."

Aaron couldn't believe it. His uncle was admitting to fraud right in front of the judge. He pivoted and faced his uncle straight on, praying for patience. "The only mistake you made was in assuming my influence here in London wouldn't have such far-reaching effects. The mistake *I* made was in giving you the benefit of the doubt and not sealing the state of my affairs prior to embarking on that voyage to America earlier this year." He glanced back at the judge and again at his uncle. "But it seems that will all be resolved very soon."

Guilt flashed in his uncle's eyes but dimmed when he caught sight of the judge. A second later, a forced penitent expression appeared. "Please, forgive me, my boy. I confess to my wrongdoing, and I know you feel betrayed. But I can't leave without knowing you might one day be able to forgive me."

So now his uncle was attempting reconciliation and a show of remorse? Although every fiber inside of him screamed to deny his uncle such a request, a still, small voice told him he shouldn't. The man would receive his just penalty for his actions. It was not up to Aaron to levy judgment on him.

With sorrow for his uncle, Aaron sighed. "I do forgive you, Uncle Clayton, and I pray you will learn from your mistakes, not repeat them."

The man nodded but didn't reply. His actions showed regret, but his eyes showed disgust.

"Mr. Stone," the judge spoke again. "I believe I have everything I need to close this case." He stood and extended his hand across his desk. "Thank you for making the journey and coming here today. I am sorry you had to come at all."

Aaron shook the judge's hand. "So am I, Your Honor, but I am glad my presence helped."

The judge didn't need to tell him twice. The sooner he left the courthouse, the sooner he could be on a return ship to America. With a nod at Merriweather, who had gathered his papers and zipped up his leather briefcase, the two quickly took their leave of the room. Once in the corridor, Aaron turned to the lawyer.

"Merriweather, I owe you a great deal of gratitude. Were it not for you, I might have never seen a single pound of my inheritance."

The lawyer nodded. "It was my pleasure, Mr. Stone. Your father was one of the most honest men I know. Once I discovered your uncle's scheme, I couldn't in good conscience sit back and allow him to get away with it. Your father deserved much better." He reached into his vest and pulled out his pocket watch. "Now, I know you have only been on land for a little more than three days, but I believe another ship departs out of Brighton first thing in the morning." Merriweather grinned. "From what you told me, there is a certain young lady anxiously awaiting your return. I shall handle all necessary paperwork pertaining to your financial affairs on this end. You go take care of your personal ones."

Aaron shook hands with the lawyer and grinned. "Yes, sir," he replied. "And thank you again."

Without further ado, Aaron headed straight for his hired hackney waiting outside. If all went well, he could be in Brighton by nightfall and ready to depart with the morning tide. But first, he had a telegram to send.

Relief washed over him. Aaron knew he'd eventually be in a position to offer much more to Lillian than he previously had been able to do, but now he knew for certain. He silently sent thanks to God for an immediate answer to prayer then leaned back and rested his head against the seat cushion. This ride would take awhile.

❧

"That box can go to the back." Lillian pointed, directing the constant flow of volunteers who had come to help with the restocking of the bookshop.

"And what about these?" Her younger brother, Geoffrey, carried a small box to her for inspection.

Lillian peered inside and squealed. Her brother rolled his eyes as she reached in to pull out one title. "These are going right up front here."

Geoffrey released the box to her and left to fetch another from the cart outside. After setting the aged copy of *Don Quixote* on the shelf hung behind the counter, Lillian turned back for more. Each title found a place of honor on display. When she reached the bottom of the box, though, she glanced back at the shelf. She reread every title from left to right twice to make sure. No. This couldn't be all of them.

"I believe this is the book you are looking for."

"Aunt Charlotte!" Lillian snapped her head up to find her oldest great-aunt standing on the other side of the counter, holding a worn book in her hands. "You came!"

A hesitant expression crossed her face. "Yes." She looked around the shop with a mixture of admiration and regret crossing her face. When she turned her gaze back to Lillian, tears filled her eyes. "Although I must admit, it wasn't easy. I must have talked myself out of coming at least half a dozen times." She reached out and covered Lillian's hand with her own. "Then, I reminded myself that you had worked hard for weeks to restore this bookshop to its former glory. And I owed it to you to make the effort to be here."

In all the time she'd spent at the shop, her aunt had never once set foot inside or even come anywhere near it. Sure, she'd granted her permission for the work to be done and given the key to Mother so Lillian and Aaron could gain access. But, though she seemed to support the idea, her verbal agreement was all she had given.

Lillian smiled. "I'm so glad you're here. I've wanted to show you the shop for weeks now, but you've been so busy."

Guilt appeared in Aunt Charlotte's eyes, and she sighed. "I wasn't busy, Lillian. I was avoiding the shop. . .and you." She reached up to catch the tears that threatened to fall. "For that, I'm sorry." Her aunt held out the first-edition copy of *Robinson Crusoe*. "If it helps, I offer this as a gift to make up for my poor behavior."

Taking the book from her aunt, Lillian smiled. "This book is going into the display case as soon as Father brings back the key." She glanced over her shoulder. "As are the others. I don't want any further dust or exposure to harm them in any way."

Her aunt sniffed. "I can see you are going to take excellent care of this shop." She glanced around again. "The way it should be tended."

Lillian closed her eyes. The time had come. She had to ask her aunt. *Father, give me strength and the right words to say.*

"Aunt Charlotte? What happened?"

Her aunt turned with sadness in her eyes. She inhaled then released a shuddering breath. Her hands gripped the counter, and her knuckles turned white.

"To the shop? To you?" Lillian continued when her aunt didn't say anything. "Forgive me if I'm speaking out of turn, but I asked Mother, and she said it wasn't her place to say, that I had to ask you."

Aunt Charlotte nodded. "Your mother is correct. And I'll have to remember to thank her for remembering the promise she made, the promise everyone made, several years ago."

"The promise about what?"

Lillian knew she shouldn't press, but everyone had been so secretive, and from what she knew, a financial crisis wouldn't be a reason to close a bookshop like this then leave it closed. There had to be another explanation.

"Let's go out into the courtyard, shall we?" Aunt Charlotte stepped around the counter, extending her arm in silent invitation for her niece to join her.

"But the books and the boxes—"

"Bethany can handle directing everyone where to put them," Aunt Charlotte replied. "You and I need to have a little chat."

They stepped outside through the back door and chose two chairs facing each other at the nearest table. Aunt Charlotte waited for Lillian to sit then took a seat herself in full view of the bookshop. She opened her mouth a few times then closed it. Pain and regret and what looked like complete sorrow played across her face. What could possibly be so difficult to say that it would have caused her aunt to avoid the bookshop completely for nearly fifteen years?

Finally, her aunt wet her lips, took a deep breath, and turned to face her.

"Lillian, you already know about the financial situation nearly twenty years ago."

Lillian nodded.

"And you know I did everything I could to keep the shop open throughout it, but a lot of people had to choose between feeding their families or keeping clothes on their children's backs, so books fell to a distant third in terms of priorities."

"But Uncle Richard had expanded the shipping business not long after the crash occurred. And he'd even branched into building railroad cars and manufacturing paper to be sold to merchants worldwide." Lillian splayed her hands out, palms up. "Surely, the profits from that would have been enough for you to not open the shop again."

Her aunt swallowed. "But money was not the reason I couldn't return." She closed her eyes, the pain of the memory causing her brow to furrow and her eyelids to squeeze shut. When she opened her eyes again, they were filled with tears and terrible pain. "Lillian," she whispered, "I lost a baby."

Wait. What did her aunt just say? A baby? That didn't make any sense. What would a baby have to do with the bookshop. Unless. . .

"I was expecting our third child, and the stress of keeping the bookshop open as well as the long hours your uncle worked to help us maintain as well as recover took its toll on me." She pointed toward the shop. "I was standing right there behind the counter when the pain struck." Tears poured down her cheeks.

Lillian reached into the pocket sewn into her skirts and pulled out a handkerchief. She handed it to her aunt then clasped her aunt's left hand, giving it a squeeze.

"Oh, Aunt Charlotte, I am so sorry. I had no idea."

What a horrific thing to happen. No wonder her aunt couldn't bear to face coming back to the shop. There were far too many memories and far too much anguish.

Lillian covered her aunt's hand with her other. "Aunt Charlotte, I understand now how difficult this has been for you. And I'm thankful you took the time to brave returning here to tell me." She squeezed her aunt's hand again. "If you are never again able to return after today, I will not hold it against you in any way." Lillian offered what she hoped was a supportive look. "But I truly hope you can. This bookshop was your dream, your passion. It wouldn't be the same without you."

Aunt Charlotte smiled despite her tears. She sniffed and swallowed several times. "Lillian, my dear, never let it be said that you are the spitting image of me, for your ability to persuade is exactly like your mother."

"But I believe Mother polished her skills while living with you." Lillian smiled. "So I consider it an honor to have a bit of you in me."

Her aunt laid the handkerchief in her lap and reached out to cover their joined hands. "Thank you, my dear. It feels excellent to have unburdened myself of that secret. And though you likely don't know how, you have given me strength to face a new chapter in my life with my head held high from this day forward." She nodded toward the shop. "Now, what do you say we get back inside and make certain our books are being treated properly?"

Lillian smiled and stood with her aunt, locking elbows with her. "I would be delighted."

Chapter 15

Lillian held the scissors in hand and carefully cut through the wide band of red ribbon strung from window to window in front of Cobblestone Books. Cheers and clapping sounded the second the ribbon split and fell to the ground.

"It's official," Uncle Richard declared. "Cobblestone Books is once again open for business." He stepped forward and pulled on the door, holding it open. "Lillian, my dear? I believe the honor of first entrance is all yours."

She beamed a smile at her uncle and led the entourage of her family and friends inside. Every nook and cranny and bookcase gleamed from the final polish. Every book had its place, and every shelf or surface containing those books had been labeled. The entire shop bore evidence of the hard work put into the restoration. It was all perfect. . .save one thing.

Aaron wasn't there to share in the celebration.

"I think I know just which book I'm going to borrow first," Chloe announced. "I've been waiting for this day and this book," she said, picking up a copy of *Emma* by Jane Austen, "ever since Aunt 'Stasia told me about it."

Lillian chuckled. "As if you need any more notions about matchmaking planted in your already fanciful mind. You do just fine on your own."

Chloe smiled. "Yes, but it can never hurt to polish one's skills and perhaps glean a little extra wisdom from someone who has gone before."

Lillian raised one brow. "You do realize that book is a work of fiction, right? That it's a story created by Jane Austen and intended solely for pleasure reading?"

"Of course I do." Chloe stuck her chin in the air. "Do you think I'm that naive?"

Naive? Her sister? Not a chance. If anyone bore that title, it would be she. Lillian tapped Chloe's nose. "Not in the least, dear sister. Not in the least."

"All right," Father announced as he hauled a crate to the counter up front. Her brother Geoffrey carried a similar crate and set it on the floor at Father's feet. "Let us all take a glass and pour the champagne. We have something to celebrate."

In short order, the champagne was poured and the glasses passed out. Father cleared his throat and once again gained everyone's attention.

"To my daughter, Lillian, for her perseverance and determination to turn this venture into such a success." Father searched the sea of faces. "And to a trio of aunts, without whose support and assistance this endeavor never would have become a reality." He held up his glass. "So, let us raise our glasses and honor these ladies for all they have accomplished."

"Here, here!" sounded from several gathered.

Glasses clinked, and chatter commenced. After a round of hugs exchanged by everyone present, Lillian stepped away from the throng of excited family and friends.

She stared out at the people she loved most in this world. But again, the one face she wanted more than anything to see right then was missing. She had hoped to hear from him by now. When would he return? How was his time in London going? Had he managed to tie up all the loose ends and restore his good name? Lillian should really be celebrating with everyone else, but her heart wasn't in it. Perhaps some time alone would help. She started to make her way to the courtyard, but Father blocked her path.

"I suppose now I should give you this," he said with a smile and handed an envelope to her. "It arrived just after you left in the carriage to come here."

Lillian glanced down at the telegram and inhaled. Unable to contain her excitement, she tore open the envelope and read the short missive inside. The greeting brought an even bigger smile to her lips.

My Dearest Lillian *Stop* Crisis averted *Stop* Returning to you on the very next ship *Stop* Arriving Tuesday next *Stop* Have an important question to ask *Stop* Wait for me on our bridge *Stop* Forever Yours Aaron *Stop*

Moisture gathered in Lillian's eyes at Aaron's brief message. She bit her lip as she looked at Father, his smile blurry through her tears.

"I trust the news is good?"

She turned to Mother, who wore an amused expression.

"Aaron—" She swallowed beyond the catch in her throat and tried again. "Aaron is coming home!"

⁊

Lillian tried for the hundredth time to calm her rapidly beating heart or gain control of her breathing, all to no avail. Tuesday had arrived, and she stood on the bridge, just as Aaron had instructed. A slight breeze stirred the air around her, but other than that, the hot summer day offered little respite from the heat. At any moment, Aaron would appear somewhere nearby. Was she truly ready for this?

A horse and carriage came into sight with a single passenger inside the hired conveyance. She'd recognize one of her uncle's carriages from the ship-yard anywhere. Aaron! It had to be. Her heart leaped with joy. Her legs trembled, and several shivers traveled up her back as he drew closer and closer.

The carriage came to a stop, and the driver opened the door for Aaron. At first, she wondered why he ambled so slowly. He should be walking at full speed in her direction. Then she remembered. Not knowing the status of her heart, he wouldn't presume without a guarantee. Waiting was pure torture. The bridge had never seemed so long.

Finally, unable to contain her excitement, she grabbed two handfuls of her skirts and petticoats and took off at a full run toward Aaron. He stopped halfway up one side of the bridge and hesitated. As if suddenly realizing her intent, a broad smile appeared on his face, and he immediately set himself to action. Closing the distance between them with just a few steps, he paused just before she reached him and braced himself to catch her in his strong arms and swing her around.

"Lillian," he breathed into her ear then slowly lowered her to the ground. "I see you received my telegram." He winked. "I have imagined this moment every day for over a week. Now, here you stand before me." He peered down at her, the intensity in his gaze nearly overwhelming. "And with affection shining in your eyes!"

"Oh, Aaron," she whispered, unable to speak as tears pooled and slid down her cheeks.

He tenderly brushed them away then touched his finger that held a tear to his lips. His eyes darkened, and his gaze fell to her mouth, and a grin tugged at his own. A second later, he wrapped his arms around her. Laughter rumbled in his chest as he hugged her to him. He pulled back just enough for her to see the sparkle in his eyes. Had she ever seen such joy spring up from his soul? His expression softened as he studied her lips. Lillian smiled, eagerly awaiting his kiss but knowing she must wait for the right moment.

"So, tell me what happened in London." She didn't want to prolong the real emotion of their reunion more than necessary, but propriety dictated her courtesy.

A smirk formed on Aaron's lips. He didn't appear too eager to delve into superficial talk, either, but she knew he would, at least for a minute or two.

"Let's just say my father's lawyer is sly like a fox. He hatched a maneuver around my uncle's scheme that effectively exposed him for the liar and cheat he is, plus restored my validity to me and ensured the smooth transfer of my father's financial estate into my name alone." He clasped her hands in his. "So, as I said in my telegram. Crisis averted."

"I am pleased to hear it all went well," she replied. "And now, you can move forward, never having to look back."

Aaron nodded. "Moving forward. That is exactly what I wish to discuss with you."

She licked her lips, her throat tight from the anticipation of the question he'd mentioned in his message. "What did you have in mind?"

&

Aaron inhaled a deep breath then slowly released it. He brushed his thumbs across her knuckles and lightly squeezed her fingers with his.

"Lillian, I must beg your forgiveness for not speaking to you sooner. Being left alone during my travels to and from London helped me realize just how special you are to me. I'm a fool for not seeing it sooner. That kiss we shared right before I departed shook me to the core. And I couldn't get you out of my mind during the entire ocean crossing. I can now only dare to hope you feel the same." He sought her gaze and held it. "All I know right now is I don't want to lose you."

A sharp gasp followed his declaration. This was it. He had to say it now.

"Lillian, your brother asked me to take care of you with his dying breath. I didn't understand it then, but I do now."

She sniffed. "Conrad asked that of you?"

"Yes. You two shared a very special bond, and it was clear how much he cared about you by seeing to it you had someone to fill his shoes." Aaron sighed. "Not that I could ever take his place, but Lillian, I love you." He grinned. "And I hope you might consider me a desirable substitute."

Lillian swung their wrists downward in an arc to interlace their fingers. Aaron glanced down at their joined hands then back at her face. Tenderness spilled forth, and tears glistened in her eyes. "Aaron, I love you, too."

He grinned and dropped to the ground on one knee, right there in the middle of the oft-crossed and dirty bridge. He reached into his coat and pulled out his mother's ring, one of the few items he'd immediately sequestered away following her death. A diamond-accented sapphire with tiny amethyst stones around the rim. He held it up to Lillian. "I spoke to your father at the shipyard the day I left for London. I didn't want anything delaying my intent the moment I returned. He of course granted his permission. So all that remains is that question I wanted to ask you." Aaron smiled big, knowing the answer before she gave it. "Will you marry me?"

A lone tear spilled and traced a wet path down her cheek. Aaron reached up and brushed it away. She stared down at him and pulled her bottom lip in between her teeth. The seconds ticked by in slow progression.

"Well, now," the familiar voice of her neighbor's eldest son interrupted. "It appears I have arrived in the middle of the most unfortunate of circumstances." Pearson paused. "At least for me."

Aaron immediately stood and turned to meet the regretful gaze of the man he'd last seen wearing a smug expression of triumph where Lillian was concerned. But that was before Aaron had whisked her away to this very bridge. He regarded Pearson with a doubtful glance.

"You followed Lillian here?"

"Yes." Pearson nodded. "I overheard her aunt speaking with her about taking a walk and thought I might join her." He looked to Lillian. "I had no idea your walk would include a meeting with Mr. Stone. So I believe I have timed my appearance a bit too late." Pearson gestured toward Lillian and Aaron's close proximity. "Or perhaps I am right on time."

Lillian started to move toward the eldest Duncan son, but Aaron held her fast. "Pearson, I—"

Pearson raised his hand and lifted two fingers, effectively silencing whatever she'd been about to say. "Please, Lillian. You owe me no explanation." He shrugged. "It's clear any presumed interest was in my mind, and my mind alone. Only a fool would see the way you are looking at Mr. Stone and not know of your fervent affection. I can't possibly interfere." Pearson took two steps backward and dipped his head. "Now, if you'll excuse me, I will retract my suit and leave you two alone. I wish you both great happiness."

Silence followed in the wake of Pearson's exit. Aaron and Lillian both stared at his retreating back, as if the man hadn't really been there. Several moments later, Aaron shook his head and turned again to face Lillian. Resuming his position on bended knee, he again took her hands in his.

"I believe there is still a question waiting for an answer," he reminded her with a smile.

Lillian startled and stared down at him. Her mouth moved, but no words came out. It was as if she stood transfixed and held captive by some unknown force.

"Say you will!" Chloe's voice broke the spell.

Lillian laughed, and Aaron joined her. Not one, but *two* interruptions? Did no one have any respect for their privacy? And just when had Lillian's sister sneaked up on them? Or had she been following behind Pearson to perhaps ensure nothing untoward occurred?

"It appears we have a mischievous little eavesdropper in our midst," Lillian said.

"Yes," Aaron replied. "But this conversation has no room for a third opinion. At least not at the moment." He cast a glance at Lillian's sister. "Chloe, we appreciate your presence in Pearson's wake, but as you can see, the situation has remedied itself. And if you do not mind, I should like to finish what I started." Aaron gave her a pointed look. "Could you perhaps return to the bookshop, and your sister and I shall join you shortly?"

An impish grin formed on her lips and lit up her eyes. "Of course, Aaron," Chloe replied. "I only wanted to tell you that everyone is waiting for you both there."

With that, she turned on her heel and walked away. Aaron returned his gaze to Lillian. "Well, you know how your sister feels. And it seems your family and friends already know the outcome." He smiled. "I, on the other hand, remain down here awaiting your answer," he reminded her.

Lyrical laughter escaped her lips. "Yes! Yes, of course I will marry you."

Aaron jumped to his feet and gave her a quick peck on the lips. He pulled back to look down into her face, seeing the same longing he felt inside. Sliding the ring onto her finger, he gifted Lillian with the iconic symbol of his love. Lowering his lips again, he positioned himself for a better, deeper kiss this time.

A few moments later, he pulled back. A chuckle rumbled in his chest. "I just realized something."

Lillian swallowed once. "What is that?"

"Your sister is likely going to rush back to the bookshop and announce to everyone present the state in which she came upon the two of us."

She smiled. "I would have you know, regardless of how Chloe had found us, she would have likely interpreted the scene in the same way. When it comes to my sister, we don't stand a chance. Like our mother before us in regard to Uncle Richard and Aunt Charlotte, you can probably count on Chloe reporting everything as though the progression of our relationship had been entirely of her making."

"That is a solid piece of advice to take under advisement," Aaron replied. "In the future, I shall be more careful around her." He grinned and winked. "After all, I should like to be given credit for my own ideas. . .especially where you're concerned."

Aaron turned and slipped his arm around Lillian's waist. They shared a special connection as they gazed up the Brandywine River and watched the water trip and stumble over itself on its way to merge with the Christina and then the Delaware. They still had so much to discuss. So many plans to make. But for now, he intended to enjoy the brief solitude and the newness of their professed love. Their joined paths might have begun with the resurrection of an antique bookshop, but the launch that had set their separate paths on a collision course with each other had been navigated by God all along.

Lillian nudged her shoulder against his side. "So, shall we make our way back and face the eager audience that awaits us?"

Aaron groaned. "Must we go so soon?"

"If we don't, they might come find us," she pointed out.

He sighed. "Very well." Turning to face her, he reached out and tipped up her chin with his forefinger. "But be forewarned," Aaron leaned down and kissed her soft lips then whispered, "I intend to steal you away again before too long."

Lillian chewed on her lower lip and grinned, a twinkle lighting her eyes. "I can't imagine anything I'd like more, Mr. Stone."

"In that case, Miss Bradenton," Aaron replied with a grin, extending his elbow out to her, "let us take the first step of the rest of our lives together."

Lillian placed her hand in the crook of his arm. "With pleasure!"